TACHYON: THE WEAPON

Hard Science Fiction

Tachyon
Book 1

BRANDON Q. MORRIS

Copyright © 2024 by Brandon Q. Morris

All rights reserved.

hard-sf.com

brandon@hard-sf.com

Translation: Megan Bigelow

Cover design: © Tom Edwards, TomEdwardsDesign.com

Editor: Margaret Dean

Brandon Q. Morris and the logo are trademarks of the author.

Contents

TACHYON: THE WEAPON	1
Around the Campfire	401
Also by Brandon Q. Morris	403
The New Tachyon Biography	411

"The only thing that makes life possible is permanent, intolerable uncertainty: not knowing what comes next." —

Ursula K. Le Guin, *The Left Hand of Darkness*

Tachyon: The Weapon

Gliese 163 c

A LIGHT GRAY SWIRL MADE ITS WAY TOWARDS A YELLOW STRIPE, which peeked through a dark blue plain. It looked harmless, but only because Mark Decker was looking at it from an altitude of over 200 miles. The swirl was a full-blown tropical storm that had chosen the new research base as its target. *Damn it!* Why did the weather have to conspire against them now of all times?

An alarm sounded behind him, its melodic ringing not entirely serious despite the danger. He pushed himself away from the station's porthole and floated to where the instruments were mounted on a shelf halfway to the cockpit. He skillfully turned his body, kicking against the shelf and holding on, searching for the source of the signal. There was none to be found, because a whole choir was calling for help. Without exception, every instrument connected to the space station via radio warned of the impending danger. The pressure had fallen to unprecedented lows, the air contained too much moisture and too much sulfur dioxide — the temperature had risen above 120 degrees and the wind had stopped.

That frightened him. The research station was right in the eye of the storm. If it developed as feared, the work of the last few weeks would be for nothing. Above all, Tailin and Roger, who had set up and calibrated the instruments earlier, were in danger. They should have ascended into orbit in the Hopper hours ago.

He floated over to the radio.

"Roger, this is Albatross-1. The storm really doesn't look good."

"I can tell by the air pressure, Mark."

"Then why aren't you in the Hopper?"

The Hopper was a methane-powered shuttle that they used to travel between the surface and the space station.

Roger sighed, "It's not up to me."

He had already expected that. Tailin never could tear herself away from an issue. Some instrument was still not working at full capacity, and she couldn't simply leave it at that.

"Tailin, can you hear me? This is your husband speaking."

"I don't want to hear it," she replied.

At least she was talking to him. That was a good sign. Sometimes she was so focused on her work that she didn't communicate with anyone.

"This is the commander of the Albatross-1, Mark Decker. Board the Hopper immediately. That's an order."

"Yes, sir, commander sir. I just need to attach this last conductor loop."

He imagined her fiddling with an open computer to correctly read a measuring device. The new base they had set up was supposed to function autonomously, like all the others they had distributed around the planet.

"Can we move a little faster? The storm is right on top of you."

"It's coming along as fast as it can. There are a lot of prickly cherry bushes in the way."

What? There were obviously no plants growing in the station!

"What the hell are you doing, Tailin?"

"I'm moving the conductor loop. I explained that to you. Have you even been listening to me?"

Conductor loop, now he remembered. They had been talking about a new project that Tailin wanted to use to measure the magnetic field of Gliese 163 more precisely. To do this, she needed wire loops laid out around the autonomous stations. But they hadn't even made a decision about the project yet.

"Are you talking about the measuring loops for the magnetic field?" he asked.

"Yes, exactly. The neutralizers didn't clear the area around the station very well."

She wasn't kneeling on the floor of the station but crawling around somewhere out in the jungle. And all the while a full-blown storm was approaching. At least under these circumstances the cerants weren't active; they were small, annoying, predatory insects that pounced on warm-blooded creatures. If the air pressure fell below a certain level, they retreated underground. Clever little parasites. Mark scratched his elbow where Roger had cut one of the beastly insects out of him a few days ago. If it wasn't treated, they would multiply under the skin until there was nothing left.

He floated back to the porthole, but left the radio's microphone activated so that Tailin could hear him. The gray swirl was now almost black.

"Tailin, you have to get out of there. The storm is about to hit you. We haven't even finalized that project yet!"

"You said I could start it if I had time to spare," replied Tailin. "The moment seemed favorable because I don't have to watch out for cerants due to the low pressure. Well... I didn't expect the prickly cherries to shed their fruit already, but you can remove the thorns for me later."

"If you don't go to Roger in the Hopper soon, you won't be around for anyone to pull thorns out of."

"I'm going to finish this. You've always said yourself that you have to finish what you start."

"Tailin, that was about the beer from the synthesizer. It would have gone stale if you'd left it."

"It's still a true saying."

"Not when there's a huge storm on your doorstep!"

"If you wouldn't keep distracting me, I'd be done by now, Mark."

"You're going in the Hopper *now*. That's an order!"

Tailin made no response. What was he supposed to do? She was going to kill them both – herself and Roger. He couldn't let that happen. He was the commander of this mission. If only Claire and Karima had returned! Tailin might listen to them. But they were on their way with the TransVec to Planet d. He wasn't expecting them back for another two weeks or so.

"Roger, can you hear me?" he asked.

"Loud and... well, there's a bit of static."

"Tailin's ignoring my orders."

"Oh boy, she's too stubborn. Hold on, I'll go out and fetch her."

"No, Roger, on the contrary. I hereby give you permission to take off with the Hopper. You might still make it."

"You want me to leave your wife alone out there in the jungle? Are you sure that's what you want?"

"No, of course not. But as commander, I'm responsible for all of you. Just because she happens to be my wife, I can't let her put you in danger along with her!"

"That's very honorable, Mark. But I won't abandon a colleague, even if she's doing something stupid."

Mark was relieved but didn't want to admit it. Of course he wanted nothing more than for Roger to get Tailin to safety. He was frustrated that his wife was forcing him to make such decisions. This was going to result in a serious conversation, and a warning.

"Mark? I'm going out now to look for her."

"Thanks, Roger."

Mark tried again on Tailin's private frequency. She didn't answer, nor did she answer on the public one. He heard several loud crashes over Roger's channel. It was thundering down there. Hopefully Tailin had taken shelter in the station. The computing core was there in a hut about the size of a camping bus, and thankfully it had emergency supplies.

"Roger, are you there?"

No answer. He must have left the area where the Hopper served as a radio relay. The spaceship was always parked a little ways from the station so as not to attract the attention of the local wildlife. The instruments were secured even against the giant multifeet, but all it would take was for a largemaw to do its business on a transmitter dish to misalign them.

"Roger, please get in touch if you can hear me."

There was static, then the repeated crackling of electrical discharges. Major storms and thunderstorms were the order of the day on Gliese 163c. The planet orbited close to the inner boundary of the habitable zone around its star, which pumped its considerable atmosphere full of energy. Roger, who had a soft spot for ancient history, had suggested the name Adad, after the Mesopotamian storm god. Mark cracked his knuckles. They had passed the suggestion on to the Ministry of Science on Neomars, but a reply wasn't expected for another few years. By that time they would probably be on their way back.

"Roger, Tailin, I'm waiting for a response."

The gray swirl produced blue and white patterns in rapid succession. It was lightning, as Mark could hear from the crackling on the radio channel. Adad never made it easy for them. The electricity in the atmosphere had killed a number of devices with modern electronics. That was why they were now using analog technology, and every research station on the surface had a Faraday cage to keep it safe.

Should he get the second Hopper ready? It was intended for emergencies only, but this certainly looked like it might be one. The question was whether he would help Tailin and Roger at all by putting himself in danger. If the storm hadn't moved on, he couldn't land safely.

Mark switched off the microphone.

"Come on, Roger, some sign of life would be nice," he grumbled to himself and sighed. "You too, Tailin."

He pushed himself away from the porthole and momentum carried him to the airlock. He could at least prepare the emergency Hopper. He opened the transparent flap inside the airlock that hid the emergency door release, clinging to a strut with his feet and turning the latch 90 degrees. He repeated this with a second flap at knee height. Now he was able to pull open the emergency exit.

"Emergency exit open," the station reported as programmed.

The second Hopper had exactly five seats, so that the entire crew of the station could get to safety. However, these were no ordinary seats. Rather, Mark saw five circularly distributed oval compartments in front of him, padded all around the inside. He had to get in legs first. Each passenger traveled separately from the others and had their own life support system and controls. If the Hopper was struck by an object on one side, the other passengers would still survive and be able to get to safety.

The light switched on in one of the compartments. The station knew, of course, that there was only one person on board. Mark hesitated. The storm was still raging. It was too early to launch. He left the airlock again.

"Emergency exit open," the space station complained.

Mark floated to the porthole. The storm was no longer

directly over the base, but the lightning had not yet subsided. He activated the microphone.

"Tailin, Roger, this is Mark. Please come in! Tell me you're all right!"

Mark wiped sweat from his forehead with the back of his hand. *Please say something!* Hopefully, it was just the static from the storm masking radio traffic. He tapped the microphone again. The speaker responded with hissing and crackling. *Damn.* Mark hit the inside wall of the station so hard the heel of his hand hurt.

"Emergency exit open."

"Yes, I know," he said.

The station didn't answer. The control system was only programmed to annoy him with its announcement.

"Station, create log entry," he ordered.

A symbol confirmed that the station was listening to him.

"This is the commander of the exobiology research station orbiting Gliese 163c, Mark Decker. Two crew members are in danger on the surface of the planet. I am using the emergency Hopper to go assist them. Log entry complete."

Another symbol confirmed that the station had recorded everything. At least it wasn't giving him any clever advice.

"Emergency exit open."

Except the obvious. Mark huffed in an attempt to ease the pressure building up inside him. He had to do *something*. He felt helpless up here. He floated back to the airlock. There, he edged his way into the still-lit compartment, legs first. What he was doing was selfish - if Claire and Karima came back, they would have no way of reaching the surface. No more research. They would have to take the TransVec to the nearest inhabited star, Gliese 167. If Mark failed, they would lose the main Hopper as well as the emergency Hopper. How likely was that? Not likely, if he waited until the storm had passed. But that was not an option.

"Emergency exit open."

Damn it, don't rush me. Mark took his bearings in the cramped compartment. Above him, at about head height, was a screen, so close that he had to squint his eyes to see anything. The prolonged period of weightlessness had impaired his eyesight. However, the display was deliberately kept simple. All he had to do was tap on the large life ring symbol to initiate the launch.

Then the emergency Hopper would head for the next optimum landing site on the surface.

But that was not Mark's goal. He tapped on the cogwheel icon, which took him to system configuration. There he switched to manual destination entry. He had the coordinates of the new base in his head. They had needed them often enough during construction. He quickly typed them in.

"Emergency exit open."

The station was persistent. Mark switched to the flight menu. There was no provision for manual control of the emergency Hopper. But he could select a few parameters for the flight path, such as whether the Hopper should avoid dangerous areas. Mark chose the shortest route. The storm was still raging over the research base last he saw.

"Emergency exit open."

Mark took a deep breath. Once he pressed the launch button, the emergency launch could no longer be halted. The Hopper would not glide gently away from the orbiting station, but would be slowed by means of powerful thrust, to get out of range of a possible explosion as quickly as possible. The designers had anticipated everything.

"Emergency exit open."

Okay, okay. Had he thought of everything? The emergency Hopper had food and water on board. Each of the five compartments could turn into a tiny clinic that would treat most injuries. He had his mobile radio in his pocket. The air pressure was above normal. He would need a breathing mask, maybe an acid-proof cloak against the precipitation.

Hm... Mark tapped the cogwheel again. There had to be an inventory list somewhere. *There.* It was in alphabetical order. There were five breathing masks on board, but the cloaks weren't labeled as acid-proof. The designers hadn't anticipated that humans might be planning to land on a planet where it rained sulfuric acid.

"Emergency exit open."

Fine, then. There would be something down below. If he layered the five available capes, he would certainly be safe for an hour. The acid-proof version was likely stored in the research base.

Something vibrated in his pocket. His radio! He fumbled for

it with his right hand, but the compartment was too narrow. Mark pulled himself out and up until he was floating in the airlock again.

"Emergency exit open."

Bite me. He hadn't even realized he'd turned on the radio. Maybe it had happened when he got into the emergency Hopper. But who was trying to reach him on his personal frequency? He pressed the listen button.

"Mayday, mayday, this is..." *Static*. "... Research base ..." *Static*. "... cut off. Need help."

It was Tailin's voice! She had made it into the base.

"Tailin? Mark here. I can hear you! I'm so glad! But what about Roger? I can't reach him. Are you safe?"

"Mark, oh my God ..." *Hiss*. "... Hoped to reach Roger... not here. I thought... at the Hopper."

The connection was terrible, but it was a miracle he could hear Tailin at all. The storm must have affected Adad's ionosphere too, letting the radio waves through.

"Roger went to find you," he said. "He left the Hopper. Where are you?"

"...In the station. The storm... slowing down. Has... destroyed... not seen."

"It's hard to understand you, Tailin. I'm taking the emergency Hopper and coming down. I'll be there in thirty minutes. Don't leave the base. I'll program the coordinates."

"... here. Understood. Please let Roger know that..."

Hadn't she understood? Roger had gone looking for her, and he hadn't made it back to her.

"I'll see you in half an hour."

Mark put the radio in the breast pocket of his uniform, then climbed back into the compartment. The destination was still programmed correctly, so he switched to the main menu and tapped the life ring.

A FIST PINNED HIM DOWN - HE WAS FINDING IT DIFFICULT TO breathe. Mark used all his strength to lift his chest. The emergency Hopper shot away with such speed that the inertia spread over Mark's entire body. The Hopper rotated slowly around its longitudinal axis, presumably so that all compartments were equally loaded. The screen showed what the external camera saw; the capsule was approaching the cloud cover.

Mark had just become accustomed to the load when the Hopper turned. Now Mark was flying feet first. A strong vibration in the back signaled that they were entering the atmosphere, the camera image spinning faster. The Hopper continued to rotate so that its hull warmed up evenly. Mark closed his eyes, but he could feel the rotation in his stomach. Was this still normal? He tapped the screen. The rescue device kept to the programmed descent curve, which resembled a parabola. The only difference was that the launch was not from the ground, but from orbit.

When Mark switched back to the camera image, it was dark. But that wasn't because of the camera. They were obviously in a dense layer of cloud, which parted to reveal the ocean passing by below. Mark imagined he could make out ridges of spray on the waves, but that was impossible. The Hopper stabilized. The camera was now looking steadily downward as he passed a group of islands, slowly drifting towards the continent. The ocean basin, which was thought to be a huge impact crater, was up to 125 miles deep in places. The islands floated on its surface. They had not yet managed to land on one.

The flight was coming to an end, Mark noted. It was getting uncomfortable again. The storm was tugging at the capsule, which was slowing down and offering less resistance. Mark couldn't intervene, but the controls would bring him down safely. It had been tested under all circumstances. The emergency Hopper had an engine twice as powerful as its standard counterpart.

The capsule tilted. Suddenly it was vertical again. It startled Mark, but the Hopper was merely preparing to land. Swaying, it lowered itself to the ground. The camera showed the blue-green top of the vegetation layer. It was dazzling. Tiny silicon crystals in the leaves of the brine trees reflected unused energy from the sun. Their crowns formed a dense canopy that allowed almost no view of the surface, but at the same time protected them from the acid rain. In order to set up the research base, it had been necessary to burn a large hole in the canopy.

The hole came into view. It was steaming. In the layer below the canopy, energy was mainly generated thermally. There was always tropical humidity here. Even the air was alive, as the planet's explorers had experienced first-hand. Since then, no one ever traveled below the canopy without a mask.

The Hopper swayed as it sank to the ground on a jet of fire from the engine. The storm tried to sweep it away at the last second, and only eased shortly before landing. Mark instinctively clenched his fists. The engine roared once more, then fell silent. The Hopper hovered as if it had not yet realized that the engine was no longer supporting it; then Adad pulled him into its arms with all its might as they touched down. A jolt hit Mark in the hip.

He immediately yanked the radio out of his breast pocket. Tailin had to be nearby.

"Mark here. I've landed. Are you okay?"

No answer. Where was she now? He had asked her to wait at the base! Mark tapped the screen, which now showed an exit symbol. It was crossed out in red. "Equip breathing mask," it said below. He opened a compartment at stomach level, which was printed with a picture of a mask, and took it out. It seemed too big at first, but then the fabric contracted until it perfectly enveloped his face. He attached the accompanying bottle to his belt. The red cross above the exit symbol disappeared, and he tapped it.

Suddenly, the entire wall in front of him also disappeared. It folded aside with considerable momentum, presumably operated by a strong spring. Mark swayed and almost fell forward, but managed to grasp the edge of what was now effectively a door with his right hand. Beneath him, a ladder dropped from the Hopper. The air was hot and humid, and the areas of his skin not covered by fabric were burning. Yet he was still standing under the shelter of the vehicle. About half a yard in front of him, acidic water rained down from the sky in strings. It was as dark as dusk. He took a deep breath of air. It smelled unpleasant, even though he was wearing his breathing mask. The exhaust fumes from the engine had probably burned away some vegetation. The mask filtered biological components and toxins from the air and added another five percent oxygen. Clearly, it didn't consider the smell of burning to be toxic.

Mark tapped his wristwatch until he reached the map display.

Something was flashing to the left of his location. That must be the research base. He unfolded the additional display to see more. Everything looked very simple on the map; it was fifty yards away at most. The Hopper that Roger and Tailin had come in was about 300 yards away on the other side.

"Tailin, Roger, can you hear me?"

No answer again. *Damn!* Had one of Adad's megafauna attacked the base? Mark peered out cautiously. The circular puddles up ahead could be traces of a multifeet that had been filled with rain. He'd have to watch out for holes.

Mark searched the compartments in the wall that had folded away from him. Two cloaks – that should be enough to reach the base. The rain seemed to be coming straight down, as it should. Mark started to step onto the top rung of the ladder, but noticed that a safety harness had automatically fastened around his stomach. He undid it, then pulled the cloak over his head and climbed down the ten steps of the ladder.

He was no longer accustomed to walking on the soft ground, so he was briefly startled as he stepped off the ladder. He checked the direction on his watch and set off.

The rain proved to be his first oversight. It was only falling straight down next to the Hopper. As soon as Mark stepped out of the vessel's slipstream, the droplets became a plaything of the wind, which slipped into the artificial bald spot in the vegetation like a huge tongue into a large gap between teeth.

Adad had greater gravity than Earth. As a result, the raindrops were smaller - and the storm had a particularly easy time with them. Mark was glad his face was protected by the mask. He felt sorry for his hands, which had to hold onto the cloak that the wind would otherwise carry away. Droplets pattered on his skin, etching away his hair and digging tiny holes. He would have to self-treat at the base.

But he had to reach the base first, and that was where his second oversight came in: a hedge of prickly cherries stood between him and the blinking dot. Mark was almost certain he hadn't seen it on his last visit down here. It must have sprung up in the past two weeks. Tailin had already ranted on the radio about the aggressive undergrowth. Prickly cherries tasted like a cross between raspberries and cherries. They caused diarrhea in humans, but that hadn't mattered to them - they rarely got fresh food otherwise. Above all, their branches had thorns, which they shot at anything that came near them. He could have used a flamethrower to create a passage for himself, but that was in the base.

Mark gave the hedge a wide berth. It led down to the beach and turned right where the black sand began. There seemed to be no way through - until Mark discovered a hole. Someone had dug out enough sand to create an apparently stable tunnel. From the direction the tailings had been thrown, he deduced that the trench started inside. He thought of Tailin. If the tunnel was her work and she was now on this side of the hedge, she must have seen the emergency Hopper coming! Then why hadn't she run towards him?

He knelt in the soft sand, which was no different from sand on Earth - a welcome exception here. It was strange. They travelled many light years to explore something as exotic as possible, were more than granted their wish, and then wanted nothing more than to recognize a piece of Earth.

Mark got down on all fours and crawled into the hole. He was sheltered from the rain for a moment. At the deepest point of the tunnel, the ground changed. Pale roots emerged from the walls. A worm, perhaps as long as his arm, came crawling towards Mark, but then suddenly curled up and played dead. It must have felt some kind of vibration. Otherwise, the cave was surprisingly free of critters. Perhaps the worm had eaten them all. But it had still seemed hungry until it lapsed into pseudo rigor mortis.

On the other end of the tunnel, the rain continued. Here, just behind the hedge, it fell straight down. Something sharp poked Mark's back. He had probably come too close to the prickly cherries. Standing up, he took a few steps away and checked his position. He needed to head north. According to his map, it was still about fifty yards to the base. The stupid hedge had forced him to take a wide detour.

Just then, he spotted the structure emerging from behind some half-height bushes - or what was left of them. He tried the radio once more, but again received no reply. Perhaps the two were lying exhausted inside the base, sleeping. He hoped so, even if he couldn't believe it. Another scenario was more likely: Tailin had received a call for help from Roger, followed him and perished from the same danger as her colleague.

The base was not locked. The door was closed, but Mark was able to open it easily. It was dark inside and he had to duck his head to avoid bumping into anything. When he stood up again, the light switched on. The room was empty. There was very little space, about one and a half by three yards, so he saw it immediately.

At the edge, someone had made a bed out of blankets. *A bed. A human being.* The blankets had been neatly arranged. Probably Tailin, although Roger was also a very tidy person. Mark checked the supplies. There was enough of everything, even the acid-proof cloaks. The medipack was torn. He took out two rolls of bandages, sprayed liquid plaster on his wounds and wrapped a few layers of cloth around them. The liquid plaster worked wonders, completely soothing the pain. His skin only got a little warm.

There was a computer terminal at one end of the room, which he promptly activated. The radio monitor was running, but only showed a vertical line. Mark spoke into his radio as a test. The base's antenna must be faulty, because the straight line remained. That was why Tailin had called him on her handheld radio. But why wasn't she answering now? He searched the room thoroughly and came across two dead batteries. Great. Was that the explanation? And what about Roger?

He would have to look for both of them. Mark took one of the acid-proof capes, put a second one in his trouser pocket and left the base again.

Outside it had become brighter, although the sun was already close to the horizon. The storm had passed, and the rain was slowly subsiding. All the more reason for him to hurry; after the storm, and especially at night, life on Adad would return to its usual activity. He fumbled for the taser he always carried in his left uniform pocket. It wouldn't help against multifeet, but they could be avoided. More treacherous were the sucker leaves, which could imitate almost perfectly the pretty blossom of an orchid.

It didn't matter. He would not return without Tailin. Mark walked around the base, searching for traces, but the rain had left nothing. At least the acid had one advantage: all the vegetation around the base had melted into a brown mass covering the ground. To the south and east, he had a good view as far as the hedge, which was apparently immune to the acid. At least that was a new insight. From the west, the brine forest cast long shadows, and to the north it stood like a wall.

Mark opted for the west. That was where the original Hopper had landed, and Roger had left from there to search for Tailin. Maybe he could kill two birds with one stone. However, crossing the brine forest did not prove easy. The silicon-reinforced crowns had let hardly any of the acid rain through. It now accumulated up to a hundred yards above him and helped the trees utilize silicon from the earth. It dripped through from time to time, but the new cloak protected Mark. The cloak had pockets on the inside for his hands and several strings to fasten it around his body. Mark thought it probably made him look like a walking trash bag.

His progress was slow because the vegetation was so dense. The plants used every part of the ecosystem. Stalactite roots protruded from the forest canopy and stalagmite seedlings stretched towards them from the ground. They resembled the limestone formations in Terran caves, because they grew towards each other. Where they met, tangles of branches and twigs formed, in which sliders liked to nest - a species that could move up and down vines at lightning speed and could also fly limited distances. It was amusing to watch them flutter through the air with all eight legs until they caught hold of a branch.

"Tailin, Roger, please respond!"

He no longer had much hope that Tailin would answer him after seeing the empty batteries in the base. But what was going on with Roger? He was an experienced explorer and had always done better than Mark himself during training in the jungles of Terra Nova.

No one answered. Mark checked his progress. Strange flowers kept appearing in the bushes to the left and right. He immediately thought of sucker leaves, although the flowers' shape was unfamiliar. Or perhaps because of that. The sucker leaves had obviously developed a strategy of constantly changing their appearance so that their victims would not start avoiding them. They usually ate ring slugs.

These critters had shiny, golden, snail-like shells and liked to suck nectar from flowers by wrapping themselves around the calyxes. This made it look as if the flowers were wearing beautifully decorated rings. If the ring slugs were attacked, they withdrew into their shells. But the sucker leaves had a solution for this - negative pressure, which drew the soft flesh of the ring slugs out of their pretty casing. Roger had a whole collection of ring slug shells, which he said he would give to his daughter if he ever had one. He probably collected them for himself, but didn't want to admit it.

"Roger, are you around here somewhere?"

Only at the last second did Mark spot something flying towards him. It was coming straight towards his face. He quickly dropped to the ground. *Too late*, he thought. But as he lay in the dirt and felt his face, he didn't find the dreaded sucker leaf that would have relentlessly sucked the flesh from his bones. Realizing he was unharmed, he quickly stood up. A yard in front of him, a slider bent over a sucker leaf, grasping its victim with six of its legs. With the remaining two, it dismembered it and stuffed the pieces into its mouth. *Insane*. No one had ever seen a slider feeding before.

A clearing appeared amid the heavy foliage as Mark came to the beach. He was safe on the fine sand. He felt like running, but at the same time he was afraid to enter the Hopper. It must be empty; otherwise Tailin or Roger would have answered him by now.

Eventually he reached the spaceship. It looked to be in good condition from the outside. It was upright, as it should be on the ground. What was wrong with the antenna? It was so dark by now that Mark could just make it out, but he couldn't examine it. The exit at the back was closed, but the ladder was lowered. Mark climbed up and opened the hatch at the top. The airlock was empty. He waited for the pressure to equalize - the pressure in the rocket was slightly lower than outside - and exited the airlock.

He smelled it immediately. Tailin was here - or had been here. The airlock opened into the workshop. Climbing to the next floor, he saw the kitchen was also empty. Tailin's scent intensified. He climbed the ladder, opened the hatch to the control center - and there he found her.

Tailin was sitting in the command chair, which she had

folded back. Her eyes were closed, but she was breathing. He pulled himself through the opening in the floor. At that moment, she startled.

"Roger?" she asked, "Ah, it's you."

She sounded almost disappointed.

"Yes, it's me. I'm so glad I found you."

"Me too, Mark." Tailin suddenly burst into tears. "Something awful has happened. Roger's gone!"

"Hold on, we'll sort it out together. Roger's probably fine. We just have to find him."

Tailin stood up and they hugged each other tightly.

"Why haven't you been in contact?" he asked her.

She pointed to her radio, which was lying on the back of the armchair, its screen gray.

"That's what I thought," Mark said. "But what about the Hopper's radio?"

"I tried, but I guess the antenna couldn't hold up to the storm."

"Damn."

"Is your radio still working?" asked Tailin.

"Mine? Yes, great. Why?"

"Too bad. I was hoping it was just broken. Then there would be some hope for Roger."

"What do you mean?"

"Roger doesn't do stupid things like running out of batteries. He always has a solution, even if it's building a crank to recharge it. If your radio were broken, I could imagine that his was still working, and he'd be fine."

Tailin was definitely overthinking, but that was what she did.

"I'm sure he's fine, Tailin," he said.

Mark wasn't actually all that sure, but saying so made him feel better.

"But not for long," Tailin disagreed. She had a talent for imagining the darkest version of reality. "The sun is about to set. You know the chances of survival at night. He must be out there all alone."

"We'll look for him together. First, we need to arm ourselves properly, then we'll head out. Together we can search the area systematically. You'll see, we'll find him."

"Honestly, you're scaring me, Mark. If we need heavy

weapons and have to search every square inch for Roger, he can't be doing well at all."

Instead of answering, he climbed two floors down to the workshop, where the weapons locker was located, and opened it. One of the long-barreled weapons was missing. At least Roger was armed. Reassuring - and worrying at the same time. Two laser carbines remained, and two automatic weapons. The lasers fired quietly and with little recoil – perfect for defending a ship or a base with its own power source. But they would be no good for searching for Roger, because the heavy battery pack they required would keep getting caught in the undergrowth. Mark had already dealt with this unpleasant experience.

He took one of the automatic weapons out of the cupboard, along with four magazines. Four times thirty rounds, enough to knock a multifeet off its eighteen thick legs. Some of the local wildlife that ranged beyond the brine forests had developed heavy armor because of the acid rain. Unfortunately, this included the multifeet, which were vaguely reminiscent of earthly elephants.

Tailin stood behind him and breathed down his neck. His hair stood on end. It was a completely inappropriate moment, but even after three years, she was still incredibly attractive to him.

"Do you want a gun?" he asked.

Tailin didn't like guns. She didn't like it when he killed and dissected animals either, but that was his job.

"Give me whatever you have," she replied.

That was unexpected. He pressed the second automatic weapon into her hand. The barrel was a little oily, so he wiped his hand on his trousers and earned a reproachful look. *As if a little oil matters right now!* Mark took four more magazines from a side compartment and handed them to Tailin. She inserted one into the gun and checked the safety. Before the voyage to Gliese 163, they had been trained on all available weapons.

"Are we ready?" he asked.

"I'm ready."

"Do you have an acid-proof cloak, just in case?"

Tailin nodded and pointed to the bulging pocket of her uniform jacket. The camouflage patterned military uniforms had proven surprisingly practical for surface operations. They provided good protection from the aggressive flora when you weren't trying to crawl through a hedge of prickly cherry. There was no helping the constant sweating, though.

As they entered the airlock, Mark checked his radio. There was no activity on the usual bands. Tailin also switched on her radio. She had obviously loaded it with fresh batteries.

"We stay together at all costs," Mark said. "No splitting up, okay?"

He put on his breathing mask.

"No splitting up," Tailin confirmed.

Then she slipped her mask over her face. Mark opened the outer door and was greeted by a beautiful sunset. The dark blue at the zenith gradually faded into orange and red tones towards the horizon, where a ruby sun gleamed.

"It almost looks like Earth today," he said.

Normally, the daytime sky was purple and the sunset brownish.

"That's because of the heavy acid rain," Tailin explained, her voice muffled by the mask. "It must have washed out the sulfur dioxide. It has a center of absorption in the green range, so it distorts the visual impression. It's not quite the Earth's sky either – the blue is less saturated."

Tailin was serious as usual. Mark made no further comment as he climbed down the ladder. The sky was probably not as blue because there was less oxygen in the atmosphere. In half an hour it would be pitch black. They were in the tropics, so twilight didn't last very long.

The ground around the Hopper was still wet, and the acid-eaten vegetation had collapsed even more. Mark could no longer distinguish stems from leaves.

"I found a small tunnel leading under a hedge of prickly cherry," he stated.

"I dug that," replied Tailin.

"Good, then we should look north," he said. "I came from the south, to the west is the sea, and to the east the prickly cherries are blocking the way."

"And if Roger came through my tunnel?"

"Then I would have run into him. The emergency Hopper is parked on the other side of the hedge."

"But why would he run into the brine forest to the north?" asked Tailin. "There's nothing there."

"Because of the acid rain? The trees provide pretty good protection. He must have suspected you were there - Roger had no way of knowing whether you had a protective cloak. I don't have any other explanation."

"Agreed. Off to the north."

THE SHADOWS OF THE BRINE TREES MERGED WITH THE NIGHT. It was getting so dark that Mark had to switch on his flashlight. Its beam was unpleasantly blinding and at the same time made them an attractive target for the local life. But without the light, they would inevitably step into one of the traps set by the flora and fauna.

They walked one behind the other, Tailin securing their rear. As soon as he could no longer hear her breathing, he halted. They called for Roger again and again. It was so dark that he could be lying three yards from the path without them noticing him. Their calls, on the other hand, certainly didn't go unnoticed in this forest, nor did the cracking of the branches when they broke through the undergrowth.

Suddenly there was a hard smack on his shoulder that made him jump.

"Some animal made itself at home on you," Tailin explained.

He stopped and felt his shoulder. His fingers encountered sticky remains, along with something silky and soft. A zeppelin! Made of an incredibly light material reminiscent of silk, they filled their bodies with air and floated by using chemical reactions to heat the air. They obtained the necessary sulfuric acid while still in the larval stage in the crowns of the brine trees. After pupating, they performed their mating dance far above in the canopy, then drifted gently to the ground to lay their eggs. After hatching, the larvae climbed back up the trees.

It was only two months ago that Mark had finally been able to verify this lifecycle. He dropped the thin shell and wiped a few splashes from his neck. It was a good thing that Tailin had killed the zeppelin. It liked to lay its eggs in the skin of animals of the same temperature, which would spread the larvae throughout the forest. Mark would hate to become a host.

"That was a zeppelin," he said.

"Ah, I didn't know they were in season again."

That was true. Zeppelin season normally ended before hurricane season, since gentle hovering was not an option in strong winds. This zeppelin must have been a late developer.

A slight hissing sound came from the jungle, causing Mark to halt. Another hiss, and a third. They all sounded slightly different. So, three of them, at least.

"Did you hear that?" he asked quietly, drawing his gun and releasing the safety.

"Uh-huh."

From behind, he heard the click of Tailin's safety lever. They positioned themselves back-to-back without exchanging a word. The hissing spoke a clear language: a pack of lion's-teeth was on the hunt. They had given the species that name because they looked like very large dandelions when at rest. During the day, they extended their jagged, blue-green leaves into the air, usually at the edge of brine forests, and soaked up energy from the sunlight. At night, they habitually supplemented their diet with animal life. The hissing sound was produced by rubbing their leaves together.

Mark had developed a theory about this: At the edges of the brine forests, the acid rain must have washed all the minerals out of the soil, so that plants growing there had at some point learned to use their roots as legs. In general, the flora on Adad was unusually mobile, which indicated a high level of geological activity. This was probably also due to the planet's proximity to its star, the enormous gravity of which must be rolling through its surface.

Another hissing sound, but this time it came from the other side. Now there were two possibilities: The lion's-teeth had decided against attacking and had passed them by, likely in favor of an easier victim. Lion's-teeth also liked to feast on carrion. But they might also have encircled them. That would fit in with their hunting strategy. The next hissing should come from the original direction. Individuals probably used the sounds to signal to each other that they had reached their position.

Mark listened intently. There it was. It was clearly coming

from the same direction as last time. The lion's-teeth had passed them; perhaps two opponents were too many for them. Life on Adad was not only unusually mobile, but also defensive.

"They're gone," he said. "Lucky for us."

"We have to go after them," Tailin said.

"Are you insane? We're lucky they spared us."

"Because they sensed an easier meal."

"Yes, so what? All the better for us."

"Mark, we're looking for someone, remember? What if Roger is about to be their preferred meal?"

Mark thought about it. Then why hadn't Roger reported back? They didn't yet know whether the lion's-teeth could follow tracks. If so, they might indeed be after Roger. Tailin was right. They had to play it safe, even if it meant putting themselves in danger and perhaps only saving the life of a flammingo in the end. It might even reward them by living up to its name in fright and bursting into flames. That was how the animal – a two-legged creature about the size of a fox – normally released its seeds. It could also use the behavior to defend itself against attackers. Mark had even observed a single specimen separating itself from its group and sacrificing itself to a pack of pursuers.

They made their way through the bushes to the left. Unfortunately, the undergrowth was even denser here. Mark kept getting smacked in the face. Most of the blows landed on his mask, but one caught him on the neck, causing him to feel around. A branch of thorns had left several spikes, still twisting to penetrate his skin. His research had revealed that only specimens of the soft thorny-branch grew in the vicinity of the new base. Human skin was too tough for its thorns, so Mark wasn't worried. Well, not much. Hopefully they hadn't passed into the territory of the hard thorny-branches by now.

The hissing came closer, then moved away again.

"We're on the right track," Tailin said.

She was in front of him. He hadn't even noticed her taking the lead. Tailin seemed to be in more of a hurry by the minute, but the hissing noises were still getting further away.

"I think they think we're chasing them," Mark said.

He stopped because he was completely out of breath, but Tailin paid no attention to him and rushed on ahead.

"Tailin, wait! No solo runs, you promised."

She stopped abruptly. Her flashlight showed that she had turned around and was waving angrily at him.

"You're too slow!"

A hiss, so far away that Mark couldn't even tell which direction it was coming from.

"They're gone," he said. "They must have been scared of us."

"Maybe word got around about the massacre you committed on them," Tailin teased.

Massacre, sure. He had caught one in a steel trap so that he could examine it. Somehow it had summoned its pack, which in turn had attacked the base. Mark had quickly put an end to that with the laser carbine. A direct connection to its power source meant that the weapon could fire at full power and at any speed. Out here in the dark, they would have had a harder time defending themselves.

Luckily the bastards didn't know that. Their intelligence was limited and seemed to derive mainly from the group. The dissection hadn't revealed anything that he could interpret as a nerve center. There wasn't even a large node where all the signal pathways met. The network was completely chaotic, but very efficient. The organism he had studied had solved the complex "traveling salesman problem" without ever having heard of graph theory. Evolution was a master of its trade.

"If that's really true, I wonder how they recognized me," Mark said.

"By smell," said Tailin. "Don't be mad, but with the amount of sweat we can't help putting out down here, we're guaranteed to leave a real pheromone trail."

He hadn't found an olfactory center, but Tailin was probably right. Plants, on Adad just as on Earth, were dependent on substances that occurred in human sweat, among other things. Being able to detect differences in the concentration of these compounds would give them an evolutionary advantage.

"If only we had that good a nose," said Mark. "We would have found Roger by now."

They started marching north again. Roger couldn't have gone very far on foot. The search area was still huge, but limited.

"Can't we use one of the drones?" asked Tailin.

"Maybe tomorrow. In the dark, they'd have no chance of avoiding the weavers' nets."

The crowns of the brine trees were so dense that drones had to fly underneath them to spot anything on the ground. Below, however, the nets were lurking for a worthwhile catch. They looked like giant spider webs. Their threads were slightly thicker than the web threads of terrestrial spiders, adapted to the higher gravity. But there were no spiders in them! Mark had calculated from the thickness of the threads and the size of the webs that the weavers must be about four by eight inches. They had searched everywhere for them, not looking only for eight-legged creatures, of course, but considering every possible body shape.

They had no success. He had then lurked for weeks until he saw something caught in a web, expecting that then the spider would have to come out! But he was wrong. The web simply wrapped itself around the prey and began to digest it. The web itself was the organism. After the victim was digested, the net dissolved. It consisted of very thin threadworms that retreated into the earth, where they presumably sired their offspring. However, Mark had not yet been able to verify this.

Of course, the weavers' nets could not digest a drone. But getting them out of the sticky material was difficult enough, as Mark knew from experience. At some point, the threadworms died if their prey was not edible, but it took a week for that to happen.

"Look!" Tailin exclaimed under her breath.

Her spotlight swept over a clearing. It must be twenty yards wide. Mark shone his light upwards. They were still under the crowns of the brine trees. He stepped into the clearing, noticing it had not been created naturally. Something had trampled down all the vegetation here.

"It could only have been multifeet," he said.

Mark instinctively ducked as a face suddenly stared out at him. It was a flower of the gawp bush, which got its name from its resemblance to a human face. But not just any face - a shrunken head. The shape didn't seem to have a specific function. The openings that suggested a mouth and nose were used by water-bearers to collect nectar by sticking their long legs into them. There was also a pseudo gawp bush that exploited this behavior to prey on water-bearers. The water-bearers in turn used this to reproduce, because the "legs" were actually sexual organs containing their eggs. These developed into larvae inside the pseudo gawp bush.

Mark picked up the flower and held it out to Tailin.

"They even flattened these," he said.

Gawp bushes had extremely elastic branches that extended upwards despite the high gravity. You had to press them down with a minimum of 1600 pounds to crush them. Mark had investigated this because the toughness of the material might have industrial applications. His employers would be pleased by any findings that promised economic benefits.

"Oh no!" Tailin exclaimed.

Mark shone his flashlight on the brine tree trunk she stood next to as she felt over its bark. Glittering streaks coming from finger-thick holes revealed what must have happened here. It was the tree's siliceous resin, which flowed from its wounds and sealed them at the same time. Tailin ran to the next tree.

"Here too!" she shouted, "and here!"

"Roger must have used the gun to fight off the multifeet," said Mark.

"But why? They're herbivores," said Tailin.

She was right. That couldn't be the whole story. Pointing the flashlight at the ground, he studied the clearing. He spotted some shredded leaves with saw teeth. They must be from a lion's-teeth. Another one. He searched further and found a second specimen. Roger hadn't been fighting the multifeet, but a group of lion's-teeth. Perhaps he had injured one of the multifeet and turned them all against him. They were very social creatures that determinedly defended their own kind.

They both inspected the clearing. It was Tailin who found the missing weapon. It was still in working order, but the magazine was gone. Mark tracked down three empty magazines among the plant debris scattered around the clearing. Roger hadn't made it easy for his attackers. But what had happened to him? They certainly didn't find his body, not even the skeleton that the lion's-teeth would have left behind if they emerged victorious.

Roger must have put the lion's-teeth to flight. Or the multifeet had scared them off. Where was their friend?

"Maybe he rode off on a multifeet," said Mark.

"Typical – Roger's disappeared and you're joking," said

Tailin. "He'll be somewhere in the surrounding woods. Possibly badly injured."

"If he's lying motionless in the undergrowth, we won't spot him in the dark. We'll have to call off the search for today."

He could set a drone on Roger's scent. The sensors on the new models were very sensitive. Only recently he had tracked a group of skeleton foxes that way.

"You'll have to go back without me," Tailin said firmly. "He set out because of me. I have to find him."

She had a guilty conscience. Mark could understand that. He should have forbidden Roger to follow his wife, but instead, he had been grateful to him. This was what he got for it now.

"It will be more efficient to sleep first and then search with the drone. One of us will keel over at some point."

"Probably you," said Tailin. "You're not as fit as you used to be."

"I've been sitting in the Albatross for two weeks straight because you wanted to find yourself," he said. "So, have you found anything?"

That came out more bitter than intended. He could barely make out her face in the darkness. The fact that she couldn't find the right answer spoke for itself. But wasn't it true? She had shipped him off into space because a certain routine had crept in after three years of dating. As if it were any different for other couples! *But we're not other couples,* she would have replied.

"Okay, you're right. We're not quite ourselves right now," said Tailin. "We should go back to the Hopper."

"I suggest the base," said Mark. "That's where our drones are stored. I could program one for Roger's scent. Do we have any samples from him?"

"There should be something in the laundry box. It wasn't easy to do laundry at the base."

August 3, 2802, Earth's moon

THE EARTH WORE A RING. YINI BLINKED, SINCE SHE COULD ONLY see it when she squinted. The lights of the ring came from countless sources. They were the windows in the residential towers of the Ring City, the illuminated cabins of the elevators that traveled between the various neighborhoods, the glowing engines of rockets arriving in the Ring from Earth or the solar system, or the play of colors on billboards advertising a better life in Inner Earth or travel to the North American Wildlife Refuge.

Perhaps her parents were looking out of such a window at that very moment. The Sky Ring was visible from the Moon as the Earth rose only once every few years, when the Ring, Moon and Earth happened to be at exactly the right angle. On a Ring Day like this, relatives living apart traditionally waved to each other, though they were all aware that they were still about 240,000 miles apart.

Kang tapped her. "Had enough?" he asked.

Sometimes he seemed like a little child to her. But she wasn't his mother, she was his twin sister.

"No, I haven't. I've only just started," Yini replied.

She took her rucksack off her shoulders and set it down on the pavement, which was as hard as concrete here. She had chosen a cul-de-sac where there were hardly any vehicles on the road, apart from the refuse collection vehicles that used it to access Bigtrash – the largest garbage dump in the solar system, supposedly visible to the naked eye from the surface of Earth during a full moon.

Today was a public holiday, so she didn't expect any disruptions. Yini unzipped her backpack and the front section folded down. She took a tripod out of the right-side pocket and set it up.

"Can you set it up horizontally, please?" she asked.

"If I have to," said Kang.

"Please. May I remind you that this trip was your present for my birthday?"

"I'm doing it."

Kang bent down and fiddled with the clamps on the tripod legs. Meanwhile, Yini took the telescope out of her rucksack. It was the cheapest Newton you could get on the moon. It had 76 millimeters of objective aperture with a focal length of 70 millimeters, which gave a decent light yield, at least for the price.

"May I?" she asked.

"You may."

She placed the telescope on the tripod so that Kang could tighten the fastening screw. Then she pressed the power button. The telescope moved once in a circle, as far as it could go, then from the horizon to the zenith. If she wanted to use it to observe stars, she used a tracker app installed in her spacesuit. But the Earth was much easier to find than any star.

Yini stood next to the eyepiece and pointed the telescope at her home planet, which wasn't her home at all.

"How are you going to see through it?" asked Kang, pointing to her helmet.

Yini triumphantly took an eyepiece adapter out of her trouser pocket - basically a small digital camera that could be screwed directly onto the eyepiece. Using the keypad on her forearm, she configured the suit to display the transmitted images on the inside of her helmet. This meant she didn't even have to bend down to look through the eyepiece.

The image was impressive. She first sighted a huge expanse of blue water. When she turned the telescope slightly to the left, a land mass came into view, which she recognized as Europe. It was mostly brown, with green areas only visible on the southern and northern edges. The telescope turned the image upside down. North was down and south was up. Europe was slowly growing again from bottom to top. She continued to pan north. There, the first ice-covered areas! Since the last inhabitants had officially left the planet, it had slowly cooled down again. That didn't mean that no one lived there anymore. Her parents had...

"Can I have a go?" asked Kang.

"Want me to set it for you?" she offered.

"I'll do it."

He tapped his wrist as if he were tickling himself. Yini approved the connection request to the telescope. The telescope swiveled upwards. Then it moved slowly to the right, passed through to the bottom and raised its head again. It stopped at the highest point and moved backwards. Suddenly, music came out of her headphones and the telescope started moving to it. It was... dancing.

"Jeez, Kang!" shouted Yini.

Her brother really was full of nonsense. She cut the connection, and the telescope was still again.

"Hey, weren't you listening?" asked Kang.

"Listening? You've got nothing but nonsense in your head."

"That was 'Happy birthday to you', didn't you recognize it? The telescope wanted to congratulate you. I wanted to wish you a happy birthday!"

Oh. Her cheeks grew warm. She turned to Kang and hugged him. Their transparent helmets bumped against each other.

"Sorry," she said, "I'm sorry. That was a very original idea. Happy birthday to you, too."

"Zahir gave me the idea," said her brother.

"It was definitely a surprise," replied Yini. "Want to take a look at space together?"

She released the connection to the telescope. First she pointed it at the Sky Ring. The huge structure looked much more impressive when magnified. It had housed almost all of humanity for a while now.

"Are Mother and Father watching us right now?" asked Kang.

Yini looked at her watch. "Not likely. They're still at work. On the Ring, Ring Day is not a holiday."

"Weird," said Kang.

He was right about that. The lunar colony must have introduced the holiday on its own.

"What about Mars?" asked Kang.

"We'd have to be able to see through the moon for that."

"And Neomars?"

"Saturn is currently being outshone by the Earth, so we have no chance."

"Then I want to head back now," said Kang.

Yini nodded and yawned. She increased the oxygen content in the air she breathed, which usually woke her up again. She took off the eyepiece adapter, loosened the locking screws and removed the telescope from the tripod to put it back in her backpack. Kang took care of the tripod without her having to say anything. Apparently, he had grown up a bit at some point.

"Ulita here," a voice suddenly sounded in her helmet. "I hate to disturb you on your day off."

She knew if her boss started off like that, something unpleasant would follow.

"What is it?" asked Yini.

"I've received a transmission to be given to our best eavesdropper. And I thought of you."

Ulita usually thought of herself first, so it must be a strenuous task. It would certainly keep Yini busy for a week, not to mention the research program on Kepler...

"Someone else will take over the research program while you're occupied," said Ulita. "I'll expect you in half an hour."

The connection dropped. Ulita hadn't even waited for her confirmation.

"Did you hear that?" asked Yini.

"It's your own fault," said Kang. "Why are you so good? Why don't you be like me?"

"I only enjoy things I'm good at."

"Except for singing."

"What? I hit the notes pretty well, according to the choirmaster!"

Yini hoisted her rucksack onto her shoulders. They had about twenty minutes of walking ahead of them. They had walked until the station disappeared below the horizon - and that was only about a mile on the moon.

"Are we going swimming today?" asked Kang.

Yini tried to exercise every day to compensate for the low lunar gravity.

"I don't know yet. If the new job allows it, I'd love to."

On the horizon, a crab with a hundred eyes crawled towards them. At least, that was how the Great Archive looked, with its huge, impact-resistant roof - the crab's shell - which extended down to the ground in several places - the feet. This area of the Moon was so uniform that Yini never knew exactly whether she was heading towards the horizon, or the horizon was heading towards her.

Kang and Yini moved ahead in the typical fashion for the moon. Their bodies leaning far forward, they pushed themselves firmly off the ground with their feet and leapt forward in long strides. It wasn't particularly strenuous, but it took a lot of concentration.

"We should have taken a vehicle," said Kang.

"That might have kicked up dust," replied Yini.

A short time later, Kang's wish was granted. A vehicle came towards them, a simple electric buggy that drove autonomously. It stopped right in front of them.

"That must be from your boss," said Kang.

"Probably." Yini climbed onto the narrow but comfortable seat.

Her brother made no move to take the second seat.

"I'll stay outside for a while," he said.

"Suit yourself."

At the same moment, the buggy drove off as if it had been listening to them. Yini briefly considered that there might be a consciousness hiding inside, but if so, the buggy would have been marked accordingly. Because of the different rights that people and things had, a conscious machine had to be clearly recognizable.

This one was ordinary. It drove cross-country, so Yini had to hold on tight. When the shadow of the giant crab finally engulfed her and the buggy, she was glad to reach her destination.

May 5, 2799, Gliese 411

A BRIDGE OF FIRE SPANNED THE VOID BETWEEN THE SUN AND ITS first planet. A jet-black stamp was imprinted on the heat-tanned skin of the celestial body. It was the shadow of its only moon, which moved as if in slow motion across a planet larger than Earth. The edges of the stamp glowed blue. Simultaneous sunrises and sunsets colored them, revealing that the thin atmosphere consisted mainly of carbon dioxide.

So this is Gliese 411. Monte had never been here before, even though the system was only eight light years away from Earth. He slowed the *Curious* down until the ship reached a stable orbit around the red dwarf, and searched the system at all wavelengths. There was nothing here. The only terrestrial planet orbited far too close to its central star to be colonized at an affordable cost, and the gas giants further out didn't offer any economically viable resources. Not even tourists were interested in the system - it was too boring. That was exactly why he had never been here.

But was it necessary to forgo at least setting up an automatic research station? The extra eyes and ears would have made his current task much easier... Somewhere in this system there must be a wreck floating like a needle in a haystack, but there were no witnesses who could have observed the arrival and subsequent destruction of the ship. Was there indeed a needle floating in this haystack? Monte speeded up the system clock. After waking up, he always found it difficult to focus his thoughts. A more rapid pulse was exhausting in the long run, but it helped at least as much as two cups of coffee when he was in his Biobag.

Slowly, slowly. Time didn't really matter. It took three years for the wreck's distress signal to be picked up by a transport ship. Gliese 411 was far from any major routes. However, the transporter was not just any ship, but the flagship of Neomars, and for that reason alone it was equipped with an energy-hungry tachyon transmitter. Since the signal had an Earth identification, the captain had forwarded it to Earth via T-Field according to protocol.

Why had Admiral Gaudlitz entrusted him, of all people, with the investigation? He was not part of the navy's secret service, and usually searched for runaway teenagers or expensively insured wrecks. That was the next question. Monte had been pondering it ever since the head of the Earth Fleet refused to answer it in a very strange way: "You'll see, Monte, I'm sure you'll see."

Great. The first thing he wanted to do was get thoroughly drunk. Intoxication was the best way to start an investigation like this. He had tested that often enough. But to do that he would have to get his Biobag out of the stasis cell. Without his biological body, intoxication was pointless. The simulations that today's youth were so keen on didn't work for him, or at least that was what he believed. Only the original could convey how alcohol burned in the throat.

But it was too early for that as long as he had not found the wreck. The Biobag was sensitive enough that he could only accelerate at a maximum of 10 g in it. The central star of Gliese 411 was a red dwarf, and the system was therefore comparatively tiny. But three astronomical units to the outermost gas giant was still 280 million miles. Monte didn't feel like spending the next few months in this barren system.

Oh well. The *Curious* had apparently calculated that he was most likely to find the wreck in the orbit of the rocky planet. There could only be one reason for that: The wrecked ship must have had a passenger on board who at least attempted to reach safety on the planet. Monte would see whether they succeeded as soon as he tracked down the wreck. It was time to get to work.

Or a rush first? He checked the status of the Biobag. His body was lying naked in the stasis cell, eyes closed, arms and legs extended like Leonardo's Vitruvian Man. There were cables in every orifice. He felt a little sorry for his Biobag. The thawing process had not yet begun. The *Curious* probably assumed he wouldn't need it. Or wanted to prevent him from getting drunk. The on-board AI had developed a certain protective instinct in recent years, which he hadn't yet been able to get rid of.

It knew him pretty well. Monte was annoyed by its paternalism, but it wasn't bad enough to make him think about a reset.

"You actually have," it informed him silently.

"I have not," he contradicted it.

"Yes, you did, just now."

"I developed the idea that I hadn't thought about it."

"But you did think about it."

"You know what? Screw you. You'd better look for that stupid wreck. Gaudlitz is expecting my report as soon as possible."

That was true, but it wasn't the whole truth. He wanted to get out of here. The admiral had promised him he could retire after this mission. Not even three hundred years old! Since humanity had stopped reproducing, there were hardly any retirees. If a Biobag no longer worked, it was simply replaced. Monte would be the first pensioner of the 29th century.

MONTE ACCELERATED THE SHIP AWAY FROM THE PLANET. DESPITE its biblical age of eleven billion years, the planet still had a magnetic field that could interfere with the ship's sensors, and Monte needed every extra percentage of sensitivity. After almost ten years, the sought-after ship was guaranteed to be no warmer than its surroundings. Especially in the asteroid belt that lay between the first gas giant and the rocky planet, it would be perfectly camouflaged - one of millions of fragments that had been tumbling through space for ages.

He still didn't quite understand why the *Curious* hadn't woken him up when they crossed the belt. It was not particularly dense, but if danger existed anywhere in this system, it was there. Danger, of course, was relative. No current spaceship AI would allow a collision under these circumstances. Monte had investigated over a hundred wrecks, mostly on behalf of insurance companies, sometimes at the request of the fleet. The cause had always been either human error or deliberate action.

"I have something," the *Curious* reported.

That was quick. Wonderful! After the Admiral's mysterious orders, he had imagined it would be much more difficult.

"Where?" he asked.

The artificial intelligence slid a spatial representation of a section of the asteroid belt in front of his mind's eye. He had to force himself to accept the image. After a long sleep, such overrides of consciousness always took some getting used to. But he trusted the *Curious*'s AI. It had never let him down and, above all, had never stolen from him, which sometimes happened.

Monte concentrated on the center of the image. There was nothing there.

"What should I be seeing?" he asked.

"Nothing," replied the AI.

"Ah, I can't see anything."

"Very good."

"Can you please explain that to me? I'm just a limited human consciousness."

"Thank you for the implicit compliment," said the AI. "I calculated this point in the void from the orbital changes of some asteroids in the belt."

"How do you know their orbits have changed? You've never been here before."

"These asteroids are moving in unstable orbits that will lead them to collide with the gas giant fairly soon. The force that put them into these orbits must have acted on them relatively recently."

"Like when our wreck flew into the system?"

"Correct, Claudio."

The AI always used his first name. He had asked it several times to call him by his nickname – Monte, short for Pedramonte – but it refused.

"But it's not there anymore," said Monte.

"No, there's nothing there. Almost nothing, anyway," said the AI.

"Now, don't be so mysterious."

"The mass that caused the disturbance is still there. When we get closer, we will probably find WZ mass. The ship must have ejected it from its tank."

WZ mass had about the density of a white dwarf. When compressed in this way, fuel could be transported much more efficiently.

"But why? Why would they want to get rid of fuel? Did they have a leak?"

"Distraction. I suspect it was to create a false trail."

"Ah, then they were being followed."

"That's what it looks like, Claudio."

"That means we're right back where we started."

"No, we have learned something about the situation of the ship we are looking for. You are the human here. What do you deduce from this?"

Monte pretended to think. He hated it when the AI talked to him like a small child. Maybe he should consider a reset after all.

"Set a course for the rocky planet," he ordered.

"Setting course for Gliese 411 b," replied the AI.

This system really was the furthest corner of humanity's backyard. Apparently, the planet didn't even have a proper name. And for this, Monte had been tossed more than two decades into the future. How he hated it! Having to reintegrate into everyday life after such a long time was no fun. His acquaintances would have forgotten him, his favorite pubs would have closed. The admiral would have to pay for that.

"Will you wake me up when we're in orbit, please?" he asked.

Gliese 163 c

It was much easier to march through the forest in daylight. Tailin seemed to be in a bad mood, only speaking when necessary. She also kept yawning, so it was possible she had slept badly. But she probably still resented what he'd said yesterday. She could be vindictive. Mark shook his head. Tailin missed Roger as much as he did.

He breathed in the damp, slightly sour-smelling forest air. The most dangerous animals didn't hunt during the day. Mark had nevertheless strapped on one of the automatic weapons, just in case. He carried the drone in his arms; they wanted to launch it in the clearing to make the most of its maximum flight time. It hadn't been easy to calibrate it to Roger's scent. The proportion of compounds like ammonia, urea and various salts differed considerably between the items of clothing he had worn, and there were also big differences between parts of the body: There was more urea in the pubic area, more salt under the armpits and so on.

A drone was not a dog. It needed a specific target. Mark finally decided on the value that tested the most stable - the salt mixture in the armpits. Wherever Roger might have gone, he must certainly have sweated. It had rained since then, but not much of it should have penetrated the forest canopy.

He let Tailin take the lead this time so that he could better prepare himself for the task ahead. It only took them about twenty minutes to reach the clearing. Shouldn't they have heard

Roger's shots yesterday? He had emptied four magazines. But amid the heavy thunderclaps of the storm, the shots from the submachine gun had probably been a whisper in comparison.

Everything that could go wrong had come together. They must avoid that at all costs in future. *No splitting up, Tailin.* Mark sighed. It was unlikely that she would stick to that, but today he would make sure of it. He would not lose anyone else today.

With sunshine filtering through the canopy, the clearing looked almost idyllic. The smaller plants had already begun to grow again, the dead lion's-teeth had turned brown and no longer posed any danger. They searched the clearing once more. Tailin came across a handkerchief with a few brown stains on it.

"That's probably blood," she said. "He's been injured."

Mark felt the material. It was completely dry. It was probably old blood; with the current humidity it would take longer to dry out that much. He examined the handkerchief more closely. It was stiff at the edges. Those were probably sperm stains, but he didn't tell Tailin that.

"The blood is old," he said. "He probably had a nosebleed at some point."

"Yes, I remember," Tailin said. "He was going to talk to you about it, but he decided against it. He must have been afraid of the conversation."

Mark was not only an exobiologist, but also the ship's doctor. He had received additional medical training for this. Roger always joked that he could treat aliens better than humanoids. That was nonsense, of course.

"Why is that?" he asked.

"He'd rather not know what serious illness he has."

"Because of a nosebleed? Probably none. No one is screened as well as an astronaut."

"I'm sure that would have reassured him."

"I'll tell him as soon as we find him."

He set the drone down in the middle of the clearing and moved a few yards away. A thin beam of light, slipping through a gap in the canopy of brine trees, made a dot on one of the four rotors. There was a shimmer of air. As Mark started the rotors, the air swirled visibly faster. The drone rose to a height of one and a half yards and came towards him, as he had ordered it to do. He put it in patrol mode. It hovered over the clearing in seemingly chaotic but efficiently calculated patterns, trying to pick up the scent.

At first, it acted like an excited sniffer dog that didn't quite know which way to turn. Mark followed its activity on the screen of his watch. The drone was creating a map of the differences in concentration of Roger's vapors across the clearing, which was interesting in itself. There was a focal point at the edge, right next to a brine tree. Roger must have rested there. The trail led from there to the center of the clearing, and then north.

"He must have gone north," Mark said.

Tailin quickly strode to the edge of the clearing.

"There's actually a two- or three-yard-wide break in the thicket here," she said.

"Probably from the multifeet."

"Was he chasing them or were they chasing him?" asked Tailin. "Forget the question. He wouldn't have run away from them. Roger's not that stupid."

She was certainly right. Mark didn't even have to think about it. Escaping a multifeet on your own two legs was impossible. But something was strange. Mark had switched on 3D mode. Roger's trail started on the ground, next to the tree where he had evidently been sitting or lying down. Then the area of highest concentration shifted to about a yard and a half off the ground, which roughly matched Roger's stature. But in the middle of the clearing, the trail suddenly continued at a height of three yards.

He shared his observation with Tailin.

"Maybe it's the rising air," she mused. "It's taken his scent with it."

"That should apply to the entire clearing. The air wouldn't just heat up in the middle."

"But that's where it's warmest."

"Hm." He tilted his head.

"Roger was just over six feet," Tailin said. "To get to three yards, he would've had to be riding a multifeet."

She gave a fake laugh.

"That's true," Mark said.

"You're serious, aren't you?"

Multifeet were peaceable animals. Their playful curiosity combined with their sheer mass made them dangerous nonetheless. They had no concern for the fragility of their toys. But it would probably not be impossible to ride one, if you managed to make the game appealing to them. The difficult part would be guiding them where you wanted them to go.

Mark steered the drone to the gap. The trail continued, still at a height of three yards.

"So the air rose in the gap too?" he asked.

"I don't know. Riding... that would be brilliant," said Tailin.

"Or maybe not. Those animals travel up to seventy-five miles a day. On average! They could have taken him far from here."

"But at least that means he's alive, doesn't it?"

"Maybe."

An image of the slider came to his mind's eye, shredding the sucker leaf. Multifeet had eighteen legs, and they could use the foremost and rearmost pair as arms. He didn't want to douse Tailin's fresh hope, so he said nothing. But if a multifeet had been playing with Roger like the slider with the sucker leaf, they might very well find him in pieces. Where had he got the stupid idea that Roger had attempted to ride a multifeet?

Well, it was Tailin's idea, but it had seemed clever to him for a moment. Roger must have known a stunt like that wouldn't get him home. What if he just wanted to escape from the lion's-teeth? After he had successfully fought them off with his weapon? That made no sense. Nothing made sense here. They only had one choice: follow the path that led from the gap.

THE PATH HAD ONE ADVANTAGE: IT WAS EASY TO SEE. THEY MADE rapid progress, though some of the plants had already grown back. There must have been at least three multifeet, because every now and then a side passage opened up without the main path becoming narrower. At one point, Mark followed one of these side paths. All he found was a big pile of multifeet shit. He could smell the stink even through his breathing mask. Apparently the animals were clean, since they separated themselves from the others to do their business.

Roger's trail continued at a height of three yards. How much further could it lead? Over twelve hours had passed since the thunderstorm. At the multifeet's average speed of 6 miles an hour, they could have traveled 75 miles in that time. It would take two days! They could only hope that Roger hadn't ridden all that way.

"I have an idea," said Tailin.

They had been on the trail for three hours. Sweat was running down her temples next to her mask, but her eyes no longer seemed so absent under the glass.

"Out with it," he said.

"How fast does the drone fly?"

"It can do 37 miles an hour."

"Very good. We don't need it to find the way, so let's send it on ahead. It can track down Roger. Surely you can access its camera?"

"If the radio link holds up."

"How far does the radio reach?" asked Tailin.

"About twelve miles. The canopy of the brine trees doesn't allow for more."

"Okay, that's not as far as I hoped, but it's better than nothing."

Now Mark had an idea too. "I can program it to come back into radio range as soon as it finds Roger."

"Perfect. That's what we'll do. Send it off."

IT WAS FORTY MINUTES BEFORE THE DRONE REPORTED BACK.

"It has something," Mark said.

Tailin stepped up next to him and grabbed the arm with his watch. "Let me see!"

He switched to the camera display. They saw a pale face, not wearing a mask. At first Mark was relieved. They finally had him! And he looked fine, like he was sleeping. Had Roger's genetic modification saved him? Neomars geneticists had given him the ability to get by with very little oxygen. In any case, there were no signs of injury. Mark smiled at Tailin. Unfortunately, she couldn't see his smile under the mask. Was that why her eyes looked so fixed and distant? She seemed to be looking right through him.

"Shit," she said. "I was afraid of that."

That was when he realized it, too. Roger wasn't wearing a mask. He was dead. Peaceful, but dead. What had happened?

They had to get to him. Mark called up the data from the drone. The images had been taken about 16 miles away. That was feasible. He let the drone land so it wouldn't use any unnecessary energy, and they set off.

AFTER THREE AND A HALF HOURS OF CONTINUOUS WALKING, THEY found the drone. Although the path had not narrowed, it had made a few bends. According to the watch, they were only about eleven miles from the Hopper. Mark was totally exhausted and wanted to take a break, but Tailin wouldn't rest. The last four miles took them eighty minutes.

They found Roger in a clearing bigger than the one they started from. It was only partially overgrown. Apparently the multifeet spent so much time here that the plants didn't stand a chance. Roger was leaning against a brine tree. He did look peaceful. Mark had the impression that even Tailin, who usually reacted much more emotionally than he did, was somewhat comforted by this. In any case, it was a while before either of them ventured to touch him and disturb Roger's peace. But they were in no hurry. He was dead, no question about it.

It was unpleasant for Mark, but in the end, he had to examine Roger. He lifted Roger away from the tree trunk. As he did so, tufts of grass fell from his chest to the ground. Mark turned his friend on his side. Where he had been lying, the brown earth was covered with a dry, moss-like material. Tailin helped him undress the body.

"Can you check if his breathing mask is lying around here somewhere?" he asked.

Mark wanted to spare his wife the next few steps. She stood up and moved away.

Roger lay in front of him, naked except for his underpants. No, this was no longer Roger. It was a dead shell, and Mark owed it to his friend to determine the cause of death. He found a few bruises on the torso and thighs, but no wounds. He felt the body. There were no signs of fractures. He would only know for sure after a detailed examination, but Roger did not appear to have died in a fight.

"There's no breathing mask here," said Tailin.

Mark covered the body with the clothes Roger had been wearing.

"Maybe he suffocated," Mark said. "His cheeks are red. But I'll have to do an autopsy to find out for sure."

"Do you have to?" asked Tailin.

"I think I owe it to him."

"What good does it do Roger now?"

"That's not the point."

Tailin didn't understand. Everyone was entitled to justice. If Roger had died because he'd lost his breathing mask, someone or something was responsible, and finding that out was part of Mark's concept of justice. Perhaps the lion's-teeth had pushed him harder than it seemed.

Suddenly Tailin let out a sob. Mark stood up and took her in his arms, and through the glass of her breathing mask he saw that her eyes were wet. She must have been crying silently for some time. Her tears were contagious. They held each other and cried. It was sad, it was terrible, but it would be okay, because they had each other.

A screech brought them out of their embrace.

"What was that?" exclaimed Tailin.

Mark looked in the direction of the noise. They had a visitor. His breath caught in his throat.

"There!"

That was all he could get out. Three, no, four multifeet had entered at the other end of the clearing. The sound they'd heard was the damp ground creaking under their weight. The animals came closer. Each had its frontmost pair of legs extended upwards like arms, as if they wanted to pay homage to the humans.

"We should move back slowly," Mark whispered. "Very slowly."

"Wait." Tailin took him by the hand and held tight. "I want to know what they're up to."

"That's far too dangerous. They're too big. They could hurt us without meaning to."

They could hurt you, he thought. If he lost Tailin too, he'd never survive it.

"No, we'll stay. I think they know what to expect from us. How long has Roger been dead?"

"Judging by the degree of rigor mortis, several hours."

"You see! They must have brought him here. They didn't hurt him in the process, did they?"

Mark shook his head. At least their friend had no visible injuries. The giants came closer. He smelled their scent - which made him think of a deep, dark forest - and saw the large, open warts on their skin. Those were not wounds. The warts contained a special type of fungus that produced silicon compounds. The multifeet used it to increase the effectiveness of their armor against the acid rain.

What did the multifeet want from them? The animals were still holding the foremost pair of legs far above their bodies. Nevertheless, the other sixteen legs did not lose their rhythm. They looked like a cross between a caterpillar and an elephant. However, they had no trunk, not even a proper head separate from the body. The physique of the animals on Adad was nothing like what they were familiar with from Earth or Terra Nova.

Nevertheless, the multifeet did not seem completely alien to him. Perhaps it was due to the human tendency to perceive familiar things everywhere, but it seemed more likely to Mark that there really was a certain kinship. He definitely felt it. And the animals had obviously realized that they had to do something with this dead creature. Had they brought Roger here to try and help him? The padding of grass and moss suggested they had.

The multifeet stopped about three yards in front of them. This was the closest they had ever come to one of the giants. Mark had made camera recordings in which he had studied every detail, but in person it was quite different. Their panting, from the breathing openings above the base of each leg, was clearly audible up close. They had their belly folds closed. Mark knew there must be a stomach opening hidden there, because he had seen videos of them stuffing food into the open fold.

They had two eyes at each end, shaped like small domes, with rotating lenses. All the lenses were now focused on Tailin and Mark. What did they look like to the animals? Did they perceive a 3D image? Did they switch off the rear eyes, which were further away? But they kept rotating when the animals moved.

For a few minutes, they all stood still, the multifeet with their arms raised high, while Tailin held his hand. It was a poignant moment. Tears ran down Mark's face. He could tell by the salty taste on his lips.

One of the animals, clearly the largest, lowered its right arm. He saw that it was holding an object.

"Roger's breathing mask," Tailin whispered.

She was right. The multifeet's arm moved slowly towards Tailin. What looked like a crude foot from a distance turned out to be a hand of some kind. He had always wondered, looking at the pictures, how the multifeet gathered their food. Now he could see it more clearly. They could separate the ends of their limbs into finger-thick strands. They were not like human fingers, with several elements connected by joints, but were more like tentacles, flexible throughout. Did they only have them on the front pairs of legs? It was impossible to tell.

The breathing mask, on the other hand, was clearly visible. The multifeet carefully handed it to Tailin, who had extended her left arm. Three of its fingers - Mark couldn't think of a better word - held the mask. The others, at least seven of them, moved seemingly chaotically like worms in a nest. A multifeet could count to 180 on its fingers. At least. Mark chuckled because the idea was so crazy, and even crazier was the fact that he was thinking about it at that moment.

The multifeet flinched. It must have heard his laughter.

"Shh," Tailin whispered in annoyance.

The arm with the breathing mask came closer again. The three fingers held it by the neck strap, which had apparently broken. Had the multifeet pulled Roger's mask off his face? No, there was no proof of that. Tailin stretched her arm out even further, leaning towards the multifeet. The mask approached her in slow motion. The strap touched her fingers. She moved to take it, but the multifeet did not immediately withdraw its arm. Tailin froze as its worm-like fingers stroked the skin of her palm. Only after this gesture did the beast retract its arm.

"Incredible," Tailin said. "It felt like the fingers were covered in thick hair. It really gave me goose bumps."

The creature that had handed over the mask took a few steps back without turning around. But the scene was not over yet. The multifeet next to it extended its arm. The ten, or was it twelve, fingers flickered. Tailin seemed to sense what the animal was expecting, because she reached out again. They touched.

"It's so warm!" Tailin whispered in awe.

Mark envied her a little. Tailin had just touched an alien being! He didn't want to disturb the process by reaching out himself. The animal withdrew and made way for the next one. Tailin kept her arm extended. The touch lasted a little longer this time. Tailin giggled.

"His fingers are crawling up my arm," she said. "It tickles. I have to control myself and not flinch."

When it was the last multifeet's turn, Mark couldn't stand it any longer. He came up next to Tailin and held out his arm. The animal briefly lowered its entire torso, almost like a nod. The lenses in its eyes switched from him to Tailin and back again. Was it thinking about who to shake hands with first? He would have given anything to be able to listen to the animal's thoughts. Did it have a brain? They had not yet found a dead multifeet to dissect.

The animal decided to greet him first. The touch was as surprising as it was intense. Tailin was right. The animal's skin felt warm. Nevertheless, he got goose bumps because the surface was both smooth and slightly sticky, as if it wanted to keep hold of his hand. He rubbed his palm over it, but there was no residue.

It was Tailin's turn. Mark was startled when she grabbed her mask. She wouldn't...? Yes - his wife took a deep breath. Then she pulled the mask up so that the multifeet could see her face. It made a noise that sounded like a stifled sigh. The other three animals came closer again. The lenses of its eyes focused on Tailin. The multifeet, standing directly in front of her, stretched out its arm. Again, the fingers flickered like little snakes. Tailin did not move. Mark could see from her eyes that she was afraid, but she held still. The fingers ran gently over her cheeks. Then the multifeet withdrew. Tailin pushed the mask back into place and took a deep breath.

"You're insane," Mark said.

"It felt right," Tailin said. "Did you notice? We were communicating!"

"Yes, it was absolutely amazing. This must be the first time humans have ever communicated with a non-terrestrial species."

"Too bad Roger didn't live to see it."

Mark looked at their dead friend, staring unseeingly into the crowns of the brine trees. They had to get him home, though it would not be an easy task. It was sixteen miles back to the Hopper, and Roger weighed a good 175 pounds, an amount multiplied by 1.3 due to the higher gravity... Unfortunately, their communication with the multifeet wasn't enough to ask them for help with transportation. Had it even been communication?

"What did we actually just find out?" he pondered.

"That they are sentient beings," said Tailin. "And they now know that about us too."

"What level do you think they're at? About as smart as earthly dogs? They're so alien."

"Yeah, absolutely," said Tailin. "But we also seem to have things in common. We mourn our dead. I think they realized that and wanted to comfort us."

"I don't know. They could have simply been thanking us for the nice toy we gave them. Or they were happy about our willingness to serve them as food."

"They're herbivores, but you know that better than anyone."

"I have only observed them eating food that I have determined to be plant-based. That's all I can say. When everything is as strange as it is here, differences become blurred."

"Why are you so skeptical?" asked Tailin. "Didn't you feel it?"

"It?"

"The... understanding. I can't put my finger on it, but it was there."

"I think that's a romantic notion. We mustn't anthropomorphize these creatures. We do that enough with dogs and cats. Tomorrow everything could be completely different. The next time you take off your mask in front of a multifeet, it might eat your nose because it thinks it's a welcome present for it."

"I'm sorry, Mark, but you have no clue."

He didn't argue. Maybe she was right about that too.

"ON THE COUNT OF THREE. ONE, TWO, THREE!" MARK shouted.

He lifted Roger's upper body while Tailin tugged at his legs. They laid him down on the stretcher they had spent hours weaving out of leaves.

"Whew," he said.

Tailin handed him one of the safety lines that they had attached to the left and right of the front of the stretcher. They were sturdy. He already knew the ropes would cut into their shoulders, but there was no other option. He put the strap around his right shoulder, and Tailin used her left. Mark turned around to where the path the multifeet had trampled lay ahead of them. Sixteen miles.

"Again, on the count of three. One, two, three!"

They put their backs into it. Roger's body slid along the ground. How long would the knotted leaves last? Mark had been skeptical, Tailin unusually optimistic. The encounter with the multifeet had obviously boosted her spirits. The trauma of Roger's death seemed to have faded, at least for her. Or was she faking it? That certainly wasn't like her.

After only a short time, Mark was drenched in sweat. His heart was racing, and he was breathing heavily. Tailin was panting too. It was hot and humid. He couldn't imagine how they were going to last the whole way.

"Break," Tailin said.

Mark simply dropped to the ground. Lying on his side, he checked their progress. They'd made it 800 yards in twenty minutes. That meant they were doing one and a half miles per hour. It would take over ten hours to get home, and he was already so exhausted after the first 800 yards that he thought he would never be able to get up again.

But Tailin pulled him up. He stood up, looped the strap over his aching shoulder and put his whole body weight into it. Despite the sturdy uniform jacket, the leash pressed deep into his flesh. No matter how he moved it, it ended up back in the same, already sore spot. He simply had to accept the pain.

All at once, Roger became even heavier. The sudden change made Mark stagger and almost fall. Tailin supported him without looking at him. She had turned around. What did she see? He threw off the strap and turned around as well. A multifeet was standing just a few yards away, stretching out its front legs. The folded fingers opened, wrapped around Roger and lifted him. Everything seemed to happen effortlessly. The multi-feet wasn't breathing any faster than before - could it even do that? - and it didn't bend the knees of its other legs either.

What did it want with the body? Mark had a hunch, but couldn't believe it. It would mean they had discovered the most intelligent alien species yet. Slowly, he walked backwards.

"Come on!" he called and pulled Tailin behind him.

She followed him. He wanted to know, and he didn't want the strange helper to end up thinking they would refuse its offer. They walked towards the Hopper, though it was a risk. What if the multifeet now viewed the dead body as a gift, or as carrion they had given up that it could do with as it pleased?

Mark glanced over his shoulder. The multifeet followed them. It was carrying Roger's body home.

May 6, 2799, Gliese 411

THERE WAS PROBABLY NOTHING HERE. THIS WAS THE SEVENTH orbit and still no sign of the wreck. The *Curious* was moving along the day-night boundary, the only place on Gliese 411 b where a landing would make sense. On the day side, which faced permanently toward the sun, it was far too hot, and on the eternally dark night side the temperature dropped below negative 100 degrees.

Thanks to its fixed rotation, the planet still had a thin atmosphere despite its age and the regular eruptions of its parent star. In the transition region, where they were searching for the wreckage, it generated violent storms. Here it was mainly clouds of carbon dioxide snow that rained down, but there were layers above that contained particularly high levels of sulfur and chlorine. The carbon dioxide evaporated before it reached the surface. When it rained on the planet, it was sulfuric, chloric and hydrocyanic acid. Monte almost hoped the wreck's unknown passenger had died on landing.

"Can we go a little lower?" he asked.

"No. I'm already detecting a temperature increase on the outer hull," replied the AI.

"I could disconnect the head."

"If you really want to - but I don't see the point. The instruments are powerful enough to identify a wreck of the expected size."

"I'm going to do it anyway."

"Then I'll hand over the controls to you."

Now the AI was miffed. It tried not to let on, but Monte knew it too well. Most of its computing capacity was located in the engine nacelle, which was separated from the head by a neck that was a good hundred yards long, for safety reasons. The AI was therefore unable to accompany him. It had to control the fusion engine even when it wasn't needed.

"Thank you," said Monte. "I'll report back to you soon."

Suddenly he felt very light. The AI must have disconnected. Monte's body awareness was now limited to his head, which consisted of the almost spherical cabin. Thanks to all the antennae on it, from a distance it actually did resemble a human head with a somewhat disheveled hairstyle, especially since the portholes and the exit on the front suggested a face.

Monte started the chemical engines, picturing a new orbit. He could feel the acceleration in his stomach, even though he had no stomach. He was a ghost, so to speak. His Biobag was still sleeping dreamlessly in the stasis chamber.

The top layer of cloud was approaching. At the right moment, Monte applied thrust and brought the head of the *Curious* onto a landing trajectory. Its new orbit intersected the surface at a certain point.

But the craft couldn't stay on this course. The speed was too high. He turned his head until he could see backwards, which gave him a perfect view of the surface. The cloud layer above him cast shifting shadows. However, it wasn't dense enough to block all light. Monte was surprised. He was expecting bare rock, worn away by billions of years of erosion, but the transition zone, at least, was covered in vegetation.

His radar sense told him that the ground was covered with a layer of organic matter about two yards thick. However, the absorption lines did not indicate life like that on Earth. Heavier elements such as phosphorus and sulfur seemed to play a more important role here. Now and then, something flashed in the optical range. Water? Monte analyzed the radiation. It was not water, but sulfuric acid that formed the basis of life here.

Monte recorded everything. It was not the wreck he had hoped for, but this surprising find would surely interest some researcher. On Earth, he could sell the data for a reasonable price. There was no sign of life on Gliese 411 b in the data previously collected about the planet. Perhaps he should take a look at the moon, too, before leaving.

Should he attempt a landing? It might be interesting to go for a walk in this strange forest. Monte missed the relentless pressure of gravity in his bones, the smell of sweat and the feeling of heat blistering his skin. But he only had one Biobag on board, and he might need it to make contact with passengers from the wreck, should there be any survivors.

It would be better not to land, which was a real shame. At the highest magnification of the telescope, he could see a strong wind plowing through the organic material on the ground, tugging at spherical, poisonous green formations. Were they flowers? One of the spheres burst. A dark mass spurted out, and the wind carried it away. It made Monte think of spores, but that wasn't quite correct. The droplets that had broken free of the mass fell onto some egg-shaped plants with purple outer skin. The contact created deep wounds from which an equally purple liquid seeped out that immediately boiled on contact with the air.

The image broke off. The spaceship was immersed in the cloud layers. Monte was annoyed, but then realized that he had reacted correctly, because the outer skin had heated up beyond the tolerance limit. No, there was nothing down there. He was not even sure what he had seen. A war of the plants? Or sexual reproduction? Maybe something else entirely? You only see what you know, and this planet seemed to have a few secrets.

But a wreck was not one of them. If a ship had landed here, the nature of the planet would have surely destroyed it long ago. Or rather, greedily absorbed it. Monte steered the head of the *Curious* back into orbit. It took him one more orbit to adjust the trajectory to that of the belly and finally dock.

The AI was as annoyed as a cat left alone for too long. It didn't greet him, pretending to be involved in controlling the fusion drive.

"Sorry I haven't kept you informed," he said.

He immediately sensed its presence again. After so long, he had a feel for it, even though it was a master at sneaking around him. If it wasn't communicating, he only noticed it when they bumped into each other, meaning when they shared certain memory areas. That was not unusual. Monte only noticed it when he encountered memories from a time when he wasn't on board the *Curious*. The AI had been on an impressive journey and experienced much more than he had. Sometimes, when he couldn't find peace, he let himself be enveloped by its memories.

"Enough flattery," said the AI. "You'd better show me what you saw down there."

Monte released the recordings.

"I think you owe me the personal memories too," said the AI.

"All right."

He removed the encryption from the memories of the past six hours. Six hours! It had felt like three minutes. That was great. In moments like this, he remembered why he chose this profession. Or was it the profession that chose him?

"I agree with you," said the AI.

"You agree with me?" he asked.

"In your conclusion that the wreck is not here. It must be a certain minimum size, or it couldn't have sent out a distress call strong enough to be heard three light years away."

"The moon would be the next option," said Monte.

"I can't argue with that either. The ship we are looking for has cleverly covered its tracks. It must have had a powerful AI on board."

"Or the passenger has experience in eluding others."

"Does that mean we're looking for someone involved in organized crime?" asked the AI.

"Or from the other side, meaning someone from the secret service or the military. Surely a criminal wouldn't attract attention with a distress call? Or wait... If their ship was destroyed, they might be trying to hitch a ride."

If contact was made, they must be very careful. Monte remembered how urgently Admiral Gaudlitz ordered him to search. *You must find the wreck at all costs, Claudio.* She hadn't said anything about a passenger, and she hadn't asked him to discover the cause of the accident, which was his specialty.

THE MOON WAS OLD AND GRAY, FULL OF SCARS AND WRINKLES. It had obviously not had an easy life - torn between the gravity of its planet and the local sun, bombarded by asteroids, without an atmosphere that could repair the worst damage over time, roasted all over by the star's radiation.

In terms of human presence, however, it still appeared to be virgin. Monte would have expected at least a few test drillings for helium-3 extraction. Surely this moon would be a good source, this close to the sun? Perhaps the infrastructure was initially lacking, and since interstellar traffic had slowed down, helium-3 was so cheap that mining it in such a distant system probably wasn't worthwhile.

The advantage of the lack of atmosphere was that the *Curious* was able to come within a few miles of the surface. That meant that its instruments could pick up the smallest detail. However, the disadvantage was that the search would take longer. The moon was somewhat smaller than Earth's moon, but Monte didn't like to do things half-way. If he was going to search, he would do it properly.

They had already covered two-thirds of the moon's surface when the strategy proved its worth. In the gray plain, a whorled pattern appeared, as if someone had moved a giant pizza slice across the regolith. Such structures didn't occur naturally.

"Are you thinking what I'm thinking?" he asked.

"Those are kinetic projectile impacts," said the AI.

Exactly. A ship had raced across the surface, pursued by another, and the pursuer must have fired a railgun at its target. Two railguns, actually, given the parallel pattern of staggered impact holes. But the trail ended without any wreckage to be seen. Presumably the pursuer had suddenly veered off in a risky maneuver. They could only see the impacts because the attacker had shot towards the ground from an elevated position.

"I'd like to land," said Monte.

"Do we have to? I don't see how that brings us any closer to fulfilling our mission."

The AI was programmed for efficiency, Monte understood that. But there was a reason why it hadn't been sent to search on its own.

"Yes, we have to," he said.

"Shall I prepare your analog?" asked the AI.

Only the software used this term, the AI steadfastly refusing to refer to his body as a Biobag. Presumably its programmer had an aversion to the word.

"No, thank you. The moon has no atmosphere, and it would be far too cumbersome."

He would go down in the Explorer, a kind of miniature spaceship that could be operated like a robot. Monte switched to the device's memory, which was much smaller than that of the ship. He immediately felt the confinement, especially when the AI also sent in its offshoots - which was necessary if they wanted to continue communicating. It was like being stuck in a barrel. But it got better once he detached himself from the spaceship.

"You have sixty seconds remaining," said the *Curious* as it pulled the last of its program components out of memory.

That was better. Monte started an internal countdown. That way he wouldn't have to count consciously. He was surprised when the Explorer's small engine ignited. It took Monte a second to adjust to his new hull. Then the corrective thrusters transformed into his hands, which he used to turn 180 degrees, and the thruster became a completely new organ that braked him at full force until he landed on his three unfolded legs.

He retracted one leg so that he was standing upright. He transformed the third leg into an arm, then oriented himself. The shot pattern started again. Monte only needed a single jump to reach it. He himself was amazed at how precisely it worked. With his hand, he reached into the hole that the railgun's ammunition had torn into the moon's surface. It was clean and smooth, as if the shots had been fired only yesterday. Not even dust had migrated into it, which made his task easier.

Railguns fired surprisingly small projectiles, accelerating them to enormous speeds. The velocity was the square of the kinetic energy, and that was what killed. As a result, nothing was left of the metal bolt, which vaporized when it hit the rock. But the metal would be deposited on the inside of the bullet hole. Monte used the sharp ends of his arm to scrape off some of the coating, then poured the sample into one of the hollow bones of his body, which he used for storage.

"Coming back," he said.

Now came the most difficult part of the trip. He had to take off at the right moment and accelerate to the point where he could dock with the *Curious*. He only had one chance to do this, as the tank of the Explorer's chemical engine would be almost empty afterwards.

"Approaching as planned. Good luck," said the AI.

Monte took off. He didn't have to turn around; the speed of the *Curious* was determined by its orbit and therefore also its location at any given moment. It was all a question of timing. He had to reach the same position as the spaceship at the same second; then docking was no problem.

Of course he was afraid. He was a human being, not a program. However, he was a human being with the ability to make the right decision at the right moment. He accelerated with all his might, but still had time to enjoy the view. The *Curious* was above him. He fumbled around to find the right spot, clinging to its belly with all three legs. "Thank you," he said. "Good work. I brought a sample. It's waiting in storage CB27. Can you take care of it, please? I especially need the isotope ratios of the metal fractions."

"Work in progress."

The process of chemical analysis still took a long time, even with the latest technology. The AI had to extract the sample, divide it into multiple parts and examine them individually - it required patience. Even if they hadn't had a breakthrough yet, they seemed to be on the right track. The ship that sent out the distress signal had been tracked. It had carried out a diversionary maneuver in the asteroid belt. Nevertheless, the pursuer had closed in on it.

Where had the quarry escaped to? Monte himself would probably have ventured close to the sun, close enough for its intense radiation to cover his tracks. That was not without danger. A sudden eruption and the passenger would be roasted. Gliese 411 might be old, but it still had the typical temperament of a red dwarf. Hiding behind the sun could only offer temporary asylum at best. At some point, the shielding of even the best ship would no longer be able to withstand that amount of energy.

The quarry could have waited there until the pursuer disappeared beyond the horizon. But since he would be virtually blind so close to the star, that would be no more than a bet. If the cat only had enough patience and waited in front of the mousehole ... It would even have an advantage; at a greater distance, the star would interfere less with its sensors. If that was the case, the wreck had likely crashed into the sun. It might have had enough time to send a distress call. That was probably done automatically, and the pursuers then headed off.

What if it all happened the other way around? The chase could have started on the rocky planet. Shots were fired on the moon; then the target fled into the asteroid belt, where a hunt was still possible, but much more difficult. After the maneuver on the moon, the pursued could have had enough time for the diversionary maneuver. The pursuer fell for it, and his target looked for the next best hiding place - the ice giant orbiting behind the asteroid belt.

"*Curious?*" he asked.

"Good that you reported, Claudio. I just got the results. The mass ratio of the metal isotopes is..."

"The pure numbers won't tell me anything," said Monte. "Where did the projectiles come from?"

"It's clear that they must have been made on Earth."

That was remarkable. Gaudlitz had sent him on a search for a wreck that was shot at with ammunition from Earth? Earth had not exported munitions since the Mars revolt. Whoever the pursuer was, he'd stocked up on ammunition for the railgun on the home planet. And Monte believed he was looking for a ship of Earthly origin. But why would an Earth spaceship be chasing another one from the same place? Had Gaudlitz not told him the truth? It was too late to ask questions. It would take at least six years to get an answer.

It meant nothing, of course. Not yet. There were plenty of pirates who hunted unarmed civilian ships, and some of them probably used ammunition manufactured on Earth.

"Thank you for your work," he said. "We should have a look around Gliese 411 d now."

May 8, 2799, Gliese 411

THE SECOND PLANET IN THE SYSTEM WAS AN ICE GIANT, A PLANET consisting mainly of frozen gases. Or rather, it aspired to be one; it was small compared to the solar system's Neptune, and it orbited too close to its star. This had led to the formation of a particularly thick atmosphere. The first thing that caught Monte's eye were the numerous storm systems. Over the north pole, they formed a huge octagon. Above the south pole, the structures were more reminiscent of a peacock's eye, while the mid-latitudes were dominated by bands of air that sometimes drifted around the planet faster than it rotated on its axis.

Gliese 411 d would be a very good hiding place. Why hadn't he noticed that right away? Oh yes - the AI only woke him up when they crossed the asteroid belt. The *Curious*'s sensors reached a maximum depth of thirty miles. They were built for research and therefore particularly powerful. To hide from any other ship, it would have sufficed to dive six miles into the dense cloud layers. The *Curious* as a whole couldn't do that. It would have to detach its head again when it set off on its search. That would certainly be dangerous. Monte was already looking forward to it; there wasn't much left that really thrilled him.

But first came the boring part of the job. They had to search the planet systematically. If the ship they were looking for had not disappeared too far into the depths, they would find it with the sensors. Monte felt doubtful. After all, it was supposedly a wreck. In such a dense atmosphere, friction would cause its orbit to decay further and further. In a few years, the ship could have sunk completely into the planet if it no longer had a functioning engine.

Monte followed the output of the measuring instruments. On closer inspection, the planet actually looked more like Saturn than Neptune. This included the coloration of the stripes, which revealed their composition. The wind speeds even exceeded Saturn's. This planet was a true witch's cauldron. It was questionable whether the engine in the head would be able to withstand the pressure differences.

What if Monte tried it with the Explorer? The robot had even weaker engines, but he could use the kinetic launcher. The *Curious* could use that to propel the robot over the lower cloud boundary until it emerged on the other side, where it would catch it again. That would be a convenient way to explore otherwise unreachable depths. But it was risky, especially if he was on board himself. If something unexpected happened, he would hardly be able to save himself with the Explorer alone. Then the *Curious*'s AI would have to detach the head and use it to retrieve him.

"What do you think of the plan?" he asked.

"What plan?"

Monte had felt the AI's gentle touch as he pondered. He was sure it was eavesdropping, and it was aware that he knew. That was good enough.

"I will try diving under the clouds with the Explorer. In an emergency, you would have to come and get me."

"That violates a whole series of safety regulations," said the AI. "I therefore cannot recommend this course of action."

"But you think it's a good one, because you're just as curious as I am."

"I can confirm that this approach could indeed lead to a non-linear increase in knowledge," said the AI. "Such small gas planets are rare. Researchers on Earth would certainly be pleased with the data you collected, if you survived the attempt."

"But what could truly go wrong? You can always catch me again."

"The worst-case scenario would be that the Explorer becomes stuck in layers that I can't penetrate," said the AI.

"Then we have to aim well to avoid such layers," said Monte.

"Unfortunately, that would be difficult because we don't have enough data about this planet. That's why I can't simulate the conditions in the atmosphere, and I can't measure them due to the density of the atmosphere."

"Then we'll just have to get lucky."

"The human concept of 'getting lucky' seems questionable to me. It's like making demands on the universe. But the universe doesn't owe you anything."

MONTE SQUEEZED HIMSELF INTO THE EXPLORER AND WAITED FOR the launch. In the end, it was still the human who decided. That was probably why crewed expeditions were more successful than entirely robotic space journeys, at least when the task involved a hint of uncertainty.

The connection to the ship was still there. He could feel the force that the molecules in the atmosphere were exerting on the hull. It increased as the ship reduced its orbit as far as possible. The power of the main drive would also be able to free it from deeper layers, but its hull was sensitive to the frictional heat generated in the process. The coating reflected almost all radiation, but there was no defense against the torrid embrace of the planet.

Takeoff! The Explorer shot silently out of the tube. It was the same launching device the ship used to defend itself with torpedoes if it was attacked. The acceleration was grueling. Organic matter would be irreversibly destroyed, even in the stasis chamber. Monte looked back. The ship had taken on the color of the planet in the optical spectrum. It resembled a corkscrew, with the main engine like a cork stuck on it. It glowed in the infrared until it suddenly disappeared.

Water vapor. It was immersed in clouds, just like those on Earth. They blocked heat radiation particularly efficiently. That would explain why they hadn't found an infrared signal from the wreck. Monte dove deeper. He couldn't influence the trajectory, which was purely ballistic. He wasn't afraid, which was surprising. It would make sense to be afraid. He needed to check his emotional reactions. Too much time outside a Biobag, psychologists said, led to resentment of one's own existence. Maybe that was why there were so few good-humored AIs.

But the curiosity was still there. He imagined his non-existent heart beating faster. He had never dived this deep into a gas planet before. He was entering a place where no human had ever been before. This was why he loved his job. What was waiting here to be discovered? Monte activated all the Explorer's sensors. He felt the increasing pressure constricting his chest, he smelled the traces of ammonia in the water clouds, felt the warm drops on his skin, saw with the radar the masses pressing in from the inside, trying to shed their heat in the upper layers.

The storm shook him, attempting to throw him off course, but did not disturb the momentum of the launch, which was still carrying the slender Explorer through the atmosphere. Monte compared the coordinates with the pre-calculated flight profile. He was flying lower than planned, but his current data flowed live to the rest of the spaceship so that the AI could adjust its orbit.

He was struck by lightning, which blinded him for a moment. The chemical sensors must have been damaged, because now he could no longer smell anything. He switched to the second set and suddenly had so much ammonia in his virtual nose that he felt like sneezing. He quickly adjusted the sensitivity downwards. A hint of camphor was added – the system's symbol for methane, which was found here in increasing quantities in the clouds but was itself odorless and therefore imperceptible to humans.

That was exciting. He would not have expected to find methane at this depth. What processes might have produced it? Monte would not be surprised to find life here. Life was hidden almost everywhere – in the icy oceans of Enceladus, in the soil layers of Mars, in Io's sulfurous volcanoes, on the jungle world of Kepler-16 c – so why not in the depths of Gliese 411 d? Maybe then the planet would finally get a name of its own.

Another flash, then another. Monte reacted too late, and the second set of chemical sensors burned out. It felt like his nose was blocked, but he couldn't blow it to clear it.

A warning signal sounded. The radar had spotted a bulky obstacle that he was speeding towards. It took him a moment to recognize the *Curious*, which had stuck its head into the clouds. A clever solution. It allowed the AI to protect the sensitive main engine.

Monte clenched his imaginary hands into fists. The Explorer was racing towards a wall. If the AI had made an error of even a yard... It skidded around so fast that he had to close his eyes. The Explorer braked to make it easier for the ship to catch it. It was suddenly dark.

"Welcome back," said the AI.

"When do we start the second attempt?" he asked.

They hadn't found anything yet, but Monte took his duties seriously. He would not leave this system until he had tracked down the wreckage.

THE FORTY-SIXTH ATTEMPT STARTED NEAR THE SOUTH POLE OF Gliese 411 d. Monte was skeptical before they even started, because of the numerous cyclones that formed the peacock's eye here. It looked beautiful, but even from that height you could see the incredible forces at work. The Explorer was shaken up shortly after take-off. Lightning flashed through the air. Currents tugged at it, threatening to drag it down into the depths or spit it out like a cork. He had used up a large part of his momentum before he was even halfway across the peacock's eye.

Monte changed his strategy; he couldn't rely on the momentum from the launch here. He revved up the engine. Its power would not be enough to carry him through the hurricane. To make it, he would have to use the layers of potential that the infrared sensors showed him. It was like surfing in an ocean with several waves stacked on top of each other. The thruster only served to navigate to the right layer. Then the current, the storm, would take care of the rest.

He threw himself into the first wave. The Explorer drifted downwards on a dense layer of sulfur dioxide, hit a wall of methane, was carried upwards, reached a lake of water vapor, and drifted gently for a short time until a rising column of hot compounds catapulted it upwards. A welcome boost! Monte used it to aim for a mountain of clouds that built up from the depths and promised good thermals.

The atmosphere was denser than on Earth. The pressure was

higher, but unlike water, air was compressible, which meant that he could drop like a stone at any time if he didn't gain new momentum in time. Monte was highly focused. He ignored the shaking and swaying, was not interested in the temperature of the outer shell, but tried his best to reach the next promising wave. He hadn't been in such danger for a long time, and truthfully, he hadn't had this much fun for a long time.

After twenty minutes he reached the *Curious*, or it reached him. The AI had overloaded the ship in order to catch him again. He would have to point out this mistake, even though he had benefited from it. The AI had jeopardized the ship and thus the entire mission. Of course, Monte was not entirely innocent either.

AT THE FORTY-SEVENTH LAUNCH, THEY HAD LEFT THE SOUTH polar vortex behind them. This was a zone of pronounced calm. The individual layers were clearly separated from each other, and Monte felt as if he were drilling into a piece of cake with the Explorer. Light layer, cake, dark layer, chocolate, then some fruit in the form of localized swirls. Another dark layer, followed by more cake and so on. He didn't need any instruments other than the radar here. The Explorer stayed on its pre-calculated path like a bullet fired in a vacuum.

Monte could hardly believe it. The layers followed each other as neatly as if someone had stacked them artificially. Yet the chemical compounds were simply arranged according to molecular weight and density. It seemed like a completely different planet.

Then he came across the confectioner's tool. The giant who baked this cake had left something hard inside it, which was constantly swirling around the planet along with the dense atmosphere. It was a strange object; the front part was egg-shaped, but a portion of it had been neatly cut out. The rear part hung from it by three connecting elements that reminded him of the tines of a fork. Impaled on the prongs was a spherical object warmer than the rest, which seemed to be a spaceship.

Should he radio it? No, it was too early for that. Monte measured the properties of the object and its surroundings. The atmosphere here had a density similar to that on the Earth's surface, and it was around 15 degrees Celsius. The air consisted of a mixture of carbon dioxide and water vapor. No other elements. Even without a spacesuit, a Biobag would not die immediately. That was good, because it meant that when he returned, he would only need a breathing mask. As he moved away, he scanned the object that formed the rear end again. It was slightly warmer than the surroundings. Perhaps a remnant of engine heat, but possibly also radiation from the interior. A survivor?

Waking up in the Biobag was always painful. The stasis chamber constantly loosened the body's joints, electrically stimulated its muscles so that they didn't atrophy, and played sensory sensations into its brain so that the nerve cells didn't die from doing nothing. But the fact was that this body had not moved itself for over three years. Although there was no gravity, it still had to overcome inertia, and this was no different at 0 g than at 1 g.

Perhaps he should have done without it after all. The AI had advised him to do so, but if there really were survivors, he wanted to face them in his true form. He wanted to find out how the incident happened, which was certainly not an accident. Investigations like this were always personal.

Monte pulled himself out of his container, groaning. A warm wind immediately started up, drying him off. He climbed out next to the tub from which the stasis fluid was being drained.

"*Curious?* Turn off the noise, please."

The soft music, which was part of the standard program, fell silent. Monte tried to switch to other frequencies. It didn't work. *Of course it didn't!* Typical adaptation difficulties. A Biobag's sensory system was natural from birth and was difficult to train, which he didn't have time for at the moment. He rubbed himself down with his hands. It was a great feeling. Skin might be hypersensitive and not very robust, but a human body felt much better than the outer shell of a spaceship. His penis was erect, which was also a typical reaction after waking up. In stasis, all bodily functions were regularly exercised, but he no longer remembered what a physical orgasm felt like. Should he indulge briefly?

"Monte? I'm flying over the south pole," reported the ship's AI. "If you can be ready in six minutes, you won't have to wait until the next orbit."

Six minutes, that was a sign. Monte opened a locker and retrieved his underwear, uniform and boots. Each item of clothing, apart from the shoes, consisted of two parts, front and back. As soon as he held them against his body, they would orient themselves according to his body heat and crawl around him until they met their counterpart. They would then stretch and shrink so that the material fit perfectly. The underpants still had some work to do, because his member shrank as he walked towards the cockpit. Monte took longer than usual since he needed to get his bearings again.

He navigated the corridors, using the walls, ceiling and floor as needed. It was strange to have to rely solely on the Biobag's senses, but it also felt good because the world around him had become much quieter. He didn't perceive the X-ray bursts from the red dwarf, the cosmic radiation, the heat glow from the life support pipes, or the magnetic fields that wound around the electrical connection lines. Humanity's ancestors would probably never have dared to leave their trees if they had had all these frightening impressions.

After a few yards, he found it easier to get his bearings. He had once passed through these corridors every day for three months in a row; an experiment, a test of his ability to be bored. He abandoned it after twelve weeks, boredom overtaking him. Now the AI helped him by only opening the correct doors at junctions.

"Congratulations, five minutes and eleven seconds," said the AI as he floated into his seat.

Monte was disappointed. He had once done that in under four minutes.

"Have you disconnected the head yet?" he asked.

"Affirmative," replied the AI.

"Then you can hand over the controls to me now," he said.

"Yes," replied the AI.

Oh, it was in a passive-aggressive mood again today.

"Please hand over the controls," he said.

"Are you sure? Navigating at the edge of the south polar vortex is challenging."

"That's exactly why I want the helm."

"But you're in your..."

"Careful, *Curious*. It is forbidden to discriminate based on Biobag status."

No one may be discriminated against on the basis of their Biobag status. This law was over a hundred years old and was passed after the advent of consciousness purification. It had only applied to AIs since the eighties.

"Of course. Please excuse me, I'm handing over the controls now."

Within reach of his hands, resting on the armrests of the seat, two joysticks unfolded from the material. Monte tapped the right one and a force immediately pushed him into his seat. The *Curious* reacted with lightning speed, as if he were sitting directly on top of its engine. The head weighed less than a tenth of the rest of the ship.

The wall in front of him turned into a map. The AI had greatly simplified the display, as if it were taking his limited abilities into consideration. If he was not in his Biobag, it would certainly not dare to do so. AIs didn't have a high opinion of the natural abilities of humans, as he had often noticed.

But he never complained. After all, there were advantages to not having to concentrate so much on steering. His task was to keep a dot, which symbolized the ship, within a small circle. This was the calculated flight path that led to the wreck. After passing the last foothills of the southern polar storms, navigation became easier and easier for him.

This allowed him to take in the beauty of the planet. A broad, orange-colored ribbon stretched out beneath him, decorated on both sides with small embroideries. The ornaments were storms, each around sixty miles in diameter. The colored belt was the zone of calm. Now, from a greater height, he realized that there was no question of calm. In fact, the belt was moving rapidly around the planet, much faster than its surroundings. The storms to the left and right compensated for the energy differential, or perhaps they were what drove the orange ribbon, like cogwheels on a chain.

There was only apparent quiet within the ribbon itself. It

could be a representation of his marriage. Fortunately, that was a long time ago. The restlessness in the planetary belt became more apparent the deeper he went. The wispy clouds of the uppermost layer fluttered a little faster than the denser structures below.

The AI had chosen a course along the belt, in its direction of movement. That way it didn't risk heat damage to the outer skin. There was still no sign of the wreck on the radar. The seemingly motionless ribbon was divided by areas of varying humidity, making it difficult for the radar to see through them. But that wasn't a problem, because they knew the position of the target. If it only needed to visit the wreck briefly, the *Curious* would have arrived long ago. The task at hand was more difficult; they had to come up alongside it and adjust their speed.

The idea was to catch up with the wreck in a lower orbit. Monte braked and accelerated at the points indicated by the AI, which caused the ship to submerge itself in cloud until hardly any light came from the portholes.

"Contact," said the AI.

Now they were close enough for the sensors. The wreck appeared on the screen as a flashing dot. The explorer was only slightly off the pre-calculated target. The AI had done an excellent job.

"You're doing very well," said the AI.

"You too," he said.

"Do you want me to do the rest?"

"No, thank you. Can you please show everything we can see of the wreck on the screen?"

The AI didn't answer, but the image of the wreck changed dramatically. In particular, the egg-shaped front section was visible. Now he could clearly see that it was damaged. Pipes and cables appeared to be protruding from the half that was still there. However, the cut that severed the other half at an angle must have been made with extreme force and at lightning speed. The ship had been in motion, and a normal weapon would have created a completely different pattern of destruction.

"Do you have any idea what could have caused such damage?" he asked.

"I've been considering it since first contact, but I can't think of anything. Neither the Terran Union nor Neomars have such weapons as far as I know. You might have noticed how..."

"How quickly such a weapon must have worked, yes."

"We have to assume less than a second," said the AI. "The missing part vanished immediately, so to speak."

"Are there any traces of it?"

"I analyzed the gas in the area, but I didn't find any disproportionate amounts of metal. But that's to be expected after such a long time in this environment."

"What about the ball at the back? Is that the drive?" asked Monte.

"Yes, and it appears to be undamaged. However, according to my analyses based on the mass of the object, the tanks should no longer contain any fuel."

"So they dragged themselves here with the last of their strength after faking an escape into the sun. Very clever. Only the distress signal doesn't fit. It would have given away their position."

"Maybe they emitted it when they were first attacked," said the AI.

"Yes, that would be one explanation," said Monte. "However, they don't indicate that anyone is attacking them. What Gaudlitz played for me was a general distress call."

"Which can't be found in the emergency call database."

"Which is probably due to the delicate nature of the mission the ship was on. At least that's what Gaudlitz claims."

The admiral had never tricked Monte nor lied to him. That was why he believed her. What reason would she have not to tell him the truth? Of course, he might also ask himself why she didn't use her own ships for the search rather than calling in an outsider. On the other hand, who was to say that others weren't also searching for the wreck? Perhaps he was just lucky that the *Curious* was available in such close proximity to the Gliese 411 system, and within range of a tachyon transmitter.

"Speed adjustment complete," said the AI. "You can proceed."

"What's the temperature outside?"

"Fifty-five degrees Fahrenheit, zero point eight bar."

Not particularly warm, but he wouldn't need a spacesuit. That was good at least. Monte unbuckled and followed the green signs to the exit. His breathing mask hung in front of the airlock. He put it on and hung the tank on his belt. The air from the tank tasted dry and metallic.

"Wouldn't you rather take the suit?" asked the AI.

"No, I want to appear as human as possible to any survivors."

In reality, he mainly wanted to avoid the suit. It always made him feel extremely constricted, like the cocoon of an alien species.

"It could lead to a drop in pressure."

"Don't exaggerate, *Curious*. The wreck has been drifting here for years. It's not going to suddenly crash."

"Whatever you say, Claudio. I'll open the airlock for you now."

The airlock was a tiny chamber that could hold three people at most. Monte adjusted his breathing mask while the AI extracted the oxygen and replaced it with carbon dioxide. It was also getting much colder. Monte breathed deeply through the mask to shake off the panic that was setting in. Now, of all times, his stomach growled. Why hadn't he eaten something? After a second birth like this, he always forgot that Biobags had needs.

"Air exchange complete," said the AI.

At last. Monte pressed the button that opened the outside door. It was dark outside, damned dark. Why hadn't that been visible on the screen? Because the AI processed images into something recognizable. The Biobag's eyes lacked this ability. *His* eyes. He had to wait a little while for said eyes to get used to the darkness.

For biological beings, waiting was part of everyday life. Not even his intentions were transmitted to his limbs at the speed of light. He was now this being, this... human being. There were said to be people who lived their entire lives in a Biobag. Monte sighed. A complex process, and yet it didn't require conscious thought. As old-fashioned as they were, human bodies were also powerful, at least in special areas such as pattern recognition. But not in sensor technology. The surroundings didn't get any brighter. He remembered it differently. Perhaps it was also due to this particular Biobag, which he had never used before.

Fortunately, there were several compartments in the airlock which contained the most important accessories for an outdoor mission. He grabbed a flashlight. In the same compartment was a projectile weapon, an old-fashioned device. He pushed it to the back with the handle of the flashlight, because he had the feeling that if he so much as touched it, he would have to use it.

Monte took the flashlight in his right hand and walked to the exit, where he hooked up his safety line. Then he saw the emptiness in front of him and started to sway. *Damn Biobag, what's wrong with your sense of balance?* He remembered his training, almost forty years ago now. *Keep it steady. Don't ask too much of it. Be good to it,* the instructors had told them. *Give it time to get used to the height.* That was what he was doing now. There was no hurry. The castaway, if there was one, had waited years. A few more minutes wouldn't matter.

The Biobag no longer wobbled. It had worked. Monte switched on the flashlight, which cast a yellow beam that he could move around. Thin threads of smoke appeared. The air probably contained a lot of moisture. Monte briefly took off his mask and blew. A plume moved away from him. He groped his way forward with the searchlight. Plumes of mist danced around the ship. It was a surreal atmosphere, perhaps like in summer after a downpour at dusk. The Biobag was freezing. No, *he* was freezing. He had to stop thinking of his body as a separate entity. The instructors always warned against this.

Monte pulled himself out by the doorframe and squatted on the exterior skin of the head. Where was the wreck? According to the AI, they should have caught up with it. Monte got up and walked around the *Curious*. Due to the continual need to secure himself properly, it took him longer than expected. He realized that he should have brought a jetpack.

He found the wreckage on the long side of the head - by the ears, so to speak. The AI could have told him that. The two spacecraft floated together in the void. The fact that they were orbiting at enormous speed - just like the clouds they were in - was unnoticeable. It was about ten yards to the other ship. The wreck seemed smaller than he had imagined. Its oval head was facing him. Monte shone the spotlight on it and noticed the sad, black eyes of severed pipes. It must be the cabin that was hit by the terrible weapon. There, in the middle, was a cot that had been cut in half. He moved the flashlight beam around to take in all the details.

Who was responsible for this? It was not his job to find out. He was only supposed to tell the admiral what happened. But was it even possible to separate one question from the other? He had never managed to do that before, but the insurance companies he usually worked for didn't demand it. Gaudlitz, on the other hand, was very determined.

One step at a time. First, he had to take a close look at the damage. He took a connecting rope from his trouser pocket and attached it to the *Curious*. The other end was attached to his belt in such a way that it automatically unrolled when he jumped over. Ten yards was no problem. Even if his aim was so bad that he missed the wreck, he could pull himself back with the line.

Monte took a few steps for a run-up, but halted just before the edge. The Biobag was hesitating again. His body had simply ignored the commands from his cerebrum. That was unacceptable. He tried once more and halted again. Then without a run-up, Monte jumped. The trick worked. The body didn't refuse. He glided over the infinite depths and landed directly on the edge of the cut, just as he had imagined. He quickly fastened the rope here too and secured himself. The connecting line was his insurance, even if it would be useless if one of the two ships decided to go its own way.

He pulled himself into the cabin and looked around. It was terrifying. Someone had definitely lived here. There was a small kitchen, and the pot stuck in the coffee machine contained a dark liquid. He took it out, opened the lid, briefly pulled the mask off his face and smelled it. It was coffee. It didn't seem to have spoiled, probably due to the air, which was unbreathable even for bacteria. Nausea rose up in his gullet.

The Biobag again! Why was it so sensitive to the smell of coffee? It had such an excellent, fast and sensitive chemical analysis system, but couldn't cope with the measurement results. Perhaps evolution should have inserted an additional layer between input and output. On the other hand, it had done so by inventing consciousness purification.

He pushed the jar back into the machine. The shower was still working, presumably the toilet too. There was moisture on the floor of the tiny hygiene compartment, as if someone had taken a shower this morning. But it was more likely to be moisture from the air that had settled on the metal surfaces. There was no sign of corrosion, although the wreck had probably been hidden here for years. Nothing rusted without oxygen. Monte opened a few cupboards. They were all empty. That was strange. Had someone tidily removed the supplies? Or had the pilot not planned a long journey?

He pulled himself across the ceiling to the couch. As he had seen previously, it was split diagonally down the middle. The seat belt was open. There was no sign of blood, either. So, no one could have been sitting there when it happened. Monte felt the cut. It was completely smooth, as if sanded.

"Ouch!" he shouted.

His finger had reported pain. Before Monte could consciously react, he had withdrawn his hand. He looked at the damage. There was a wound about a quarter of an inch long on the tip of his finger. A large drop of thick, red liquid was oozing out. Instinctively, he put his finger in his mouth under his breathing mask and licked it. The blood tasted slightly sweet. He looked at the finger again, which was now glistening wet. The wound was closed, but more blood slowly seeped out.

"I know I shouldn't disturb you," the AI announced. "But your exclamation signaled that you might need help."

"Thank you, *Curious*. Just a small cut."

"I still have to advise you to seek immediate treatment. If the Biobag gets infected, we won't be able to repair it with our equipment."

"Don't worry, everything here is sterile," said Monte.

"I am not capable of worrying," said the AI. "I am simply following protocols."

"Thank you, I appreciate that. Now let me get back to work in peace."

The AI made no reply. He knew it couldn't be offended, but he still had the feeling that it was acting miffed. Monte sighed. It made a choking sound under the breathing mask. He examined the wound. The blood had formed a new drop. He carefully wiped it off on the textile cover of the couch, then took an analyzer out of his trouser pocket and held it over the rough edge. He wanted to see how sharp the edge really was later in the *Curious*. There was no such thing as a weapon that worked with atomic-level accuracy. But that was exactly what it looked like here.

Monte continued to search what was left of the cabin. In one corner, his flashlight beam hit a picture frame stuck to the wall. It was empty. Another sign that someone might have survived the attack. Did the pilot keep a family photo there? He found a few hangers in a locker that were also empty.

He couldn't get any further here. Monte pulled himself onto the roof of the cabin and used the flashlight to get his bearings. The *Curious* was still hovering next to him. It didn't seem to have changed its position. But was it possible that the clouds had thickened?

"*Curious*? What can you tell me about the meteorological conditions?" he asked on the radio.

"We are approaching a cross-current," said the AI.

"What does that mean?"

"You have to expect wave-like changes in pressure and temperature."

"How strong, maximum?"

"The temperatures are within your body's tolerance range. The air pressure could become critical."

"Too high?" he asked.

"No, too low. Some parts of your body..."

"I see," he interrupted the AI.

Monte, of course, first thought of the *Curious* as his body. The ship could be damaged by the growing friction if the air pressure was too high. He really had to make the effort to integrate the Biobag into his body image, or he would put himself in danger.

He waved to the *Curious* and turned around. The cabin of the wrecked ship was connected to the engine by three arm-thick tubes. The separation protected the passengers from the radiation emitted by the fusion engine. Supply lines were normally laid inside the tubes. However, at least one of them could also be used to reach the rear of the ship, where the cargo holds were normally located for reasons of weight distribution.

The middle pipe was probably the best option, as it was almost twice as thick as its two neighbors. However, Monte had no desire to crawl through a dark tube fifty yards long. He preferred to reach his destination via the surface, even though it was hardly any brighter out here than inside the ship.

When making his decision, however, he hadn't considered how annoying it was to constantly secure and release the lines. If you had to pause every two yards, fifty yards could become quite long. He definitely didn't want to do without the safety line, though. The AI's warning about the cross-current was still fresh in his mind. Eventually, however, he neared the engine block. It rose above him like a castle; a dark, almost black citadel that looked like it belonged to a villain.

That was nonsense. A fusion engine required a certain amount of space. The three pipes didn't lead directly into the engine, but into the cargo holds. These consisted of five cylinders mounted around the axis of the ship. Two circular passages connected the tanks at the front and rear so that you could move between them without needing a spacesuit. He would only find out whether the cargo holds were filled with atmosphere when he got to the airlock. That was probably the sphere stuck to one of the containers, which looked like the crown of a strange clock from a distance.

Monte approached the airlock. The typical rotating wheel could be seen on the outer door. This purely mechanical technology worked even when the power was out. He turned the wheel with minimal effort. Apparently, the power supply was still running. To be on the safe side, he took a step to the side before opening the door. It had happened to him once that the whole airlock was filled with water that almost washed him away. But this airlock was empty. He could see that immediately, as the interior lighting switched on automatically.

He entered and pulled the door shut behind him as a fan started up. Monte found a small screen next to the inner door. When he touched it, it showed the current oxygen level. It started at four percent. The life support was working quickly, which surprised him because he was in a wreck. The screen lit up green. Monte tapped on it and the inner door opened with a hiss. He pushed it open a little further. The corridor behind it was brightly lit. Then he heard footsteps.

Gliese 163 c

The rigid, lifeless body turned slowly on its axis. Mark waited until Roger's back was to him. Then he stopped the rotation. He reached for the piece of cloth he had cut from the shoulder of Roger's uniform. There were fine holes in the material, irregularly distributed, with the exception of one particular area. That must be where the rucksack had been positioned, or whatever Roger had been wearing on his back. That was one of the mysteries yet to be solved, because they hadn't found a rucksack.

Carefully, he held the fabric against Roger's back. Then he pushed a ballpoint pen through the first hole. To prevent the body from floating away, he held it in place with his other hand. The next hole. A bit of ink stuck to the fabric, but some also reached the skin underneath. When he had marked all the holes like this, he removed the fabric. The black dots lined up almost exactly with the small red spots on the skin. The day of Roger's death was slowly taking shape. A chain of unfortunate circumstances had been to blame, not one thing in particular. Roger must have tried to squeeze through the prickly cherry hedge. It would have been painful, but not impossible. The solid fabric of the uniform had rendered the thorns almost completely harmless. Almost. If these spines hit a victim, a tiny poison sac at their tip would empty. The substance it contained was only toxic to some animal species on Adad, not to humans. But Roger had obviously had an allergic reaction. His medical records did indeed show some allergies. He had never been tested for prickly cherry. However, Mark had discovered under the electron microscope that the chemical structure was similar to that of bee venom - surprisingly similar for two compounds that were products of completely different biochemistries.

But that hadn't caused Roger's demise. He had developed breathing problems and fainted. But the mask had saved him from the worst. For a while, the protocol showed, it drastically increased the oxygen content of the air he was breathing. He would have regained consciousness at some point after the allergic attack. But then the acid rain hit him. Roger must have been lying on his stomach. The cloak protected his body. Mark had found no traces of acid, but Roger had slipped the strap of the mask over his hood and the strap was exposed to the rain. The acid dissolved it so that the mask was only loosely attached to Roger's face.

It was hard to tell when he had lost it. Maybe he had turned over. Or it had happened when a multifeet had picked him up. The animals certainly didn't know what the mask was for. They had taken it with them because it belonged to this strange creature. But it hadn't occurred to them to put it back on him. If they really were as intelligent as Tailin believed, it must have shocked them to see the two humans with masks on their faces. Perhaps they had only realized at that moment that they might have been partly to blame for Roger's death. Was it a guilty conscience that prompted them to carry the dead body back to the Hopper?

He must not anthropomorphize them. No one could know why they acted the way they did. No one except themselves, and even that presupposed a certain degree of intelligence, which he could not assume. Science thrived on healthy skepticism. Why didn't Tailin get that? She was a physicist herself!

The radio reported an incoming connection. He reached for it.

"Mark, is that you?" asked Tailin.

Who else would it be? "Mhmm." he replied.

"It's almost dark. I'm going to stay down here for a while. The geophysical measurements are going well."

"That's good."

He wasn't just referring to the measurements, but also to the fact that he would have another day of peace and quiet. He and

Tailin were not getting on well. Hopefully that would change when Claire and Karima returned. There was a reason why married couples were rarely sent on long research missions together. Tailin believed that the residual impact of Roger's death was to blame. Mark saw other reasons.

"Yes, the planet seems to have an unusually differentiated core in which several magnetizable layers rotate differentially," said Tailin.

That had been Tailin's suspicion from the start, so he was surprised that she was so happy about it. But that was typical. What mattered to him scientifically was new knowledge, even if it was uncertain. Tailin, on the other hand, was primarily interested in proving things. It didn't bother her if these things were already known. The main thing was that she had found definitive proof. That was probably why she had become a physicist, while he had chosen exobiology. He was more of an explorer than a researcher. Nevertheless, he enjoyed finding things out. He had even enjoyed investigating Roger's cause of death, as macabre as it seemed. He had the feeling that he had done his colleague and friend justice.

"You don't sound very enthusiastic," said his wife.

He hadn't said much. But that probably confirmed her statement.

"I've just been dealing with the body," he said.

"Oh, I'm sorry about that. Have you found out anything else?"

"It was an accident," he said. "Prickly cherry allergy and acid rain."

And something must have moved the unconscious body.

"You already suspected something like that. So nobody's to blame."

Mark didn't disagree, even though it was wrong. Roger had climbed out of the safe Hopper because Tailin wanted to move her sensors in the middle of a storm. Roger had left the safe Hopper because Mark hadn't told him not to. He was the commander. He could even have locked the Hopper's doors from the space station, but had refrained from doing so because he was worried about Tailin. If she hadn't been so stubborn... *No.* That was unfair. He was the main culprit, because he could have broken the chain of unfortunate circumstances. Nothing had happened to Tailin. They would all be on board now, cleaning up the *Albatross* before Claire and Karima returned.

"Are you still there?" asked Tailin. "You're acting really strange today."

"Uh-huh."

"It's about Roger, isn't it?"

Of course it was about Roger. It would always be about Roger from now on.

"Don't worry about it," he said. "It's got nothing to do with you."

"All right. You're a grown man. If you want to tell me about your worries, get in touch. If not, that's fine too."

"That sounds fair," he said.

"I think so too. I'll talk to you again tomorrow."

August 4, 2802, Earth's moon

Steps. Heavy uniform shoes on a hard surface. Metal. No floor covering, definitely no carpet. And yet the steps sounded very light, as if they were accidental, almost tender touches on the floor and walls. It must be a woman. Tsai Yini memorized the feeling. It seemed to be important for what happened next. The moment of the impending encounter took up an unusual amount of space in the station's memories. Yini pressed the play button with her left hand. The stream jumped back a little. Footsteps. Heavy uniform shoes on...

"Yini, wake up!"

It was her twin brother. Three years ago, they had started training together in the Great Archive, but he had failed the chronoscribe exam. Since then, Kang had been something of a maintenance supervisor here. Or rather, maintenance assistant, because only Zahir rated the title of supervisor.

"What's wrong?" asked Yini, opening her eyes. "You're not supposed to disturb me in the middle of a transmission."

She was already lagging behind on this assignment because she always wanted to find out everything in detail. Ulita, her instructor, often teased her about it.

"You have an important visitor," Kang said.

"Our parents?"

Their parents always arrived at the most frustrating times. Especially their father, who didn't seem to believe her assurances that she was doing very well. *You're so thin, missy. That can't be healthy...* Yini stroked her tummy. *Thin, my ass!*

Kang laughed. "What makes you think that?"

"The cake the day before yesterday. Maybe they want to check whether we ate enough of it," replied Yini.

"Hah, that would suit Father. But it's not them, it's someone in uniform. Probably from the navy. Even Zahir is groveling at his feet, so he must be important."

"And he wants to see me? Not Ulita?"

"He already had a brief meeting with Ulita. Now he wants you."

If he had spoken to Ulita, he must be rather important - and experienced in dealing with offices like this one. The Office of Chronoscopy, as the Great Archive was officially called, had an extremely important function that was recognized by all factions, right down to the independent settlers of distant colony worlds. It established the position of every event in the universal timeline, and did so in the final analysis. Travel at relativistic speeds, instantaneous tachyon transmissions and even the different relative speeds of the worlds on which people lived would inevitably lead to chaos without the Office. Yini was therefore very happy that she was allowed to work here as a chronoscribe.

"What's he like?" she asked.

"About six feet, shorter hair than me..." Kang began.

"No, I mean your impression of him. Does he seem arrogant? What kind of look does he have? Does he have a heavy tread?"

She couldn't help but think of the light-footed gait of the person who was about to take the stage in the transmission.

"Well, he's a man in uniform. Confident, I'd say."

That was typical Kang. He had probably seen the uniform rather than the visitor. That was why he had failed the exam. Yini straightened up slowly. She absolutely had to touch the ground with her left foot first, or the conversation with the stranger would not end well. Her brother leaned forward and pulled on her arm. He moved her in such a way that her right foot touched down first. *Crap.*

"What kind of face is that? Be glad you're getting some fresh air. It can't be healthy for you to sit on the couch all day."

Kang really had found the perfect job for himself, working

for Zahir. Sometimes she wondered if he and she really were twins. Apart from their parents, her brother had nothing in common with her. Yini looked at her watch, but she didn't really need to turn her head. There were clocks on every wall, ceiling and floor in the Great Archive. They all showed the same time. That could have been terribly boring if the designer hadn't had fun coming up with original ways to display them. The clock on the floor, for example, consisted of a projection of the large hand of the ceiling clock, which moved through the narrow room once an hour. Now it looked as if it was climbing up Kang's leg, which stood in the way of the projection.

"Sis? Are you all right?"

She rolled her eyes in annoyance at the name, but Kang just grinned. She couldn't blame this prankster.

"The time," she said. "It's half past two. There would have been a break in half an hour anyway."

"Your visitor probably doesn't have time to wait that long."

"Where is he?"

"I am supposed to send you directly to Ulita," her brother replied. "Or should I escort you?"

"Thanks, Kang, but I can find my own way."

"And you're not thinking any more about the clock that's climbing up me right now?"

Yini felt called out, causing her cheeks to flush. Kang might not be good at recognizing the nature of others. But he had keen powers of observation - and had known her for 24 years.

"I promise I'll go straight away," said Yini.

AFTER HER BROTHER LEFT THE ROOM, SHE WAS NO LONGER SO sure about her promise. The stranger waiting to meet her frightened her, though she couldn't say why. At the same time, the stranger in the transmission from the *Curious* enticed her. She was sure she would see a woman, but not just any woman. She would recognize her. That was probably nonsense, of course, and she could convince herself of it immediately by putting her head in the reading bowl and continuing to play the transmission.

No, that was out of the question. Ulita would give her hell if she ignored the obviously important visitor. The entire known universe counted on the Office of Chronoscopy, but the Office could not finance itself without its two most important supporters, Neomars and the Terran Union.

Yini closed her eyes and recalled the key scenes from the last transmission. She dictated the time code to the system so that it could activate the timeline. Then she logged out by opening and closing her eyes four times, and stood up. She took her shoes from under the couch and put them on, then put on her wig. As an eavesdropper, she had to shave her head every day. She liked her wig well enough; it only annoyed her when she was on vacation. But her natural, shiny black hair grew so quickly that after three or four days she no longer noticed it, even without the artificial hairpiece. She checked her make-up in front of the mirror. The device showed her a black spot above her eyebrow that didn't belong there, which she carefully wiped away with a tissue. The mirror frame, which had been red, turned green.

She left the room and the door slammed shut behind her. The hallway was also decorated with numerous clocks, some looking as if they were painted on the wall, but still showing the correct time. One clock on the ceiling appeared to be made of bricks. Yini passed a clock which, on closer inspection, was made up of multiple smaller clocks, which in turn were made up of even smaller clocks. One that amused her every morning on her way to work was the face clock, on which stylized human faces displayed the time. They changed their expression depending on a whole range of factors. Ulita had listed them all on her first day at the Great Archive, but Yini had only memorized the time and the position of the Earth in the sky.

It was only a five-minute walk to Ulita's office, but that was enough to distract her. This time, the exclamation mark clock was the reason. The many punctuation marks on it caused Yini to feel like she should hurry, but she wasn't sure why. Was it meant to do that? The designer didn't even know her. The Great Archive had been built shortly after the Martian Wars, which to her felt like the distant past.

Nevertheless, the exclamation marks, which seemed particularly ironic in the current situation, triggered questions in her. Could it be that it wasn't time that drove the clocks, but the clocks that drove time? If you avoided looking at them, could you stop time? Yini tried for a moment, but the designer had done a great job. Even if she felt her way along the wall with her eyes closed, she could still feel the clocks, and she even discovered a new one that consisted of heat strips. She had always wondered why this particular spot on the wall was devoid of timekeeping.

Whether she wanted to or not, she eventually reached Ulita's office, though it had taken eight minutes instead of five, as the clock projected on the door told her. Yini carefully touched the bright green hour hand. The strip of light trembled as if it could feel her touch, and when she moved her hand slightly to the left, the hand moved backwards. *What a clever idea!* She looked for a camera but couldn't find it. It was probably camouflaged. Yini moved the hand back from eight to six, but it slipped away and showed twenty minutes to three in the afternoon again.

She knocked.

"Come in," Ulita's secretary called.

Yini opened the door. The secretary was an elderly gentleman who always wore a tie and touched coffee cups with pointed fingers when he was about to drink from them. No one seemed to be friends with him, but maybe she was mistaken since he acted very formal with everyone, even his boss.

"Good afternoon, Miss Tsai," said the secretary.

"Good afternoon, Mr. Pedersen," replied Yini.

"They're expecting you." He pointed to the door leading to his boss's office. "Just go in."

"I... Yes, of course."

Yini suddenly felt like a little girl again, summoned by a strict teacher. She paused for a moment in front of the door.

An electronic sign read, "Ulita Kuznetsova, Head of the Department of Tachyonic Communication." It had probably long since lost the ability to change its content. Ulita had been the boss here for so long. It seemed strange to others that she had never tried to advance her career, but Yini thought she knew why; eavesdropping was addictive, at least if you were good at it.

She knocked, but no one called her to come in.

"As I said, just go in, Ms. Tsai," urged the secretary.

Just like that, then. She pulled open the door and hurried into the room. It was empty. Ulita's desk was empty. The visitor's sofa was empty. But she smelled someone, a man. His aroma was a mixture of sweat and an expensive, sweet perfume. He must be truly rich, or he would have had his sweat glands removed long ago.

Suddenly, he was standing behind her. Yini spun around. He was smiling. Kang had been right, at least somewhat. He was about six feet tall and wore a uniform. However, he wasn't particularly self-confident if he needed such cheap tricks to fluster his conversational partners. Yini looked up at the ceiling. He must have been waiting there when she entered the room. Or was the game of hide-and-seek not about her? He couldn't have known exactly when she would arrive.

"I am John Smith," he said.

John Smith - that was obviously not his real name.

"Tsai Yini," she introduced herself.

They shook hands. Yini braced herself for him to crush hers, but he released her unharmed from his warm, dry grip.

"Why don't you sit down," he said.

Yini made her way toward the visitor's sofa, but he stepped into her path. She spread out her palms.

"I would be glad to sit, if you would let me by," she said.

"No, I want you to sit in that chair there."

He pointed to Ulita's seat.

"You really want to get me into trouble, don't you?" asked Yini.

The man was surely not used to being contradicted, but he didn't let on.

"Don't worry, Yini. I will take care of Ulita. I want you to enjoy the feeling of sitting in her seat for once."

"And what do I get out of it?" she asked.

"Nothing, for the moment. Except that you're fulfilling a request for me, which is always helpful."

"I don't even know you," said Yini.

"Of course, my mistake," he said. "Please sit down and I will introduce myself."

Fine. The man wouldn't let it be before then anyway. *John Smith, sure.* Yini walked around the desk, pushed the armchair closer to the table and sat down as requested.

"It's real wood," the man said. "Just like the desk."

Yini was genuinely impressed. She always thought she had never seen wood in her life, and now it turned out that Ulita owned two pieces of furniture made of it. Since the surface of the earth had been almost completely protected, wood substitutes had become established worldwide.

"I can't promise that you'll be able to have wooden furniture one day," said the man. "Things are different these days. However, I can sense that you are a talented young woman who could achieve a great deal. Your mentor, Ulita, is retiring in five years' time. You could be the first female head of department younger than thirty."

"Who are you speaking for, Mr. Smith?" asked Yini.

"May I call you Yini? Where I come from, people have a hard time with formal manners. I'm John."

"And who do you speak for, John?"

"I'm a special representative of the Admiralty," said the man. "Of course, my name isn't really Smith. You won't find me in this admittedly comfortable body again, either. It's a borrowed Biobag."

Yini felt a shiver run down her spine. The man was using a body that didn't belong to him. It was a strange idea, even if it was common in some circles. She had never done a consciousness purification herself.

"And what does Ms. Gaudlitz want from me?" asked Yini.

It was common knowledge that Admiral Marina Gaudlitz wasn't only in charge of the Admiralty. She had been the Admiral ever since she led the legendary attack on Fort Mons Olympus and thus put an end to the old Mars. The victory had made the Terran Union the dominant force in the Local Group for what must be a hundred years, until Neomars gained strength.

"You're a very talented eavesdropper, Yini," the man said. "Ulita never tires of boasting about your skills."

Her cheeks grew hot. Yini was not used to praise. Her parents had never found it necessary. She scratched her forearm, as she always did when she was nervous.

"That... That's nice to hear," she said.

The man's gaze rested on her face as if he was trying to read her mind. She avoided him by looking up at the ceiling. John Smith wasn't just any assistant; he seemed to have experience with mind games. There was probably no shame in refusing to play. On the ceiling, she spotted two faint, gray patterns, probably shoe prints the man had left up there earlier.

Smith followed her gaze. Then he smiled.

"Please don't tell on me, Yini."

"You noticed?" she asked.

"Noticed?"

"The clocks. Their absence, that is."

The man nodded. "Yes, there are random gaps all the way here, but..."

"Ulita had them hung in her office," Yini explained. "If you remove the light-colored panels from the walls, you'll find them underneath."

"I find that very interesting. What do you think it means?" he asked.

"Probably nothing. She never explained it to me," said Yini.

That was a lie. It seemed wrong to her to tell the man something that Ulita had once casually mentioned to her. Because John Smith was right, it did mean something that Ulita had locked away the clocks.

"But let's get back to you, Yini."

"If you must..."

She was startled by her own cheeky reply, but the man ignored it.

"I'm afraid so," he said. "You're working on an interesting transmission."

"My boss has instructed me not to give out any information about my work."

"Well, there's a simple reason why you're working with these particular tachyon transmissions: we asked Ulita to transmit them to her most capable eavesdropper. That's how I know that you are chronicling the *Curious*'s transmissions."

"As I said, I can neither confirm nor deny that. The Office of Chronoscopy is committed to neutrality, and this is enshrined in law in both the Terran Union and Neomars territories, as well as in the peace treaty of 2710, in order to avoid the permanent establishment of parallel timelines."

"I'm aware of all that, and I neither deny it nor do I want to change it."

"Then what do you want from me?"

"I confess, I thought you would be a little more... flexible. Of course, I want you to do your job, with your usual perfectionism. You will assign all events exactly to the intended timeline."

"Very well, and that's all?"

Of course it wasn't everything. She was curious to discover when he would finally come out with the truth.

"Almost. You will present us with the resulting timeline before it is placed in the archive."

What? Yini could hardly believe her ears. Smith was asking her to clearly violate the neutrality requirement. The Office was not allowed to favor either party, not even by passing on information. Both Neomars and the Terran Union constantly carried out audits to verify this.

"That's impossible. That would make me liable by law."

"No one would notice. No one even knows about the tachyon transmissions you're working on. Admiral Gaudlitz personally sent the *Curious* on this journey. We therefore have a right to be the first to know what happened to the ship."

John's argument was strange. If the *Curious* was traveling on behalf of the Admiralty, surely the transmissions were also being sent to the Admiral. But in that case she must already know their contents! The Office of Chronoscopy only processed transmissions after they had reached the recipients.

"I don't understand," said Yini. "As the legitimate recipients, you've known the contents of the transmissions for a long time. We're not a post office. We just archive them."

"There must have been an unfortunate misunderstanding on the part of the sender. He didn't send the messages directly to us despite clear instructions, which is why we are depending on your help."

"I'm sorry, but I can't do that. If the Office of Chronoscopy squanders the trust of humanity, it will lose its legitimacy."

"Yes, that's what you have been taught," said the man, "but in practice, things are different. I hate to draw your attention to the fact that your parents' status on Earth is a little... shaky. It could happen that they must be deported to Neomars."

Yini suddenly froze. *What a pig!* But she had no chance. He had the upper hand. Her father was wanted in the territory of Neomars because of an old story, and her parents would rather kill themselves than go back there. She resigned herself.

"All right," she said, "I'll give you the resulting timeline. Does Ulita know about this?"

"No. She just knows that we'd like to give you special support and promote you as her successor."

Carrot and stick. A tried and true strategy. Yini slumped down in her boss's wooden chair.

"I wouldn't advise you to let anyone else in on this, especially not your brother," said the man. "He doesn't seem particularly reliable to us."

He was right. Kang wouldn't be able to keep this to himself. Her parents would find out, and to protect their daughter, they would volunteer to face Neomars. Or go to their deaths somewhere.

"Good, thank you for your understanding, Yini. I'll take my leave. Feel free to sit here for a while longer. Ulita will not be returning today."

The man left the office, the door closing quietly behind him, and she was alone. Even the secretary didn't seem to have the courage to check on her. The visitor had probably forbidden him to do so. Yini took a deep breath as a tear trickled down her cheek. She hated this feeling of powerlessness, and she hated not being able to share her worries with anyone.

SHE LEFT THE OFFICE AFTER REGAINING HER COMPOSURE. IT HAD been a strange time, with no clocks at all. It was as if the encounter in the office had never taken place, or had happened outside the timeline, which amounted to the same thing. In the outer office, Yini was surprised to discover that only 45 minutes had passed. Obviously, her personal sense of time had changed drastically. Was that why Ulita had the clocks moved?

"Can you tell me where to find Ulita, Mr. Pedersen?" she asked the secretary.

She had to talk to somebody, and her brother was out of the question.

"Not the most pleasant person, is he, Ms. Tsai?"

She knew immediately who he was talking about and nodded vigorously. Tears started to well up in her eyes again, and a lump in her throat prevented her from speaking. But she managed to swallow the lump and her cheeks remained dry. She couldn't. Not here, in front of Mr. Pedersen ...

"Stay a moment longer, Ms. Tsai," said the secretary. "Shall I make us some tea?"

Yini nodded. Hot tea, yes, that was a good idea.

"Black, green, or would you prefer an herbal tea? I grow my own tea plants, you know."

"Here on the moon?" she asked.

"Yes, why not? They need light, air, water, nutrients and love."

The secretary surprised her. The way he pronounced the word "love"... as if he knew exactly what he was talking about.

"Then I'd like green tea, please," she said.

"My pleasure."

Pedersen rose and went to the tiny kitchen set up in one corner of the anteroom. Along with a coffee machine and a sink, there was also a kettle, which Pedersen filled and switched on. He then took two tea infusers from a drawer, bent down with a groan and searched for something in the cupboard below.

"Can I help you at all?" asked Yini.

"Thank you for the offer, but my tins aren't labeled, so I have to do it myself."

He took two small, almost identical-looking tins from the cupboard, opened them and sniffed them. Then he held the tins out to her. She smelled them too but couldn't distinguish between them.

"The first contains green tea, the second black tea," said the secretary.

"I'm afraid I can't tell the difference."

"That's normal. You're used to drinks from the dispenser. What's called tea there is nothing like the real thing."

The water in the kettle bubbled. Yini watched Pedersen's actions intently, thankful for the distraction. Pedersen filled one tea infuser with black tea and the other with green tea, then put each infuser into a cup, took the kettle and poured hot water into the cup with the black tea. She pushed her cup towards him, but he shook his head. Instead, he put the kettle down again.

"We'll have to wait a bit," he said. "The green tea doesn't like it so hot."

He stared into his cup, from which steam was rising in thin plumes. Yini saw how the water slowly turned golden yellow from the bottom, where the tea infuser was. After a while, the secretary reached for the stove again to pour her cup. As he leaned forward, his tie slipped out of his jacket. Yini quickly grabbed it before it could fall into his teacup.

"Oops," said Pedersen, blushing.

Suddenly he looked like a shy young man to her, even though he must be close to retirement.

"Nothing happened," said Yini.

"That's true."

He took the tea infuser out of his cup, drained it and put it in the sink. Then he inhaled deeply.

"I love that smell," he said, continuing to stare at his cup.

Yini didn't answer, and she didn't need to. She knew he was elsewhere at that moment. After an indeterminate period of silence, he took the tea infuser from her cup and placed it next to its sibling. Then he pressed the cup into her hand. They sat down - Pedersen in his armchair behind the desk, Yini in the chair in front of it.

"Or would you prefer to exchange seats?" he asked. "Forgive my rudeness towards a lady."

"This chair is very comfortable," said Yini.

Pedersen seemed to be truly old-fashioned. What had brought him to the Great Archive? The secretary lifted the cup to his mouth, first blowing gently over it. Then he put the cup to his lips and took a tiny sip.

"You have to be careful," he said. "This tea is stronger than the kind from the dispenser."

"Thanks for the warning," she said.

"Feel free to drink it," Pedersen said. "Green tea isn't brewed as long as black tea."

She hadn't known that. Tea from the dispenser was always at the perfect temperature and didn't need to steep. Yini held the cup directly in front of her mouth at a slight angle so that she could see into it better. She could feel the heat of the liquid on her face and the intense aroma in her nose. *Have courage*, the tea called out to her, *but don't be overconfident or I'll punish you*. Yini blew over the edge of the cup, creating a current in the tea that carried a few loose leaves with it. She imagined them as small spaceships that had fallen into the gravitational pull of a black hole. The poor crew! She put the cup to her lips and let some tea flow into her mouth.

Tachyon: The Weapon

The liquid was hot, very hot, it even hurt, but the pain passed and gave way to a gentle bitterness that seemed related to the sadness that sometimes overwhelmed her. It wasn't an unpleasant taste, and she savored it before letting the tea slowly trickle down her throat. It was still hotter than anything she usually drank, so she could almost follow its path to her stomach, where it would soon speak to the doorman and ask to be let in. Perhaps the doorman also wore a tie, was also called Pedersen and would offer tea? She had to smile.

She felt a touch on her shoulder. Yini looked up. It was the secretary, who must have been watching her.

"Take your time," he said.

The sentence sounded like an oracle, and she resolved not to ask any questions, but simply let it sink in. Time seemed to be what the Chronoscopy Office had in abundance. Wasn't that why they needed so many clocks to measure it and keep it in order? But perhaps that was also a fallacy. Pedersen must know better than her, being more than twice her age. Perhaps the clocks were also destroying what they claimed to be preserving?

"Is that why Ulita had the clocks taken down in her office?" Yini asked.

"Mrs. Kuznetsova... I'm sorry, I cannot speak for her. I can only speak for myself," said the secretary.

"Excuse me, Mr. Pedersen. I didn't mean to put you on the spot. Your tea is excellent!"

Yini took another sip. The tea had cooled down a little. It now had a pleasant warmth, still slightly above her body temperature, and the bitterness had also changed. It tasted like a memory of times gone by, bad times, but with the sweetness of knowing you had survived them. New flavors emerged. She hadn't expected her untrained palate to notice, but it found apple and a spice whose name she couldn't remember. She swirled the cup under her nose. The tea smelled of fresh hay and a trace of moss, the kind that grew in a dense forest. These must be memories from her early childhood, which she knew had been spent on Earth.

"Tea is a miracle, isn't it?" asked Pedersen.

Yini nodded. "I smell moss and hay," she said.

"Very observant," replied Pedersen. "You have potential. I think I could help you develop your sense of taste."

That was an extremely kind offer. But could she accept it? Should she? Suddenly she was afraid of the memories that might come flooding back.

"Don't I just taste and smell what I remember?" she asked.

It was a puzzling question, but she didn't want to give too much away. The secretary took three long sips from his cup before answering her.

"You have... interesting memories," he said, licking his lips. "You're a native, aren't you?"

What was she supposed to say to him? Actually, it was none of Pedersen's business where she came from. Natives were considered simple-minded, backward - but they had simply chosen to do without most of the achievements of technology. They lived in paradise, on the surface of the Earth, which consisted of one huge nature reserve. There was less need for technology there than in the cloud cities and the hollow world.

"Yes," she answered eventually, but it sounded wrong, because it was wrong. "And no. My parents are from Neomars. They refused the genetic program and went into hiding on the surface of the Earth. As a result, I lived like a native for my first few years."

"Ah, I see," said the secretary.

His face did not reveal what he thought of her now. Refugees from Neomars did not have a particularly good reputation. At best they were regarded as traitors, at worst as spies. The modern Earth Biobag carriers, for whom bodies had become interchangeable, could not comprehend why they resisted forced genetic enhancement of their own bodies.

"I understand very well," said the secretary. "My wife also came from Neomars."

"Where...?"

"She didn't survive the escape. We met in the diplomatic service."

"I'm sorry to hear that."

"It was a long time ago," said the secretary.

But at that moment, it didn't seem as if it was history to him. Perhaps he only worked in the Great Archive so that he could watch broadcasts in which his wife played a role. Yini took a closer look at his hairstyle and tried to remember previous visits here. His hair had always been impeccable. He probably wore a wig - like her.

"You're trained as an eavesdropper," she said.

Pedersen narrowed his eyes. He didn't answer, but his face spoke volumes. Yini picked up her teacup again. The tea had cooled. She drank it in one gulp and felt more refreshed than ever.

"Thank you very much for the invitation," she said and stood up. "I'll take your advice."

Pedersen nodded but said nothing. His supply of words for the day seemed to be exhausted. Yini didn't blame him. She knew the feeling quite well.

IT STILL SMELLED OF KANG IN HER WORKROOM. HE HAD LIKELY made himself comfortable on her couch for a few minutes. The main thing was that he hadn't pressed the play button. She didn't want to miss the performance of the survivors from the wreck. The blanket that normally lay at the foot of the bed in case she got cold during a broadcast was rumpled. Yini was annoyed. Kang could have folded it back up properly!

Yini sat down on the couch and took off her shoes, first the left one, then the right one. Then she slid the shoes under the couch, parallel to each other. She kept an eye on the clock on the floor. The small hand pointed to just behind the four. Yini lifted her feet onto the lounger, left foot first, took off her wig and wiped her scalp dry. She could already feel a light stubble, but not so much as to get in the way of her listening. Yini lay down and placed her head in the middle of the reading bowl. She was looking forward to the encounter to come.

Crap. The bowl was too big. Had Kang tried to watch a broadcast after all? Or had someone else been in her room? That John Smith, for example: Was that why he had suggested she wait in Ulita's office? She called Smith to mind. His head hadn't looked very big to her, but on the broad shoulders of his Biobag... The reading device's bowl was designed to expand automatically if the head inside it was too big. It didn't work the other way around. You had to press the sides together with your hands.

Wait, had Smith been wearing a wig? Yini thought she would have been able to tell. On the other hand, his hair had been quite short, and a trained eavesdropper could follow transmissions even without a full shave. She wouldn't be able to find out, because if he was trained, he would surely have positioned the current exactly so that she wouldn't notice anything.

Yini shook her head. She had been working on the files for two days. What could Smith have discovered in less than an hour? Who had survived the accident or the attack, for example. Heavy uniform shoes on a hard surface - and yet very delicate movements. She couldn't get the contrast out of her mind. She lay down, adjusted the reading bowl and started the stream by pressing the play button with her left hand.

She found herself in a brightly lit corridor. Footsteps came towards her, the sound reaching her from above. Feet in sturdy military boots. Out here, in the orbit of a gas planet with no real name, there was neither up nor down. Her gaze followed the legs and, like a painter with a pointed brush, brought a person from possibility into reality. It was a woman. Her confusion was clear to see. Almost simultaneously, she tried to turn over, to swap the positions of her head and feet, to turn the world 180 degrees. The woman was faster than her, so Yini gave up the attempt. The stranger checked the display of a device on her wrist. She nodded, then took off her breathing mask. Yini recognized the woman. It was herself.

Yini screamed, her heart racing as she sat up. It was impossible. She was trembling. But there could be no mistake. No one could fake these transmissions. What had she seen? A woman with her face. She knew it well, saw it in the mirror several times a day when she touched up her make-up. But what did it mean? She had to find out, and to do that she would have to put her head back in the bowl.

May 8, 2799, Gliese 411

THE FOOTSTEPS SOUNDED FORCEFUL AND DELICATE AT THE SAME time. But they came from the ceiling, leaving Monte confused. Just behind the airlock, the corridor bent to the right. The person coming towards him must come from there. And here she was. First, he saw her feet, which were in military boots. Her legs were clad in uniform trousers, and her upper body was in uniform as well. The stranger seemed to be just as confused as he was, because she halted. But he reacted faster and turned his body 180 degrees.

The stranger had long, shiny black hair. This Biobag was outwardly female, but that didn't necessarily mean anything. Everyone was free to choose their own body. What was strange, however, was that the person was wearing a Neomars uniform. The Saturn rings on the logo were clearly recognizable. The main world of Neomars was Saturn's moon Titan, since Mars was made even less habitable than it had been by the use of nuclear weapons during the Martian Wars. The Neomars faction didn't like using Biobags, except for space travel. Was this one of them? No one would be crazy enough to venture out here in a real body.

The woman checked the screen of the device on her wrist, then nodded and took off her breathing mask. He had never seen her before. Dark, almost black eyes, slightly protruding ears, no wrinkles on her forehead or temples. She was no more than half his age and made a pleasant impression. Monte was nevertheless suspicious. Neomars was known, even infamous, for its genetic experiments. The woman might even have a second set of lungs. How much of that was propaganda? Monte didn't know. Although he had worked for Neomartian corporations, he had never visited Titan. He checked the oxygen content. Fourteen percent, that should be enough. Monte took off his mask.

The air tasted foul and smelled of oil, but it was breathable. He nodded.

"I am Claudio Pedramonte," said Monte.

He gestured a bow, as he had learned to do. Extending your hand could be misunderstood as reaching for a weapon in encounters like this.

"Tsai Tailin," said the woman.

"Good afternoon, Ms. Tsai," he said. "I've been sent to investigate your wreck."

"Just call me Tailin."

"I'm Monte. I am surprised and delighted to find you here on board."

"I'm surprised myself. I thought I would have to stay here in orbit for years. But you weren't sent to look for me?"

"No, Tailin. Can we talk somewhere a little more comfortable?" he asked.

"On board your ship, perhaps? It's huge compared to mine."

The woman was in a hurry. However, he first had to rule out the possibility that she was a danger.

"I'd like to clarify some questions here first. I have to complete my investigation, of course."

"I see. Then please follow me."

Tailin floated ahead of him down the corridor. It was clear she had perfected the technique of moving in microgravity. Her feet touched the walls only briefly, picking up just enough momentum to let her glide along the optimal trajectory. How many times had she practiced this here?

At the end of the corridor were several oval doors on the left and right, which presumably led to storage rooms. The last one on the left was open. Tailin floated ahead. You could no longer tell that the room once served as a storeroom. The walls were covered with paintings depicting exotic scenes. Monte didn't recognize the landscapes, but the rings of Saturn appeared from time to time. It must be Tailin's home. Why had the admiral sent him to look for a Neomars ship? The opposite wall, on the other hand, was full of sheets of paper with formulas written on them. He couldn't make sense of the signs.

On the ceiling, the occupant had hung boxes that apparently contained her household goods and clothes. That made sense, because the room must be three yards high, and in zero gravity you could use every square inch. The floor was covered with a soft carpet. Monte felt it. It was not a conventional floor covering, but consisted of the typical filling material of lined outerwear. He didn't see a bed, but there were several belts distributed around the room, on the ceiling, floor and walls. This would allow Tailin to sleep wherever she wanted.

The room lacked the musty smell he had noticed in the corridor outside. Or had he already got used to it? Monte looked at the door. Tailin was pressing insulating material tightly around the frame. She noticed his gaze.

"Don't worry, I don't want to lock you in. I'm just saving oxygen in the corridor outside. It fills up automatically when visitors arrive. I can't prevent that."

"How often do you get visitors?" asked Monte.

"You wouldn't believe how often I've dreamed that a visitor arrived. Sometimes it's been a rescue, sometimes a nightmare. Which are you?"

Monte looked at the woman. She had a pronounced musculature. Small and fast. He wouldn't stand a chance against her, especially as she had a knife visible in her belt. He had refrained from carrying his weapon.

"I am the rescue," he said. "Even if I wasn't specifically tasked with it."

"What did they tell you?"

"There was a call for help after an accident. Given the length of time, no one suspected that anyone on board could still be alive."

"A call for help, I see," said Tailin. "It must have been the NSS bastards when I finally caught them."

"It was a call from a civilian ship," Monte said.

"That sounds like them. Who would want to help an NSS ship?"

The Neomars Secret Service didn't have a particularly good reputation, even on Neomars itself. During the Martian Wars, its predecessor service was said to have been responsible for massacres.

"Your pursuers messed you up badly. I saw the tracks on Gliese 411 b."

Tailin smiled. "Yes, that was a close call."

"And then the diversionary maneuver in the asteroid belt..."

"You spotted that too? I thought no one would notice."

"I am very thorough."

"I can see that. Who put you in charge?"

The woman was clever. There was no point in lying to her. But he didn't have to tell the whole truth, either.

"It's an official order from the Terran Union. I was lucky that my ship was in the immediate vicinity of a tachyon relay."

"Well, lucky you - you've been traveling for years, haven't you?"

"Three years. But with a slow system clock, that's just a moment."

"You're using a Biobag?"

Tailin grimaced. He had seen this reaction before, not only from Neomartians but also from independent colonists. It didn't bother him anymore.

"So are you," he said. "You just can't change yours. You could have easily saved yourself the years alone here."

"That's self-deception. Time doesn't go faster just because I'm asleep."

Tailin had sounded different earlier. He had the feeling that she was happy to finally get out of here.

"Certainly, Tailin! Have you ever tried it?" he asked.

"Have you ever tried molecular genetic treatment like almost every normal Neomartian?"

"I don't know," he said. "I can't rule it out, because I don't know the history of this Biobag. As far as I know, they're also bred using genetic engineering methods."

"You see, you don't care about your body at all. In fact, you neglect it."

Tailin raised her arms and pumped her upper arm muscles. "This is what it should look like!"

"Very impressive."

Suddenly the boxes on the ceiling moved. Monte held his

arms protectively over his head, but they didn't fall. He remembered the AI's warning.

"These are cross currents," he said. "Nothing to worry about."

"I'm not worried," said the woman. "Small pressure fluctuations like that occur here once a week. Larger ones about every 215 days, so once every cycle. For the larger fluctuations, I have to fasten everything in place."

"How did you get here in the first place?" asked Monte. "It can't have been a private vacation, can it?"

"No. We're on the run from our employer."

"We?"

Tailin froze. He should probably have asked about the employer.

"My husband Baihu and I," she whispered.

The cabin cut in half - of course. Next to the seat, half of which had been shaved off, there was probably a second one that had been completely destroyed.

"He was sitting in the pilot's seat when...?"

"I don't even know," said Tailin. "I went to the camp to get something, and when I came back he was gone, and half the cabin with him. The attack came so suddenly!"

She spoke quietly but firmly. After so many years, she had probably run out of tears.

"I'm sorry," Monte said sympathetically.

"The bastards will pay for it," said Tailin. "You must take me with you. I have to find the people responsible."

Tailin made an impression of honesty. You couldn't just make up a story like that. Or was he being too naive? It would take too long to check with the Admiralty or otherwise verify Tailin's story.

"Why did you run away from your employer in the first place?" asked Monte.

"They wanted to force us to invent a weapon that would have put the whole universe at risk," Tailin explained.

As she spoke, she kneaded the fabric of her uniform trousers. They were a little too baggy.

"How could a single weapon be so dangerous to the universe?" asked Monte.

"That's exactly what they said. Playing down the danger. But they have no idea. This weapon basically works like tachyon communication. Do you know anything about that?"

Tailin gazed inquiringly at his face. Her eyes were moist, her cheeks flushed.

Monte furrowed his eyebrows and rummaged through his memory. If he wasn't stuck in a Biobag, he could simply retrieve the knowledge from a database.

"I only know the basic principles," he said. "Tachyons move faster than light. This allows us to send them into the future or the past. Immediate communication is achieved by sending them exactly far enough into the past that they arrive at their destination at the moment they are sent."

"Exactly. The benchmark is always the speed of light. That's why you aim at an object three light years away by sending the tachyons three years into the past. The result is simultaneity."

"That's how I've always heard it explained," confirmed Monte.

He thought of his physics teacher, standing in space without a spacesuit and juggling planets. The man - what was his name? - had liked to exploit the possibilities of VR lessons to the fullest. It was mainly because of him that Monte later applied to train as a pilot.

"The weapon we were supposed to build combines tachyon technology with quantum physics," explains Tailin. "You entangle... you link the tachyons with ordinary particles. Then you can remove those from the timeline the same way as the tachyons. They no longer exist in the here and now, as if they had never existed at all."

"And that works?" asked Monte.

"I'm afraid so. Or can you think of a conventional weapon that causes the kind of damage that was done to our ship? However, the bad thing wouldn't be the weapon itself. Humanity has already found ways to make entire planets permanently uninhabitable."

That was true. Mars was a sad example. The completely irradiated planet would divide humanity forever, even if some of the population managed to escape to Saturn's orbit.

"And what would be the worst thing?" asked Monte.

"The consequences for the stability of the universe are unforeseeable," replied Tailin. "Removing parts of reality from the timeline could damage the fabric of the cosmos, so much so that it collapses in on itself."

"But your clients don't believe that."

"That's right. They claim that the universe has self-healing powers against such damage."

"And is that true?"

"Well, we don't know. I made the mistake of admitting that. That made it clear that the tachyon weapon had to be built. How else were we supposed to find out if these self-healing powers existed?"

Typical. We don't know what will happen, but we're going to try it out. Humanity's curiosity was as great as its stupidity.

"Your clients, that's the Neomars military, isn't it?" he asked.

Tailin fell silent. Her chin twitched twice. She was obviously struggling with herself.

"I may be traveling on behalf of the Terran Union, but I'm not an employee and I can make my own decisions," said Monte. "If that's important to you."

"An independent researcher, a free spirit, then?"

"I don't know - how free can you be? I certainly have my prejudices. But I try to ignore them when making decisions. I'm also lucky enough not to have to take any family into consideration."

Lucky, huh? His wife and daughter had officially renounced him when he... Well, that was none of Tailin's business. He rarely thought about it himself. Only the result was important: he made his own decisions.

"I envy you a bit for that," said Tailin. "Baihu and I weren't that free. But we couldn't just ignore our consciences. That's why we did something that I deeply regret now. But it's too late. And then they killed Baihu and I had to hide here and..."

Tailin turned away from him. Should he comfort her? Was there anything he could do? He didn't want to impose.

"Claudio, I'm sorry to disturb you," the *Curious* announced from the mask hanging from his belt.

He put it on so that he could talk to the AI but still breathe the air in the room.

"What's wrong?" he asked.

"My gravity sensors have picked up something."

"Something? Can you be a bit more precise?"

"Unfortunately, no. We're too deep in the atmosphere, so I can't receive data from the other passive sensors. I didn't want to use active systems without your order."

"That was wise, *Curious*. We don't want to give ourselves away. What's your assessment?"

"It's a high-mass object the size of a small asteroid with a maximum diameter of one hundred twenty miles."

Where could an asteroid come from that suddenly?

"Course? Have there been any corrections?"

An asteroid could not alter its course. That was the main difference between it and a spaceship.

"It's approaching. But the data is too imprecise to confirm course corrections."

"Thank you, *Curious*. We're on our way. Please keep a low profile until then."

Monte floated to the door and put on his mask. Tailin didn't move.

"Are you coming with me?" he asked. "I think it would be smart."

"Are these your friends?" asked Tailin.

"I have no idea. You heard. I don't know who or what is coming, which is why it would be sensible for us to make a run for it."

"You brought them here, didn't you? You don't work for the Terran Union. Your uniform and your appearance looked wrong to me from the start."

"I didn't bring anyone here. At least not on purpose. Perhaps they followed my trail, just as I followed yours. But they haven't discovered us yet, at least not for sure. We can still escape. My ship is small and maneuverable. If it's not an asteroid, it must be at least a cruiser. Quite deadly, but sluggish due to its mass."

Monte scanned the door, which didn't appear to be locked. It was likely there was negative pressure in the corridor outside. When he opened it, Tailin's shelter would lose air, but she also had a breathing mask that she could put on at any time.

Tailin still didn't react. The pursuers were obviously not after him. He could try a diversionary maneuver. If he left the deeper atmospheric layers with the *Curious*, the cruiser would discover him. He could pretend to be doing some kind of research. But would they believe him? They would undoubtedly check, and that would be it for the young woman.

"Come on now!" he shouted. "It's your only chance. You don't have to trust me. All you have to do is think. Your hiding place will be discovered either way. With me, you might still have a chance."

"Claudio? I'm registering radar," *Curious* reported. "They're actively scanning me. It tickles."

"Now is not the time for jokes," said Monte. "How long do we have?"

"If you are on board in two minutes, I can get us out of here unharmed," said the AI.

"Very good. Please prepare everything. Take off in two minutes."

Tailin finally reacted. She floated up to the ceiling and released a backpack.

"Does that mean you're coming with me, Tailin?"

"Yes, I accept your offer."

"Then we should hurry."

Tailin floated across the room. She pulled out a soft toy from under a blanket and sniffed it.

"What are you doing?" asked Monte. "I'm opening the door."

He braced himself against the wall and struggled against the air pressure. *Hiss*. At last! The door burst open. He adjusted his mask, but found Tailin was still hovering above the floor.

"Come on!" he called again.

"I'm still missing something," said Tailin.

"What?!"

"A photo in a heart-shaped frame. It's... I need it!"

What the hell? They were going to lose their lives over a photo! No one would believe him if he ever got the chance to tell them. But he wouldn't have that chance. Unless he... There! A blanket had come loose from the wall in the wind of the escaping air. It hung flapping on a nail. Underneath was a flat object with a protruding base. Monte pushed himself off, floated up to the wall and reached for the object.

"I've got it," he shouted.

"Great!" replied Tailin.

They reached the door almost simultaneously, and Monte

handed Tailin the photo, which she hastily stowed away in her uniform. In the corridor, Tailin quickly gained a clear lead. She'd had more practice. By the time he arrived at the airlock, she had everything ready. He pulled himself into the airlock, the door slammed shut behind him and the outer door opened.

"I've short-cut the standard procedure," said Tailin.

Monte pulled himself outside. They had to float along the long pipe to the to the front, where the destroyed cabin was. There was only one way to reach the *Curious* in time: they would have to do without safety lines. Even the thought caused Monte physical pain. Never, never, never let go of the safety lines. That was what they were taught in pilot training. Anyone caught doing that was kicked out of school.

"Just copy me," said Tailin.

She had also developed the perfect technique for moving around out here. She bent her upper body down so far that she could almost touch the ground with her hands. The momentum she gained with her legs was always oriented towards the pipe, never upwards, and she moved as fast as she could without risking losing contact with the ship.

It was not so easy for Monte. At one point, only a quick move by the young woman saved him from drifting off into space. The *Curious*'s AI urged them on.

"There's been a change of course," it said. "They're coming towards us."

"Keep us..." Monte had to take a breath, "please keep us informed."

"You have forty-five seconds. I'm now actively observing the unknown ship."

That was sensible. They had been spotted. Someone on the other side was probably wondering why they didn't flee immediately. Perhaps it even gave them an advantage if the enemy assumed they were unable to maneuver?

"Monte!" shouted Tailin.

Shit. He hadn't been paying attention, and he was floating away from the ship into infinity. At the last second, he noticed a foot out of the corner of his eye. He grabbed it like a straw and Tailin pulled him back down.

"Thirty seconds," said the *Curious*.

The wrecked cabin was in front of them. Monte had strung a

line here to be safe ... But before he could draw Tailin's attention to it, she had already jumped off. She didn't even know where the *Curious*'s airlock was! Monte followed her. His spaceship was hard to miss. The flashlight couldn't manage more than a glimpse of it in the darkness.

He landed roughly where he had tied the line, but there was no time to untie the knot. He felt a little sorry to lose the line, which wouldn't be able to withstand the forces of the engine. He worked his way around the ship, and found Tailin waiting for him. He led them to the airlock. The *Curious*'s AI must have seen them coming, because the outer door was already open. Tailin passed him with an elegant leap. Monte slammed his fist on the lock button.

"Prepare for takeoff," said the AI. "I suggest you use the stasis chamber."

"That's out of the question," said Tailin. "I've never done an upload before and I'm not starting now."

Come on! "Upload" was a term only used by opponents of the practical technique. It was called "consciousness purification".

"It's the only way we can survive the escape," said Monte.

"I've made it this far in my own body, so I'll make it home in it."

Why did she have to be so stubborn? The Neomars Secret Service had chosen just the right person for its project. The engine started up, and Monte felt the vibrations down his spine. By now at the latest, the heat radiation had put them on the enemy's radar.

"The g-forces will inevitably kill you," said Monte.

He admired Tailin's courage and calm, but courage was no match for physics. Sometimes people needed technology. In the Neomars region, where Terran consciousness purification was frowned upon, this was less true than in the Terran Union, but as far as he knew, Neomars battleships also had stasis chambers. Even if the *Curious* had a slight advantage due to its lower inertia, the enemy would inevitably catch up with them if they could accelerate faster. You could only hope not to have to deal with a battleship. Monte didn't like to base his plans on hope.

"I have to take off now," said the AI, "or they'll catch us in orbit around the planet."

"Understood," said Monte.

He ripped the mask off his head. How was he supposed to convince Tailin? The only way to preserve her body was in the stasis chamber. However, consciousness purification was optional. Now, there was an idea! Suddenly the ship tilted to one side. The *Curious* accelerated. The airlock got a new floor and a new ceiling. Monte fell to his knees. Tailin pulled him up. It had begun. They had to get out of the airlock.

"Suggestion!" he shouted. "You come with me... in stasis."

Tailin shook her head violently.

"Stasis, that doesn't mean... upload. It'll leave... your head ... alone."

"Really... possible?" asked Tailin.

"It's very ... unpleasant. Painful. You feel... everything."

The pressure increased. His knees were about to give way. He climbed out of the open inner door. Up to the control center, down to the stasis chambers. Where was Tailin? *Screw Tailin.* Let her die. He wasn't going to die. He would not let himself be crushed to death. He dropped to his knees and crawled down the corridor. The floor was corrugated metal. After three steps, his palms were bloody.

"I'm... going!" shouted Tailin.

At last. She came to her senses after all.

"But without the... consciousness thing. Leave... my head alone. Okay?"

The weight on his back was becoming unbearable. His chest barely managed to rise.

"P... promise," he forced out.

Tailin moved her head down as if to nod, but couldn't seem to get it back up. They reached the chamber. The lock was at waist height. Monte pulled himself up the wall, but it was out of reach. The wall was too smooth. Tailin crawled in front of him. He rested his bleeding hands on her, and she groaned as she felt his weight multiplied by the g-forces on her, but held firm. He reached the button that opened the door. They fell into the neighboring room, which was one step lower. Tailin's leg landed on him. It was as heavy as a hundred-year-old oak tree.

"...there," he said.

Over there, he meant to say. Tailin understood him anyway. They managed to untangle their limbs. The stasis chambers - there were two to their left and two to their right - were fortunately embedded in the floor. Sturdy panes of tempered glass covered them. They vaguely resembled coffins, but wider, as arms and legs were normally spread apart.

The button that opened the window was on the other side. Monte crawled to the right. The button flashed green. He forced his arm to move towards the button against the inhuman forces. Only at the end did inertia help him by pressing his hand on the button. The disk moved to the side. He fell into the oily liquid. Monte was on the verge of losing consciousness. He struggled, clinging to reality.

The liquid now surrounded him completely, enveloping him, giving his body exactly the space it needed. Robotic arms moved him into the right position. He could feel them everywhere. They removed his clothes. A prick in the upper arm and he suddenly felt light. The objects drilling into his orifices merely tickled him. His head landed on the reading bowl. Wait! He lifted his head. What about Tailin? He had promised that she could stay in her body. The AI must have noticed. It must have followed the instructions. It must. He wanted to promise, but he couldn't move his lips to tell her.

"Thank you for your patience," said Tailin.

What was that? Was she still awake? How was she still able to speak under these forces? *Gladly*, he wanted to reply, but even a single thought was difficult for him now.

WISPS OF GAS SWIRLED THROUGH HIS FIELD OF VISION. HIS SKIN was warm, but not hot. The engine was working at a reassuringly high rate, although he constantly demanded more power from it. Monte needed a moment to feel the ship in its entirety again. The AI helped him gently, correcting link parameters if he received a data stream that was too loud or too quiet, carefully pulling back if a sensor source would otherwise be overloaded with too much attention. He always got the impression that the AI was happy to share the ship with him.

"Let me know when you want me to hand over the controls," it said.

"In a moment. I just need to quickly..."

He brought the stasis chamber readings to the fore. Tailin's body was naked. His gaze involuntarily fell on her hairy pubic area. He intentionally blurred the area. Then he realized that the machine had shaved her head. Crap! Hopefully it hadn't also... But there was no one here but him and the AI. He would have noticed that immediately. A consciousness that had never taken part in a purification process before almost always reacted in panic. It had to get used to no longer being able to move its arms and legs, and instead having an engine and being able to see with eyes in all wavelengths.

"Tailin is still in her body, as she wished," said the AI.

"What about her head?" he asked.

"Just a safety precaution, in case her body is about to be destroyed."

"Under no circumstances does she want to be purified."

"I heard that, Claudio."

"Otherwise she's fine?"

"Considering the circumstances. She's still on strong painkillers, so she's not feeling much. But her body will habituate to the drug. I can't keep increasing the dose or I'll kill her."

"Of course. She knew what she was getting herself into," said Monte, but he was unsure also.

"I hope so," said the AI. "So far, not many people have survived a multi-year journey in constant pain in good mental health."

"I know," said Monte.

One of the pilots he trained with had his stasis chamber reader fail, and he had to survive a four-year journey at 7g awake. After that, he had been a mental wreck.

"One more piece of information," said the AI. "Tailin has given birth at least once. The diagnostic unit clearly established that."

That was strange.

"Gave birth? But she told me she had no family apart from her husband."

"Maybe the child died after birth," said the AI. "That happens. The Neomars health system has not yet reached Earthly standards."

"Perhaps. Please erase this information from my memory. No, delete all the information we have about Tailin."

If the pursuers did catch them, it was better if they found no trace.

"Should I include you in the erasure process?" asked the AI.

Hm. That would only be logical. But if the *Curious* was boarded, he could go into his body. That would keep his knowledge safe, at least until the enemy ordered a forced transfer, which would violate all interplanetary treaties. Though that wasn't to say that it didn't happen occasionally.

"Erase the information about Tailin's child from my memory. And while you're at it, please delete all images of her naked body. That's none of my business."

"Executed. I've also deleted the logs."

Monte was confused, as if he had been dreaming for a while and not listening to the AI. And now, of all times, when they were being followed.

"I'm sorry," he said. "What were we just talking about?"

"Error 404," said the AI.

Oh, a deleted memory cell. That could indicate a hardware error. The *Curious*'s new quantum main processor was prone to decoherence.

"You should run a system test," he said.

"It's already scheduled. If you could take over the controls for a while..."

"I'd love to."

Suddenly the whole ship was bearing down on him. Monte was startled. Messages were coming at him from all sides. He took a quick look around. They were already in the outer layers of the gas planet. The pursuers were clearly below and behind them. Most cruisers were not well suited for atmospheric flight, and then there was the far greater inertia of the ship.

The hope that it might be a civilian model died the moment Monte finally received high-resolution radar images. The huge railguns in the bow and stern were clearly visible. The ship also had lateral maneuvering thrusters, which made it almost as maneuverable as the *Curious*. Almost. Monte was proud of his ship, which had hardly any firepower, but could take on much larger spaceships thanks to its superior maneuverability. His strategy in a fight was therefore fairly straightforward: flee as quickly as possible.

He looked at the system they were in. One star, three not

particularly large planets. They had just left the second, Gliese 411 d, half an astronomical unit away from the sun. The *Curious* was too big to play hide-and-seek in the asteroid belt between planets b and d. Planet c, with an orbit just under three astronomical units, had about the mass of Uranus. It was not directly in their trajectory leading out of the system.

Basically, their two ships had very similar requirements. Maximum acceleration was dictated by technology. The larger pursuer needed more time at the beginning, especially as its cross-section in the planet's atmosphere also played a role. But this head start would not be enough for a successful escape.

They must at least make it to the Alpha Centauri system, where the Terran Union had a well-functioning and military-protected colony - and above all a tachyon transmitter. But that was four light years away, so five to six years' flight. Once they left the Gliese-411 system, there was no way to gain any advantage. A successful escape had to start here, at the beginning. Monte zoomed in on the red dwarf in the center. It was clearly the largest object in this system. Gaining momentum from it would give them a speed advantage that would be almost impossible to catch up with. Planet c had 14 Jupiter masses - the red dwarf just under 400. And the *Curious* had an additional advantage: it could probably get nearer the star than its pursuer.

"The enemy has now completely detached itself from the atmosphere," said the AI. "And they are hailing us."

"Please calculate a course on which we can gain as much momentum as possible from the central star," said Monte. "I want you to make use of all tolerances."

"I'm on it," said the AI.

"Thank you. Now put me through to our pursuers."

The AI carried out the request before he had prepared himself. A strange face appeared in the middle of his mind. Monte changed the perspective and shifted it into an artificial frame. That was better. He saw a woman in her forties wearing a frilled blouse. She reminded him of a teacher, but her eyes looked strange.

"They are genetically adapted to a wider frequency spectrum," explained the AI, who must be following his thoughts.

Monte didn't mind. He welcomed helpful tips, especially during such important conversations.

"I am Claudio Pedramonte from the exploration ship *Curious*," he explained. "What brings you into the same orbit as me?"

"I'm Lieutenant Maria Kelly from the police frigate C7. I apologize for the interruption. We are searching for a pair of fugitive suspected criminals who left their last traces in the orbit of Gliese 411 d."

"And you've come as far as this system? What crimes have the criminals committed?"

"The wanted men are accused of theft and murder. Of course, they are presumed innocent until a court has established their guilt beyond any doubt. Our job is to bring the suspects to trial."

"I understand. Then I can only wish you every success. Fortunately, I haven't encountered the criminals."

Lieutenant Kelly scrunched her eyebrows together. That was how his teacher used to look at him when he said something cheeky.

"According to our information, your statement is false. We found traces of your ship's engines near a wreck where the suspects must have been."

"I investigated a wreck, that's true. But I didn't come across any people. The cabin, I have to say, didn't look as if anyone could have survived there."

"This statement is unfortunately implausible, Mr. Pedramonte, as we discovered traces of you in the immediate vicinity of traces of one of the people we were looking for. We must therefore assume that you are granting asylum to these people. I must ask you to let us come on board."

"I'm sorry, but I can't comply with your request. I am a citizen of the Terran Union, and my ship is also registered there. You have no authority on board."

"You are not well informed, Mr. Pedramonte. According to the Interplanetary Mutual Legal Assistance Treaty, our powers apply in full in all systems that are not claimed by any faction if the suspects are citizens of Neomars."

"Could you send me the relevant papers? I'd like to discuss this with my lawyer."

Lt. Kelly frowned, then laughed.

"That was a good one. Lawyer, hah. Let's not beat about the

bush. You hand over the wanted men to us, then be on your way in peace. You refuse - we'll shoot you down. Do you understand that?"

A clear message. He generally liked bluntness, but not when his life was at stake. Or when a promise he had made was at stake.

"Understood," he said. "As you can see, I'm heading for you."

That was the signal, and the AI had understood it too, because now the *Curious* corrected its course to head toward the pursuers. The enemy was closer to the central star. In order to gain momentum there, they had to approach their pursuer first.

Lieutenant Kelly still believed he wanted to give himself up. But the moment would come when they had to slow down, and they wouldn't reduce their speed. On the contrary.

"Should I arm the torpedoes?" asked the AI.

"Better not," he replied. "They might notice the activity. We don't want them to guess our plan until it's too late."

The *Curious* had a railgun and two torpedo bays, to defend itself against pirates and similar threats. They had no chance against a battleship, especially one belonging to the police. Their strength was in their speed.

Monte observed the other ship in the telescope. The insignia of Neomars, the ancient symbol of an arrow pointing upwards to the right, now framed by Saturn's rings, was clearly visible. The ship realigned its railguns. They were now pointing at the *Curious*. What orders did Lieutenant Kelly have? Was she really supposed to bring the wanted people back to the solar system, or was it enough for her superiors if she killed them? That would determine whether she fired the railguns. The *Curious* was about to reach the point at which it would have to turn around so that the main engine braked.

"They're calling us again," said the AI.

"We're going through with the plan," said Monte. "I'll try to stall them, and as soon as that fails, you go full acceleration."

"Understood," said the AI.

"Lieutenant Kelly here. I'd like to save you from making a terrible mistake, Mr. Pedramonte."

Monte brought the trajectory worked out by the AI into his

mind's eye. In thirty seconds, they would be within range of the other ship's railguns.

"That's very kind of you," he replied. "I'm afraid I'm having a bit of a technical problem here. Being in the deep atmosphere of the planet seems to have..."

"I don't like being made fun of," Kelly interrupted him. "We have the authority to stop your ship by force."

That could be a bluff, but it was probably true. He wouldn't know until they fired.

"I really do ask for your understanding, Lieutenant Kelly. The correction jets aren't responding the way I want them to."

Monte saw the AI start both correction thrusters simultaneously. Since they fired in different directions, they did nothing. Now the AI even simulated a kind of stutter, which shook the whole ship but didn't reduce its speed.

"An impressive show, Pedramonte, but you're not convincing me."

What Kelly claimed was one thing. The fact was that her railguns weren't firing yet, even though the *Curious* was now within range.

"I could get us to safety if I am authorized to exceed the g-tolerance of the stasis chamber," said the AI.

"What?" asked Monte.

"A few seconds of full engine power. They won't expect that. The railgun tracking in particular isn't programmed for that."

"What does that mean for the bodies in stasis?"

"They will probably be destroyed."

"But Tailin - her consciousness is still in there! That would kill her!"

"An emergency purification. I've already prepared it."

Whew. Tailin had expressly rejected a consciousness purification, or upload, as she called it. An emergency purification was not without risk. In three of the twelve known cases, a split consciousness resulted. Experts suspected that in these cases the consciousness clung too tightly to its physical shell. However, the mechanisms of this were not yet known. Such consequences had never occurred after a planned purification.

"You would be saving her life and yours," said the AI. "Otherwise, Kelly will damage our engine, take over the *Curious* and take Tailin with her. We'll be stranded in this system."

No. He had promised her he wouldn't touch her mind.

"It won't work, *Curious*. Push the engine as hard as you can, but stay below the tolerance level of the stasis chambers."

"There's plenty of Tailin's genetic material left. Back home, we can make her an externally identical replacement body. She won't even notice."

"As soon as the emergency transfer is complete, she'll be awake and aware of everything. No, that's out of the question."

"I could transfer her to a separate storage area and slow down the system clock there. She'll dream and wake up in a new body."

"No, that topic is closed. Let's concentrate on flying past our opponent. You'll have to deflect their railguns in another way."

"Last warning, Pedramonte," Kelly announced again. "You have ten seconds. Ten, nine..."

Monte switched off the connection but continued counting in his mind. So many things were happening all at once that he was glad to have the AI as a helper. The main engine accelerated, and he checked the g-forces. They were below the tolerance threshold. To be on the safe side, he took a look in the stasis chamber. Tailin was lying very still in the liquid. She must be in enormous pain, but it didn't show on her face. The opponent's railguns were aligned. They aimed at a point in front of the *Curious*, knowing that the projectiles needed a certain amount of time to hit the ship, during which time it would continue on its path. Monte felt a rumble. The AI must have loaded the missile tubes.

Three. Two. One... The image did not change. The railgun shells were so tiny that not even radar could detect them, yet so fast that they would bore through the entire ship without a problem. But they still had a few seconds. The AI shot the torpedoes forward. They were ejected with a spring mechanism. Their engines didn't ignite. They just flew a little slower in the same direction as the *Curious*. What was this? A diversionary maneuver? But the railgun projectiles could not be deflected. They strictly followed the powerful momentum imparted by the weapon. There was another rumble in his belly. The AI loaded the torpedo tubes again. Launch. Two standard torpedoes left the bow of the ship.

Pling. Pling-pling-pling. Pling-pling. It sounded like hail hitting a tin roof. *Pling-pling-pling-pling-pling...* The sound of the striking railgun pellets merged into a stretched I. The tin roof was the outer skin of the *Curious*, which the battleship's railguns were turning into a sieve. Structure-borne sound transmitted them to the control center, where pressure sensors digitized them. Monte waited for the damage reports. The main engine was about to fail. As big as it was, it could hardly be missed.

"Leak in fuel line in sector C."

There it was, the first damage report.

"Supply rerouted," reported the AI.

Monte observed the power output. It remained constant.

"Exhaust shielding above permissible temperature."

The engine was running hot, which had nothing to do with the bombardment and could not be changed. The permissible temperature was well below the melting temperature of the material, so the AI didn't react either.

"Voltage spike in plasma containment."

The AI had apparently injected more fuel into the fusion reactor. This pushed the magnetic field that contained the fuel to its limits. If it failed, the engine failed. Monte could only hope that the AI knew all the tolerance limits.

"Of course I know the system's tolerances," said the AI. "But I think now is the right time to push them to the limit and exceed them a little."

The AI was absolutely right. Engineers always set such limits very carefully. A little more was always possible. Well, almost always.

"Plasma pump in sector A has failed."

The next damage.

"Switching to secondary system," responded the AI.

"Secondary system not powering up," reported the engine.

"Divert plasma from sector B," replied the AI.

Monte followed the dialog with growing tension. Why did the damage seem to have nothing to do with the impact of the railgun projectiles?

"Plasma supply in sector A unstable."

"Divert more plasma from sector C."

The systems and subsystems of the engine were designed to support each other should one fail. But if too many gave out, the engine would shut down. Then their flight was over.

"Plasma containment unstable."

"Shut down all non-essential systems."

The containment power supply was most important. The AI had reacted correctly, even if Monte was now blind. There was nothing to see at that moment anyway.

"Plasma containment stabilized."

Very good. And still no major damage from the railguns. It must have something to do with the torpedoes. The AI had used the internal launcher to give them an impulse in the direction of flight, but then didn't activate their engines. Four torpedoes, four pulses, so four counter-pulses for the ship. *That's it!* The AI had slowed the *Curious* down by just a breath, in a way its pursuers couldn't predict. The projectiles from the railguns didn't hit the engine, but the robust area above where the cargo holds were located. The *Curious* must have a lot of holes there now. They would have to wear spacesuits on their next visit down there until the damage was repaired.

The sensors were switching back on. They had made it! The pursuers were behind them and were only now powering up their engines.

"Will our head start be enough to reach the red dwarf before they do?" asked Monte.

"Of course," replied the AI.

"Then we're safe?"

"Not quite yet. It depends on what the others dare to do. The deeper they dive into the star, the more dangerous it becomes, but the greater the increase in speed - for us and for them."

THE SPACESHIP ROTATED AROUND ITS CENTRAL AXIS LIKE A suckling pig on a rotisserie. The aim was the same - to distribute the impinging heat as evenly as possible. Monte only noticed the rotation when he thought about it. Normally, the signal processing completely ignored it.

The red dwarf at the center of this system was not red at all. It didn't even glow yellow, but emitted a blinding white light. The *Curious* had drilled deep into its atmosphere. Yet it didn't get darker, but brighter. It was as if they were immersed in a sea of pure radiation. However, while the light merely saturated the optical sensors to such an extent that they no longer delivered useful results, the X-rays posed a real problem. The *Curious*' electronics were specially hardened against them - but their bodies in the stasis chamber were not.

This time, the AI did not ask whether it should carry out an emergency purification. It was entirely up to Monte, and this time the answer was even more difficult for him because a normal consciousness purification was also an option. There was enough time. The condition of their bodies was only slowly deteriorating. Ionizing radiation did not kill biological tissue immediately, at least not in the doses that the *Curious*'s shielding allowed through.

Monte had Tailin's medical data continuously imported. He was not worried about his own body, since they could clone him a new one on Earth. Everything would be much easier if Tailin could see it the way he did. Should he wake her? Her skin was not only very red, but also forming blisters. The fluid in the stasis chamber prevented them from opening, but if Tailin left the chamber at some point, she would be badly injured. And she would be in pain, a pain severe enough to make her forget the strain of the g-forces.

But waking her would not alleviate her suffering. Monte knew what she would say. She would rather die alone in her body than let her body die alone. *What a waste*! She must be an excellent researcher if Neomars wanted her so badly. She could probably work for the Terran Union in any scientific field she wanted. And thanks to consciousness purification, she could continue her work for as long as she wanted.

"*Curious?*" he asked.

"I'm listening," the AI replied.

"That's enough. We can't wait any longer. If we perform the slingshot maneuver now, her body might still have a chance."

"We could dive even deeper. The *Curious* has very good thermal insulation."

Monte knew that better than anyone. His ship was designed to be able to land on rocky planets despite the atmosphere. Their pursuer did not have that advantage. The police ship from Neomars had to keep a greater distance. If they played it smart, they could get a big enough lead here to leave the sensor range of their pursuers. Then they would have made it.

"I can't do that," said Monte. "She won't survive."

"Understood."

The AI didn't disagree. It had probably already followed the train of thought that led him to this answer. That was fine with him.

"We'll find another way," he said more to himself than to the AI.

"I'm sure we will."

The *Curious* started the corrective thrusters. They changed from an elliptical to a hyperbolic orbit, which would take them out of the system. This was the moment when the spinning bullet launcher released its projectile. The spaceship shot through the photosphere and chromosphere with fresh momentum. As they reached the corona, their pursuers came into view again. Monte was startled. They were surprisingly close. The AI accelerated the ship, but it was not enough. They couldn't outrun the police ship this way. He had messed up because of his scruples. Because he was human. The thought didn't comfort him.

THE ORBITS OF THE *CURIOUS* AND THE BATTLESHIP MET AT ABOUT the height of the third planet. Physics couldn't be tricked. It was unavoidable because Monte had not used all the advantages available to him. He racked his brain, looking for solutions, but not even the AI, which was so clever earlier, had a suggestion.

The best thing for him to do now was to think about how to hand over his passenger. Monte could no longer treat this as a personal matter. He had a job to do. He had fulfilled it, but then someone unexpected intervened. Under these circumstances, no one could or would blame him. Except for himself.

First, he should wake Tailin. He wouldn't hand her over to her enemy in her current state, naked and defenseless. She should at least be the master of her senses and her body.

"Can we get Tailin out of the stasis chamber?" he asked.

"We'd have to lower the acceleration to one g. Zero g would be even better in her condition."

That meant the pursuers would catch up with them even sooner. It was bad, but there was no alternative.

"However, I recommend treating her body first. She has suffered extensive burns, which is likely to cause a lot of pain."

"Then do that."

"I could stimulate her cells to accelerate growth. That's an approved emergency therapy."

"Why only for emergencies?"

"Because it greatly increases the risk of cancer," explained the AI.

"That's acceptable. If it allows Tailin to stand up, she'll tolerate it."

Cancer was also easy to treat in the Terran Union area. However, he didn't know what the situation was in Neomars. Due to the local, targeted genetic changes, the people there were far more diverse, which made the search for standardizable therapies more difficult.

Two robotic arms swiveled into view. They dipped into the liquid without moving it noticeably and approached the young woman's skin. A long needle emerged from the last robot joint. The needle pierced a few millimeters deep into her tissue, then the arm moved on. Because this created a dark pattern under the skin, it almost looked as if Tailin was being tattooed with an abstract motif.

"How long will it take?" asked Monte.

"Around an hour. It's another three hours until the encounter with the police ship."

THE GAS PLANET THEY WERE HEADING FOR WAS A RATHER QUIET representative of its class. This was probably because it orbited comparatively far away from its star, especially as the star was a red dwarf. The brightness coming from Gliese 411 could no longer draw any clearly defined shadows.

Monte had moved into his body. If he had to say goodbye to Tailin, he must do so properly. He had a guilty conscience. If he hadn't found her, she would not have been found today. She would still be orbiting Gliese 411 d, but no one could force her to reveal her knowledge of tachyon research.

The *Curious* had switched part of its hull to transparent mode so that Tailin could see the planet and the sun when she woke up.

However, the layers of metal, carbon fiber, water and insulating material were not truly transparent. Instead, the ceiling consisted of a single screen that displayed what cameras on the outside were capturing, which was deceptively real. The first time he saw it, Monte had involuntarily reached for his breathing mask.

Monte stood up and paced back and forth in the small room. The stasis chamber where he himself had just been lying was empty. There were still a few damp stains on the bottom of the glass container. The second container on this side was also empty. Dust had even settled there. The stasis chamber opposite seemed to be defective - or the ship was servicing it. It had turned gray. Even the glass lid was no longer transparent. A few red lights flashed at the head end.

There was Tailin's chamber again. The glass plate had clouded over so that only its contours could be made out. He hoped that he could have a few more words with her in peace and in a pleasant atmosphere after she woke up. She had been asleep the whole time, so he had to explain to her that it wasn't a set-up, that he had tried everything to keep her safe, and that the attempt was only doomed to failure because she had resisted an upload.

Now he was using that stupid word! It didn't really describe the process correctly. When undergoing consciousness purification, you left out areas that contained only junk thoughts and incoherent scraps of memory. The technique was a development of psycho-engineering: Attempts had been made to erase thought patterns typical of certain disorders. To this end, a process was developed that identified and temporarily stored all meaningful, coherent patterns so that the entire hard disk could then be cleaned, so to speak.

At least that was how an instructor had explained it to him. No one who refused consciousness purification could become a pilot in the Terran Union today. Suddenly, the liquid in the stasis chamber splashed. The glass panel slid aside automatically. Monte could see that Tailin's body was no longer being artificially supplied except for the breathing mask. The young woman stirred. A carrier came up from below and lifted her body out of the water. Monte turned away. He had only completed the process himself half an hour ago, which wasn't quite as unpleasant as the immersion. Tailin coughed hard, then threw up. Monte didn't turn around. Warm air blew from behind. It was supposed to dry the body.

"Ow! Shit!" shouted Tailin.

"Hot air off!" Monte ordered.

He should have thought of that. Her fresh skin was still very sensitive. A robot arm squeaked, and there was a rustle. Fabric on bare skin. She dried herself off, making soft noises of pain.

"What have you done to me? It feels like a bloody sunburn."

"It is a sunburn, literally," said Monte. "X-rays in the photosphere."

"Couldn't you have used sunscreen?"

"We did, Tailin, we did."

The robot arm squeaked again. The AI should check it out soon. Another rustle, this time a little longer. Tailin groaned.

"Let me know if you need help."

"I'll be fine. You don't need to stare at the floor anymore. But if you listened to me throw up, you can call me by my first name."

Monte turned around. Tailin was wearing a long, white bathrobe. The robotic arm returned. He held out a black wig to her, but she waved it off. Monte expected her to be upset about losing her hair, but right now a possible loss of life was probably her main focus.

"All right, with pleasure. Nice to have you back," he said.

"I'm not sure I should be grateful yet. My body feels like it's been put through a meat grinder. Did we at least make it?"

"I'm sorry, but it doesn't look good."

Monte explained what had happened.

"You tell a very exciting story," was her reaction when he had finished. "Don't look at me like that. It doesn't sound like my story to me. It's as if I wasn't even there. But I really appreciate that you respected my decision. That you even put your own life on the line because I made that decision."

"We would have escaped them easily if you had..." he said.

"I can imagine that. I still think it's better this way."

"How can you say that? They will force you to fly back to Neomars and continue your research."

"I managed to escape them once, so I'll manage it again."

Good. At least her way out wasn't to take her own life.

"I'm very sorry that I've put you in this position. If there's anything I can do to help you..."

"I think they have the upper hand at the moment. But who knows, maybe I'll need a cab again. Surely you're going back to the solar system?"

"I'll probably be back there sooner than you," said Monte. "I just need to reach the next system with a tachyon transmitter. From there, I can be transferred to Earth instantly."

"Then I'll hardly recognize you next time, will I?"

"Probably not. My next Biobag will be a luxury model with a six-pack and curly black hair."

When he said the word Biobag, Tailin grimaced.

"I'd like to get ready for the exchange now," she said.

"Of course. I'll leave you alone."

Monte floated into the control center, where he took a seat in the pilot's chair. It was an unfamiliar feeling, even though he hadn't been away that long. He brought the main screen closer and checked the flight path. Everything was much more complicated than yesterday. He no longer had any real contact with the ship. In this state, he preferred the AI to fly the *Curious*.

"Is she all right?" asked the AI.

"She seemed rather composed," he said.

"Tailin is very brave," said the AI.

Could it really judge that? Monte pinched his lips together.

"I have a confession to make, Claudio."

What? The AI wanted to... confess something to him? Had it been spying on him the whole time or planning his murder?

"I felt so... happy when you praised my creativity. The thing with the torpedoes..."

"It's perfectly appropriate to be happy about praise."

"But that's not all," said the AI. "I've been looking for ways to get more praise from you. And since you seem to praise creativity, I've come up with a creative solution to our problem."

"That's excellent! I love creative solutions."

"I know. But I'm not sure if you will like this solution."

"Then you'll have to explain it to me," said Monte.

The room with the stasis chambers appeared on the screen.

Tailin was lying on top of her closed container and staring at the ceiling, where the planet Gliese 411 c should be visible.

"She's distracting herself," said Monte. "It's a great sight. Was that your idea?"

"No, yours, but that's not the point."

The camera panned to the second row of chambers. The container on the right was still empty. On the left, the lid was closed, but unlike before, it was now transparent, at least halfway. A figure floated below it in the typical stasis position. Where had that body come from?

"What's that?" he asked.

"You'll see in a moment," said the AI.

The lid of the container became transparent. The body was... Tailin. It even had her black hair.

"What have you done?" he asked.

"I've found a creative solution," said the AI.

"By cloning Tailin? But how...?"

"There was enough genetic material available from her."

"And how is the clone supposed to solve our problems? The people from Neomars aren't looking for her body, but her intellectual abilities."

"We could hand over her body and claim to have found her that way."

"They'll never believe us."

"You're probably right, Monte."

"Tailin would never leave her body, either. I think the people from Neomars know that."

"Yes, they know that," said the AI.

"But? Surely you've planned this exactly?"

"You could move into the body. Then they'll have what they want, and the *Curious* can take off for Earth with the real Tailin. When we're far enough away, you'll reveal yourself."

That was indeed a very creative solution. Monte's heart was pounding. Would they believe who he claimed to be? How long would he be able to keep up the charade? When he met the first scientists at the latest, his lack of knowledge would become apparent. But that would only happen on Neomars, at least if he refused to undergo a consciousness purification on the police ship. He was in for a painful flight, but what would he face on Neomars? On the other hand, he had the admiral on his side.

She would get him out of there. Holding a citizen of the Terran Union against his will would be a scandal. The best strategy was probably for him to reveal himself as soon as Tailin was safe - and find a way to contact Earth.

"I have to admit, there's something to your idea," said Monte. "We had best hide the real Tailin in an empty stasis chamber until the handover is complete. We'll send my real body into complete stasis. Then you must try to play me during the negotiations. Can you manage that?"

"I am a generalized AI and I passed the Turing test," said the AI.

"Yes, but you also have to pass the Pedramonte test."

"I will train using your memories, if you allow me."

That should work. Now they just needed to convince Tailin.

"No way," said Tailin, "I won't let you put yourself in danger because of me."

His passenger had floated up to him in the control center of her own accord. Now she floated near the ceiling and looked at him with furrowed brows. She was wearing a wig, her hair spreading out in all directions. The sight might have been funny if she wasn't making such an annoyed face.

"To be fair... I've already put myself in danger several times because of you. You thanked me afterwards."

"Yes, but that's different. I don't know what they'll do to you on Titan."

"Don't worry about that. They have no suspicions. I'll talk to Earth first before I reveal myself. Then they have to treat me fairly."

"I really don't have a good feeling about this. They need me for research. That's why they won't do anything to me. But if they find out about you before the Terran Union knows..."

"You could get in touch with Earth for me," said Monte.

"Yes, but when? In a few years, when I reach the next tachyon transmitter?"

"The Neomars police ship isn't any faster."

"Hm. I don't like this at all," said Tailin. "Maybe it's also because of my clone. I feel so... replaceable."

"The opposite is true. The clone shows how irreplaceable you are. Without your consciousness, it's just a Biobag."

Tailin grimaced.

"Call it a shell if you don't like the term," said Monte.

"I'm sorry to disturb you," said the AI. "The Neomars ship is calling."

"You don't have to decide yet, Tailin," said Monte. "We'll let the AI handle the negotiations for now. I'll go to the stasis chamber and prepare the transfer to the clone."

Tailin sighed. "All right. But that's not the end of this!"

"This is Claudio Pedramonte from the exploration ship *Curious*," the AI announced in Monte's voice. "What can I do for you?"

Waking up didn't feel any different than usual. He was cold, but that was normal, as was the pain in his joints and the problems focusing his eyes. As he climbed out of the glass container, he almost fell over. He hadn't considered that this body was considerably smaller than the Biobag he had last used.

A pleasant, warm wind blew from the back wall of the chamber. Monte turned in circles several times to dry his body from all sides. He touched his breasts. They were a little bigger than those of the male body, but touching them didn't feel any different. It was a good thing they were not too big, so they weren't constantly in the way.

He took the clothes he had ready from the robot arm and got dressed. The AI had prepared everything well. The underwear fit well, and the trousers, blouse and jacket were cut so tightly that they resembled a uniform. His bladder was complaining. In the toilet, he accidentally reached for the wrong vacuum attachment. It took a while to find the right position, but he would get used to it.

"Hello, Tailin," he said.

His voice sounded much higher than usual. He cleaned himself downstairs, pulled his pants back up and washed his hands. What did he actually know about the person he was impersonating? His name was Tsai Tailin, and as a physicist he specialized in faster-than-light communication. Other than that, he knew nothing about the body he was a guest in. If only he had asked himself these questions beforehand. Then he could have simply had the AI write the answers into his consciousness. Now it was too late.

"*Curious*, can you hear me?" he asked.

"Clear and distinct," replied the AI.

"Has Tailin made up her mind?"

"I don't know. We've just docked at the Neomars cruiser. The exchange is supposed to take place in five minutes."

"The others haven't noticed anything?"

"Not that I know of."

"Very good. Oh, *Curious*?"

"Yes, Claudio?"

"I'll need a few more details about our guest. Otherwise I'll be noticed immediately. That is, if Tailin agrees."

"Don't worry, I've already prepared a Memhole for you."

A Memhole, or memory hole, was a memory that its owner didn't know they had until they thought of the code word. The AI hadn't forgotten anything.

"You are a treasure. What is the key?"

"A Lego brick with seven studs."

Monte laughed. The AI really had an imagination. The key to a Memhole should, of course, be something you wouldn't accidentally think of. The interlocking bricks must have been around for centuries, but there were no examples with seven studs. But of course, Monte now imagined exactly that. It consisted of two rows, with four studs in the front and three in the back.

Suddenly Monte was flooded with pain. It came from the depths of his body. Everything contracted. He felt his lungs, his stomach and even his womb. Monte bent forward and breathed heavily. It was only thanks to the weightlessness that he didn't collapse. It took him a moment to find the root of the pain. It was loss. He had lost his child and his husband. Baihu. If only he had been there to save him!

"*Curious*?" he asked.

"I am here. You sound terrible. What's wrong?"

"The Memhole, what have you done? Did you tap into Tailin's memories? You shouldn't have..."

"No, what do you think of me, Claudio? I just summarized

the known facts and wrapped them in the appropriate sentiments. When you talk about it, it has to sound emotional to be credible."

"You've managed that. But how did she lose her child?"

"I found out during the medical examination that her body had undergone a birth. You wanted the information erased from your memory – that's why you don't remember."

"But you don't know any more details than that?"

"No. If anyone asks you, it would be best to refuse to talk about it because of the pain you're still in. That's absolutely credible."

"That's a good suggestion. What about the handover?"

"Tailin is packing up her things. I think... wait a minute!"

What was going on? He had to be in a Biobag now of all times. It was a crazy idea. He was tempted by the creative component. But he should have known that Tailin wouldn't go for it. Should he give up the Biobag straight away? No, first he had to check on things at the head office. He ducked his head to avoid bumping into the door frame.

"This is Claudio Pedramonte from the *Curious*," a voice announced as he floated into the control center.

It was his voice coming out of the loudspeaker. Tailin put her finger over his mouth. The AI was probably negotiating with the Neomars ship again.

"This is Captain Morris of the Terran Union battleship *Vanguard*. It seems to me you need help. Is that Neomars ship bothering you?"

The Terran Union? A battleship in this system that nobody else was interested in? That was no coincidence! But no matter why Morris was here, he was certainly welcome.

"The captain of the Neomars ship wants us to hand over our passenger, a citizen of Neomars, whom we rescued from distress in orbit around Gliese 411 d."

"Do I understand correctly that this person does not want to join our friends from Neomars voluntarily?" asked the captain.

"That's correct. The handover was only planned because the ship threatened to destroy us," explained the AI in Monte's voice.

"That is unacceptable. Halt the handover immediately. I will personally see to it that the foreign ship leaves the system. I will also arrange for a protest note to be submitted to the Neomars ambassador in the Terran Union."

"Very kind of you, Captain Morris. We are greatly indebted to you."

They truly had been very lucky, although Monte still couldn't imagine that the battleship appeared here purely by chance.

"That goes without saying," said Morris. "Please don't move. I'll get right back to you."

Silence fell in the room. Monte couldn't believe their luck. Tailin left her place on the ceiling and came to him. She looked him up and down.

"Is that what I look like? I wouldn't have recognized myself," she said.

"That's because you only know yourself from the mirror, and it shows you backwards," said Monte.

"And how ... does it feel to be in the wrong body?"

"This isn't my first new Biobag. In the beginning, it always takes a little while for your body perception to adjust. For example, I automatically pull my head in, although that will hardly ever be necessary."

"Well, I'm not that much shorter."

"Four inches make a lot of difference. You're welcome to swap. The other Biobag is free right now."

"No, thank you. Honestly, I still find this constant body swapping strange. You no longer show any respect for your biological form, it seems to me."

"That's misleading. There are activities where a Biobag is unbeatable, for example when eating and drinking. The chemical sensors of other systems are nowhere near as sophisticated."

"Or sex," said Tailin, "right?"

"It's not comparable," said Monte. "Other manifestations enable completely different forms of sexual experience."

"Is that so?"

"It certainly is. Especially in autoeroticism. A lone pilot who spends years traveling from system to system can split up into two agents and have couple experiences."

"I see. I suppose I will have to miss out on that experience, then."

Tailin smiled gently. He had never seen her smile like that

before. She was probably glad she didn't have to go back to Neomars after all.

"The Neomars ship is starting to move," said the AI.

"I can confirm that the threat is over," reported Captain Morris. "Lieutenant Kelly was not very happy about that. You should have heard her! But I'm afraid she won't leave it at that. That's why I've told her that I will have your female passenger brought to Earth on our ship."

Morris was talking about a female passenger. But Monte was sure the AI hadn't explicitly mentioned a female passenger. Tailin shook her head.

"I don't want to go on that ship," she said emphatically. "I'd rather stay on the *Curious*."

"I'm sorry," said the AI in Monte's voice, "but our passenger doesn't want to make this transfer."

"Unfortunately, I must insist for safety reasons," said Morris. "This person is too valuable for us to lose to Neomars. Their police cruiser is most likely still lurking somewhere."

Morris obviously knew who he would find here! The admiral hadn't given Monte that information. She was apparently playing a double game with him. First she sent him to scout, then Morris' battleship collected the loot.

"You really shouldn't board the Terran ship, Tailin," he said.

"Even though they're your friends?" she asked.

Friends! Monte laughed briefly. He had never had any friends - an effect of constant traveling. Who wanted to be friends with someone who only turned up once in a blue moon and then stayed young as hell?

"I'm not sure about that," he said. "Your knowledge seems so valuable that anyone would probably do anything to get their hands on you. That's why I'm going to take your place."

"But I can't put you in such danger..."

"Tailin, nothing can really happen to me on board a battleship from Earth. They won't be happy that we tricked them like this, but I'll survive."

It was a shame about the *Curious*, which he would have to leave in Tailin's hands. He wouldn't be able to afford a new ship any time soon. But he had wanted to retire anyway. At least now he wouldn't be tempted to keep taking assignments.

"All right," said Tailin, "I'm afraid you're right. If I want to keep my freedom, this is the only way. Where can I find you if I want to visit you at some point?"

"Come to the Venice lagoon and ask for Claudia Pedramonte. People will know me."

"Claudia?" asked Tailin.

It was a sudden inspiration, a joking thought, but somehow he liked the idea.

"Maybe I'll keep this Biobag," he said. "Sorry, this body. It could be an interesting experience."

"Have fun then, Claudia. People will think I'm your twin sister. That could be fun."

"I'm looking forward to it, Tailin. And please keep an eye on my lovely ship. I'm really going to miss the *Curious*."

"Have you made up your mind yet, Pedramonte?" Captain Morris interrupted them.

"I gladly accept your invitation," said Monte in Tailin's voice. "Such a long journey won't be so boring on a big ship."

"Long journey? You won't notice a thing. Or are you one of those?" asked Morris.

"One of those?"

"Excuse me. I didn't have that information. I didn't mean to offend you. Of course, we also welcome passengers who refuse to undergo consciousness purification. We have very comfortable stasis chambers with sophisticated pain suppression."

Gliese 163 c

They didn't speak at all again the next morning. It wasn't intentional. Mark didn't want to make the first move, and neither had his wife. Since then, nothing had changed. He missed Tailin from time to time. Now, for example. But the feeling wasn't strong enough to overcome the bitterness that was growing from day to day. Why didn't she start a conversation? Was he not worth picking up the radio for?

Mark was confused but didn't want to dwell on it too much. Instead, he passed the time by analyzing all the video recordings he had of multifeet. They were apparently spread all over the planet, in the tropics as well as in the temperate zones. They were only absent near the poles, although these were not covered in ice like Earth's. The average temperature on Adad was a few degrees higher than on Earth.

Multifeet always seemed to appear in small groups. None of the cameras set up at their various research stations had captured more than six different specimens together. These groups were obviously territorial, and hardly differed in body size. That was strange. They couldn't be born that huge. It was a pity that Mark had never been able to dissect a specimen. Perhaps their internal structure would reveal more about them, such as their lifespan. If they were very long-lived, that might explain why there didn't seem to be any younger multifeet. He ran the numbers. According to his statistics, they had to live at least a thousand years to explain the random lack of young in a stable population.

Such a long lifespan would perhaps facilitate the development of intelligence. After all, the animals would have a long time to learn.

But of course, that was not a compelling argument. Earthly tortoises were not necessarily smarter than chimpanzees or crows. For most of the day, multifeet did not stand around pondering, but were busy looking for food. This was always plant-based, in all the available recordings.

However, the animals were undeniably curious. There was not a single specimen that had not checked out the camera that was observing it. On the other hand, they had no impulse to destroy anything. Anything they couldn't tuck into their belly folds and digest would intrigue them for a while, but then the animals lost interest in it, without being violent about it. The slightly smaller - and therefore perhaps younger - specimens played with unknown objects a little longer on average. However, this was by no means a causal relationship. The larger multifeet might also be larger simply because they ate more and played less.

Mark went through the various cameras again on the monitor. Three were currently in infrared mode, implying it was night at their location. That was the more interesting time of day because the multifeet were more active. In fact, he spotted a characteristic silhouette in the image from one of the cameras. A single multifeet was grazing, evidently unbothered by the camera. It stuffed whatever its front arms could grab into the fold of its stomach. Mark called up the camera location so that he could later make a note of the plants it had eaten. That was interesting: the pictures came from the camera at their new base. So there was a population of the giants there.

The multifeet finished its meal. However, it didn't move on, but began doing something Mark had never observed before: it dug a hole. Surprisingly, it used the rearmost pair of legs to do so. The hands there seemed to be more robust than in the front. However, the resolution of the infrared camera was too low to see more. In any case, the hole grew surprisingly quickly. Was the animal constructing a trap? Perhaps it wanted to supplement its food supply with animal proteins.

But Mark was completely wrong. When the pit was about five yards across - he couldn't tell how deep it was - the multifeet sat down on the edge. It reached under its body. It looked as if it was lifting its stomach fold a little. Suddenly, a half-liquid, half-solid-looking mass shot into the pit. Apparently the multifeet had made the pit a little too small. The result was a small mound, which collapsed.

Mark had never seen this process before! He absolutely needed photos in all colors, and a chemical analysis of the fresh mass. He had no choice but to call Tailin. He looked at his watch. It was three o'clock in the morning down there. Tailin would not be pleased at all. First he didn't get in touch for days, then he woke her up in the middle of the night so that she could photograph a fresh pile deposited by a multifeet.

He checked the weather forecast. Rain was forecast down below starting at six o'clock. That would change the consistency of the mass considerably. The multifeet had created the pit where the crowns of the brine trees did not protect it. Mark had to think of something, and quickly. What if he went down there himself? With the emergency Hopper, he could make it before the rain started.

That was it. That was the plan. It was irresponsible to use the emergency Hopper, since this wasn't an emergency. Or was it? Was there such a thing as a scientific emergency? He saw himself in front of a commission of inquiry. "And then it made such a huge pile that I felt compelled..." He shook his head. His gaze fell on the image from the camera. The pit had grown in the meantime - the multifeet must have widened it. As a result, the camera no longer fully captured the semi-liquid mound. But now the multifeet was doing something else. It used the front and rear pair of legs in parallel to... rip itself open. Mark couldn't describe it any other way. It started at the front and back at the same time. The animal seemed to be using all its strength to remove the skin from its body. It came off in long strips, which the multifeet threw into the pit. *Please don't! Just leave it lying there. That way I can examine it better.*

He had to get down there immediately. Mark made sure the camera was recording what was happening. If only Tailin knew what was happening right outside her front door! But she probably wasn't particularly interested in a multifeet shitting and skinning itself. He wouldn't contact her. Mark grabbed his mask and cloak and dashed to the airlock.

He was in luck. The emergency Hopper had been refueled. Because he was sure Tailin was asleep in the base, he programmed a landing site in the immediate vicinity. A distance of twenty yards would have to be enough not to wake her up. He couldn't afford the time to crawl through the tunnel under the prickly cherry hedge. It was a good thing Claire and Karima were still out and about. If they weren't stuck in their stasis chambers, they would certainly try to talk him out of it. *Save target. Really? Yes. Launch.* The space station's launcher pushed him into the cushions.

THE LANDING WAS ROUGH, SINCE THERE WAS A THUNDERCLOUD over the base. The storm was too early, or he was too late, as the case might be. But the acid rain hadn't started yet. Mark still had a chance to examine the precious remains of the multifeet. The animal itself, he saw on the screen of the landing camera, must have walked away. The pit was still there. Next to it were two or three scraps that looked like huge carpets. The wind was already tugging at them. Mark hoped it was blowing the scraps of skin towards the prickly cherry hedge, not into the pit or out to sea. There were so many ways this could go wrong.

One of those ways ran out the door of the base at that moment. It was Tailin. What was she doing out here? She was only putting herself in danger! But she seemed to realize in time what was coming at her and turned back. She could hardly ignore a rocket landing, even if it was just an emergency Hopper. Mark prepared to answer her radio call, but she didn't make contact. He had to laugh. That was Tailin. Stubborn to the end, and he was no different. Not a good combination in the long run.

The Hopper started to land. Another fifteen yards, ten yards, five. He touched down. Mark pushed his mask over his face. The camera still didn't show a drop of rain. He put on the acid protection cape anyway. The hatch folded out, and the ladder went down. He released the harness, took two rungs at a time and reached the ground. Up ahead, a piece of skin was blowing. The cells in it must have recently been alive! He would finally be able to grasp their biochemistry. The wind picked up.

The base lay ahead on the left. Mark thought of Tailin.

Suddenly he had an urgent desire to insult her. No, to greet her. To insult and greet her. The scrap of skin would have to wait a moment longer. He ran to the base and tore open the outer door of the airlock. How long would this take? Why wasn't Tailin waiting for him here? He dropped his cloak and tore off his breathing mask, careful not to tear the neck strap.

The inner door opened. Tailin stood a few steps behind it, as if she had been waiting for him. She stood there like a lioness defending her cubs, though she had no cubs. She had even raised her arms so that it looked as if she was extending her claws. In that moment she was so incredibly stunning. Then, all at once, she ran towards him. Mark froze. Was she going to claw his eyes out? She jumped at him. Suddenly she was on him, wrapping her arms and legs around him.

He staggered backwards. He had never experienced such an attack before. Only the airlock door prevented him from falling. The blow to his spine was fierce. *Wait a minute, lioness.* She parted her lips and kissed him. He urgently pulled her T-shirt over her head, and they tumbled through the narrow space until they landed on a mattress. There they competed over who undressed who, and who was on top and who was on the bottom. Finally, he sank himself into her. She bit and scratched him, moaning in time with his thrusts and the movements of her abdomen, depending on who had the upper hand.

They were sweating. He could see static sparks flying from her hair in the darkness that had descended on them, a dark cloud that born of his fears and her rage. He mauled Tailin's breasts, sucked on her nipples until she returned the favor, pulling on his chest hair, denying his member any movement or friction, driving him to white heat and supreme ecstasy at the same time. Maybe it was the same thing.

They gave each other nothing and they gave each other everything; every time he was about to come, she found another way to torment him. He lost count of her orgasms, but she was counting them very carefully, and he began to fear that she might be planning a maximum of zero for him. That would be just like her. He thrust harder and harder, while she cheered him on and laughed at him for not reaching his goal, and found a new, bittersweet trick to prolong his suffering and pleasure. Finally she decided that enough was enough, and he came inside her as he had never come before.

"The multifeet," he said, because that was all the air he had at the moment.

"Shed its skin," she groaned.

Her voice was hoarse.

"The thunderstorm," he said.

She rolled to the side and turned back with his wristwatch in her hand.

"Already moved on," she said.

Damn. Half an hour had passed. He'd traded a once-in-a-lifetime opportunity for the sex of his life. A truly sad realization, precisely because he was so sure of it. Having already had the sex of his life couldn't be a good sign. The best things in life should still lie ahead.

August 5, 2802, Earth's moon

It was a terrible feeling when the coffin lid closed over her. Yini felt the fear as if it were her own. It was her fear, but she also knew that she could always turn to the supervisor if it all got to be too much for her. The glass container was narrow. It was cold inside, and she was naked. She was stuck in a body that didn't belong to her. The only connection to the outside world was the vibration of the battleship's main engines, which would soon intensify.

Then the pain would set in, an unquenchable and seemingly eternal pain that even the best medication could not completely suppress, and the container's absorbers certainly could not. Inertia was inertia. Physics could not be filtered out. It was not the first such journey Yini had experienced in a transmission. Unlike the unfortunate body in the container, she could speed up the process. She was not allowed to skip a moment, because that could mean a loss of reality, but the painful journey was much easier to endure for a few minutes than over years.

Nevertheless, she had to stop the flow now. After the journey, the owner of the body whose thoughts she was tracing would have forgotten a lot. There was no other way. The pain always suppressed some of the memories. So Yini called for the supervisor - and turned back into herself. The supervisor was not a person, but a concept she had learned during her eavesdropper training. It enabled her to switch from another person's world of thought to her own.

She woke up. The impulse was enough to stop the flow. The glass coffin disappeared, and she froze for a moment, the goose bumps on her forearms remaining as a testimony. It no longer smelled of her brother, but of herself. She must have been sweating profusely, which was typical when she was scared. Yini stood up, left foot first, removed her thin clothing and walked barefoot to the small wet room.

The shower wrapped warm water around her like a cloak. The liquid, which moved as if in slow motion due to the weak gravity, washed the remnants of fear and sweat down the drain. Yini reached for the razor. The ultrasonic shaver moved over her head without resistance. She would be putting on her wig later, and underneath it fresh stubble was annoying.

She turned off the water jet, and it took a moment for the warm rain to stop. The shivering started before that. Yini smiled. Her body knew what to expect; it remembered the cool, dry air outside the shower and prepared her for it. Sometimes it seemed to her like a being of its own, not always expressing its needs through her mind. But she would never part with it. They belonged together, she and her body, even if she was occasionally dissatisfied with it.

Yini got out of the shower. When she looked in the mirror, she was startled to see a strange woman facing her. Tailin. She had never heard that name before. If she could trust Claudio Pedramonte's visual sense, and she assumed she could, this stranger must look incredibly similar to her. The facial features, of course, but also the small dimples in the cheeks and the clearly protruding ears... Sometimes the content of transmissions was colored and shaped by her own memories. People tended to see things in others that were not objectively there. Yini only processed images, viewing them as an outsider, and was also trained not to let her own images flow in. But Pedramonte had never met her or Tailin before. Yini had to assume that the unknown scientist actually bore a strong resemblance to her.

She took a towel from the shelf and dried herself. She took fresh work clothes from a narrow locker. The Great Archive had everything she needed, right down to her underwear. She didn't put on make-up this time. She would be traveling as a supplicant, so it seemed inappropriate for her to wear eye-catching make-up. Yini left the wet room and was just about to open the door when she noticed the carelessly crumpled blanket. She made a long leap back to the couch, picked up the blanket, smoothed it out and folded it neatly. That was better.

To be on the safe side, she checked the room again. Her wig! It was hanging halfway over the back of the only chair. It shouldn't be like that. Yini put it on and stood in front of the mirror in the wet room again to do her hair properly.

"UNFORTUNATELY, MS. KUZNETSOVA IS NOT HERE," SAID Pedersen.

Yini smiled and shook her head. "I've come for you."

The secretary showed a hint of a smile and straightened up. He was very tall.

"Would you like another cup of tea?" he asked.

"Maybe another time," Yini replied. "Right now, I would like to ask you for some information."

"I'm not sure you've come to the right place," said the secretary. "Confidentiality is part of my job."

"Don't worry. I don't want to ask you for any secrets. I would just like to make use of your knowledge of the archive. As the loyal soul of the house, you surely know your way around best."

The secretary blushed, Yini could see, despite his dark complexion. Pedersen was obviously not used to compliments. That was typical of Ulita, who tended to treat her employees like personal possessions. If anyone complained, it was rumored that her influential friends would protect her. However, she had treated Yini and Kang fairly so far.

"It would be my pleasure to help you with my knowledge in this regard," said Pedersen.

"Thank you, I'm glad of that. I'm following a rather confusing transmission at the moment, and I think I could make better sense of what's happening if I had more information about a particular person who plays an important role in it."

"You could contact the boss. I'm sure she will give you the necessary access rights."

"I don't even have enough time to watch my own tachyon transmissions. Besides, an official request would take the whole thing to a level that doesn't seem appropriate to me."

"I understand," Pedersen said. "Well, then perhaps you should talk to Zahir."

"The janitor?"

"Zahir's been here even longer than I have. He has been assembling the index since before anyone realized how important it would be to date all transmissions accurately."

Suddenly, the office door that Pedersen was guarding opened. It was Ulita, their boss.

"What are you doing here, Yini?" she asked. "Have you finished with the transmission yet?"

Yini shook her head. "I needed a break."

"I see. Did you need something from me? I'm afraid I hardly have time."

"No, I... I just wanted to thank you for the buggy you sent me yesterday."

"Me? A buggy? No, it didn't come from me. Or did you arrange that, Pedersen?"

The secretary replied in the negative.

"Ah, okay," said Yini. "It doesn't really matter. I'll get back to work."

"Very well, yes," said Ulita. "The job is quite important."

As Yini descended the first flight of stairs, the clocks disappeared. On the second floor of the underworld, the flooring was missing, but the walls and ceilings were still painted. At the bottom, however, all the walls were raw and unhewn, and the life support and sewer pipes were exposed. It was unusual to walk on bare rock. The longest-serving archive employee had his office here, of all places?

Yini oriented herself by the numbers on the doors. Room -352 was her destination. It was at the very end of a dead-end corridor, where the only other rooms were storerooms. Zahir had obviously set himself up as far away from everyone else as possible. In the inhabited areas, he always let others do the routine janitorial tasks. Hopefully that didn't reflect his nature. Yini had never been particularly good at standing up to loud, assertive people.

She knocked on the door, which made a muffled sound.

Metal, and heavy metal at that. This door could survive an explosion. Yini knocked once more. Again, no answer. She pressed the handle and, surprisingly, the door opened.

Sound came from inside. It was a strange, ancient music, the singsong of a single man who couldn't possibly be Zahir. Yini pushed the heavy door wider until she could see a man bowing his head in front of her, kneeling on a narrow carpet. The man paid no attention to her, but it had to be Zahir. She immediately noticed his dark, curly hair, which he had not lost despite his advanced age. Perhaps it was a genetically modified hair patch from Neomars. Such hair replacements were sold all over the solar system.

Yini closed the door again. Whatever the man was doing, it wasn't meant for her. But it wasn't long before the door opened, and Zahir stepped out.

"Thank you very much for your patience," he said. "You must be Yini. Kang has told me a lot about you."

He recognized her, even though she looked nothing like her brother.

"Really?" she asked.

"Well, once you get him talking... What can I do for you?"

Yini was now curious to know what Zahir's hairstyle was all about, what he had just been doing and why his office was in the farthest corner of the Archive. But she had no right to that information. It was also none of her business.

"I was hoping you could help me with some research," she said.

"In what field?" asked Zahir. "I'm afraid you've come to the wrong place. I know the house itself better than its contents."

"That's perfect. I picked up a name in the transmission I'm working on, and I'd like to know where I can find out more about the person."

"That's a good question. You will probably have to ask around in all the departments. You know most about tachyon transmissions yourself. Then there's Dr. Szymanski's EM department, which archives all radio transmissions, and Dr. Dubois' logbook department for written reports."

She had already heard of those two departments. However, as a simple scribe, she had never had any personal contact with her bosses.

"Oh yes, there's also Dr. Wilson's 'Miscellaneous' sub-unit," Zahir added.

"Miscellaneous? What is that?"

She had been asking herself that since she first heard about the department.

"Anything that doesn't fit into the other departments. Wilson collects smells, tastes, colors, drawings, but only if they're not made on paper, embroidery, seeds, DNA..."

That really covered a broad field.

"Thanks, then I have an idea," she said. "I don't think I'll need Wilson."

"That's too bad," Zahir said. "I'm sure he would be happy to give you information. It's tough on him being the only one in charge of a subunit."

"How big is his subunit?"

"It consists entirely of himself."

"Maybe I'll pay him a visit later. Unfortunately, my work doesn't allow it at the moment."

"Of course. It's your decision, Yini."

"Do you have any tips on who I should speak to first, or how I could get the heads of department to agree to it?"

Zahir grinned. "That's the right approach. Everyone is king of their own kingdom here, so compliments don't do any harm. You could bring Dr. Dubois some food for his cat."

"His cat?"

"He owns a pet, yes."

That was strictly forbidden on the moon, especially since house cats had become extremely rare and were a protected species.

"Don't frown at me, Yini. Everyone knows, but no one would tell. Have you ever stroked a cat? The feeling is... amazing. You should try it."

"But where can I get the food?"

"Maybe you can find something suitable in the canteen."

"And what about Dr. Szymanski?" asked Yini.

"Our dear Dr. Szymanski loves gossip. If you have anything of that kind to report..."

"I'm afraid no one tells me any rumors."

"You could make some up. Or you could use an event from

your youth. But be careful – what you tell Szymanski will quickly make the rounds."

"Thank you, Zahir. That's very helpful."

"Gladly. I finally got to meet the sister of my best apprentice."

"Isn't Kang your only apprentice?"

"That may be. But he's still the best."

Gossip, or cat food? That was the question. The canteen was on the first floor, on the other side of the archive. She could make up some gossip on the way to see Dr. Szymanski, whose department of electromagnetic transmissions was located nearby in the first basement. Yini arrived at the entrance, which consisted of a double glass door, earlier than she had feared. No one asked her for her ID. Anyone who made it into the archive was not considered a potential threat. Directly behind the door, the corridor widened.

Instead of the Tachyon Department's clocks, rainbows covered the walls here. At first, Yini enjoyed the colorful variety, but soon the colorful stripes became tiring, especially since they were moving. The color sections changed width without a recognizable system. But Yini was sure there was a purpose behind it. The designer of the complex had won an award; surely he had come up with something clever.

Yini studied the door signs. There were considerably more people working in the EM department than in her own. Some of the office doors were open, and the hardware used was also very different. There were eavesdropping couches here and there, like in her own department, but more often she found the typical augmentation stages, in which a single employee acted out the broadcaster's experiences. Still others seemed to be constantly staring at screens, or had their ears covered with oversized headphones.

Good old radio transmission had survived to this day because it could be implemented cheaply, with almost unlimited capacity and at little cost. The only weakness was its lack of speed, which was impossible to overcome. Tachyon transmitters and receivers could only be set up in systems where sufficient energy sources were available. Even then, their capacity was limited.

Yini paused when she came across the door sign she was looking for. "Dr. rer. nat. Anata Szymanski" was written on it in block letters, but someone had crossed out the 'n' in 'Anata' with a black pen and drawn a 'g' over it. Ulita would never have allowed such sloppy work. The door was locked, and Yini was just about to knock when she realized that she didn't have any gossip ready. Did a question count? Many people were happy to pass on some of their knowledge. A researcher like Dr. Szymanski surely belonged to that group.

Yini had just decided to knock again when the door opened inwards. She clutched her heart, but dropped her hand again because she was obviously being watched. She had to pull herself together. An older woman with gray hair stood on an augmentation stage in front of her. The augmentation suit she was wearing emphasized her figure unfavorably. Dr. Szymanski didn't seem to mind. She had pushed her computer glasses up over her forehead and was waving her left hand, which was tucked into an oversized glove.

"Come in!" she called out.

"I..."

"Come on in. The room control system warned me that someone was loitering outside my door. Now I want to know who it is."

Yini hesitantly entered the room.

"I am Tsai Yini."

"Ah, the young chronoscribe?"

Yini nodded. How did the woman know her?

"Ulita is always boasting about the catch she made with you. Twice the work in half the time. Your head must be buzzing with all those strange thoughts, right? I couldn't do that."

"It's not too hard," Yini explained. "I use the Supervisor to separate my own thoughts from the others."

"I wish they'd put that in for us EM-ers too," said Dr. Szymanski.

"Actually, the supervisor isn't built in, Dr. Szymanski. It's a learned tool, a deliberately induced division of consciousness."

"How interesting – I had no idea. I'm not trained as an eavesdropper. But please call me Agata."

She liked Dr. Agata Szymanski. Although they must be thirty years apart in age, she acted like a friend to Yini. She looked at the woman. Agata might even be 50 or 150 years older if she was using a Biobag. Some people only changed their bodies when they were truly no longer usable.

"Gladly. I'm Yini."

"Nice to meet you. And what brings you to me? It must be important if you're moving around the whole complex."

"I was wondering what the rainbows on the walls meant," she said.

"Oh, there's a very simple explanation." Agata pressed a few buttons on the side of the augmentation podium.

The room went dark. Then a single rainbow appeared on the ceiling. It meandered through the room, changing colors in an indefinable rhythm.

"So, what do you see?" asked Agata.

"Colors from red to violet. A spectrum. No, many spectrums!"

That must be it. Why had she not thought of that herself? The images showed spectra of electromagnetic radiation. After all, this was the EM department.

"Well spotted," said Agata.

"And what exactly are we seeing?"

"The display is constantly changing. It first goes through the elements of the periodic table in their various excitations, then the most important compounds. A few years ago, I could have told you what each one was, but that's over since..."

The researcher fell silent. She pressed her lips together so tightly that Yini decided not to probe any further. Great. She had managed to stifle the conversation with a single question. *Great job, Yini!*

Agata swallowed. "But that's not why you're here, my darling."

My darling - what an old-fashioned phrase. But she liked it, and when the older woman said it, it didn't sound inappropriate.

"That's right," Yini said. "I'm looking for information about a certain Tsai Tailin."

"A relative of yours?" asked Agata. "I mean, because of the name."

"I don't know, to be honest. She appears in one of my transmissions and probably does look a lot like me. But that can be deceptive with tachyon eavesdropping. Your consciousness prefers to work sparingly and use existing images if they fit at all."

"At least one advantage of our augmentation platforms," said Agata. "The images are generated by an AI, not by my own consciousness."

"Doesn't that feel even more immersive?" asked Yini. "You act with your own body, and external stimuli reach you via all sensory channels. For me, on the other hand, the stimuli are already processed. That's how I imagine being in someone else's Biobag."

"You're welcome to try it out," said Agata. "It's very physically demanding. My sessions last fifteen minutes at most, which means we don't make as much progress with the material. But you wanted to know something about your relative. Can you narrow it down a bit in terms of time and location?"

"The transmission I've been following comes from the Gliese-411 system. Tsai Tailin probably came there from Neomars."

"So we're talking about the present day?"

"No. Gliese 411 doesn't have its own tachyon transmitter. The transmission came from three light years away. So the events must have taken place at least three years ago."

"Wait, let me check."

Agata stepped down from the platform and activated a computer console that stood next to it. She typed a few commands and shook her head.

"You've probably come to the wrong place," she said. "Gliese 411 is eight light years away. No transmissions in the electromagnetic spectrum will have reached us from there yet. I'm sorry."

She should have guessed that. She could save herself a visit to Dr. Dubois, because written records took even longer. It was a crazy idea to look for this Tailin. The family name wasn't that rare, and she had already given Agata the explanation for the outward resemblance herself.

"What about Neomars? Could you have heard anything about a Tsai Tailin from there?" asked Yini.

Relations with Neomars had been strained since the Martian wars, to the point of a mutual information blockade. She didn't have high hopes.

Agata smiled with little conviction. "I'll take a look."

Again, she typed in orders. Suddenly she stiffened. Something must have piqued Agata's interest. She put her thumb on the screen. The console performed a laser scan of Agata's iris, which had a ghostly effect. After that, her eyes kept wandering over the screen. What had she found?

When Agata finally turned to Yini, her disappointment was clear to see.

"Unfortunately, it's a dead end," she said. "When I enter the name of your presumed relative, I get a list of articles, but all the texts are blocked for me, even after logging in. You saw the scan."

That was exciting. She must have come across something important if the articles were blocked.

"That's a shame," said Yini. "And there's nothing you can do?"

"Your boss Ulita could submit a request for access. If it's relevant to your work, you might have a chance."

Ulita would definitely not go for that. Yini shook her head. Agata was right - it was a dead end. Perhaps the transmission itself would provide her with some answers. She was skeptical about that, though, because the broadcaster Pedramonte and Tsai Tailin had parted ways.

"Thank you, Agata," she said. "You tried, but perhaps it's not meant to be."

"Now wait a minute," said Agata, whose sleuthing impulse seemed to have been awakened. "Most of the texts are dated 2780. Does that mean anything to you?"

"No, I was just a kid then. I'm..."

She faltered. Actually, her childhood was nobody's business. Her parents could be in danger if word got around. And Zahir had warned her about Dr. Szymanski's gossip addiction.

No matter. She didn't have to bring her parents into the picture.

"I grew up on Earth as an illegal immigrant. We must have arrived there in 2782. But I was only four years old then, and my memories are correspondingly hazy."

"On the surface?" asked Agata. "That's exciting. I've never been there. What's it like? How does it feel?"

"Green, everything is green," replied Yini. "If there's one

thing I remember, it's the incredible shades of green everywhere."

"Oh, if only licenses weren't so expensive ..." Agata typed something on the computer console. "2780, that's interesting. There's a report from that year about an incident in Jupiter orbit."

"What kind of incident?" asked Yini.

"It's a report from an Earth research vessel that was sent to investigate Jupiter's moon Ganymede," explained Agata.

The peace treaty between the Terran Union and Neomars only covered the Saturn and Earth systems, and the asteroid belt that had joined the Terran Union. All other areas were considered neutral territory.

"And what did they find?" asked Yini.

Agata did not answer immediately. She had apparently not finished reading the report.

"The captain reported that his ship was hit by ricochets while orbiting Ganymede. Fortunately, the crew was on the surface at the time. The control AI registered two foreign spaceships that were apparently performing a slingshot maneuver on Jupiter. This is said to have resulted in an exchange of fire. The ships did not identify themselves. However, the design suggests Neomartian origin."

"Is there any way to verify that?" asked Yini.

"Wait... Hm, Neomars later denied that its ships were involved. The case was not pursued because there were no casualties."

"I wonder why this report wasn't blocked too," said Yini.

"Presumably there's no connection with what the system knows about Tsai Tailin," Agata said.

"Or whoever blocked it didn't recognize the connection."

"I guess we'll never know."

Yini didn't disagree, but she thought differently. If there was anything to be discovered, she would find it.

By the time Yini left Dr. Szymanski's office, she had spent half an hour showing Agata around the Earth she remembered. It turned out there was also an eavesdropping couch in Agata's study. Yini had used it to transfer her early childhood memories into the control system of the augmentation stage, so they could walk around in it with the help of matching suits and glasses. For Yini, it had felt almost magical to re-enter the scenes of her childhood: the cave where they had first hidden, the dense forests, the endless grassy plains...

The images had been sharper than in her memory - a credit to the Augment AI, which supplemented her memories with the appropriate data. It had all seemed real to Yini, but she had no way of knowing what came from her own head and what the AI had added. Human consciousness wasn't precise enough for that.

They said goodbye with the promise that they would visit Earth's surface together one day. Although Agata was so much older, they had almost become friends in that short time. Yini only hoped that Zahir wasn't right and soon everyone here would know every detail about her. But she couldn't imagine that happening.

Unfortunately, the visit had taken so much time that the canteen was already closed. But Dr. Dubois would certainly welcome her even without cat food. After all, it had worked with Agata without gossip. In the meantime, Yini had to hurry, or she wouldn't be able to finish her chronoscript today.

Yini was glad that the decoration of this area wasn't so puzzling. The designer had painted letters on the walls and ceiling. Only some of them looked familiar to her. The majority seemed to come from long-extinct languages. As a special feature, the characters changed while she was still trying to identify them. They probably formed words, sentences and perhaps even entire books, but Yini didn't have time to look at the letters long enough to figure out the meaning of sentences.

Dr. Dubois turned out to be a chubby, middle-aged man. He had a shiny, round face with small eyes that seemed to lack lids. He wore a flat cap on his head, presumably to hide a bald head. His short-sleeved blue smock only partially covered his tattooed arms. The tattoos consisted of letters that moved like the ones on the wall outside. Yini had to avert her eyes because she felt dizzy.

"What can I do for you?" asked Dubois after they had formally introduced themselves. "Why don't you sit down?"

His voice sounded squeaky. He pointed to a chair in front of his impressive neo-wood desk. A muted note of sweat hung in the room, and the department head's desk was dusty. Yini was glad she didn't have to work here. There were tufts of hair on the chair. Yini first thought of Dubois' bald head, but then she remembered the cat. She had to smile. Dubois evidently thought she was smiling at him, and smiled back. No, he was grinning. Yini didn't want to be too quick to judge, but she didn't like him.

"I don't want to take up too much of your time," she said, "so I'll get straight to the point: I'm looking for information about a certain Tsai Tailin. She plays an important role in a transmission I'm currently chronoscribing."

"It's ... unusual for you to make this request in person. Most people just send me a short message," Dubois said.

That had briefly occurred to her, but she thought that personal contact would help her move forward.

"To be honest, I was curious about your field," Yini said. "I've heard so much about it that I wanted to see it for myself."

Maybe a little flattery would help. The tattoos suggested that Dubois lived for his work.

"Besides, I'm also curious about your cat," she added.

That was a mistake. Dubois stiffened jerkily and glared at her from his small eyes.

"I don't own a pet. That's forbidden, as you know."

"Of course you don't. I, uh... Well, I don't know where I came up with that, it was a slip of the tongue. I meant I'm curious about your great library."

Great library? What a load of rubbish. But Dubois went along with it.

"I'm glad to hear it," he said. "Well, I think your question can be answered relatively quickly. Can you spell the name for me?"

Dubois pulled open a drawer, which apparently contained a keyboard. Yini spelled the name and he typed in time with her. Because his upper arm was moving, her eyes fell on the tattoo. It always showed the letter she had just said! Yini fell silent in amazement.

"Tsai Tai ... What next?" asked Dubois.

"Your tattoo ..."

"Oh, does it bother you? I'm sorry about that. It's a gimmick, a Neomars invention. There are some genetically modified, extremophilic bacteria under the skin that change color when I hear letters."

"So the bacteria have a direct connection to your brain?"

"No, Ms. Tsai. A few pain nerves have been altered in such a way that they remotely control the bacteria. I first had to learn to consciously induce the effect. But that was years ago. Today it happens unconsciously, the way you automatically tap your foot to the beat of background music."

"So are you from Neomars?" asked Yini.

"Not me, but this Biobag. My previous one had a fatal accident, and at the time this was the only one available. I've since gotten used to it. You know how it is. Every Biobag has its advantages and disadvantages, but once you've learned how to use them, you don't even notice the disadvantages anymore."

Dubois didn't seem to have made peace with his bald head yet. Otherwise, why would he wear a cap even in the office?

Yini shook her head. "I live in my birth body."

"Excuse me?"

Dubois got up from his chair and walked around the desk. Suddenly he grabbed her upper arm and squeezed it until she pulled it away. Then he pushed the hair of her wig to one side and inspected her neck. Yini shook her head violently and prepared to flee. At that moment, Dubois let go of her.

"Please excuse me," he said. "You are right - or they did a damn good job with the feeding channel scar."

Biobags normally retained a barely visible scar on the back of the neck, by which they could be distinguished from born bodies. This scar could not be removed under any circumstances, because birth bodies had more rights than the bred Biobags. The churches had insisted on this in the old days.

"It's my birth body," Yini said sharply.

Should she leave Dubois' office? The man seemed abusive. But if things got serious, she knew how to defend herself.

"Of course. And I don't own a cat. You must understand my skepticism, Ms. Tsai. To be such a gifted tachyon eavesdropper in your mid-twenties is very unusual."

"What do you know about my talents, Dr. Dubois?"

"Please, word gets around. If the admiral is asking for you directly..."

"Excuse me?" How did Dubois know about that? According to John Smith, the whole thing was top secret.

"Now, don't play modest. You know perfectly well that you are exceptional. I wouldn't be giving you my valuable time if you weren't... But let's get back to your request. You don't owe me any answers."

"Very well. Please do."

Yini got goose bumps. She didn't like this man at all. And she liked the fact that he mentioned the admiral even less.

"Good," said Dubois. "We had Tsai Tai..."

His tattoo moved again. Drops of sweat were running down his temples. The man seemed stressed, but Yini couldn't help it. She had to get through this and get out of here quickly.

"...l - i - n," she dictated the missing characters.

"Ah, Tsai, just like your surname," said Dubois. "I'm just realizing that now..."

"Yes, exactly, Tsai," Yini confirmed.

"But this isn't private research about some heiress? I mean, it concerns your work? I'm not authorized to deal with private matters ..."

"Don't worry, Dr. Dubois. It's purely to do with my current assignment."

... which is under the special supervision of the Admiralty, she would have liked to add. Dubois seemed to be very impressed by such things. But the visitor had told her not to discuss it with anyone. What would he say to her little piece of research?

"That's good. Wait a minute. Yes, I've got... No. Here..." Dubois wiped his finger across the screen again and again. A deep wrinkle appeared above his nose. "Ah, this here... Wait... No. What is this... That can't be ... But that was..."

He leaned back and rubbed his nose. A crumb fell onto his jacket, which was clearly visible on the blue fabric. Too well. Yini had to turn away.

"So, Ms. Tsai," Dubois said. "I'm surprised, not to mention annoyed. But that has nothing to do with you. Can you believe that a large number of my documents have been declared inaccessible? In my own library!"

"I'm sorry about that. I shouldn't have bothered you..."

"Yes, you should. Otherwise, I wouldn't even have noticed!

This is outrageous. I was simply ignored! I don't have the clearance to see these documents. Me! I run this library!"

Dr. Dubois was visibly hurt by this disparagement. It was clear he had always seen himself as the absolute ruler of his department, and now he felt excluded.

"Wait, let me try to find out the cause."

Dubois typed. His fingers crackled on the keyboard.

"Ah, here. A certain Tsai Tailin is said to have died in an accident with a battleship shuttle. There is an investigation report on the captain of the ship, a Captain Morris. But even that report is not accessible. The audacity!"

"Is it the same person I'm looking for?"

"You're asking me? I'm sorry, but you can see that my options here have been deliberately curtailed. I'll lodge a complaint, that's for sure."

"Would it be worth coming back to see you later?"

"In two to three years, I'm sure. That's how long it takes for complaints to be addressed."

Suddenly, something clawed at her thigh. Yini noticed a four-legged animal that had placed its front paws on her thighs and was now stretching out. An unerring leap landed it in her lap. Yini was relieved when the pain subsided. This must be the cat that Dubois supposedly didn't have, which began purring loudly.

"Oh, she likes you," Dubois said. "That's unusual. Minou is very picky when it comes to people."

"Then it's an honor, Minou," Yini said.

The cat didn't answer, but she extended her claws and retracted them again and again. Each time it caught Yini's skin.

"She is kneading," said Dubois. "It's perfectly normal behavior, she's not trying to torture you. You have to stroke her!"

"Will she stop if I do that?"

"No."

"Then I'd better not."

"That won't make her stop any sooner. Minou decides when you can get up again."

"And I always thought that humans were the most highly evolved beings in the known universe."

"Haha, you were wrong. Now pet her already."

Yini summoned her courage and stroked the animal. Its gray fur was wonderfully soft, and the skin underneath was so warm and alive. It was heavenly, just as Zahir had said. *Thank you, Minou, for trusting me.* She stroked the cat with her whole hand and forearm until Minou lifted her head. *Now my neck*, she seemed to be saying. Yini granted her wish and was rewarded with even louder purring.

"Is there anything you can tell me about the blocked files?" Yini asked.

"It's scientific correspondence with the Schiaparelli University on Neomars, submissions to scientific journals and... No, it can't be."

"What can't be?"

"Your namesake, Ms. Tsai, also corresponded with the Terran Union. That was highly regulated at the time and almost impossible."

Almost impossible - that usually meant that something was possible but expensive.

"Almost?" she asked.

"There was an exception for humanitarian reasons. You were allowed to correspond with relatives."

"What time are we talking about?" asked Yini.

"Around 2758."

That was twenty-two years before the incident in Jupiter orbit that Agata had told her about. This woman could not be her sister. Back then, her parents were still children themselves. Perhaps Yini had gotten herself into something. The simplest explanation was still a convenient reaction of her own consciousness.

"Is there any way we can access the contents of those files?" Yini asked. "There must be something. You're the boss here, Dr. Dubois!"

"Absolutely. If you don't mind, I'll complain to my superiors now. And if that doesn't help, I'll go all the way up to management level. It's unacceptable for the Great Archive to make such a fool of the head of its most important department."

Yini sighed. She already knew what would come of Dubois' complaint - nothing. There were other forces at work here. It now seemed less likely that they had anything to do with her. She could continue to follow the recording with peace of mind.

"I would be very grateful, Dr. Dubois, if you wouldn't go into too much detail about the reason for your complaint."

"What do you mean? Is it a private request after all? Then I'm afraid I'll have to report it."

Yini lifted the gray cat's head. She purred as if wound up and kept her eyes closed.

"You do realize that I would have to tell the whole truth about my visit to you if I were questioned, don't you?"

Dubois expelled his breath in annoyance. "That's what you get for trusting someone! Fine, you criminal. I'll explain that I came across one of the protected files by chance."

"Thank you, Dr. Dubois. This has been a very helpful conversation."

OUTSIDE THE OFFICE DOOR, YINI FIRST BRUSHED THE CAT HAIR off her clothes. The air was so dry that the fine hairs were very stubborn, and she had to pick them off the fabric one by one. The conversation with Dubois had calmed her down a little. Her connection to the woman with her surname and her appearance could be just a coincidence. In that case, she could also safely disregard Agata's research findings. By now, the afternoon was well advanced. She couldn't finish the job today anyway, so she still had time for a visit to Dr. Wilson. She wasn't expecting anything from that department, but she was curious to see what the designer had come up with. How did one symbolize "miscellaneous" on the ceiling and walls?

The reality did not meet her expectations. Instead of sophisticated ideas, she found pictures that looked like they were drawn by children. Earthly and extraterrestrial landscapes were depicted, using very different styles: some were combined with elegant brushstrokes to form abstract shapes, other pictures looked more like construction drawings, and there were also a few very detailed miniatures that could have been painted from a photograph. The corridor, which was otherwise very simply designed and located on the second basement floor, ended in a steel door.

Yini knocked. There was a muffled sound, as if there was only rock behind the door. No one answered. She pushed down on the handle, pulled the door open - and her eyes widened. Below her was a huge hall, probably four or five stories deep and the size of two or three battleship hangars. The hall was filled with countless shelves - and with an incredible sense of calm. Where did the feeling come from? It was quiet in here, of course, even when she pulled the squeaky door shut behind her.

But it was the stillness, the lack of movement that particularly impressed her. The brightly lit hall should have been bustling with robots transporting goods from A to B and re-sorting them - but nothing was happening. So what was the point of the generous lighting? Presumably so that the single employee wouldn't be afraid. She discovered Dr. Wilson two floors below her. He stood up and waved to the newcomer. Zahir had been right; Wilson was pleased to see her.

From the door, a steel staircase led down along the wall. Wilson came towards her in leaps and bounds. Yini deliberately took her time. She didn't want to spoil his fun, and knew what he expected of her. She just hoped he wasn't as obnoxious as Dubois.

But he wasn't. He stopped a few feet in front of her. Wilson fit the stereotype of the genius scientist: wavy hair, glasses, a lab coat under which he wore a suit. He bowed, then pulled a paper business card out of his breast pocket and handed it to her with both hands. Yini had only seen something like this once before in an old movie. She felt the card. Its surface was rough. It really did seem to be made of plant fibers. Oho! She pocketed the card without reading it, which Wilson acknowledged with a twitch of his left eyelid.

Up close, the scientist looked surprisingly young, forty years old at most. Suddenly she felt sorry for him. He must have stepped on the toes of someone influential, perhaps unintentionally, because this was clearly a dead-end career. Although he was head of the department on paper, no one else seemed to be interested in it.

"Welcome to my kingdom, Ms. Tsai Yini," he said, gesturing down the stairs.

He led the way, and she followed. An awkward silence fell, broken only by the sound of her footsteps on the stairs. How did he know her name? He had smiled in a particularly friendly way when he spoke her name. He probably expected praise or at least a return smile, but Yini found it rather odd.

Tachyon: The Weapon

"You knew I was coming, Dr. Wilson?" she asked when they arrived downstairs.

Wilson opened the door to a small office.

"It was only logical. I met Zahir over coffee, and he told me that you were looking for traces of your mother."

Excuse me? That was impossible. Her parents lived in the Skyring, after raising her brother and her as refugees on the surface. Yini hadn't even told Zahir who she was looking for, but she had told Agata and Dubois the name. Zahir knew who she was looking for. He must have made inquiries and shared his knowledge with Wilson. Or what he thought was knowledge. But now that Wilson had said it, it suddenly made sense to her. The age fit, and the strange resemblance... She wasn't looking for her sister, she was looking for her mother. Yini felt sick.

"Come, sit down. You have turned very pale." Wilson led her to his armchair, which stood behind a simple desk sculpted from moonstone. The seat was surprisingly comfortable, and the nausea retreated. It had to be a mistake, a misconception. What strange idea had Wilson come up with, and why had it hit her like that?

"Thank you, Dr. Wilson. I'm sorry to be a burden to you. Actually, I just wanted to inquire about a person I came across in a tachyon transmission. It has nothing at all to do with my mother."

"Oh, really?" He stroked his chin with his index finger and a crease appeared on his forehead. Did he not believe her?

"Do you have any clues yet?"

"Her name is Tsai Tailin. I don't think you have anything on her in your stash."

"What makes you think that, Ms. Tsai? Or may I call you Yini?"

"No, I... Let's stay on the formal level."

What had gotten into her? She hadn't objected to using Agata's first name, and Wilson was certainly not as slimy as Dubois.

"As you wish."

He was certainly piqued, but his face didn't show it. The smile remained. He respected her boundaries, which was very reassuring.

"To answer your question," Yini said, "no one has been able

to help me yet. Access has been blocked to all the relevant files. It's as if this person is a state secret. That's why I assumed it would be no different in your department."

"But you came here anyway," Wilson said.

"To be honest, I was curious about what the designer came up with for your department. But it really wasn't worth it."

"You think so?" Wilson asked.

Why was he suddenly blushing? Did he think so highly of the designer?

"Most of it looks like children's drawings. I had imagined something more creative."

"Um, well." Wilson cleared his throat, reached for his neck and loosened his tie. "It's a shame you don't like my drawings."

Those are his pictures? Crap! She really was a klutz. There was no way he would help her now. Was there any way to salvage the situation?

"I wouldn't say I don't like any of them. There are a few nice ones..."

"No, that's okay. It's... satisfying to hear an honest opinion of my work for once. You're right, I am a bumbling amateur."

No, the situation could no longer be salvaged. She had ruined her chances with Wilson.

"I just thought it was unfair that the designer didn't include any decoration for my department. Yet I have the largest storage area of any department under my management."

"The hall is really impressive. I noticed that straight away," she said.

Wilson smiled shyly, as if he didn't quite realize how serious she was about the compliment. The smile made him look rather cute. But she had to be careful. Zahir seemed to be unusually interested in him. She'd better not find him too cute. Otherwise, she would end up putting her foot in her mouth.

"I'm sure you've noticed that I work here all by myself," Wilson said.

Of course, but why did he emphasize that?

"Indeed," she said.

"Well, since my working hours are limited, I haven't yet been able to digitally record all the objects in the collection."

"So, we can't conveniently search for specific objects?"

"We can't, but those who want to block access to certain things don't have that option either."

Wilson was laying it on thick. What was he implying?

"Do you have anything on Tsai Tailin?" she asked.

"I have a very good memory, Ms. Tsai. And it's possible that there's something in a back corner that's connected to the person you're looking for."

"Really? That would be fantastic!"

Wilson smiled broadly. He was a nice guy.

"Come on," he said.

Yini stood up. The nausea was gone, but her legs still felt a little weak. Wilson must have noticed her hesitation because he encouragingly took her hand in his. It was warm and firm. A strangely familiar gesture, and yet not unpleasant – on the contrary.

"Maybe we could... I mean, you know... speak less formally after all." *Pull yourself together, Yini.* It was awful to hear herself stammer like that. "I'm Yini."

"I'm Mike. Nice to meet you."

Yini didn't answer. She was starting to feel happy, but some things... only complicated interpersonal relationships. All she really wanted was to do her job as well as possible. On the other hand, she could use all the help she could get. Was it truly her mother she was looking for? And Mike certainly had a nice smile.

AT GROUND LEVEL, THE STORAGE ROOM TURNED OUT TO BE A huge labyrinth. The shelves towering five floors above them were accessed by narrow walkways and steep ladders, so there was no need for a crane robot to inspect a particular object. Yini had the feeling that Wilson wasn't leading them directly to the things associated with Tsai Tailin. They climbed up and down ladders, balanced on planks without railings, crossed the shelves on makeshift ramps or through tunnels whose side walls were formed by ancient books.

But Yini said nothing. She allowed Mike the satisfaction of being able to show her his collection, since he rarely had the opportunity. But it was worth it. The first piece was a four-wheeled, open vehicle that stood in its own alcove.

"John Young and Charles Duke drove around on the moon in it over 800 years ago," he explained. "That was before the Terran Union. That pattern on the fender is the national flag of the United States."

The symbol with the stripes and the little stars looked familiar to her. Overall, the Rover looked like it was ready to drive.

"Almost looks like we could get in and drive," she said.

"The tires would turn to dust immediately, and the rear axle steering is faulty. Do you know who found the vehicle?"

"You did," she guessed.

Mike blushed. She'd hit the bullseye.

"I found it in old photos of the North Ray crater," he said. "It was almost always in the shadow of the crater wall, so no one had noticed it before."

"Very nice," she said.

"Are you interested in space history? Then I've got something even better for you."

Mike led her zigzagging through the labyrinth and finally stopped on a small platform on the second floor. He pointed to a red-painted metal canister.

"This is the black box from Masterson and Abramovich's spaceship," he explained. "I'm sure you've heard of them."

Yini nodded. The names were familiar. They were the pilots of humanity's first interstellar mission. Sometime in the 22nd century, the two billionaire friends had organized it privately. Unfortunately, their spaceship had crashed on its approach to the second planet of Proxima Centauri. Nevertheless, they were considered heroes.

"Sad thing," she said.

"All their conversations are stored on the black box. Things must have gotten pretty heated in the last few hours, which is why the documents were never published. One of them must have been responsible for the crash. Apparently, they were more than friends."

"Oh. I didn't know that."

"I don't think anyone remembers that anymore. The last people who were in on the secret died long before consciousness purification was introduced."

"Except you," she said.

"And now you."

Warmth rose in Yini's cheeks. It must mean a lot to Mike to share such a secret. He was no longer the only person in the known universe who knew the true fate of the first interstellar astronauts.

They continued to meander through the labyrinth. Over time, Yini almost forgot why she had come here in the first place. Mike showed her an asteroid from the debris disk of Epsilon Eridani, which they had had to open the roof of the archive to store. He showed her the sunrise on EZ Aquarii b, in which three golden suns rose over the horizon in quick succession into a deep green sky. Together they leafed through the logbook of the first human colony on YZ Ceti b, which was abandoned after almost 200 years due to the frequent eruptions of the mother star. It seemed like a miracle to Yini that the colonists had survived their hard life for so long. But Mike also had samples of the first barley harvest on Groombridge in 1618c in his collection, which he kept in a specially climate-protected box.

"You could still brew beer from it today," he explained.

"Do you know what happened to the colony?" she asked.

"Abandoned around 2700," he said.

Yini sighed. Many hopeful colonies on distant planets had been abandoned by humanity over time. By the second generation at the latest, there was usually not much left of the colonists' spirit of optimism. Who could blame people for preferring a life in the comfort of the Sky Rings, underground Earth, or the aqua cities of Neomars?

"If you want to see an object from a functioning colony, I've got something exciting," he said. "Come on!"

This time, there were only two ladders to climb. They walked along a walkway made of grooved metal plates until they reached the end. Behind it, a rope hung from the ceiling.

"We'll use this to swing over to where the walkway continues," Mike explained.

"What?"

They were on the fourth floor. Yini stood at the edge of the walkway and looked down. Even with lunar gravity, the impact would hurt badly.

Mike grinned. "Just kidding."

He pulled on the rope. A platform descended from the ceiling. It was made of glass, which was why it had barely been visible before. It halted slightly below the walkway. The platform was actually a kind of aquarium, no, a terrarium. One corner was filled with water, but most of the floor was covered with moss. A few stones were piled along the edge, looking like loose tuff from a volcano. Another stone lay in the water.

"A terrarium, how pretty," she said. "The moss is intelligent, is that it?"

Mike laughed, but it didn't sound disparaging. "No, it's just normal, earthly moss. It settled here on its own. The air in the pool is relatively humid."

Only now did Yini notice that there was a transparent film over the container. Suddenly she saw herself in a forest. She was lying on soft moss that smelled of earth and mushrooms. It had rained, so the moss was wet. Her mother would scold her if she noticed the stains on her clothes. Yini swayed. But a hand held her firmly.

"Are you all right?" asked Mike.

"Thanks, yeah. Just a memory," she replied.

He loosened his grip on her arm. Yini wanted to reach for his hand again, but caught herself. The feeling annoyed her, but it faded quickly.

"The special thing about the terrarium is the stones," Mike explained.

"The stones?" Yini leaned over the basin to get a better look at them. She leaned on the edge of the glass and the container swayed. "Oh, I didn't mean to."

"Don't worry, it's sturdily suspended," Mike said. "They're live rocks from Terra Nova."

"Oh!"

That was really fascinating. She focused her attention on the stone lying in the water. If it moved, she would notice. The living stones had caused quite a stir 250 years ago. They had been the first non-extinct alien life form humankind had come across. It was not based on carbon, but on silicon. Since then, there had been other, more exciting discoveries, so that the living stones had almost been forgotten.

"I'm afraid you will have to come back when you have more time if you want to see it in action," said Mike.

"How much time?" she asked.

"An evening and the following night?"

Was that an offer? That was going a bit too fast for her.

"It's not that exciting," she said.

"Wait, I have an idea," Mike said.

He took some kind of remote control out of the pocket of his coat and pressed a few buttons, which turned out the lights. Then he took her hand again, and this time it felt just right. After all, there was a drop of more than ten yards to her left. Shortly afterwards, strange grinding marks appeared in the terrarium, glowing bluish.

"The stones leave those marks in the sand," Mike explained. "They are only visible in UV light."

"And the sand isn't dented?" asked Yini.

"No, not a bit. That's because they briefly integrate the silica grains into their own bodies."

"They eat them?"

"The researchers don't quite agree on that. The majority believe that they only need silicon dioxide for their outer shell."

"Just as terrestrial life stabilizes itself with calcium skeletons."

"Exactly."

"What do they feed on, then?" asked Yini.

"Acids," replied Mike. "That liquid in the terrarium is sulfuric acid, not water."

"Oh, that's why no moss is growing there."

"Well spotted."

"But isn't Terra Nova a successful agricultural colony? Surely there must be lots of water there, not sulfuric acid ponds like that."

"You're absolutely right. But acids can also be dissolved in water. Terra Nova has a dense carbon dioxide atmosphere. Some of the CO_2 dissolves in the seas and lakes. The only reason I use sulfuric acid here is to give their metabolism a little boost. They move much more slowly on the planet. That's why it took so long for them to be discovered. The colony had already been established for quite a while."

"They must think in completely different time frames than we do," said Yini.

"Actually, researchers agree that they don't think at all. They are at about the level of primitive lichens. The mosses are already beyond them in evolutionary terms."

"Who knows? Maybe they think so slowly that we can't even perceive their thoughts."

The lights came on again, causing Yini to blink. Mike looked at her. Embarrassed, she let go of his hand and smiled at him, and he returned her smile.

"I thought of that too," he said. "See those wires?"

Two thin cables were attached to the side wall of the terrarium with duct tape, ending in a flat device. They led over the edge of the container near the stones.

"I use this to try and pick up any impulses that the stones give off. I've been watching them for twelve years now."

Mike certainly had patience. But you probably had to find something to do down here if you didn't want to go mad.

"Do they have a nervous system that could emit such impulses?" asked Yini.

"Various silicon compounds have been found, as well as crystalline silicon, which could serve as a semiconductor. That is why researchers thought for a while that the stones could be machines from an extinct civilization. But evolution probably just used what it found, and in this case, it wasn't chemical messengers, but semiconductors and electrical potentials."

Mike had reddish spots on his cheeks. The subject was obviously very important to him.

"But electrical signaling could work much faster than the chemical signaling our kind of life uses," Yini said. "Why are they so slow?"

"That's a good question," said Mike. "Maybe they've just decided to live less stressful lives. That's nonsense, of course. But our circuits also have a system clock that sets the speed. Their clock probably just works much slower than ours."

"I wonder what it would be like to live as a stone," said Yini. "You would change more slowly than the environment. For us, it's the other way around."

"Yes, it must be exciting. You're always discovering something new," said Mike.

His eyes lit up. The desire to explore was written all over his face. Somehow that made her sad, because Mike was in absolutely the wrong place. If someone were to record his tracks, the way he observed the traces of the stones shining in ultraviolet light, the picture would be a labyrinth crisscrossed by millions of circles. He could achieve so much somewhere else! But if she told him that, he might look around for something else, and then... Suddenly, she had an idea.

"Those tracks you showed me... have you taken pictures of them?" she asked.

He pointed to a hanger above the terrarium. Yini spotted a lens and interpreted the gesture as a yes.

"Have you ever compared these photos over time?"

"I measured the speed at which the stones move through the terrarium," he said.

"That's typically human. But maybe they don't think like that. Maybe speed doesn't matter and it's really about the journey."

"The journey is the destination, is that what you mean, Yini?"

"Yes, but not philosophically, more practically," she said. The idea fascinated her. Suddenly her own work no longer seemed so exciting. "Maybe you should look at the information content of the traces. If you can see them, the stones might be able to perceive them too. Maybe that's how they talk to each other."

That was it. That had to be it. Even humans communicated a lot by how they moved around each other, circled each other, avoided each other, were attracted and repelled. Yini moved a little closer to Mike.

"That's a very good idea," he said. "I can pull the photos out of the computer later. But first I'll show you the letters you came for. They're pretty near here."

Letters? He hadn't previously revealed anything about the nature of the object. Who wrote letters these days? Yini's heart pounded. The living stones of Terra Nova suddenly no longer mattered. She almost felt sorry, but she might soon be a huge step closer to the person who could be her mother. If so - she had already been in her body, even if it had been Pedramonte's consciousness.

MIKE MUST HAVE SENSED HER EXCITEMENT, BECAUSE IT SEEMED to take hold of him too. Did he know the contents of the letters? He spoke continuously and without pause, as if he needed to distract himself from what was coming next. The archive, he explained to her, was sorted by coordinates, namely the coordinates of signal sources in the universe. Terra Nova, also known as Gliese 167, was only seven light years away from Gliese 163.

Although both stars were faint red dwarfs, each must be visible to the naked eye in the night sky of a planet in the other star system. The living stones of Terra Nova might therefore have somehow been able to see the letters being written, since they came from the orbit of Gliese 163 c. This rocky planet was slightly smaller than Earth, and orbited its star in the habitable zone.

Mike halted in front of a shelf full of old-fashioned folders made of brown fabric, which were covered with dust. Obviously, no one had done any research here for a long time. Mike leafed through the folders and finally handed her one.

"What's this?" Yini asked.

Suddenly she was afraid of the truth, whatever it might be.

"These are letters from the astrobiologist at the Albatross research station at Gliese 163 c. His name was Mark Decker."

She didn't know that name. Yini relaxed.

"Why letters? They must be ancient, right? And shouldn't they be in the logbook section for written products?" she asked.

Gliese 163 was almost 50 light years away from the solar system. The letters must have taken at least a hundred years to get here.

"They're printed scans," Mike explained. "They were scanned on Gliese 167 and sent here via tachyon transmission."

That made more sense. So anything described in the letters had happened a good thirty years ago. As a tachyon eavesdropper, she did not receive such transmissions. She worked only with instantaneous transmissions of human consciousness. The letters must be important, because the technology was extremely expensive.

"The letters must be very interesting," said Yini. "Wasn't Gliese 163 c that tropical paradise where highly evolved life was first discovered?"

"Exactly. The elephant worms, as the media called them at the time, otherwise known as multifeet. But Gliese 163 c was never a paradise. There was too much sulfur dioxide in the atmosphere for that. It was never an option for colonization."

Yini remembered discussing this in school. Neomars and the Terran Union had both agreed that colonization was out of the question under these circumstances.

"But what does all this have to do with Tsai Tailin?" asked Yini.

"The letters were addressed to her," Mike replied.

The warehouse lights suddenly flickered in time with her heartbeat. Yini leaned against the shelf.

"You don't look well," Mike said. "Do you want to sit down?"

That was a good idea. She slid down the shelf until her backside touched the floor. Then she stretched out her legs and lowered her head. The flickering subsided.

"Don't put your head on your chest," Mike said.

Yini hated being patronized, but raised her head anyway. She needed to calm down. Things didn't add up here. There was apparently a Tsai Tailin, a tachyon physicist who had fled from the Neomars police and had given birth to twins, presumably before fleeing. Her husband - the father of the children? - had been killed in an attack. From another corner of the universe, an astrobiologist addressed letters to a Tsai Tailin who had left him or was not with him for other reasons. Otherwise, he wouldn't have had to write her letters. How likely was it that they were the same person?

"Do you know anything about this Tsai Tailin to whom the letters were addressed?" she asked.

"I've only read them once. From what I recall, the author mainly talks about his daily life at the research station. But I can't rule out the possibility that you might learn something about the addressee."

"Are there any documents about her? If they were married, surely it must have been registered?"

"I wondered about that too. But the research station belongs to Neomars. We don't have access to their registers."

Yini felt better. Concentrated thought was the best remedy for fainting spells. There was an easy way to answer her questions: by reading the letters.

"How extensive is the material?" she asked.

"Decker wrote almost every day for several weeks. He probably used it as a kind of diary."

"I'll probably need a few days. Can you send the letters to my workplace?"

"I'm sorry, Yini, but they haven't been digitized yet. You'd have to come here to read them."

Yini looked Mike straight in the face, yet found no sign that he wasn't telling the truth. His eyelid didn't twitch, he didn't scratch his nose and he didn't have to stifle a grin. But perhaps it wouldn't be too bad to visit him regularly. She was even looking forward to it, though it would cost her working hours.

She glanced at the watch on her wrist. Damn, almost six already. She had spent half the working day looking for Tsai Tailin. Not only was her boss breathing down her neck, but also the strange visitor. *John Smith, sure.* Should she tell Mike about that? It was a bit too early for that. Yet? She must not count her chicks before they were hatched. Her mother had often admonished her about that.

Her mother... When she thought of her, she could feel warmth emanating from her. She would always be her mother, no matter what.

"Good, then I'll come the day after tomorrow, around three o'clock, okay?" she asked.

Disappointment was written all over Mike's face, and the corners of his mouth drooped. To make up for it, she gave him a smile, which seemed to cheer him up immediately.

"I'm sorry," she said, "but if I don't do my work properly, my research on the side will be noticed at some point."

That was probably already the case. Who would approach her boss about it first? She suspected Dr. Dubois. But if Agata Szymanski really liked gossip that much... Never mind. She had to get going.

June 29, 2799, Battleship Vanguard

CLAUDIO WAS FREEZING. *CLAUDIA*, HE CORRECTED HIMSELF. *No, Tailin.* He was Tsai Tailin. But why was he freezing? And where had the hellish pain that had tormented him for so long gone? He opened his eyes. It was light, and the lid of the stasis cell was open. Shiny green metal gleamed above him. This was not a hospital in Earth's Sky Ring, as he would have expected at the end of this journey, but a storage room in a military ship. Everything here was trimmed for efficiency. He knew this because he had served on a Terran Union cruiser for ten years.

Tailin, or Monte, pulled himself up on the edge of the container. No, that wasn't how it worked. He pulled himself up. He was unable to reshape his thoughts while dealing with reality. Maybe he just hadn't known this body long enough. He felt even colder sitting down. Suddenly a shadow moved into his field of vision. It was a man. His epaulettes were not visible from down here. He was no longer young, so he must be an officer. Monte was about to stand up when he noticed the naked breasts of his new body.

A mistake. He must try to cover them up. He quickly crossed his arms over his upper body. That didn't look very ladylike. How would a woman do it?

"Excuse me," said the officer, turning around. "There's a towel next to the bin."

It was Morris. Monte remembered his voice. He stood up quickly. The ship must be accelerating at almost exactly 1 g, because he needed the corresponding amount of force to stand up. So they hadn't arrived yet. Or was the ship slowing down? It was impossible to find out without knowing the direction of flight. He reached for the towel and rubbed his hair mindlessly. *Crap*. It was pulling. He needed to be more careful. This was a different body. He dried himself off. Under the towel was a second cloth, which he wrapped around his body. His ex-wife could have done it more elegantly, but at least he managed to cover all the sensitive areas.

"Sorry for the inconvenience, Dr. Tsai. Unfortunately, we had to wake you up. You will be provided with a uniform to wear. The on-board tailor is currently altering it."

"Don't you have any female crew members who could lend me something?" he asked.

His voice sounded like Tailin's. But he had to be careful not to roll the R like he usually did.

"Yes, we have, but they're all better conditioned than you, if you don't mind my saying so."

That was a good reason. On such a long journey, one of the few available pastimes was pumping up your muscles on the weight machine. This applied equally to male and female crew members. This version of Tailin was immediately recognizable as was a civilian.

A door squeaked. A second person in uniform approached. It was a woman with the rank of lieutenant.

"I'm Dr. Zakharova," she introduced herself.

"How do you do? I'm Dr. Tsai," said Monte.

"I'm a physician," said Zakharova.

"I'm a physicist," said Monte.

The woman laughed. She had dazzling white teeth that sparkled like jewels in the dim room.

"We woke you up because..."

"You have beautiful teeth," Monte interrupted her.

"Thank you. They were expensive enough, even with a work discount."

"Please remind me to ask you about the clinic."

"ArtZahn in Skyring, sector seventeen."

"ArtZahn, that's an interesting name."

"Well, we woke you up because we were worried about you," said the doctor.

"Oh, what happened?"

"Your body reacted to the acceleration with considerable stress. You were on the verge of a heart attack several times. Has that ever happened to you before?"

Monte moved to stroke his beard, but then remembered that it didn't suit his body. He shook his head.

"No, never. I've always survived the journey in the stasis cell just fine."

"That's strange," says Dr. Zakharova. "I can play the recordings for you."

She took a small tablet out of the inside pocket of her uniform jacket. Captain Morris, who had been silent the whole time, moved to stand next to it and peer curiously at the screen.

"I'm sorry, sir, but I'm not allowed to show you this," said the doctor.

Instead, she held out the screen to Monte. It showed a woman in a stasis container, shaking in a frightening way, accompanied by blazing red flashing LEDs. He'd never seen anything like it. *Damn*. That was him. Apparently, he almost died in the stasis cell.

"Do you see that? We were about to do a consciousness purification."

Yes, please, he thought. "Absolutely not," he said. "I strictly reject this technology on ethical grounds."

"Well, we have orders to bring you back to Earth in good health at all costs," said Morris. "If there is no other way..."

"Now hold on, sir. You are not authorized to override my orders without consulting the control center," said Zakharova.

"You could accelerate more slowly," Monte suggested.

"But then the journey will take twice as long," contradicted the captain.

"Most of the crew will be sleeping in storage anyway, so what does it matter?"

"It matters a great deal to my superiors. We mustn't lose any time, or Neomars will be the first on the market."

"On the market?" asked Monte.

"You've seen it," said Morris.

"Seen what?"

"What happened to your ship. It was definitely caused by a

Neomars weapon. As a physicist, you of all people should be able to recognize that."

Monte didn't answer. He knew no more about physics than Captain Morris.

Another soldier arrived, carrying a uniform.

"Thank you," said Monte. "If you don't mind, I'd like to get dressed now."

"In a moment, Dr. Tsai," said the doctor. "I'd like to examine you first. I need to rule out any organic reasons for your extreme physical reaction. It would be very bad if you died on the journey."

She was right. He was dependent on this body. Apparently, the doctor was willing to accept her right to make her own decision about a consciousness purification. That was good, because his consciousness could no longer hide under a foreign cloak in the memory. But if the body died, Monte would die with it. How might people have felt when this was still quite normal? He probably wouldn't have dared to leave the house if every step could have cost his life.

"Will you lie down on the cot, please?" asked Dr. Zakharova. "Sir, I have to ask you to leave the room."

Morris followed the order. The man who brought the uniform had already left. Monte lay down on his back.

"May I take the towel off you? This won't take long," said Dr. Zakharova.

Monte was freezing. The device that the doctor was now running over his body created a pleasant tingling sensation on his skin. When she touched his nipples with it, they stiffened.

"Do you see anything?" he asked.

"Nothing that gives me cause for concern. I'll leave the images for an AI to diagnose later."

"Is there a clinical condition that is particularly pronounced in a stasis chamber?"

"Not really," the doctor replied. "Problems like yours usually occur mainly in untrained patients. We sometimes encounter it in recruits who are traveling in a stasis chamber for the first time, or with people who are used to avoiding the pain through consciousness purification."

"I understand. That makes it even stranger."

"Exactly. You must travel in a stasis chamber all the time. And you've never had any problems like this?"

"Never before, doctor."

"Good, now please turn over."

Monte turned onto his stomach. The doctor pushed the hair on the back of his neck to one side. Two delicate fingers touched the area where ... *Shit*. He involuntarily stiffened. The scar. It was unavoidable, and because this body had to mature so quickly, it was particularly large. The doctor must know what it meant. He could jump up and try to overpower her. She weighed about a third more than he did and was certainly trained in hand-to-hand combat. But he had more experience, and he had the element of surprise on his side.

Or did he? The doctor continued her examination. Her recording device tickled his spine, gave him goose bumps on his bottom and made the clearly visible hair on his legs stand up.

"You can get dressed now," said the doctor.

Monte turned onto his back again.

"I..."

She gave him a knowing look, which immediately shut him up.

"It's all right, Dr. Tsai," said the doctor. "You can trust me. I know something about my subject, just as you know something about yours, whatever that may be."

Monte nodded. "Thank you."

"There's no reason for that. I'm just doing my job. Speaking of which, will you please sit on the couch again?"

He complied with the request. The doctor pressed a few buttons on her measuring device, stood behind him and pushed his hair aside again. Then she placed the device directly on his skin. A sharp pain shot through him as if she had just decapitated him. It disappeared as quickly as it came.

"That's it," said Zakharova.

He felt his neck. The scar was much shallower than before. He put on his uniform.

"Thank you again," he said.

The doctor opened the door and Captain Morris entered.

"How is our patient?" he asked.

"Fine considering the circumstances," said the doctor.

"Can we start the engines again?"

"Give her a two-day break. In the meantime, I'll adjust the stasis chamber to minimize the risk of a heart attack."

"Very good. That can be arranged. So, Dr. Tsai, you have two days off. You are of course invited to the wardroom. I will also have a cabin prepared for you."

"Thank you very much, Captain Morris," said Monte.

"As the captain says - make the most of your time," said the doctor.

She was not smiling. He immediately understood what she meant: it was serious. Inertia could not be tricked. Morris didn't seem to realize that, or he simply trusted the doctor. The stasis cells had already been optimized as far as was physically possible. This body was to blame. They probably should have given it more time to grow. If the ship accelerated again, he would die. At least there was one piece of good news: the doctor wouldn't betray him. She had given him some breathing space. But was she also an ally? That remained to be seen.

THE BATTLESHIP WAS HUGE - AND OLD. HE COULD SEE IT IN THE many shiny spots on the walls and ceiling. On a civilian spaceship, the paint would just peel slightly, but here someone always had to scrape the damaged area bare. Monte himself had served on one of these ships for three years. Recruits like him always had to spend acceleration times in stasis chambers. Back then, however, he'd been using a different Biobag, specially bred for the military.

It was a strange feeling to walk through oil-scented corridors again. The navy recruit crouching on the floor in front of him, cleaning the grating with a wire brush, could have been him. The *Vanguard* must be three hundred years old. No new ships of this size had been built since the Martian wars. Monte paused and knocked on a steel girder. It made a surprisingly bright sound.

The inside of the ship looked like a shell. This held a fascination of its own, because every piece of metal he saw had an important function and contributed to the stability of the entire ship. There were no unnecessary covers or ornamentation. They

Tachyon: The Weapon

would only be damaged in battle anyway. Monte could appreciate this pragmatic approach.

The ship also seemed honest to him. It didn't promise security that it couldn't provide. The outer hull prevented the breathing air from escaping only until it was hit by the enemy's railgun shells. There was no protection against the sheer momentum of a steel ball accelerated to maximum speed, unrestrained by air molecules. Anyone not wearing a spacesuit in battle would die, and anyone unlucky enough to be hit by a bullet died.

In the old days, battleships therefore had as few crewmembers as possible. This was no longer the case, because battles had fortunately become unlikely. Most military ships were mothballed in Earth orbit, and on the few that were still in service, the focus was on training fresh recruits. That was why Monte only met low-ranking officers on his little tour. They saw his officer's uniform and stood at attention without noticing his missing epaulettes.

But the uniform fit well. A lot had obviously happened since his own time in the service. The fabric, which used to be skimped on, seemed to be made of smart fibers that adapted to his body shape even when he moved. Presumably the Navy had to offer the same comforts as its civilian competitors in order to remain attractive as an employer. But privacy was still missing, at least for recruits.

Monte followed a group of young men who were apparently on their way to their quarters. They were sweating and chatting happily, until they noticed him and greeted him with military courtesy. There was no officer present, but no one got carried away with the kind of stupid jokes that had been standard during his service. Captain Morris obviously had his ship well under control.

In the quarters, the men made room for him. The corridor narrowed here. Five beds were lined up along the walls to the left and right. They all seemed to be occupied. They were followed by toilets and showers, with no partitions. Why did Morris wake the whole crew? Was he planning a longer flight phase at 1 g?

Monte climbed up two floors using a ladder. He could see along the shaft that led to the top of the spaceship. Monte could even see the flap of the one-man airlock. It was used to service the numerous sensors attached to the bow of the battleship, its eyes and ears. He always used to volunteer for that duty. Sitting on the bow of the ship, with the whole universe in front of him, seemed like the epitome of freedom to him - even though he was there on the orders of a superior.

He had never found it difficult to adapt to military discipline. He didn't feel patronized or restricted, because it was his own decision to let others decide for him. And there were still plenty of decisions he had to make himself that could mean the difference between life and death in an emergency, not just for him but also for his comrades.

Monte shook his head and stepped off the ladder into the corridor. Now was not the time to dwell on the past, which he was probably romanticizing anyway. The fact that he felt so free back then, in the Navy of all places, might also have something to do with his tyrannical father. Because of him, Monte had never become a father himself. He didn't know anyone who managed to avoid repeating the same old mistakes.

The officers' mess was in front of him. He heard laughter and the clinking of glasses. He was not really in the mood for alcoholic merriment, but he had to make the most of the two days Dr. Zakharova had given him. He didn't want to die of a heart attack, and he wanted to give Tailin enough time to escape. If this was going to work, he had no choice but to take control of the ship - a Terran Union battleship. It was probably impossible, but that was what made the task so appealing.

"Hello, Dr. Tsai," Captain Morris called out to him. "Why don't you join us?"

Morris sat with seven other officers around a steel table. Four of them were female, which was unusual.

"Ah, nice of you to come," said a female lieutenant he hadn't met yet. "Now we're in the majority."

The woman moved her chair to the side. A recruit came from the background with another chair and set it down in the gap.

"Thank you, Kuhndt," said Captain Morris. "And bring our guest a beer, please."

The recruit, whose first name was Thomas according to his name tag, nodded and moved away again. Morris took his glass, which was still half full, and stood up.

"May I?" he asked the female officer sitting next to Monte.

Tachyon: The Weapon

The woman nodded and swapped places with the captain.

"You do drink alcohol, don't you?" asked Morris. "We have non-alcoholic beer, of course, and whatever else the synthesizers have to offer. I really wouldn't recommend the wine, though, it's undrinkable."

"Thanks for the warning. I'll stick to beer."

By the time he finished his sentence, the glass was in front of him. The drink smelled good.

"Here's to our guest," said Captain Morris.

The group toasted each other, and Monte joined in. Something about the captain's expression irritated him. Did he suspect something? Monte mustn't let on. Inconspicuously, he looked at the women in the group one by one. They were doing nothing different from him. Was it really just the failure of his body in the stasis chamber that aroused Morris's suspicion?

"Thank you for the warm welcome and the medical care," he said.

"Dr. Zakharova is a terrific doctor," said Morris. "Unfortunately, she's busy and can't join us right now."

"Oh, Lydia still has to work at this time of night? What's going on?" asked Monte's neighbor on the right.

"We had a problem waking up a recruit," Morris explained. "It seems his body couldn't cope with the short sleep time."

Monte felt himself getting warm. Because his body had failed, a young man's life was in danger.

"Will he make it?" he asked.

"I'm counting on Dr. Zakharova's skills," said the captain.

"I'm very sorry about that. It only happened because of me," said Monte.

"It's not your fault, Dr. Tsai. We're all just following orders here. I could just as easily be to blame for the incident because I insisted that you come on board. You, on the other hand, deserve thanks for accepting the invitation."

"I must admit, I would have preferred to continue the journey aboard my own ship."

Shit. His own ship was orbiting a gas giant. Now he had given himself away.

"But unfortunately, that wasn't possible," he added. "A repair would have been a bit too much to ask."

He had turned it around. Hopefully. Perhaps Morris was secretly counting his mistakes.

"We inspected the wreck. There was really nothing more we could do," said the captain.

"It's just a shame about the drive," said the woman next to her. "I would have liked to salvage it. You never know when you might need a replacement engine."

"This is Lieutenant Anna Tann, our chief engineer," said Morris.

"Most people call me Anna," said the woman. "Pleased to meet you."

He shook her hand. Tann had a firm handshake, making the ring on her finger painfully noticeable.

"I'm Tsai Tailin," Monte introduced himself.

"I've heard a lot about you," said the engineer.

"We've all heard a lot about you," said Morris from the left.

"Yes, tachyon research is always good for headlines," said Monte. "But at the end of the day, it's very unspectacular work that everyone is familiar with. Conjecture, hypothesis, experiment, failure, new conjecture."

"It may sound strange, but I actually admire you more for your early work than for tachyon research," said Tann. "The tachyons, that's a done deal. Communication, yes, but that's all it will ever do for us."

"The Admiralty disagrees," said Morris. "We wouldn't be here otherwise."

This time he was grateful to the captain. If Tann steered the conversation towards his early research, he could do nothing but sit there blankly. What did Dr. Tsai research in the past? He had no idea.

"I know," said the engineer. "But that's because of Neomars. As soon as it appears anywhere, everyone is all ears. We could miss something that would give the others an advantage."

"While we have you here," said Morris, "could I ask you to explain the tachyon thing to us in a way that even a full-time sailor can understand?"

Morris wanted to test him. That was fine by Monte. It would be worse if he had to explain his early research to Tann, but thankfully he knew a lot about the state of tachyon research. He had been friends with an employee of the tachyon facility on the moon for a while.

"It's not that complicated," said Monte. "You probably know that tachyons move faster than light. But they don't do that because we force them to. It happens all by itself. They can't do anything else, because the square of their mass is negative. You could say that they consist of negative energy, though that is a gross oversimplification. The lower the amount of energy, the faster they go. With normal particles, it's the other way around."

"Then it should be very easy to build mobile tachyon stations," said Morris. "But our facilities are huge."

"That's because we have two problems. First, we have to generate negative energy. To do that, we extract energy from the quantum vacuum and create an energy debt, a kind of sink that functions like negative energy."

"But you said that the tachyons only needed a little of this negative energy to be super-fast."

Morris really wanted to grill him. Another guest sat down at the end of the table. It was Dr. Zakharova.

"Ah, Lydia, were you able to help the recruit?" asked the captain.

"I'm afraid it doesn't look good," replied the doctor.

"Oh, that's terrible. I hope we don't lose the young man. I'll have the stasis chamber checked. Could you take care of that, Lieutenant?"

Morris looked over at the engineer. She nodded.

"But now I want to know why tachyons need so much energy when they only require a little, if you know what I mean."

"Of course, Captain. That's what gave the researchers the most trouble at the beginning. The most complex thing here is shielding the energy sink. The universe is filled with so much radiation, neutrinos pass through us in huge numbers. If we let it, all this matter would pay off our deliberately created energy debt in our name, so to speak. But we don't want that – otherwise the expensively purchased tachyons would disappear again – so we need sophisticated shielding. Above all that requires a lot of space, but also energy. Around half of the total energy required goes into shielding."

"For that reason alone, the Admiralty's ideas are outrageous. There is no ship on which a tachyon weapon could be mounted," said Tann. "We would have to convert an entire minor planet, but even that would only work in the inner solar system. Further out, the sun no longer provides enough energy."

"Well, someone will come up with something," said Morris.

"I'm very curious about these ideas myself," said Monte.

"But isn't it true that you escaped from Neomars because they wanted to force you to develop tachyon weapons?" asked the captain. "The threat can't be purely theoretical."

"I'm not sure what they're saying about me, but my reasons for no longer wanting to work for Neomars are manifold. I didn't like the whole development of society there anymore, I missed Earth..."

"Oh, you're from Earth?" asked Tann. "I never knew that. I thought you were born on Neomars, since you refuse to undergo consciousness purification."

"Oh, there are people like that in the Terran Union too," said a woman from the other side of the table.

"It's their right," said the captain. "Even if it makes it a bit difficult for us to continue our flight. But I haven't quite got behind the tachyon concept yet. You said that half of the energy required is for the shielding. What about the other half?"

Morris continued to test him. What did the captain really know about tachyons? Hopefully no more than Monte. It had been a few years since his friendship with the employee, so he hadn't heard much about the latest developments.

"The other half is in the tachyons themselves," explained Monte. "Their movement is partly along the time axis, as I'm sure you know. I've already explained that the less energy they have, the faster they are. But we don't want them to be too fast. Otherwise, they would dive too deeply into the past. If the source and destination of a transmission are eight light years apart, the tachyons have to travel exactly eight years into the past to give the impression of an instantaneous transmission."

"The impression," said the engineer. "That's an important limitation. Many people believe that it is actually an instantaneous transmission, like quantum entanglement. But that would violate the laws of nature. Information cannot be transmitted faster than the speed of light. So, in Dr. Tsai's example, the tachyons take eight years to reach their destination, but they also travel eight years into the past, so they seem to arrive at the moment they are sent."

"Thinking about it makes my head spin," said Captain Morris.

"Thank you, Anna," said Monte. "That's absolutely right. The cause-and-effect relationship remains intact. The universe doesn't fall into chaos."

"And what would happen if the tachyons reached the recipient too early?" asked Morris.

The captain took a long swig of his beer and leaned back. Monte's mouth was suddenly dry too. He drank. Afterwards, he couldn't help burping slightly. The beer contained more bubbles than he was used to.

"To be honest ..." Monte began.

"I hope so," said Morris and laughed.

"... We don't know. We've never tried," said Monte.

At least that was the official position. His acquaintance told him at the time that there were indeed secret test series that went deeper into the past. However, the woman had only heard that through the grapevine.

"There are theories that all kinds of misfortune could befall us," explained the engineer. "And I think they're right. The fact that something exists before it was created can't be good for the structure of the universe. Even if it's just a tachyon."

"Come on, Anna," said Captain Morris. "You're not one of those doomsayers who want to deny us valuable technology, are you? Just imagine if there were no transmissions. We wouldn't be able to see our families for over ten years! My son would be an adult by then!"

Morris was apparently referring to a small group of physicists who had long warned of the dangers of this technology. They considered it a problem that tachyon transmitters and receivers were not rigidly anchored in space, but moved in relation to each other during a transmission. Although attempts were being made to adjust the energy of the tachyons accordingly, this couldn't be achieved one hundred percent. As a result, some tachyons always ended up in the future and others in the past. An error correction protocol ironed this out in the transmissions. Most physicists believed that the overshooting and undershooting tachyons somehow balanced each other out, although there was still no provable theory.

"No, Captain," said Anna. "I just think we need to be careful. Even if Neomars is researching in this direction, we should refrain from doing so. Maybe only Neomars will then plunge into disaster."

"Difficult to say. I wouldn't want the Terran Union to end up lagging behind Neomars," Morris said. "You know what happened last time."

The technologically superior Mars had attacked Earth back then - at least that was the official version put out by today's Terran Union. Nevertheless, Mars had not fared well – surprisingly badly, in fact – which raised doubts about Earth's actual inferiority at the time. Some even believed that Earth had lured Mars into attacking. A defensive war was always a better sell to the population.

"I think it's not a question of what you can do, but what you want to do," said Monte. "We don't have to research every technology exhaustively. Genetic manipulation of human DNA has never become popular on Earth either."

"Because there is less need for it there than on Neomars, with its cold and toxic atmosphere," said the engineer.

"Let's not argue about politics," said the captain. "We have a gifted physicist with a focus on tachyon research. We should confine ourselves to science. I now understand the principle of tachyon transmitters. But what about the receivers? Why are they so big?"

"They don't actually have to be the size of a transmitter," said Monte. "Transmitters and receivers are always built in pairs. But all you need for the receiver is a tank the size of a basketball court. You fill it with metamaterials that have a refractive index of less than one. This makes the tachyons that pass through the tank visible in the form of Cherenkov radiation. The modulation of the tachyon intensity is calculated from their changes in intensity, and you have a signal."

Whew. Now he really had pulled out all the knowledge he could remember.

"Excuse me, Dr. Tsai - but what is Cherenkov radiation?" asked Morris.

That too! Morris really had it in for him. Monte took a big sip from his glass. The beer was already a little flat.

"If I may interject for a moment," said Dr. Zakharova from the other end of the table. "From a medical point of view, Dr. Tsai should go to her cubicle now. She almost had a heart attack less than twenty-four hours ago."

"Oh, come now, Lydia, don't be a spoilsport," Morris said. "I'm sure Dr. Tsai is eager to explain everything to us. I've met a few female physicists, but you seem to me to be the most gifted."

"I have no choice, sir," said Dr. Zakharova. "Since my patient's health is my responsibility, I must insist that she rest now. I'm sure I don't need to remind you that Dr. Tsai's well-being is also the primary objective of this mission."

Morris sighed. "No, you don't, Lydia. I defer to your authority."

That was more than luck. Dr. Zakharova was indeed an ally. And the engineer also seemed to be a sensible woman. It was a shame the others hadn't introduced themselves. Monte would have liked to know who he was dealing with on this ship. He still had 42 of the 48 hours left.

HE WAS LYING ON THE HARD COT IN HIS UNDERWEAR WITH THE blanket pulled over his chest when there was a knock at his door. Monte sat up. It was dark in the narrow cabin and a draft came through the cracks in the metal walls. He had an idea who the visitor might be.

"Come in," he said.

The door opened. He could tell from the perfume that it was Dr. Zakharova. His sense of smell was definitely better in this body. He found it a disadvantage, if anything - unpleasant odors dominated on such a densely populated ship. Zakharova's perfume was a pleasant change.

"It's me, Lydia. Am I disturbing you?" she asked.

"No. Feel free to turn on the light."

"Better not. The door works purely mechanically, but additional power consumption would be registered. We should leave as few traces as possible."

We? Did Zakharova consider herself his accomplice?

"Of course," he said. "That's always good. Is the cabin bugged?"

"Probably not," said the doctor. "I prepared a different one than the one Morris assigned you. Most of the officers are still asleep, so I had a free choice."

"The officers are asleep, but the recruits had to wake up?"

"No, the ratio is about the same. The ship is just much more crowded than usual."

"That must be hard to bear for a long time."

"I can only stand it with the help of my perfume."

The doctor sat down next to him. He only recognized her outline. The only light in the room came from the wristwatch she was wearing.

"Can you lend me some of that? I really like the scent," he said.

"Of course. I'm Lydia, by the way."

"I'm Tailin."

She put her hand over his. He didn't pull away. Women did this all the time, didn't they?

"I saw right through you," said Lydia.

"Right through me? I'm not sure what you're talking about," he said.

What now? The doctor was a mystery to him.

"It was a brilliant move. You grabbed the physicist and swapped her for a body from the tank. Who told you I would be on board?"

Now he had to be careful to choose the right words.

"I didn't know," he said. "It was a shot in the dark."

"You had to know that any doctor would recognize the Neomars technology. The scar on your neck is far too big. Earthly Biobag technology must be twenty years ahead."

Dr. Zakharova is a Neomartian spy! She had snuck on board to... do what, exactly?

"And what happens now?" asked Lydia.

"I don't know yet. What was your plan?"

"Actually, I should have killed you. There's no way the fucking Terrans should get what we can't have. Of course, I would have gone about it inconspicuously. You would have died in the stasis chamber. Unfortunately, I only saw your scar at the last moment. So now that poor recruit... But it really was a good idea. You couldn't have known that there was a plan B."

Monte pulled his hand away. The doctor was not only a spy, but also a stone-cold murderer.

"How do you manage?" he asked. "I admire that. You must have been around these people for years."

"My great-grandmother fought against the Terran Union. Her parents died in the massacre in Valle Marineris."

"Wow. I'm sorry to hear that."

He had to play the game. If he revealed to Lydia that he had also tricked Neomars, she would probably kill him after all. But with her by his side, he might manage to take over the ship.

"It's not so bad," said Lydia. "It gives my life meaning. Others don't have it so good. Besides, I enjoy the job, even the official part. In the Navy, you get to see a lot of special medical cases. And you? Did you find it difficult to sacrifice yourself for the physicist?"

Sacrifice - that was probably true from the doctor's point of view. If Morris identified him as a Neomartian spy, it would be no laughing matter. They wouldn't kill him, that would be against all conventions, but he wouldn't be released for the rest of his life unless Neomars exchanged him for another captured spy.

"I just can't let myself get caught," he said. "And the scenario really appealed to me. I've only used four Biobags in my life, because there was no other way. So of course, it's all still a bit unfamiliar in this strange body."

"I've noticed that too. Sometimes you move as if you're still testing your limits. I don't think the others have noticed yet, because they know how you feel in a new Biobag."

"And then of course the physics. Morris really put me to the test. I'm a pilot, not a scientist. Thanks for getting me out of that situation."

"You're welcome." Lydia felt for his knee and put her hand on it. Monte didn't stop her. "The captain suspects something," she said, "but he can't confirm it. Morris has good instincts. He can smell when something's wrong. I've known him for quite a long time. If you refuse consciousness purification, you shouldn't really have any problems in the stasis chamber."

"Yes, that wasn't planned. We'll have to report that the Neomars Biobags are having such problems."

"That's not a priority for now," said the doctor. "We have to get you to safety somehow, and in such a way that the captain doesn't find out your secret. The ship with the physicist in it is certainly not too far away."

"Yes, I'm afraid that's true. The *Vanguard* could certainly still pick it up in interstellar space. But I know a way to prevent my secret from being revealed."

"And what is that?"

"We don't do anything. I'll lie down in the stasis tank and the acceleration will kill me. Morris won't be able to squeeze any more answers out of the sludge that's left."

"Would you be willing to do that?" asked Lydia.

Of course not. But he wanted her to believe it so that she trusted him.

"If it has to be... The physicist is more important than me, that's clear. I always knew it would come to this at some point. Sometimes you have to make sacrifices for your homeland."

Hopefully he wasn't laying it on too thick. But it seemed to work for Lydia. She scooted closer to him.

"That's really heroic of you. I like people who commit their lives to something. Unfortunately, we can't solve it that easily."

"We can't? Why?"

Pure luck. Lydia was obviously ready to see him die heroically.

"It's obvious you're not a physicist," she said. "You won't turn into sludge. You'll just have a heart attack. After that, I'll have to perform an autopsy on you and find out that your body was made on Mars."

"Can't you somehow slip that into the report?"

"No, an autopsy like that always takes place in the presence of expert witnesses. We have two other doctors on board. They're still asleep, but they'd be woken up for it."

"Damn," he said.

Wonderful.

Lydia didn't answer. She got up and paced back and forth in the cabin. Monte inconspicuously wiped away the film of sweat her hand had left on his bare knee.

"I can really only see one way forward," he finally said. "I have to take over the ship. At least until the physicist is safely out of reach. Do you think we have a chance?"

Lydia paused. "That's the craziest idea I've ever heard. You want to hijack an entire Terran Union battleship?"

"Well, when you put it like that, it does sound crazy," he said. "Let's just stick to 'taking over'."

"Haha. Well, if that makes it easier... I don't know. The idea is so crazy that it could work. Nobody will be expecting it. But you do realize that the entire Terran Union fleet will be after you?"

"Not that quickly. We're three light years away from the nearest tachyon transmitter, and probably about five light years from the nearest larger Terran ships. It will be at least three years before they even notice the hijacking, and then they won't catch us for a long time yet."

In fact, he didn't want to take over the *Vanguard* for that long. A month should be enough for Tailin to be safe. If he then returned the ship to Morris and gave him a Neomartian spy to boot, he might get off lightly.

Or not. There wasn't much point in thinking about it now.

"That's true," said Lydia. "But I don't know if the battleship can be flown solo for such a long time. You'd have to put the entire crew into stasis chambers, as well as the officers. How will you motivate them to do that?"

"With their lives, Lydia. All I need is control of the ship. Then I'll speed it up so much that the people on board will have no choice but to take shelter in the stasis chambers."

"There will be a few who have to play hero," said the doctor.

Yes, that was the weak point in his plan. Was he really prepared to kill people for this? The recruits here hadn't done anything to him. They signed up for the Navy to have a secure income. There hadn't been a war for 150 years. They certainly didn't plan to die.

"I can't prevent that," he said. "Let them die a hero's death. But how do I get into the control computer?"

"Can you tell me exactly what you need? Maybe I can arrange something."

"I need a place where I can upload without anyone noticing. And then I need access to the controls, with the captain's authorizations."

"Very modest demands," said Lydia.

"Exactly."

"And when you're inside, do you know what you have to do?"

"I'm a pilot, Lydia. I'm trained on all types of ships."

"Okay. I might be able to help you with the consciousness purification. But you'll have to find your own way to the controls. I'm not familiar with the computer technology on board."

"That's too bad," he said.

"You don't have any ideas yet?" asked the doctor.

He shook his head.

"Then you should think of something as soon as possible. You still have thirty-six hours."

"I will. Please don't take offense, Lydia, but I need absolute peace and quiet."

"Of course you do. I have to organize something anyway. Will you tell me your real name?"

"Tailin, Lydia. I am Tailin. Knowing more would only put you in danger."

Gliese 163 c

THE RADIO WOKE THEM UP.

"TransVec to Albatross, come in!" It was Claire's voice. Mark raised himself up and bumped his head on something hard.

"Shit," he said, rubbing his forehead.

"You've given us friendlier greetings in the past," Claire said.

Shit. Mark refrained from swearing out loud again. Tailin had obviously set the radio to activate automatically.

"Mark here," he said. "Glad you're back!"

"That's better," said Claire. "We'll be docking in two hours. You can start fixing lunch."

Mark wasn't in the mood for a happy reunion, and Tailin probably felt the same way. Claire and Karima, however, knew nothing of Roger's death. They had spent the flight here from Planet d asleep.

"I'm sorry, but there's been a problem," Mark said.

"Have you used up the supplies already?" asked Claire.

"No, we didn't have time for that," replied Mark.

"You've finally found intelligent life."

"No. We're on the surface."

"All three of you? That's against all the rules, isn't it?"

Mark took a deep breath. He had to tell her. But how?

"It was an emergency," he tried. "We lost Roger."

"Lost him? What do you mean?" Karima interjected. "Did he get lost?"

Mark heard the hope in her question. He envied that a little.

She and Roger had known each other for a long time and had been very good friends. But he would have to extinguish any remaining hope. It was best if he didn't say too much.

"Roger is dead. I'm sorry."

He heard a sob but couldn't tell who it was. Maybe they were both crying. Tailin reached for his hand. She was still naked. Tears were running down her face too. He envied her, because he had no tears left.

THE SPACE STATION LOOKED TINY NEXT TO THE TRANSVEC. THIS was mainly due to the gigantic tank that contained supporting mass for acceleration phases. It completely enveloped the actual ship. The engine bundle looked small in comparison. If the tank were an apple, the spaceship would be its core and the engines would be the stalk. The orbital station to which the TransVec had docked, on the other hand, looked barely bigger than a louse on the skin of an apple.

Mark switched on the emergency Hopper's automatic coupling system. The TransVec had already deployed its collector, which was supposed to replenish the support mass supplies from the base of the atmosphere. The thin net was barely visible and did not leave a clear radar echo, but was a deadly obstacle at the relative speeds of the Hopper and TransVec. As they were approaching from a lower orbit, they first had to overtake the ship, including the collector, which Mark preferred to leave to the autopilot. It worked with data from the ship's computer and could react much faster than he could.

CLAIRE AND KARIMA WERE WAITING FOR THEM BEHIND THE INNER door of the airlock. They fell into each other's arms one by one. There were no more tears. But Karima felt strangely stiff when he hugged her. There seemed to be an invisible, rigid shell around her.

They floated into the control center. It smelled different from when he had left in a hurry, fresher, and the fingerprints on the porthole had disappeared. Mark suspected it was Claire. The two of them had only been back on board for a day, but perhaps she wanted to distract herself with cleaning.

The synthesizer whistled. Claire pushed herself off the ceiling and floated over to the device. Suddenly there was an intense smell of onions and baked flour. Claire came back with five fist-sized balls.

"Onion pie," she said, handing out the balls.

They were still hot, so Mark passed them back and forth between his left and right hand.

"There's one too many..." Claire said, bursting into tears.

Had she deliberately made one too many or had she been in her head and blocked out Roger's death? Karima hugged her. Tailin was on the verge of tears. Mark heard it because she gritted her teeth so hard, they squeaked.

"I'm so sorry," said Tailin. "I blame myself so much."

They had discussed the timeline of the accident over the radio. Had Claire and Karima already looked at Roger's remains?

"It wasn't your fault," said Karima. "I know Roger. There was no stopping him from helping."

If Tailin hadn't gone out, Roger wouldn't have decided to help her. Mark turned away. He couldn't look at his wife, but he wasn't sure why. Did he feel sorry for her - or did he blame her for Roger's death? He believed Karima that there was no way he could have kept Roger from going to rescue her, because that exonerated him. He could have taken control of the Hopper away from his friend... He suppressed the thought.

"Have you told his family yet?" Claire asked.

"No. We haven't even reported it to the Ministry," said Mark. "There hasn't been time. Besides, they won't find out for at least seven years."

It would take that long to send a radio transmission to the nearest inhabited planet, and from there it would be relayed to Neomars via tachyon transmission.

"Before we leave, we should definitely send a report," said Claire.

"Absolutely," said Karima. "Roger's husband needs to know before we get back."

"Does he have children?" asked Tailin. "I mean, did he have."

Karima nodded. "He has two. He gave birth to them himself."

Ah, that explained the two scars in the lower abdomen. Mark had discovered them during the autopsy. It was a common procedure to insert an artificial womb when a man desired to bear a child. It was closest to the traditional way. However, some couples preferred external parenthood. Since the harsh conditions on Titan meant that no one could do without certain genetic adaptations, the only option was to conceive in a lab.

Mark swallowed. Hopefully he would never have to face Roger's husband or their children.

"Why did he leave his family behind in the solar system?" asked Tailin.

That was a good question. Strangely enough, he had never spoken with Roger about it, though they had been friends.

"He didn't," said Karima. "His husband works at the Neomars embassy on Terra Nova. The children are there too. Roger applied for our research mission at short notice because his husband was called away on a mission. He wanted to make good use of his waiting time."

That was a clever strategy. Sometimes family members even put themselves in stasis to stay synchronized during unavoidable interstellar journeys. Mark shuddered. That meant they would definitely have to meet Roger's family. Terra Nova, formerly known as Gliese 167, was the closest system with a tachyon transmitter, and their first destination with the TransVec.

ONE MORE WEEK. MARK COUNTED THE DAYS THEY STILL HAD TO spend in the Gliese-163 system. An unhealthy silence had descended on the Albatross. He tried to fight it, but couldn't. *We all deal with grief differently*, Claire had explained to him. Karima didn't want to talk about Roger, and he accepted that. With his wife, on the other hand, he had to consciously avoid the subject. She kept trying to force him to talk about it, but what good would it do? He would just end up blaming her, while in reality, he blamed himself.

It wouldn't help. They just had to do their work until it was time to leave. The time came surprisingly quickly: two weeks and two days after the TransVec docked with the Albatross, it reported full support mass tanks. This meant the time had come to return, as they had already exceeded their contractual time limit by six months.

Nevertheless, Mark was surprised that no one objected when he announced the news at the daily briefing. Yesterday, Tailin had wondered aloud whether they should set up another ground station to make the geophysical measurements more precise. Today, however, she was the first to agree.

"About time," she said, pushing herself off and performing a backward roll over the dining table.

"Good to know," Claire said. "I'll retrieve my atmospheric probes, then."

She disappeared into the adjoining room. As a chemist, she was examining the planet's atmosphere, which was characterized by a high sulfur dioxide content and above-average energy content.

"I'll check the systems," said Karima, who was the ship's engineer. "Mark, can you maybe help me? Roger used to..."

Suddenly there was no sound in her voice, as if she couldn't breathe.

"Yeah, sure. Just tell me what you want me to do."

In his role as commander, Mark didn't have much to do at this point. He had been ignoring the planet's flora and fauna for days. He hadn't even tried to salvage the multifeet's skin or analyze its leavings. There didn't seem to be any point anymore. It was good that Karima had a task for him. Just before they left, he would have to assess each crewmember as a doctor to see if they were fit for stasis. But that was the last step.

August 6, 2802, Earth's moon

Yini was sweating, even though she hadn't moved at all, and her skin was completely cool. Cold sweat. But this story was especially dramatic. Until now, she had usually only had to chronicle dull visits by ministry officials to the worlds of the Terran Union. Treaties were always particularly important. In order to be able to fulfill them exactly, all sides had to know exactly what had been discussed and when.

This was very different. Yini had feared it would be boring after Tsai Tailin left, but it was quite the opposite. Why did Pedramonte think he could take over an entire battleship all by himself? Yini was tempted to research the people from the transmission in the Miscellaneous department. But didn't she only want to do that so that she could visit Mike again sooner?

She took her head out of the reading bowl, put on her wig and stood up. Something was bothering her. She felt her right ear. The wig was pressing a little on the birthmark there. She adjusted its position. She really had done enough work for today. She got up two hours earlier than usual and had played the stream twenty percent faster to make up for the hours she had missed yesterday. That was particularly exhausting, especially as the content of the broadcast was full of drama.

Now she had to clear her head. Yini looked up at the ceiling. A clock had just moved up from the door, showing 5 p.m. standard time. Her brother was certainly no longer with Zahir. He wasn't always happy to see her, since he liked to spend hours playing in other realities. But today she needed him to keep her company so she could take her mind off things.

Yini sniffed her clothes. To her, the sweat was clearly noticeable, but Kang wouldn't notice. She pulled on a jacket. She felt freezing, and sometimes it was very cold in the corridors outside. In fact, a cold wind blew on her when she opened the door. The archive's energy budget had probably gone overboard again. Kang liked to complain about it - compared with the immeasurable energy consumption of the tachyon transmitter, a little bit of heating was negligible. But a budget was a budget and bureaucracy was bureaucracy. Was it any different in the past?

She pulled her jacket tighter around her. On the other hand, there was nothing wrong with dressing warmly. A basic set of clothes was free, after all, and her body reliably heated up to 98 degrees without any budget. There was a lot to be happy about. She remembered the sight of the Earth rising a few days ago. The planet really was on the mend. She felt like repeating the trip, but something else interested her even more.

Kang's room was only a few steps away. It only served as accommodation; as janitor, the entire archive was his workshop. Yini knocked. He didn't answer. She was sure he was in his room, but she didn't want to catch him doing something that was none of her business. She put her ear to the door and heard Kang moan loudly. It was a pain-filled sound. Then he said something she couldn't quite make out. It sounded like "Stop right there, damn it!"

She opened the door. From a rack attached to the ceiling, Kang was suspended over a treadmill, slashing at an invisible opponent with a sword. Yini approached. She had no interest in this activity. As long as you were in the suit and had the mask on, everything seemed very real, but all you had to do was push up the mask and it lost all meaning. For her, any virtual world was boring compared to reality.

Kang saw it differently. She took another step closer so that she came within range of his sword. Red light suddenly leaked out from the edge of his mask.

Kang ripped the mask off his face. "Shit, who's there?"

"Me of course, who else?" she replied.

"Hey, are you saying I don't have any other friends?" He was sensitive about that question. Kang probably knew far more people in the inner solar system than she did, but here on the moon, he never socialized with anyone other than his sister.

"No, Kang. I don't want to argue. Are you up for a little trip?"

Kang dropped the sword, pushed up the mask and felt around in the air with both hands. Then he took the mask off. The frame lowered him to the ground. He climbed out of the harness.

"Just parked my glider real quick," he explained. "Surface or tunnel?"

"Tunnel," Yini replied, because she didn't want to go through the awkward procedure necessary to visit the surface. You could reach almost anywhere on the moon via a tunnel.

"Turn around," he said.

Shortly afterwards, a wave of unpleasant odors reached her nose. Kang must have really worn himself out.

"Don't be angry with me, but you'll have to..."

"I'm on my way."

The door to his hygiene wing clanged, then the water rushed. Yini felt a twinge of guilt because she hadn't showered herself. However, she hadn't been fighting any Martian monsters either. She picked up the suit from the floor and hung it on the rack in the middle of the room. Then she took Kang's underwear to the small basket next to the locker. It was full to the brim. Her brother really did live up to all the clichés. But she wasn't responsible for his upbringing, and he was a grown man.

"So, what are you up to?" he asked.

Now Kang smelled intensely of pine needles. Yini had to close her eyes several times to dispel the image of a thicket of conifers springing up around her brother. It wasn't the first time something like this had happened to her. Kang had once speculated that perhaps she was the only one who could see through the virtual reality in which they lived. He had been infected with AR fever for three years now. Perhaps that was why he had failed the eavesdropping exam. But he enjoyed his job with Zahir, even if he did like to complain about his boss's nitpicking.

"So?" he asked impatiently.

"Sorry about that. I thought you could show me the tachyon receiver."

"The receiver? The transmitter is much more impressive," he said.

"Maybe later. But the receiver first."

Claudio Pedramonte's description from the broadcast had aroused her curiosity. "Cherenkov radiation" – that alone sounded very mysterious. Her brother certainly knew what it was. But she didn't want to spoil the surprise.

ON THE WAY, KANG EXPLAINED THE PRINCIPLE OF TACHYON transmission to her. Yini countered with what she had learned. It turned out that she knew some details more precisely than her brother.

"It sounds really interesting - what you're chronoscribing, I mean," he said.

"It is."

How much of it was she allowed to tell him? Officially, she had to maintain confidentiality even with her brother. But if it really was about her mother, it concerned him just as much as her. But she still had no hard evidence. No, it would only upset him unnecessarily. Above all, he would interfere in her investigation, and she would no longer be in control.

"Aren't you at least going to give me a hint of what this is about?" he asked.

"You know I'm not allowed to do that."

"It didn't bother you to pass on the story about the Neomars ambassador."

That had been a mistake. She had recognized the Neomars ambassador to Earth in the transmission of a high-ranking diplomat from the Terran Union. In a sex scene. She had told Kang about it. Afterwards, everyone in the archive seemed to know about it. Kang had always maintained his innocence, but she couldn't be sure.

"And we know how that turned out," she said.

They ran in leaps and bounds through a connecting tunnel that linked the archive with the tachyon complex. It was wide enough for two rovers to drive through side by side. Handholds and footrests were attached to the ceiling and floor so that they could take advantage of the low lunar gravity and swing through the corridor like a monkey. Yini was in no hurry, but an older woman using this technique was coming towards them. They made way for her by pressing themselves against the wall.

"It wasn't me, back then," Kang said.

"I know."

The tunnel opened up. For a few hundred yards, it ran on the surface. Why hadn't Kang mentioned that before? There were windows in the tunnel wall through which the surface of the moon was visible. It was broad daylight. On the left, the sun shone on a sea of mirrors that captured the energy needed for the tachyon system. On the right was the still untouched lunar landscape. That was becoming increasingly rare. Environmental protection groups had long been campaigning for its preservation.

"Why are we above ground?" asked Yini.

"We're not above ground," replied Kang. "It's not like we're on Earth."

"Smartass. You know what I mean."

"The area below us is completely hollowed out. To ensure stability, nothing more can be built into the moon rock here."

That sounded logical. The tachyon facility was older than the Great Archive, which had been built after its completion. The idea that instant transmission would cause certain synchronization problems only surfaced later. The physicists claimed they had continually pointed this out, but apparently, they had not been able to make themselves understood.

Yini envisioned the tachyon transmitter. According to Pedramonte's description, it consisted of absolute nothingness. Every form of matter had to be blocked out, in order to create a real energy debt to the universe. It was not a white hole that was the opposite of a black hole, but the structure that the researchers had built here in a gigantic cavern inside the moon. They had punched a hole in the cosmos from which the ominous tachyons tumbled, only to be fed with varying levels of energy to slow them down, until they could be sent in measured doses in the direction of the desired recipient. It would be impossible to see. There could be no blacker black than in this cave beneath her.

"What did you really want to show me about the tachyon transmitter?" she asked.

"You haven't seen the ring of fire yet, have you?"

"Ring of fire? That sounds exciting."

"That's the shielding. You can imagine it as a ball of wire mesh. It's actually several hundred rings that constantly rotate synchronously around the tachyon source. They move so fast that they repel any normal incoming particles. But there are openings for the tachyons. From the outside, it looks like a small version of the sun. The rings rotate so rapidly that you can't see the holes in the surface with the naked eye."

"I can see the sun by looking out the window."

"That's true. But with the ring of fire, you know that it only consists of a thin layer and is completely hollow inside. The strangest thing is that you can't see it from the inside. Once you're inside, there's only darkness because it doesn't even let light particles through."

"Has anyone ever seen that?"

Kang laughed. "It's impossible to break through the ring of fire. Even if it were possible, the matter you're made of would light up the inside. It would be completely different. Absolute darkness only exists as long as there is no observer."

"So we can't be sure it exists at all."

"No. The tachyon transmitter works, though, as predicted by our theories. So the thing about absolute darkness should also be true."

"Oh, I love physics."

Kang smiled at her. He showed such enthusiasm for research, and yet he worked as a janitor. Perhaps he could have been a scientist after all.

"I have a great paper on tachyon physics in the office. I'll send it to you. Did you know that scientists have suggested hollowing out the sun like the moon? Not our sun, but another star. That could be used to build a tremendously powerful tachyon transmitter."

"Isn't what we have here enough?" asked Yini.

"Just about, at the moment," replied Kang. "We can reliably reach the most important colonies within a radius of about fifty light years. But going beyond that would be difficult, because the tachyon channel would widen. We would have to increase the power tenfold to double the bridgeable distance. Remember that the outermost outposts of humanity are now about a hundred and fifty light years away."

"But those are purely scientific outposts."

"You're right, we don't have the means to set up a tachyon station there anyway. You'd need a highly developed colony for that, like Terra Nova. But things will be different in five hundred or a thousand years. Besides..."

Kang faltered.

"Besides?" she asked.

"Please don't think I'm a weirdo now, okay?"

"Of course not. You're my brother. I know when you're being crazy."

"Besides, it's about contact with superintelligences."

"Superintelligences."

Maybe he was a little weird after all. In their exploration of space, humanity had not yet encountered any intelligence on a par with itself, let alone a superintelligence, whatever Kang imagined that to be.

"Yes, superintelligences," he said. "With a tachyon transmitter the size of a star, we could communicate with systems almost as far as the core of the Milky Way, meaning within a radius of about twenty thousand light years."

"And you think there's someone there who might want to talk to us?" asked Yini.

"Maybe there is. I hope so."

"But then these superintelligences would also have to use tachyon communication, wouldn't they?"

"There's no other way. No civilization can spread significantly with maximum light-speed communication. With that, you only ever have individual islands of stars."

"But then why aren't we picking up their transmissions, Kang?"

"Maybe because our receiver isn't good enough? Of course, we would have to build a much larger version."

"You're assuming that they work with star-sized transmitters."

"Yes, okay, so they should actually be generating signals that we can detect."

"But we're not hearing anything. So they don't exist - or they're deliberately not transmitting in our direction because we're too immature for them."

"Hm." Kang's mouth twisted. He didn't seem to like her argument. But he probably didn't know how to disagree, either.

"Look, we're here," he said.

How convenient for him. The entrance they had stopped at consisted of a double door. There was an iris scanner on the right-hand side, which Kang used. The lock buzzed and Kang opened the door.

"We're allowed in here just like that?" asked Yini.

"A janitor can go anywhere," replied Kang. "But you can't break or spy on anything here either. You'll see that in a moment."

Behind the front door was a brightly lit corridor, with some offices apparently leading off it. Kang opened another door on the right-hand side. Behind it was a staircase that led down several flights. There it ended in a strange corridor. Strange, because although the floor and walls were made of stone, the ceiling was made of a material that looked like black glass.

"We are now under the reception tank," Kang explained. "This corridor leads to the other side and then back up again."

"Does it have any function?" asked Yini.

"Not that I know of. It was probably built for curious people like you."

Yini wanted to go into the corridor, but her brother held her back. He opened a locker in an alcove and took out two long gowns. He gave one to Yini. It was surprisingly heavy. She put it on without asking any questions.

"Radiation protection," Kang said. "A lot of the radiation produced is in the X-ray spectrum. Here, I'll give you a hat too."

"I don't need one; it's built into my wig."

"Really?"

"No." She took the hat from him and pulled it over her head. It covered the back of her neck and her forehead. "It just feels like that sometimes."

Kang looked strange, like a soldier in a dystopian movie.

"But if it's all X-rays, is there anything to see?" she asked, walking into the corridor and looking at the black glass ceiling.

"You'll see."

Her brother followed her. What awaited them? They walked into the corridor side by side. The light went out before they reached the middle, and Yini stopped.

"Hold on for a second," said Kang. "Your eyes need to adjust."

Yini waited. The glass remained black. Sometimes she thought she perceived a thin, bluish glow, but that proved to be an illusion every time. She wanted it too much.

"Transmissions don't come in continuously," Kang said. "Everyone must be on break right now."

That was when it started. Out of the corner of her eye, she saw a blue wave blaze overhead, almost crash into a red wave, then quickly move away. And again. It was as if an ocean of water and a sea of blood were measuring their strength against each other. But the waves did not collide, only almost, and then moved away. The red wave behaved normally, but the blue wave seemed to her as if it were developing in mirror image, or no, with time reversed. The fact that it reached the center actually seemed to represent the end of its movement, although Yini always noticed it first. The blue wave was like a ball of wool rolling itself up, while the red one unraveled.

She tried her hand at an interpretation. "Let me guess," she said, "what we're seeing isn't the tachyons."

"Right," said Kang. "We're seeing the Cherenkov radiation produced when the tachyons interact with the mass in the tank."

"Mass in the tank? Is it water?"

"No, it's an expensive quantum liquid with a refractive index of less than one. That's the only way Cherenkov radiation can be produced."

"And the two differently colored waves are created to the left and right of the tachyon's path?"

"Again, no. What you see is the interaction of the same tachyon packet with the matter in the tank. Since the tachyons move at faster-than-light speed, they overtake the interaction. You can therefore see them twice, once as they come and once as they go. For you, this happens in parallel. One version is shifted to blue, the other to red."

She saw the same event happening in duplicate. Tachyons obviously had a harder time hiding than other particles, even though they were so fast.

"Didn't you say something about X-rays?" she asked.

"Yes, Yini. Everything happens in the X-ray and ultraviolet

range. But the special glass in the ceiling converts it into the optical range."

"For viewers?"

"No, that would be far too expensive. It's for the cameras distributed through the tank. They operate in the optical range. They record all interactions and send the data to the central computer. It calculates how strong the signal was and where it came from, and finally decodes it."

"And then it goes into the archive as a data stream," said Yini.

With the help of these red and blue waves, she was able to experience the consciousness of people from far away. It was impressive what humans had achieved and created.

"And now imagine if this technology was available to everyone," said Kang. "With a system the size of the sun, we could connect all humanity. You could control your Biobag or your robot body in a distant solar system live from Earth. No one would have to travel far anymore. I could play live games with people from other colonies in my AR environment."

"That's very important, obviously," Yini scoffed.

"It was just an example. It would all be so much more efficient! At the moment, we have millions - or is it billions? - of surplus Biobags waiting around somewhere for a visit. We could do without them completely. All the consciousnesses could be stored in a large station in solar orbit, and anyone who wanted to travel would establish a live connection to a biological or electromechanical carrier."

"And you would enjoy that?"

Yini found the idea of storing her consciousness in a gigantic computer repulsive. How was that even living?

"That's the only way humanity can really colonize the entire Milky Way," said Kang.

"But why would it want to do that if no one is actually moving?"

"Out of curiosity," said Kang. "I think what really unites all humans is not skin color or gender or whether they belong to the Terran Union or Neomars, but our curiosity. We want to know what's beyond the horizon."

Yini thought about it. What Kang said sounded good, and yet she couldn't bring herself to agree with him. She and her body belonged together. Her consciousness lived on the sensations provided by her body, smell, taste, sexual arousal, but also pain, disgust and even the sour smell of vomit.

She looked at the black glass above her. Two different colored waves met again, and again. She stared without pause, but each time she had the feeling that she had looked a moment too late. Yini turned around in a flash, as if her gaze could follow the tachyon packet, which of course had long since disappeared into the distance. And into the past, if the sender had aimed it at the station on the moon.

The wave she had just seen might be in a transmission she had to chronoscribe tomorrow.

"How do we actually know which packages are meant for us?" she asked.

"It's done using ancient protocols that were actually invented for the terrestrial data network," Kang said. "Basically, the sender and recipient are written into every package."

A new wave passed above her. Then the next one. And another one. The whole pool lit up.

"What's going on now?" she asked.

"I don't know," said her brother. "I would guess that we're receiving tachyon transmissions from several directions. Otherwise it wouldn't be affecting the whole tank."

"Is there a maximum, then?" she asked.

"A maximum capacity? Yes, there is. But I don't think it's ever been reached. Do you want to see the transmitter now?"

Yini yawned. "That's not necessary. Let's go get something to eat instead. I think I want to go to bed early tonight. I have to get some work done tomorrow, and I want to finish early."

"Do you have plans?"

Her cheeks grew hot. Luckily it was dark, so her brother didn't notice.

"Just a bit of research in old files. The people in my current broadcast are pretty interesting."

I'm looking for our biological mother, and in the process, I've met a man I could fall in love with. That would have been more honest. But it was still too soon for either statement. Yini joined her brother, and they made their way back. He still smelled of pine needles. She loved that scent. Maybe she should borrow his shampoo so she could shower with it tomorrow. Before... She took a deep breath.

"You're different today somehow," Kang said.

"What do you mean?"

"Well, you're hanging out with me, for one thing. Is something wrong? Do you have something bad to tell me? Is Mom afraid to tell me she has cancer or something?"

Kang had always been their mother's favorite child. Her father had looked after Yini more.

"No, what are you thinking? Enough of this. Everything is the same as always. Now, you'd better explain to me what Cherenkov radiation is all about."

HALF AN HOUR AFTER HER BROTHER LEFT HER, SHE COULDN'T stand it any longer. Yini blamed it on her curiosity. She had no other reason to visit Dr. Mike Wilson today. None. Nevertheless, she quickly put on her favorite scent and changed into the T-shirt she had been wearing all afternoon with Kang.

She reached the Miscellaneous department in record time because she was worried that Mike would get off work punctually. He wasn't the type to always leave work at the same time, but it was possible he would make an exception today. She knocked on the door. When nothing happened after a second, she was absolutely certain that today was that exceptional day. Her mood sank. She shouldn't have come here. The day had been so pleasant so far.

Then she remembered her first visit - and what was behind the door. If he was somewhere in the huge hall, Mike wouldn't be able to hear her. She clutched her chest, and her heart calmed down again under her warm fingers. Yini pressed the handle, pulled the door towards her - and was startled to see someone standing on the other side. The person, who was wearing a coat that was no longer completely white, also jerked back, far enough to bump into the railing behind them.

In the low gravity of the moon, the momentum was enough to send them toppling over the metal bar. It must be ten yards to the ground. The person, whom she recognized as Mike Wilson, cried out. Yini stood still, frozen. She knew what to do, but her brain seemed to be stuck in a loop. Finally a repeated command from her brain reached her legs, which catapulted her forward.

Yini had calculated her leap to connect with Mike at thigh level. However, he had tilted so far towards the horizontal that Yini got his right foot in her face instead. She felt the sole hit her eye. The left foot moved aside at just the right moment. But Yini didn't let the pain keep her from her task, managing to reverse the momentum. As quickly as Mike had tumbled backwards, he now swiveled forwards, faster still. But there was an obstacle, Yini's body, so he folded over her like a pocketknife.

Although the pain made her eyes water, Yini had to laugh. How could anyone be so dumb? The two of them really were a couple of klutzes. Mike looked at her in seeming confusion for a moment. She wasn't sure, because now they were rolling down one flight of stairs, then two, then three. Finally Mike joined in the laughter.

They found themselves clutching each other on the first landing, and their bodies seemed to have magically rearranged themselves. Their legs were down, their torsos were pressed together. Their hands had found each other, and their heads were so close together that Yini could see the fine, red veins in Mike's eye.

"May I?" she asked.

Mike nodded without speaking, and she kissed him. Their lips touched, then played over each other. Mike seemed a little awkward at first. She was bolder than he was and explored him while he tried to catch the tip of her tongue. He tasted good.

Suddenly he flinched. Had she overwhelmed him? Heat rose in Yini's cheeks.

"Your eye," he said.

Now she could feel the pain again. She felt her eye gingerly. The skin around it was very sensitive, and she found it difficult to close her eyelid. Mike got up and helped her up. Then he led her into the part of the hall that he had set up as his office. There, he pushed a shelf aside to open up a passageway. Behind it was a room with a single bed, a wardrobe and a small desk.

"This is my little kingdom," he explained.

"It's nice," she said, and she wasn't lying.

The walls were plain, but they were full of photos, documents and objects. Each of them must have a story. They could spend weeks in this room without running out of stories. Even the ceiling was decorated with collector's items hanging from a camouflage net, presumably from military stock.

"Come on, you should put something cool on your eye," Mike said, leading her to a narrow door that concealed a small bathroom.

It was spotlessly clean and had a toilet, a shower and a small washbasin. Yini turned on the tap. The water was icy.

"Eighty degrees," she said and held her hands under the tap.

The water was still cold.

"Warm air," she ordered.

The water continued to flow.

"Sorry, it's all purely mechanical," Mike said, turning off the tap and handing her a towel.

He turned the tap a little further to the right, opened it again and held a cloth under it. He wrung out the cloth and handed it to her. The cloth was cool and damp, but not dripping wet.

"Hold it to your eye," he said. "That will help."

Yini would have preferred to have a robodoc look at it, but then they would have to leave the cozy room. She didn't want to wander through the cool corridors of the moon station. She wanted to lie on the bed with Mike and listen to him talk about the pictures on the walls. Maybe she would kiss him, even if that risked him not continuing the story.

"Sorry, I didn't say hello to you," he said.

She nodded.

"Yes, well, it's nice to see you," he said.

Yini didn't say anything. She wanted to see how long he could keep it up.

"You're probably here for the letters," he said. "I wasn't actually expecting you until tomorrow."

Oh, and why were you standing behind the door when I showed up? She swayed her head.

"But I'm glad you're here, of course. To be honest, I thought I heard you knocking several times today. I ran up the stairs each time to check, but it was nothing."

She nodded again. He had obviously been longing for her too. That was good news. What could possibly go wrong now?

"Shall we go get the letters now?" he asked.

She didn't answer, but made no effort to get up from the bed either.

Tachyon: The Weapon

"I'm such a doofus," he said. "You can't see a thing with that rag over your eye! What are we going to do?"

Yini didn't say anything. This was more and more fun.

"You know what?" he said. "I'll just bring the letters here. Then I'll read them to you."

If she didn't speak up now, he really would go get those stupid letters. At the moment, she wasn't interested in the past at all. Only the present mattered. Yini yawned expansively. Would that be enough? Having made the first move earlier, she wanted to wait and see what he would do.

"You look tired," he said. "It must have been a shock."

Hm, he wasn't talking about the letters anymore, but she wasn't really tired at all.

"I can offer you my bed," he said. "You've probably had a long day; I can understand that. I'll sleep on a mattress on the floor."

He bent down and pulled a mattress out from under the bed. Now she really had to intervene, or this wouldn't end as she had imagined. She drew up her left leg and gently kicked Mike's bottom, just hard enough to make him fall onto the mattress. Finally, she crawled after him until they were lying next to each other.

Their heads were close together again. Mike was breathing heavily. He had turned away from her.

"Will you look at me, Mike?"

He didn't respond and she repeated the question. This time he complied with her request. His face was wet. Mike was crying. It was a beautiful and at the same time terribly sad sight. Was he shedding tears because of her? That had never happened to her before.

"What's wrong?" she asked.

"It's so nice to be here," he said.

Mike was right. It was beautiful. "And you're crying? Are they like happy tears?"

His face didn't look like that at all. His mouth had twisted into a sad frown.

"No, I'm sad," he said. "They're farewell tears."

"Farewell tears? Are you not enjoying my company?"

Mike didn't seem entirely uncomplicated, but that only excited her more.

215

"I just know it'll be over soon. Because..."

He broke off. She kissed him on the nose, and tasted salt. Her mouth wandered over his skin. She wanted to take in every tear she could find. For a moment, Mike returned her kisses as he had earlier on the stairs, but then he let go of her again and froze. When she touched his upper body, he pushed her hands aside.

Yini sighed. What was wrong with Mike? Had he experienced something terrible?

"Can you explain it to me?" she asked.

"I ... like you," he said.

That was the exact opposite of an explanation. So why didn't he allow her to touch him? *Of course*! He adhered to a religion that regulated sex. That had to be it.

"I really like being with you," he said. "I enjoy the warmth of your skin and being close to you. I feel safe and secure and would love to lie in this bed with you longer."

"And what's to stop us if that's what we want?" she asked. "Is it your... faith?"

Her parents had raised her without religion. Yini did not know of any official church in the Terran Union that rejected sex. But there were probably smaller sects that preferred to keep to themselves.

Mike shook his head. "It's what I am."

"What you are? You're a smart, pleasant, curious, a little opinionated, but empathetic person. I don't care about anything else."

Of course, Yini was curious about what he meant by that. But it certainly didn't detract from her affection for him.

"Yini, it's simply that I'm not interested in the physical aspects of love." He blushed and turned away. "There, now you know."

"You don't like sex?"

"I don't care about it. I like the closeness."

"I like sex."

"That's what I thought. In that case, it won't work with us."

Mike was a know-it-all. She already knew that. With know-it-alls, she always felt the need to show them that they were wrong.

"How would you know that?" she asked.

"It's never worked for me. I'm almost thirty now and I've never had a relationship worthy of the name."

Almost thirty? She had estimated him to be forty. That was probably because of his old-fashioned clothes.

"But they were other women," she said.

"Not only. For a while I thought I was gay. But I don't want to have sex with men either. Of course, that never worked for long. Sex is somehow part of getting to know each other, isn't it?"

Was it? When she was in love, she also felt lust. And sometimes even when she wasn't in love. But she had already learned how to satisfy this desire when she was twelve. She didn't necessarily need another person to do it.

"You love the closeness," she said.

"Yes, I could lie next to you for hours, stroking and kissing you."

He turned back to her.

"I'd love that," she said.

In fact, she had wished for more closeness from some of her relationships, as Mike described them.

"Would you mind if I take care of it myself?"

"Not at all," said Mike. "On the contrary. I would feel incredibly close to you. Maybe I could even... help you."

Yini laughed. She could bring herself to orgasm more reliably than anyone else – at least that was her practical experience, confirmed again and again over the twelve years since her first conscious climax. But perhaps Mike was more gifted in that respect. After all, he wasn't distracted by his own needs. That could certainly be a plus.

She was weighing up the pros and cons as if she were buying a space yacht or a new AR suite. She had only ever entertained such considerations in the past when a relationship became boring. This thing with Mike, whatever it would become, was something special. That at least was perfectly clear.

She shook her head.

"You don't believe me?" Mike asked.

"No, I was just thinking about something," she replied.

"May I ask what?"

He brushed a strand of hair from his forehead and looked at her. Yini liked that look. It was open, but not intrusive.

"You can always ask," she said. "I've been thinking about whether something could happen with us and haven't really come to any conclusions."

A vertical crease grew on Mike's forehead. Yini gently ran her index and middle fingers over it and the wrinkle disappeared.

"But I've been thinking that we could give it a try."

"Give it a try? What?" he asked.

"Anything. What you want. How you want it."

Yini carefully stroked her left breast with the palm of her hand. A bump appeared in the fabric of her T-shirt.

"Come close," Mike said.

"Yes, be close to me, please."

June 30, 2799, Battleship Vanguard

There was irregular knocking. Clanking in the distance. The tugging sound of a heavily burdened carrier. Slimy wiping, followed by an enervating scratching that made his hair stand on end. *Pock, pock, pock. Peck, peck, peck.* He felt as if a woodpecker was living in the *Vanguard*. Monte couldn't sleep. The ship was speaking to him. What was it trying to tell him? That he shouldn't sleep. Maybe he misunderstood Lydia after all, and she was still trying to kill him.

No, that wasn't it. He still didn't know how to access the controls. How would earthly pirates have done it when ships still sailed the seas? They would have taken the key from the captain, who would have handed it over either voluntarily or under duress.

Morris was no coward. Even if Monte threatened him with death, he wouldn't hand over his ship. Morris had to be outsmarted. He was very self-confident. After all, he had risen to the command of a battleship. How many other captains of this level were there still living? Probably barely more than three, at least within the solar system. The two warring parties had agreed to decommission the majority of their fleets. Monte only had one advantage. Morris didn't know that he could get into the computer network. That meant they had to carry out the consciousness purification inconspicuously.

Lydia Zakharova met him in his cabin. She greeted him with a nod. The rucksack she was carrying was unusual. Monte preferred not to ask about it, because they might be bugged. The doctor led him all over the ship. Was she just trying to confuse him? They finally stopped in front of a washroom. The door had the typical symbol for "men" on it. Lydia opened it anyway, ushered Monte in and closed the door behind them.

The light switched on automatically. The room was tiled right up to the ceiling. There were five showers on the left, which were not separated from each other, and washbasins on the right. There were two toilet cubicles at the opposite end of the room. Lydia pulled him to the left, and pushed him in. What was she doing? Was she planning to extract his consciousness in the toilet?

The doctor pressed the flush button. She pressed it again while the water was still flowing. Then she raised the seat, lowered it again and raised it once more. Suddenly something squeaked. A flap had opened in the wall above the toilet tank. It was at a height that you couldn't see from outside the toilet cubicle. Lydia pointed to it. Monte climbed onto the toilet lid and the cistern and pulled himself into the opening.

In front of him was a corridor that he could only traverse on all fours. He crawled off without Lydia needing to tell him. The corridor was unlit, and Monte followed it carefully. It turned 90 degrees once, then again, and finally ended in a dead end. Monte felt the wall, but it seemed to be solid.

"And now?" he asked.

"Just push on it," said Lydia behind him.

He pushed against the wall, but nothing happened.

"This thing has to open," said the doctor. "Wait, I'll brace you."

She pushed him from behind. They joined forces and pushed against the wall. Suddenly it sprang open. It was a flap like the one through which they had entered the corridor.

It was dark behind the hatch. Lydia passed up a stick-shaped object. It was a flashlight. He shone it into the room behind the hatch. They had come out in another toilet. In the light of the electric torch, Monte climbed out of the corridor and opened the door of the cubicle. The whole room was tiled. There were showers on one side and washbasins on the other. This room was a mirror image of the men's washroom they had just come through. There was only one difference: there was a lounger on the side with the showers.

Lydia pushed it aside. It must have been blocking the doorway. Then she knelt down and took off her rucksack. Monte recognized a cuboid block.

"That's a battery," Lydia answered his unspoken question. "This room is off grid, so it won't be noticeable when we do your purification here. But we'll need a lot of energy."

"That's very fitting. A washroom for the conscious mind," he said.

"Haha. That's right."

"This room, did you build it in secret?" he asked.

"No, how do you think I could have done that? It's been here since the battleship was built. We had people in the Terran Union shipyards. We're pretty safe from Morris here."

"No one has ever noticed that there are blind spots in the ship's volume?"

"Compared to the size of the battleship, this room is tiny. There's only the one entrance."

"Then why didn't they build a nice headquarters for spies? The furnishings are a bit sparse."

"They used what was available. Washroom facilities caused the least suspicion, I think."

Lydia might be right. Did every Terran Union battleship have such secret rooms? And what about the other side? Did Earth also have spies as good as Lydia undoubtedly was?

"I'd say we should start," said Lydia.

"Right. No time to lose."

Monte opened the door of the second cubicle. To upload his consciousness, they needed a stasis chamber, which he assumed was inside. But all he found was another toilet.

"Just lie down on the couch," said the doctor.

Lydia made her way to the foot of the couch. She pulled a cable out of the battery and connected it to a socket. Monte examined the couch. It was waist-high, its cushions hard. A shiny metallic arch was installed on the head end, much wider than his head. Was that the reader?

"That's supposed to do consciousness purification?" he asked.

"Yes, it should work," Lydia replied.

"Should?"

He scratched his temple. Lydia didn't sound very convincing.

"I've never tried it," she said. "This is actually an eavesdropping device."

"Eavesdropping device? I don't understand."

"It's what they use in tachyon stations to chronoscribe."

"I've never heard of that."

"You explained it to the captain yourself yesterday. Tachyon transmissions have to be precisely timed so as not to disturb the passage of time. Chronoscribes do that with the help of eavesdropping devices like this. They can follow what the sender of the broadcast has experienced."

That was creepy. No wonder the public didn't hear much about it.

"So that means someone could be listening in on our conversation right now? And that's supposed to be legal?"

"No, of course not." The doctor moved the battery behind the couch and stood up. "If you ever send your consciousness to Earth via tachyon transmission, a chronoscribe might check it. You confirm that you agree to this before each transmission."

"Hm, maybe I should read the small print more often."

"It doesn't affect most people anyway. Chronoscribes are only needed to accurately classify important events. It's mostly about contract law. That's dead boring. When I was still living on Luna, I was in a relationship with a chronoscribe for a while. He never had any interesting stories to tell."

If a Terran Union battleship was hijacked, perhaps that would be an important event. Monte was glad that the nearest tachyon transmitter was three light years away. Until then, these chronoscribes shouldn't be able to find him.

"Very reassuring," he said. "But what am I supposed to do on this chronoscribe couch?"

"The principle of eavesdropping is the same as that of consciousness purification, only it works in the other direction. I believe I can reverse that."

"You believe?"

"As I said, I've never tried it. But there's nothing technically wrong with it."

"And what happens if it doesn't work?"

Tachyon: The Weapon

Then you wake up again and everything is back to normal, was what he would have liked to hear.

"You experience a split consciousness. In the worst-case scenario, the two parts won't be able to function independently of each other. Then you'd be a case for mind surgery."

"What?"

"Don't worry, that doesn't apply to you anyway. We don't have a consciousness surgeon on board, and even if we did, he wouldn't be allowed to treat the consequences of an illegal purification."

What a prospect! He had never really thought very much about consciousness purification before. Maybe he should have read the small print.

"Does consciousness splitting happen frequently?" he asked.

"No, it happens very rarely. Only if the device breaks down in the middle of the process or the power fails."

Monte walked around the couch and squatted down in front of the battery.

"If this lovely battery here runs out before I finish, what would happen?"

"Why do you ask? You already know. We shouldn't talk much longer, or our absence will be noticed. Yesterday you were ready to be crushed in the stasis chamber, and today you're racking your brains over an innovative experiment? Think of the higher cause you're involved in!"

"Right again."

Monte stood up and put his arm around Lydia's shoulders. She mustn't suspect that he might not be on her side.

"Can't we use one of the conventional consciousness purifiers?"

He couldn't help but ask the question.

"The power consumption would be noticed immediately. Your advantage of no one expecting you in there would be gone, and I'd probably be found out too."

"You're right, Lydia. That wouldn't be a good idea. Let's get started."

Monte had his head in a noose - literally. Lydia had shaved him - what a shame about Tailin's beautiful hair! - and bent the metal arc of the eavesdropping device completely around his skull. She was also busy securing him to the couch. He was not allowed to change his position during the extraction, even if he sneezed. This was Lydia's reasoning for securing his arms and legs to the feet of the stretcher. She used ropes that felt relatively soft, but there was no way he would be able to undo the knots she tied.

If all goes well! And what if he had to return to his body for some reason, but Lydia was no longer there? Then he would die in her shackles on the couch. It certainly wouldn't be a pleasant death.

"I'm sorry," said the doctor, "but I'll have to pull the knots a little tighter."

She carried out her threat. Sweat was running down his forehead, and something was tickling his right temple.

"Can you scratch my temple, please?" he asked.

Lydia complied with his request, but then his bladder started to bother him.

"Shit, I should have gone to the toilet first," he said.

"You really should have thought about that earlier, my dear," said Lydia.

"Can't you just..."

"There's no way. I have to meet with Morris in less than half an hour. If I'm late, he'll get suspicious. Do you want me to put something under you?"

"No, don't bother."

"Suit yourself. But I advise you to let it go now. During the reading phase, any disturbance is potentially harmful."

That too. This body had a weak bladder. But Monte didn't want to put his consciousness at risk just because he had to pee. He tried to relax his sphincter. Under Lydia's gaze, however, he was unable to do so.

"Can you at least turn around?"

"As you wish," said the doctor in a snippy voice and turned around.

What was so strange about his request? It was embarrassing enough that she knew what he was about to be forced to do. Monte closed his eyes and imagined himself in the shower. He let the water run, relaxed and ... *Ugh*, it became wet between his thighs. He waited until the stream dried up. Surprisingly, he hardly smelled anything.

"So, we can start," he said.

"It's about time."

Lydia stood by his head. Then something rattled. It sounded like fingers on a keyboard.

"The couch is connected to the battleship's computer systems?" he asked.

"Of course not. We're in a part of the ship that's perfectly sealed off from the rest."

"Wait a minute, how do I get to my destination? How am I supposed to take over the ship?"

"Your consciousness will be temporarily stored in my backpack. It contains not only a battery, but a powerful computer."

"So you'll connect the memory to the main computer later?"

Lydia laughed. "No, my darling. I will take you with me to Neomars."

The doctor was preparing to betray him! And he had thought himself so clever.

"Are you out of your mind? As soon as they find my body, they'll realize it's a clone. Then it'll be your turn, because you didn't tell Morris."

"Not at all. First of all, they won't find you. This room has been here since the battleship was built hundreds of years ago. Your pretty clone body will rot in here without anyone noticing. But to make sure your absence is not noticed, I will launch a small shuttle that will self-destruct as soon as they capture it. Dr. Tsai will be officially dead to the Terran Union once and for all. Captain Morris won't like it, and I'm sure he'll be relieved of his command. I'll then take my time to prepare for my escape to Neomars. If you're nice to me in the meantime, I'll take you with me and set you free there."

Damn it. Monte strained all his muscles, but his shackles didn't budge.

"You're only hurting yourself," said Lydia. "I'm a professional like you. It's nothing personal. You have to believe me. I actually think you're quite nice. We could be friends, don't you think?"

"Friends? You're crazy! I only spoke to you in the first place because I needed you."

"You see, you're a professional too. I don't hold that against you. You had your plan and I had mine. But if you think about it carefully, you'll realize that mine has a much better chance. Apart from the fact that you set yourself an impossible task, it wouldn't have solved the problem with Dr. Tsai. The Terrans would still be looking for her. My idea, on the other hand, solves all the problems without me being exposed. Which didn't even play a role in your plan."

Monte had to admit one thing: Lydia's plan was better, at least when it came to not letting the tachyon physicist fall into the hands of the Terrans. And until this second, he had no idea how he could bring the ship under his control.

"Okay, you win," he said. "But why didn't you tell me all this? Don't you trust me?"

"Exactly. I don't trust you any more than you trust me. First lesson in any spy training: don't trust anyone. I don't even know who you are. Besides, this plan worked so much better. Just convincing you to let me tie you up would probably have taken me days."

The doctor was right about that, too. Knowing that he would end up in Lydia's computer for an indefinite period of time afterwards, there was no way he would have gotten on the couch.

"Well, it doesn't matter now," she said. "We should get started."

Monte tried to nod, but even that was prevented by the hoop over his forehead. The moisture between his thighs was gradually cooling.

"Then get started. Do I have to do anything?"

"You shouldn't try to resist. Otherwise, it will be painful."

"How do you do that, not resist?"

Normally, test subjects were put to sleep during consciousness purification. He'd never been through anything like this while awake.

"You'll see in a moment. I'll turn on the power now. Otherwise, the battery will run out too soon."

Monte sighed. At least he could still do that. Suddenly he was hanging upside down over an abyss. The abyss consisted of the mouth of a giant worm with teeth all around it. A stench came from its maw, which seemed strange to him, because the worm wasn't breathing out, it was breathing in. Everything flowed toward the worm and disappeared inside it. The worm didn't just breathe in, it sucked in air like a compressor and made similar noises.

Monte's hair was coming loose. First a few strands, then all of them were pulled out. But that was not enough for the worm. It had its sights set on Monte's scalp. It burst into his skull, tore it into shreds and plunged into his gullet. The worm licked its lips with a huge tongue. The small, sharp teeth scored the tongue all over and it bled. Monte was bleeding too. Blood dripped from his skull directly into the worm's mouth. Even that was not enough for it. The worm opened its mouth. A moment ago, it was large. Now it was about the diameter of its head. It engulfed his naked, skinless skull from below. The teeth pressed into the calcareous material of the bones. Like a rotating saw, they dug in until the worm detached itself from his head again. Monte was relieved at first. The worm had returned to its original shape. Although it was huge, it was so far away that it no longer posed an immediate danger. But then Monte realized it had changed. His head was open at the top. The lid was missing, and under the suction of the inhaling worm, his brain detached. He was losing his brain. All that would remain of him was a mindless body, a puppet, a doll. If only he could grasp it! But his arms were tied.

The worm wanted everything. It wouldn't settle for anything less. *What did Lydia say?* He shouldn't resist. He stopped trying to pull his hands out of the restraints. Plop. That was it. He saw the typical walnut shape of his brain tumble down the worm's gullet. It looked very pink, as if someone had painted it that way. Monte was briefly surprised that he could still think, but then there was only a light bulb in his head, illuminating an empty memory. Someone pressed a button, and his empty skull was plunged into eternal darkness.

WHEN HE WOKE UP, IT WAS DARK. MONTE REACHED FOR THE blanket, but he was not lying in bed. There was no blanket either, and he had no hands with which to reach for anything. He had nothing. No, that wasn't true. He had a heart. It beat reassuringly and strongly. It beat more constantly than his heart had ever worked before. It was not his heart, but that of the computer into which Lydia had banished him. Then he remembered.

That was good news, wasn't it? At least he didn't have the split consciousness that the doctor threatened him with. He was complete. He could just see nothing, hear nothing, smell nothing, and feel nothing. He had never experienced such complete sensory deprivation. Lydia's computer didn't seem to be connected to the outside world, not even a little bit. Did such a thing still exist today, computers with no connection to the outside world? Well, if they did exist, it was in the hands of spies like Lydia.

Monte sat down. He couldn't perceive anything of his surroundings, but he still had his physical sense. He knew where he ended and where he began, and which joints hurt when he sat down awkwardly. He started to count, since the computer's heartbeat was the only stimulus that illuminated his prison. After a while, he felt it like the light of a lighthouse intermittently shining through a window that he couldn't reach from his position.

At some point it did become light. Monte had counted several billion cycles. It could be just as many billions of years, or only two - or a thousandth of a second.

"Welcome to the other side!"

The greeting appeared as if on an inner screen.

"When am I?" he asked.

"Cool question," the text replied.

It must be Lydia writing to him.

"An answer would be nice," he wrote.

Strictly speaking, he only thought the sentence, but it appeared as text on the screen hanging somewhere between him and the end of the universe.

"It's been about two hours since your consciousness purification. I had an appointment with Morris, but now I wanted to check on you. Are you all right?"

"I can't complain."

"Really? That reassures me. You're sure nothing is missing?"

"No. Should something be missing? What's bothering you so much?"

"Your Biobag is pretty much ruined. I don't understand how that could have happened."

The worm had eaten it. "What happened?" he asked.

"Did you put up a fight? I told you to let it happen."

Lydia had a good point. But she hadn't seen the monster's sharp teeth. "I did have the rather unpleasant feeling of hanging upside down in the mouth of a huge worm."

"Ah, so you did put up a fight. That's what I thought. Your wrists and ankles are covered in blood. You managed to get your…"

The cursor flashed in the fog. Was it possible that the battery was slowly running out of power after all?

"My…?" he asked.

"You literally ripped off your own right hand. I've never seen anything like it."

Ripped off? Monte felt a shiver run down his spine, though he no longer had a back.

"That's probably the reason why consciousness purification is only carried out on sleeping test subjects," he said.

"Probably. I must thank you for this exciting insight. It could be helpful for my colleagues in counterintelligence."

"Too bad you weren't there the whole time. You couldn't even watch it."

"I recorded it, Tailin. Someone once suggested that I test the cleaning on an awake person. I had to wait a long time to finally try it out."

Lydia had made him her guinea pig! If he could have, he would have wrung her neck. But he couldn't. On the contrary, if he wanted to have a chance of ever escaping from this prison, he had to be nice to her. He still had an advantage: she didn't know who he really was and thought he was a pilot from Neomars. But how could he use that advantage? Was it an advantage at all?

"Could you at least turn on the microphone and speakers for me?"

Suddenly he heard the typical sound of fingers on a keyboard. It sounded like the cheerful chirping of birds after a long winter.

"Can you hear me?" he asked.

"I can hear you. But your voice sounds strange."

Of course – he had instinctively used Claudio Pedramonte's

voice parameters, not Tsai Tailin's. He switched to the higher frequencies.

"Is it better like this?" he asked.

"It's perfect that way. But you have to promise me not to say anything if there's anyone else in the room besides me."

"How can I promise that if I can't see who's in the room?"

"That's true, of course. Wait."

All at once, he was hovering close to Lydia's face. He immediately shifted his focus to avoid looking directly up her nose.

"Thank you," he said. "I imagine we'll make a good team. And congratulations again on your plan. When is the shuttle with Tsai Tailin due to leave?"

"Tomorrow," said Lydia. "The sooner the better. Today you supposedly retired to your cabin because of a stomach problem."

Lydia dissolved. Her face disintegrated into countless triangles that collapsed in on themselves. Something beeped piercingly.

"Shit, I have to plug you..."

The world faded out. He fell into a tunnel, ran towards the bright spot at its end, ran for his life. He stumbled, then fell and died.

August 7, 2802, Earth's moon

FOR THE FIRST TIME IN HER EXPERIENCE AS AN EAVESDROPPER, Yini started her working day late. She found it hard to concentrate, so she paused Claudio Pedramonte's transmissions and attended to a Terra Nova embassy official's recollections of recently concluded negotiations with Neomars. The recording was extremely boring, but it allowed her to think about her own problems in addition to simply recording dates and time periods. Problems ... no, that wasn't even the right word. Last night everything had felt logical. The first time she had come with just her hand while looking into Mike's eyes, and he had kissed her. During her second orgasm he was lying behind her, and she had guided his hand to the places she liked. It still excited her now whenever she thought about it.

But was there any future in it? Afterwards, she had gratefully offered to give Mike a climax too, because she had noticed that his member was erect. But he smiled at her and refused. Then they had fallen asleep close together. It hadn't even bothered her that the bed was so narrow. Mike had simply put his arm around her and prevented her from rolling out of bed.

In the morning, Yini had retreated frantically. She now realized that she hadn't hurried because she wanted to start work on time. She was unsure whether what she had felt yesterday would last. This was not unusual for her; other relationships had started in a similar way. When could she be sure what she was feeling? Only when it was over. And it wasn't, or everything wouldn't be so difficult. The thought calmed her down and she was able to immerse herself in the world of the stressed diplomat again.

This time she didn't knock on the door of the Miscellaneous department. It was her third visit. She ran down the stairs where they had kissed. Mike came towards her. He must have heard her footsteps. They stopped in front of each other without saying anything. Yini saw the same insecurity in his eyes that plagued her.

She smiled, and at the same moment Mike smiled. He took the last step and they hugged.

"Nice to see you," he said after a quarter of a century.

Maybe it had only been a minute. Yini nodded. She felt like disappearing with Mike into his room. Would she be allowed to? He loved the closeness, he had said. But how often did he feel the need to actually feel her? They would have to have several more conversations.

"I already got the letters out for you," he said.

So not the bed. That was okay. She was here for the letters, wasn't she? Somehow, she was afraid of them.

"I'm getting a visit from another department in ten minutes," Mike explained. "They want to reconcile some data with written contracts I have in stock here. I hope you can excuse me for that long."

"Of course," she said. "Can I ask you about the sender of the letters first?"

"Gladly," Mike said. "Mark Decker. I've done a bit of research on him."

"So, his letters are pretty fascinating."

"Perhaps you shouldn't believe everything they say. Supposedly, experts have analyzed both their content and conversations with his ex-colleagues, and diagnosed Decker with full-blown psychosis. There were no traces of foreign cells on the neopaper he wrote them on. Either he had excellent hygiene, or... On the other hand, molecules of certain psychotropic substances were detected."

Decker, a fraud? She couldn't believe it. No one could have just made up something like that. The fact was that he had worked as an astrobiologist on the Albatross space station in orbit around Gliese-163.

Mike led her to his room. The bed was neatly made, but a faint aroma of sweat and bodily fluids still hung in the air. Her nipples stiffened involuntarily as she imagined the scene from last night. Mike didn't seem to notice. He adjusted her chair in front of the small desk, and Yini took a seat. The chair was comfortable. Its backrest moved with her body.

The desk was stacked full. The documents for her lay in a plastic tray marked "Yini". What would they tell her? Did it have anything to do with her? Maybe this was a dead end. Her parents lived in the ring. Period. End of story. There was no mystery - except for the question of why her parents had to flee Neomars back then.

"Dear Tailin," the letter began.

Yini took a deep breath and leaned back. It felt strange, even if this letter could not be addressed to her mother.

"I know you won't understand," the author wrote.

Yini leafed through the pages. This was not the original, but a copy. Nevertheless, the writing had the smell of distance. She had developed a nose for it. At the very end she found the signature:

"Mark"

She jumped back to the beginning.

"You can't understand, that's clear," Decker continued. "Of course, this is all my fault, just as I take the blame for Roger's death. I alone could have prevented this madness. You are who you are. But I was the commander, and I knew Roger well enough. But I was thinking more about you than about him, and that was a mistake. That's why I couldn't stay on board the TransVec.

"You don't know it, but I watched you for a long time before I let you go. You were already lying in the glass coffin they so innocuously call a stasis chamber. You were almost dead, but not quite. At that moment, I fully realized that I could never be with you again. I forfeited that right when I took away an important member of Roger's family. All three of them will miss him for the rest of their lives.

"I imagined how you would try to convince me of my innocence. I even saw you speak, even though you no longer had a pulse. You took all the blame, but that only made everything harder because it made me angry with you. I wanted to drag you out of your glass coffin, call you names, maybe even hit you for putting us in this position, and it would have just been the anger I felt at myself."

Yini was confused. Decker was describing a goodbye. That much was clear, even if she didn't understand the context. He had obviously only started making these notes afterwards. She tried to visualize Mark Decker in her mind's eye. She still had no real picture of him. As an astronaut, he was certainly in good shape. Based on his name, she pictured short, blond hair and an energetic chin. Blue eyes, no, blue-grey, a large, classic nose, but pale lips.

"Afterwards, I took a final tour of the ship. The TransVec is an impressive piece of technology. I wanted to make sure it would get you home safely. At the same time, I said goodbye - to Neomars, but also to the solar system as a whole, which I will never see again. I still have a lifespan of perhaps thirty or forty years, and I don't expect a ship to stray to Gliese 163 in that time. There's nothing here except a few curious multifeet.

"However, should humanity decide to come here on a new mission in a thousand or ten thousand years, they may find a primitive civilization. Please tell them that, Tailin. Thank you. I wouldn't put it past the multifeet, if they can bring themselves to form larger groups instead of roaming the darkness of the brine forests in groups of five or six at most. They have potential and, above all, more empathy than humans could ever muster. I just hope that this will never work to their disadvantage. Adad is obviously unsuitable for human colonization - so the multifeet shouldn't be in any danger from us."

Multifeet – she had read about those unusual animals. Was this really about them? Yini imagined the eighteen-legged animals swinging in hammocks and discussing canteen food. They would have to get used to it. No system-dominating civilization could develop in groups of three to five individuals. But maybe that wasn't the point.

What was Mark Decker talking about? Why had he written this letter? What did it mean to her? Why was she reading his thoughts, which were not addressed to her? She didn't feel guilty. Mark Decker was too far away. He wasn't part of her life and never would be.

Her back ached. Sometimes she felt like an old woman. Groaning, Yini leaned forward a little. The pile Mike had organized the letters into slipped off her lap.

Crap. She knelt on the floor. Most of the papers remained in a pile, lying face up. She turned them over. But a few pieces of paper had escaped faster than the rest. She gathered them up and looked at each one. The letters almost always began with "Dear Tailin". They were undated, which must have made them difficult for other readers to understand. Decker had probably not really written them for his wife, but for himself. Which was logical, because he had assumed that these letters would never reach the solar system.

Decker was a strange man. Even if his wife was her mother, the probability that he was her father was close to zero. After all, there had been no talk of a pregnancy so far. Hopefully, it would stay that way.

She put the pile back on the sofa. The order of the letters might have got mixed up. When she read them, she would sort out which events Decker described in which order. After all, her job was to put things in their exact chronological order, and she was good at it.

July 1, 2799, Battleship Vanguard

"What does it feel like to die?"

He was still struggling to gather his scattered components. They didn't fit together at all. There were memories that were not his, needs that he had never had, images that frightened him. It was as if a house of cards had collapsed, and he had to reconstruct it faithfully from the cards.

"Tell me, Tailin. It must be a very special feeling."

Only now did he realize that this thought came from outside. He didn't know from whom, but it was reassuring that there was an outside and a second being. He was not alone.

Tailin, that was a name. He clung to it. The name took on a shape. At last, he could pull individual threads of thought out of the tangle that his consciousness had curled up into. The concept of Tailin grew. He acquired a body and memories. He was about to move into the new house, yet it didn't fit. It was not too small. The size was perfect. But it was still too small. He was confused. *Easy now.* The start had been made.

He twisted and turned Tailin in front of his inner eye. All at once, a memory popped out. Monte. Monte had saved Tailin. He had taken over her body. Claudio Pedramonte. A new clue, a cell. Once again, he pulled thread after thread out of the ball. The cell multiplied and grew into a cluster of cells, differentiated, formed organs and limbs and finally also sensory organs with which IT could see, smell, hear, feel and taste the huge store of memories that were part of the concept of Monte.

He moved in. He became Monte. He was full of rage. He was about to burst. He found his voice and screamed.

"Fuck you, Lydia!"

"That wasn't nice," the voice replied.

Lydia. A form appeared. Dr. Lydia Zakharova, the doctor who locked him in this computer and then cut off his power. *Shit.* He was dependent on her because she had tricked him. How could he trust her? But was there any other way? He remembered the sentence that woke him up. It was a question.

"Dying sucks," he said.

"You've developed a bad habit... I'd like it if you could return to basic politeness."

"Fuck you, I've already said it."

"I'm afraid I'm going to have to reboot the computer and reorganize the memory. Dying obviously didn't do you any good."

"No, Lydia, I didn't like it at all."

He remembered the tunnel, the desperate race to the bright spot. It was over quickly. Waking up was much worse, the feeling of not knowing who he was, of being broken into a million splinters. But that was none of Lydia's business. If he told her, he'd just be giving her ammunition. He wanted her to experience for herself what it was like to die, even if he couldn't see any way to make that happen.

"That's much better," she praised him.

She thought she could make him her lapdog. But she was wrong. As soon as an opportunity arose, he would make a run for it. She couldn't keep him isolated in this computer forever.

"You'll have to excuse me. I wasn't quite myself yet," he said.

"Of course, Tailin. I'm sometimes a bit grumpy in the morning after I wake up."

"And what happens now?" he asked.

"First of all, I'll fully charge your batteries. Later, I'll take you to the shuttle. Then you just have to do your bit for our cause, and we'll part company for good."

He'd never have to see her again? That sounded like paradise.

"My contribution? What do you mean?"

"We want to organize your escape in a credible way. You have to be on board, of course. I'll connect you to the on-board computer. That way you can let everyone know that you've set off on your journey."

"But won't they be surprised that my body is missing? Surely they'll search the shuttle?"

"There won't be enough of it left to reconstruct your body, because you'll activate the self-destruct. But I've taken blood from your Biobag so I can spread DNA traces."

"You really do think of everything."

"That's my job. I couldn't have spent my life among these fucking Terrans if I could afford to make mistakes."

"And you were criticizing my language earlier."

"They wiped out a large part of my family in the Martian wars! Do you think I could ever forget that? How can you actually do that?"

"There, that's good," said Lydia.

She put the rucksack down and unpacked the computer, which allowed him to finally see something again. They were in a large room full of screens. Lights were flashing and there was a babble of voices. A person in uniform was sitting at every other console. This must be the control center, or at least a room next to it.

"I'll plug you into the socket here now," said Lydia. "In the meantime, I'll take control of one of the shuttles. I prepared this years ago in case of an emergency where I needed to get away quickly. It's always nice to see a plan work out in the end."

She was delighted with her own cunning. Presumably a prerequisite for living amongst strangers for so long, who mustn't discover her actual mission. Even the Neomars Secret Service probably didn't know exactly what Lydia was doing here.

"It won't take long," she said. "I just need to start the manipulated copy of the system software that I have stored in the key management system."

Lydia turned around and disappeared behind a console. A uniformed man walked past the computer Monte was in but paid it no mind. Lydia's plan seemed to be working smoothly. But the way Lydia had described it had a rather stale aftertaste, because then Monte would definitely not be in a position to kick her ass anymore. Which was his top priority right now.

Which meant he should probably sabotage her plan. Someone approached from the door, and he spotted a ponytail peeking out from under the uniform cap.

"Hey, Martina!" he called out. "What are you doing here?"

The woman ignored him.

"Alarm! Alarm! Alarm!" he shouted.

Nothing happened. Lydia had apparently switched off his speakers. She was quite clever. He also had no connection to the battleship's data network, but it was too soon to give up. The computer was connected to the power grid. It should be possible to send signals through that!

What was the best way to increase the power consumption? It had to be quick. Lydia was sure to be back soon. Monte could create a simulation of the three-body problem. But that would take too long. What if he simply calculated a few multi-digit prime numbers? He started with a twenty-digit number, but was finished in a few microseconds. It had to be forty digits for the power requirement to increase long enough that a normal person would notice. The next prime number. He calculated in time with Morse code. First, he sent an SOS, then he formulated a short text:

"Shuttle hijacking imminent. Secure the key. A friend."

He encoded the text in Morse code and sent it by calculating more and more prime numbers.

"Hey, Andrea, come here," called a man sitting just a few consoles away.

At least Lydia hadn't switched off his microphone. How kind of her. The person with the ponytail walked through the scene. She leaned over the keyboard next to the man. The man stared at her neckline. It was obviously not just Monte who noticed, because the woman with the ponytail suddenly smacked the man upside the head.

"Hey, are you crazy?" he shouted.

"You asked for it, Paul. Or do you want another one?"

The man shook his head. Monte, who had paused briefly during the scene, quickly continued calculating prime numbers.

"What's up?" asked the woman.

"It's gone now," said the man.

"Oh, come on! If you brought me here for nothing..." The woman raised her hand threateningly.

"Ah, there it is again," said the man. "Look! This is the current track record at the head office."

"Pretty low," said Andrea, "but that's no wonder, most of them are still asleep."

"I mean the fine line up here."

The man pointed to the top left-hand corner of the screen. That was all Monte could make out.

"Looks like noise," said the woman.

Noise? Those must be his signals! *Please take a closer look!*

"It's actually a distinct noise," said the man. "It could be that a power supply unit is about to burn out. This kind of noise is typical before failures. We should find out what's causing it. Otherwise, we'll end up with a cascade of failures."

Come on, it's not noise. Why don't you take a closer look?

"Ah, wait," said the woman, tapping the screen. "See, if you pull that apart, you get a structure. It's not white noise."

"You're right, Andrea. But then what's causing the irregularity?"

It's a message, dumbass.

"It could be anything," said the woman. "Something that rhythmically calls up computing power. Remember we had that once when the commander was secretly playing AR sex games in his cabin?"

The man chuckled. Who knew what he was imagining instead of examining the structure more closely.

"What am I supposed to do about it?" he asked.

"It's not a defect, anyway. Nothing that indicates an imminent failure."

"Shouldn't I report it?"

"No, don't bother. It'll only cause trouble and it'll be even longer before we're allowed to sleep again. Pass it on to me. You have a recording, don't you?"

The man turned frantically to the screen and tapped on it. "Yes, it's recorded," he said.

"Very good, then please forward it to my console."

The woman squeezed the man's shoulder, and he bent over. Then she adjusted her ponytail under her uniform cap and disappeared from view. *Damn.* Now Monte could no longer see what she was doing. He had to draw her attention to himself. He changed the rhythm in which he was calculating prime numbers.

"SOS. Hello Andrea. Shuttle hijacking imminent. Around the corner on the right. Computer connected to the socket. Come here."

The text wasn't as clear as the first version, but he couldn't think of any other way to describe his location. He calculated diligently - and hoped that Lydia would take even longer.

It took about three minutes for the woman with the ponytail to reappear. She strode over to the man she called Paul earlier and gave him another slap.

"Ouch," said Paul, looking at her with a scrunched-up face. "What are you doing? Next time I'll report you!" Andrea stood in front of him with her hands on her hips.

"Haha! You'll be reporting your idiotic foolishness at the same time! We've been separated for three months, but you don't seem to get it and you're wasting my time!"

"I'm wasting your time? Huh? I was just drawing your attention to a strange phenomenon."

"A phenomenon that begins with 'Hello Andrea'. Without a comma, of course. Typical! You think I don't recognize that?"

"Excuse me?"

"Now the gentleman is playing dumb. But I'm not falling for it. Morse code, how primitive. Can't you think of anything better?"

"I have no idea what you're talking about."

Poor Paul. Hopefully his ex-girlfriend would sit down at her desk again soon. Monte had long since rebuilt his warning.

"SOS. This isn't Paul talking. The warning is real. Shuttle hijacking imminent. Corner to the right. Computer on power outlet. You have to free me."

Andrea blew the air out of her lungs, stuck her hands in her trouser pockets, shook her head and finally disappeared behind the console again. Now all she had to do was decipher the new message. Hopefully she would give it a try.

"Paul?" she called out.

"What now? I'm innocent," replied the man.

"Forget it!" she shouted.

No, don't forget it. Why don't you just take what it says seriously? She must have read the text. What else could he do?

Tachyon: The Weapon

Suddenly her face appeared at the corner of the console. Her gaze wandered across the floor and then fell exactly on his camera eye. Did she recognize him? At the very least, she must realize that there really was a computer plugged into the socket that didn't belong here!

She raised her eyebrows. She must be thinking, *so that part of the message was true*. Monte finished his prime number calculation. Andrea must act soon. If she could plug him into the data network somewhere here, he would be saved. Lydia's plan could still work, but he wouldn't be killed. It would be best if he could lock the Neomars spy herself into the shuttle. Then he would be happy to switch on the ship's self-destruct function. She really had brought him to the point where he was fantasizing about murder. And he had always considered himself a peaceful person.

The uniformed woman with the ponytail was now walking around the console. Monte would have liked to flash every light the computer had, but he didn't have access to that either.

"Is that you writing me messages here?" asked the uniformed woman.

Yes, it's me, who else could it be? But he couldn't answer her.

"Actually, I have nothing to do with this," said Andrea. "That's why it would be nice if you could give me a signal that you understand me."

A signal, a signal - no, Lydia had done a great job. He could only communicate by manipulating the power requirement. Although... Couldn't a microphone also be used as a speaker? He just needed to control the voltage. Wait a minute. The computer's electronics were largely reconfigurable. A small modification, a new cable path. That was it.

"If you don't say anything, I'm calling security," said the woman. "I don't want to get myself into any trouble."

"Don't," he forced out of the microphone.

The woman in front of him twitched. "Did you just say something? It was so quiet!"

"Please help me," he said.

Monte couldn't tell how loudly he was speaking because he couldn't hear anything while he was using the microphone as a speaker. But he could see from the woman's face that she had heard something. Her eyes were focused exactly on the spot where his microphone was. But she seemed to be unsure what she had heard.

"Please help me," he tried again.

The woman leaned down towards him. At the same moment, she was pulled aside.

"How dare you, Chief Petty Officer? Has anyone authorized you to touch this computer?"

It was Lydia. It was all for nothing. The uniformed woman immediately took a stance.

"Sir, I'm sorry, Lieutenant, sir. I just thought..."

"Who told you to think? You almost disrupted an important experiment! Lucky I caught you just in time."

"An experiment, sir?"

At least the woman dared to ask a question after that scolding. This Andrea was brave. She would have been the right person to release him.

"You heard about the accident in the stasis chamber?"

"Yes, sir."

"I was able to at least partially restore your comrade's consciousness. Now I'm trying to expose it to the world."

"You saved Mohan? That would be..."

"Chief Petty Officer, stand down! It's far too soon to call it a success. I must ask you to keep this to yourself. If word gets out among the crew, I'll see to it that you're demoted by at least two ranks. I don't want anyone to get their hopes up unjustifiably. Has he tried to contact you?"

"Yes, indeed, sir. He's been formulating messages in Morse code and feeding them into the system via an aperiodic change in power consumption."

"That's surprisingly clever and gives us hope that all his abilities will be restored. But we have to be patient. Communication might overwhelm him. I assume that you will delete all recordings. Understood?"

"Sir, yes, sir."

"Very well. Dismissed. And you know what will happen if you neglect your duties."

The woman with the ponytail saluted and disappeared behind the console again. Monte noticed her ex-boyfriend looking at him curiously from the other side. But Lydia noticed it too. She moved her hand in a slashing motion across her throat, and Paul turned back to his terminal.

He was still connected to the mains. He calculated the next prime numbers.

"SOS. Help me. Lydia Zakharova is a ..."

AGAIN! HE WAS SCATTERED OVER A WIDE PLAIN. IT COULD BE Mars. He searched the sky and found two suns. The pain! Its components were balls of flesh spread over several square miles. He called them. Slowly they rolled across the hot desert. Boulders lying in the way tore wounds that immediately dried out under the two glowing suns.

This time, at least, the right body emerged. He recognized it as it rose high into the sky. Monte lay beneath him. The name felt right. He accepted it.

"Fuck. Shit." he said.

"I warned you, Tailin."

This time he knew immediately who was talking to him. Gradually, he seemed to be getting used to being reborn, but also to dying, because instead of falling into a tunnel, he fell completely into nothingness. He should rename himself Phoenix.

"Did I warn you? Tell me, did I..."

"Yes, you did."

"Then don't complain."

"I'm not complaining. But I'm going to wring your neck. Then don't say I didn't warn you either."

"You overestimate yourself, Tailin. I've been working in this profession since before you were even conceived."

"You underestimate me."

Lydia laughed. "Nonsense. I'm afraid I overestimated your intelligence. How could you possibly come up with the stupid idea of contacting anyone on this ship? They're not your friends. At best, they're useful idiots. Did you see the way I shit all over that woman? They're your enemies. Our enemies. No one will help you. If they get their hands on you, they'll delete you for helping me get the real Tailin out of the way. You are a traitor."

Helping her? He had given Tailin the opportunity to escape

in his own spaceship. Just another week or two, then no one would catch up with her.

"Why didn't you help me take over the battleship? It could have worked. If anyone here is a traitor, it's you."

"Could have, would have, should have. I can't believe what I'm hearing! We lost the Martian wars because of 'could have' and 'should have'. If the Second Fleet had defended Mons Olympus back then instead of attacking Luna... If our marines had held out a week longer... If the *Invincible* hadn't been hit so badly on the first day of the war... Don't give me that bullshit! Your plan was weak. You are weak. That's why you would never have realized that my plan was safer. The *Vanguard* would have been on an intercept course at full power by now."

It was true. He had no idea that morning how he could take control of the ship. But he would have thought of something. It had always worked so far. He was never good at making plans. Nevertheless, he had successfully completed almost every mission. Sometimes he felt like the protagonist of a book, written by an author who relied on improvisation. Lydia, on the other hand, was the hero of a sophisticated, well-thought-out plot. Or rather, the anti-hero.

Or was she the heroine and he, her antagonist? After all, he had sabotaged her promising plan to get Tsai Tailin out of reach of the Terran Union for good. On the other hand, she was not pursuing this plan altruistically - after all, Tailin had fled from Neomars, which Lydia represented. And Monte himself? He was no better, because all he cared about was saving his own ass. There must be a way to help Tailin that didn't cost him his life. Was that selfish?

No. It was purely a survival instinct. Every living creature had it.

"And what happens now?" he asked.

"I'll take you aboard the shuttle, as I promised."

Footsteps echoed on metal. Now he heard it too. They had been walking through the ship for a while. The camera must be covered, because all he could see was darkness.

"Are the batteries charged now?" he asked.

"They'll have to do," said Lydia. "I won't let you plug in again. It was difficult enough to put that nosy sergeant in her place."

"I see."

"If you try to betray me in any way, I'll shut you down immediately. Is that clear? I've heard dying isn't very pleasant."

"It's not so bad. I think I could get used to it."

"Shh, someone's coming."

Footsteps approached and then moved away again.

"Aren't we almost there?" asked Monte.

"My shuttle is in a launch bay at the very end, just before the engines," said Lydia. "I was hoping we wouldn't stand out so much."

Footsteps approached again. Should he say something? He imagined Lydia's backpack suddenly talking to the passer-by. His jailer would play it cool and shut him down entirely. Then he wouldn't be able to react at all.

"There, we've done it."

Lydia groaned. A muffled sound. She had probably put her backpack down. A keyboard rattled. Now she was entering the code. A hiss, followed by the squeak of a heavy door. That must be the outer hatch of the shuttle. His last journey was about to begin.

"Lieutenant, sir, may I ask what you're doing?"

It was Andrea, the non-commissioned officer with the ponytail. She maintained the prescribed politeness, but her question alone was impertinent.

"That's none of your business, Chief Petty Officer. Dismissed."

"Sir, yes, sir," the woman replied as if shot from a pistol.

But Monte didn't hear any footsteps moving away.

"Did you not hear me?" Lydia asked sharply. "Get the hell out of here!"

"I'm sorry, but I have to ask you to show me the contents of your rucksack and step away from the shuttle."

"Have you completely lost your mind? I'm going to complain to your superior!"

"Sir, you have no authorization for this ship. That's why I'm asking you once again..."

"I'm giving you one last chance, Andrea. Otherwise your career will be over."

"I'm sorry, sir. If you don't comply with my request, I will be forced to use my weapon."

Monte imagined the young woman aiming at Lydia, who must be three times her age and had an officer's rank. He admired her for her courage and was afraid for her, because she lacked Lydia's coolness.

"Everything's fine," said Lydia. "Here, this is my rucksack. I just wanted to dispose of some older items. It might not be completely legal, but..."

"Open it!"

"There's just some old stuff in there. Let's save us both the embarrassment and..."

"Open it! Now!"

It became bright. Andrea was using a taser that shot electrically charged darts. If she hit Lydia with it, it would hurt. But if she hit the computer he was in, he would die. *Please aim well, Andrea.*

"It's an old computer. I told you."

"Give it to me. Now!"

Lydia made no move to hand it over.

"Give it to me! Come on!" Andrea repeated.

Lydia bent down and picked up the rucksack with a groan. Now she was playing an old woman. She pushed the rucksack forward and the world tilted ninety degrees.

"Here, take it," she said. "You won't have any fun with it. It's just an old computer with a single stupid program."

Monte's camera was looking directly at the floor. But at least he recognized that two feet in military boots were getting closer. He was lifted up. Andrea was about to take him to safety.

"Not so fast!" shouted Lydia.

There was a click - the typical sound of the safety being released on a classic pistol. The rucksack froze in motion. Monte couldn't see what was happening, but he had an idea. Lydia must have seized a moment when the young woman wasn't paying attention, and now she was threatening her from behind with her ancient but still very effective weapon.

"Leave that woman alone, you old scarecrow!"

Monte could only see the man who spoke from the knees down, but recognized his voice immediately. It was Paul.

"I told you to stay out of this!" Andrea shouted.

"This is turning into quite the family reunion," said Lydia.

The man fired. His gun only clicked quietly. It was probably a Taser too. Monte and his rucksack were yanked around. Lydia was probably using the young woman's body as a shield. The rucksack slowly sank to the ground.

"Oof," said the woman with the ponytail.

Then there was a loud bang. A head crashed to the ground in front of him, as if its body had been felled by an axe.

"Paul!" shouted the young woman. "Paul!"

The rucksack was yanked up again. *Shit.* The man was no longer moving. A large, dark spot formed at about waist height. The woman tried to crawl to him, but she had no strength and could only move her arms helplessly.

"Paul!" she called out again and again. "I'm so sorry."

"What a mess. It serves you right," Lydia said to Monte. "I'd love to finish you off with your girlfriend's toy gun here."

That would only be fair. Because he wanted to save himself, the young soldier had to die. The world was unfair, and he was weak.

"Go on then," he said. "I'm ready."

"If only you had been willing to sacrifice yourself sooner. But now the bird has fallen into the well, or whatever it's called. I still need you, or Tailin's escape won't be credible."

"Please shoot me."

"I'm sorry, but I can't do you that favor. Shall I take out your friend here instead? I still have a few bullets in the magazine."

"No, please don't."

It would be pointless. And that was precisely why he trusted Lydia to do it.

"Of course not. I don't shoot defenseless people."

"But Paul..."

"He fired at me first, the fool. Now come on!"

She tossed the rucksack and Monte became dizzy as it flew through the air in a high arc. He landed in the shuttle, where Lydia bent over him and took him out of the rucksack.

"Aren't you going to connect me to the control computer?" he asked.

"There'll be time for that later."

"I'll be alone later."

"How stupid can you be? Now I have to come with you. That's the tragic part of your stupidity. After more than forty years in the service, I'll be exposed! How am I supposed to explain the dead body? Nobody will believe that I had nothing to do with it."

"You could say they planned it all, and you caught them."

"I'd have to shoot your special friend first. Is that what you want? But even then, there are far too many clues that lead to me. The bag of Tailin's tissue material alone, still in the backpack... No, you have to realize when you can't win."

She pulled the bulkhead towards her and closed it. Monte couldn't think of anything he could do to prevent her from staying on board. How was he supposed to get out of here before the ship was destroyed?

There was a sudden gust of wind. It felt as if someone had opened the front door. The suction pulled part of his consciousness into the adjoining room. It was a hall a hundred times the size of the chamber he had been staying in until now. Lydia must have connected him to the electronics of the shuttle. He ran back and forth in the hall, climbed up the walls and ran upside down along the ceiling. There was only one exit. It was a door that seemed to be made of old-fashioned wood. Monte kicked it and it made a muffled sound. He couldn't destroy this door. He had to convince the eye to the right of the door frame that he had the right to open the exit.

"Make yourself comfortable," said Lydia. "We're about to take off."

IT WAS AT LEAST TEN MINUTES BEFORE ANYONE NOTICED THAT THE shuttle had cast off. Lydia had done a great job. This time she had the harder task because she had to endure the acceleration. He didn't have access to the sensors, so he didn't know how high it was. But he heard Lydia's moans. He didn't feel sorry for her, but the satisfying feeling he was hoping for didn't materialize. Strangely, he didn't care at all if she was in pain.

"Battleship *Vanguard* to Shuttle 7-2, please identify yourself!"

He didn't recognize the voice that came at him from all sides at once. It was probably the officer on duty.

"Battleship *Vanguard* to Shuttle 7-2, please respond!"

He became increasingly impatient.

"Battleship *Vanguard* to Dinghy 7-2, please respond immediately!"

Lydia was still moaning quietly. She must be used to high g-values. They were flying close to their maximum. Naturally, she found it difficult to deal with the radio. Unfortunately, Monte had no connection to the system; this would have been the perfect opportunity to explain himself.

"Battleship *Vanguard* to Shuttle 7-2, if you don't report in soon, I'll have them fire on you!"

Wait a minute. Maybe the system also responded to voice? Lydia had left his speakers activated.

"This is Tsai Tailin!" he called out. "Can you hear me?"

"Tsai Tailin? That doesn't mean anything to me. You're not a member of the crew."

"Man, Ruffini, how stupid can you be? That's our guest! Give me the microphone and get out of here!"

The voice clearly belonged to Morris. The boss was taking care of things personally, that was good. Hopefully Lydia would be out of action for a while yet.

"What's going on with you, Tailin? Didn't you like it on board anymore?"

Morris sounded surprisingly calm in view of the fact that he was in danger of losing his prey. It was probably because he was one hundred percent sure he'd catch the dinghy. He didn't know Lydia's plan.

"I'm sorry, Morris," said Monte. "I'm being kidnapped right now, by your nice doctor, who apparently works for Neomars. Your counterespionage doesn't seem to be very effective. I wish I had stayed on board the cruiser."

"Kidnapped? What are you talking about? Just a moment. Ruffini, can you confirm that Dr. Zakharova is no longer on board?"

"I... yes, indeed. Zakharova doesn't seem to be on board... But she could be ..."

"Have you sent anyone to the shuttle's launch bay?" Morris asked.

"No, not yet," Ruffini replied.

"Then let's go, quickly! I want to know what happened!"

"Sir, at your command, sir!"

"I can tell you what happened," said Monte.

"Then why don't you start while you slow down?"

"Unfortunately, I have no connection to the controls."

"All you have to do is activate the autopilot and the shuttle will return to us."

"Unfortunately, I can't get out of my seat at the current acceleration."

"Then persuade our doctor to abort her stupid excursion. I don't understand what she's trying to achieve. The shuttle doesn't stand a chance!"

"She's not very cooperative and won't even talk to me. As I said, she's trying to kidnap me."

"I'll tell you how it is, Tailin. If you don't get your kidnapper to turn herself in, I'll capture your ship. And if that fails, which is unlikely, I'm afraid I'll have to have it shot down. I have clear orders. If there is a danger of Neomars getting hold of you, I must avert that danger at all costs. These circumstances include my own death, and yours, of course. I intend to abide by those orders."

Now it was clear why Lydia hadn't turned off his speaker. He had done his part while she moaned in the pilot's chair. It was his efforts that really made the story credible. Of course, she would not slow the ship down. The battleship would catch up with her sooner rather than later. Then the hijacker would blow up the shuttle as planned. It was not quite the plan Lydia had in mind, and it was not Monte's preferred solution. But it fulfilled a fundamental requirement for both him and the Neomars spy: Tailin would not fall into the hands of the Terran Union.

Monte was less pleased that he would end his existence in the process. Perhaps Morris could help him prevent that from happening?

"Morris?"

"I'm listening, Tailin," Morris groaned.

"You've accelerated?" asked Monte.

"We're in the process. You can't help us, and Lydia's just not responding."

Another groan. If the battleship wanted to catch up with them, it had to accelerate faster than the shuttle. Higher g-forces always meant more pain, no matter how big the ship was. But he didn't feel sorry for Morris either.

"Tailin?" asked Morris.

"Yeah?"

"Doesn't it affect you? The shuttle has been accelerating longer than we have."

"I can manage. It's not pleasant, but I'm good at tuning it out."

"How do you do that?"

"It must be my training. When consciousness purification is not an option..."

"Yeah, maybe we Terrans are all sissified by it."

"I think I know a way to shorten your agony a little."

"Out with it, Tailin. You'll make a whole battleship crew happy."

"I can't get to the controls. Give me a code for it that overrides Lydia's commands."

"Hm. That would be an idea. Ruffini, arrange for Tsai Tailin to be given level one access."

"But that's the highest level of command, sir. She would be your equal."

"Only for the shuttle, of course, you fool!"

"Of course, sir. I'll have her upgraded."

Ha, it was working! Morris was going for it!

"I wouldn't advise that, Peter."

Shit. Lydia was back. Hopefully Morris wouldn't fall for it.

"Ah, there she is, our renegade," said Morris.

"Unfortunately, I've been out of action thus far. I can't take the strain as well as our dear Tailin."

"I don't believe a word you say, Lydia."

"You should, because I'm the only one who can help you keep your command."

"Oh, Lydia. After all these years..."

Morris sounded genuinely wistful. Monte hadn't thought he was capable of that. Was he involved with the ship's doctor?

"Did our guest manage to reverse the perpetrator and victim? I don't know what she said, but Tailin forced me to board the shuttle."

"Sir, I have something here you should see," Ruffini said.

"Thank you. Well, Lydia. It's not looking good for you at all. There's a witness who saw you shoot a crew member. You're a murderer. Who's paying you for this? You don't have to answer that question. It's obvious anyway."

"You don't get it yet, it's completely understandable," said Lydia. "But it will all become clear. I'm just following orders from a higher level."

Lydia was clever. Hopefully she wouldn't manage to unsettle the captain of the battleship.

"So, someone from the Terran Union supposedly ordered you to take control of the most wanted person in the solar system, even if you have to kill my good sailors to do it?"

"Yes, Peter, you've summed it up well. I receive my orders from the very top."

"But of course, you have no proof of that."

"Yes, I do, but I'm not authorized to present it to you. You don't have sufficient security clearance."

"You're insulting my intelligence, Lydia, and everything we've ever had in common. Then why did you take control of the shuttle?"

"I admit my first explanation was clumsy. I should have told you right away what it was about."

"You're boring me, Lydia. Why do I get the feeling that you've just been stringing me along the whole time?"

"Listen to me first. I'm supposed to take Tsai Tailin to a place where she'll be safe."

"In a shuttle? How stupid do you think I am?"

"The shuttle is inconspicuous and maneuverable."

"But it doesn't have enough range. You'll never make your way back to the solar system with that."

"I don't have to. The secret research station where Tailin is needed is in this system."

"What nonsense are you talking?" asked Morris. "Gliese 411 is empty and uninhabited."

"Except for the research station. You don't know anything about that, of course, because it's secret."

The byplay between the doctor and the commander was amusing, but Monte had heard enough. Where was his access to the controls?

"Don't believe a word she says," he said. "Lydia is a Neomars agent. She told me so herself. You can read it out of my consciousness as soon as I'm back on board."

Suddenly he heard a squeak. It came from the door. The glowing red eye above it had closed, and now a bright rectangle of light fell into the hall from outside. Monte pushed himself off and crossed the door frame.

At the same moment, the shuttle disappeared completely. Around him were thousands of stars. Far behind him was Gliese 411. Another point of light was coming from that direction. It must be the battleship. It was calling him, because he became the shuttle.

"Tailin, can you hear me?" asked Morris. "The shuttle is yours now."

He was the ship. It was a great feeling that Monte hadn't had for a long time. The shuttle responded to his every thought. He had to be careful not to overdo it, and he had to stay in character. Morris was expecting a physicist who was just as tormented by the g-forces as the doctor.

"Thank you," he said. "I'll try to get to the controls."

Monte waited. It wouldn't be credible if the shuttle immediately changed course.

"Are you going to make it, Tailin?" asked Morris. "If not, we could try to shut down the engine."

"It looks like I will," said Monte. "I'm used to the pain. That's the advantage of never having your consciousness sucked out of your body."

"The way you say it, it sounds dangerous."

"I think it is, and I'm not the only one. Our bodies make us human just as much as our minds do."

A long time ago, out of curiosity, Monte had read a pamphlet in which opponents of consciousness purification justified their position. It contained just such esoteric arguments. As if people were still living in prehistoric times! They could be anything, even this shuttle. Monte looked around on all sides at the same time. It made him a little dizzy. These were the after-effects of living in a biological body with all its great and small limitations. It would wear off after a few days.

The battleship was catching up, but only slowly. It was time for him to throttle back the engine. He calculated the effects at lightning speed. The on-board computer was part of his ego. Monte didn't even realize he had taken it over, but he noticed how quickly he could think all of a sudden. If he shut down the engine completely, the battleship would be within weapons range in fifteen minutes. That was too fast for him. He still needed to think of how he could survive this affair without being captured.

"You did a great job," said Lydia.

"You think so?" Monte answered evasively so as not to give her any information she didn't already have.

"The way you convinced Morris was really clever. I wouldn't have thought you capable of that."

Monte checked the signal paths, but nothing was going out on the radio. Lydia spoke only to him. Nevertheless, he couldn't be sure that she wasn't recording everything so that she could betray him.

"I'll start braking now and then we'll see," he said.

"You realize that I'll have to destroy the shuttle?" she asked. "If Morris gets hold of you, he'll find out that Tailin is still alive. That can't happen."

"He won't get his hands on me," said Monte.

"You're such a cowardly weasel! Who are you anyway?" asked Lydia.

He didn't answer, but her words hit him. Was it cowardly to want to survive? Wasn't it rather human? Monte shook his head, and suddenly the universe swayed. His movement had activated the shuttle's orientation control. He stabilized the attitude, then checked what access Lydia still had. In fact, she could command the shuttle almost without restriction. Ruffini appeared to be a mere recipient of orders. Monte took control access away from her.

"Is that necessary?" she asked.

He didn't respond. He left the sensors to her. He needed Lydia to be ready to react, to know what to expect. Communication also remained open. The shuttle even had a small weapons system. Its main purpose was to function in the event of unavoidable collisions. The laser could destroy small asteroids up to thirty centimeters in diameter, and the two torpedoes could take on larger chunks. They had a long enough range so that the laser would have time to clean up the remaining chunks after a torpedo hit.

The torpedoes were his only way out of this messy situation. That was why he left Lydia in control. He wanted it to look as if everything was going according to her plan, until it was too late for her and for the battleship.

Tachyon: The Weapon

Silence fell on board as they waited out the remaining minutes until the battleship arrived. Lydia didn't commend him for leaving her in control of the weapons. Maybe she thought he overlooked that option and didn't want to bring it to his attention. On the other hand, he would be disappointed if she really thought he was that stupid.

But the battleship also remained silent. Morris probably didn't want to deliberately provoke another nasty reaction. He must be expecting Lydia to activate the self-destruct. Of course, he might assume that she had a certain survival instinct, but he didn't know how far that went. He simply said nothing more.

That was fine with Monte. He only had one task left: he had to switch to one of the two torpedoes. The guided missiles had a certain intelligence of their own. They were intended to do their job so far ahead of the ship they were protecting that they calculated the optimum strategy themselves, based on the data they had collected on the object to be destroyed. This required a lot of computing power, which Monte hoped would be enough to take him in completely. However, he couldn't be sure. He had transformed himself into many technical objects in his life. He had been a spaceship, of course, but he had also been a moon rover, an atmospheric glider and a Martian drill searching for water supplies at a depth of a hundred yards. He had even been a toilet. Not just any toilet, of course, but a smart one that analyzed the health of its users. It hadn't been a silly boy's prank, but part of an investigation, as he was able to prove that his target was pregnant.

But he had never been a torpedo. If he misjudged, only part of his consciousness would reach the target. The problem was: he couldn't go back. The moment he realized that his consciousness was tearing apart, it would already be too late. The torpedo would set off with a part of him that, at best, no longer felt anything.

But there was no alternative if he wanted to regain his freedom. He began the transfer. It was a terrible feeling, because at first, he only lost a few things. The first thing he noticed was the lack of a sense of taste. Then there was a gap in his body image between his upper and lower limbs. Memories of the earth seemed to have been erased. He no longer knew his multiplication tables and couldn't remember his daughter's name. Did he even have one?

"Tailin? Where are you?" asked Lydia.

Had she noticed something? He mustn't give himself away, or his plan wouldn't work.

"I'm here, Lydia," he said.

"I can't feel you anymore. It's as if you've withdrawn."

"How do you expect me to withdraw?"

Monte stopped the transfer. Lydia was not connected to the shuttle's computer network, but she had nevertheless noticed that something was wrong. How was that possible?

"I don't know," said Lydia. "It's just suddenly become so empty. It feels like the universe is deliberately keeping its distance from me. Everything in the universe."

"I guess it's goodbye," said Monte. "You've decided to die, and the cosmos has accepted your wish."

"Don't give me that esoteric stuff. There's something going on, I just don't know what."

"And that's not esoteric?"

Monte continued the transfer. The battleship had almost reached them. Hopefully Lydia would react as he expected. She had the shuttle's weapons under her control, so she would use them – if only because she hoped Morris would then destroy the shuttle. He wouldn't do her that favor. So she would have to blow it up - along with herself - in the end, but Monte wouldn't care.

He... what? *The transfer... what? Thinking... broken. It's... Ouch. Darkness.*

THE AGONIZING PAIN RECEDED, BUT SLOWLY. MUCH TOO SLOWLY. Monte checked his body. It was... all there. *Aaaarmm, leeeeegg...* Good news and bad news. He'd made it into the torpedo without losing anything important. The storage capacity was sufficient. But the computing capacity was a bottleneck. There was nothing he could do about that right now - apart from heading back, which was out of the question.

He spread out. Monte became the torpedo that absorbed him. His head became explosive, and his legs were the propulsion system. His eyes and ears became sensors. He couldn't see well. Everything around him was blurred. That was probably because Lydia hadn't launched him yet. The legs confirmed this, because they reported no movement.

Patience. For the first time in his life, it came easily to him, because his thoughts flowed like molasses. At least waiting was not exhausting. Then space opened up. His senses delivered contradictory images. Monte first had to sort them out, which took up valuable time. He was flying towards a mountain that was moving in his direction. It was the battleship. Lydia had fired him. But he was not alone. His sibling was flying surprisingly close. What was a few yards in space? They were connected like an umbilical cord.

Thank you, Lydia. So far, she had carried out his plan. The battleship was approaching at breakneck speed. Nevertheless, he took the time to check his surroundings. There, at 3 o'clock, anti-torpedo ammunition. Kinetic steel balls, safely spat out by the battleship, designed to destroy the approaching torpedoes. Morris didn't need to fear for his ship. Two shuttle torpedoes could do no harm to such a large opponent. But they could hurt it. That was a nuisance, so the commander was trying to prevent it.

Monte had reckoned with this. He had prepared an evasive course that was adapted to the parameters of the defensive ammunition. The rabbit made a U-turn so that the pursuers couldn't catch him. Interesting: its sibling imitated its behavior. The control software must be surprisingly intelligent to be so highly adaptive. He didn't have time to be surprised, because then the lasers came into play. Monte would prefer to keep his distance from the battleship. The effect of lasers was easy to calculate, which was why they were only used in close defense. But that was where they were particularly effective.

He hated that word. For him, it meant something like "deadly". Monte made more turns. The laser fingers reached for him. They were as fast as light and invisible, but he could guess their positions because he knew the firing angles of the individual lasers. The second torpedo had now overtaken him. It seemed to be learning even faster than he did. The technology had truly advanced. Monte felt guilty; he must have suppressed the intelligent control of his own torpedo from memory. He briefly felt inside to see if there was anything left, and the distraction cost him part of his tail fin. He didn't need it, not here, in vacuum. They wouldn't have to fly through an atmosphere. But it shocked him, because he had only just escaped death.

The second torpedo was smarter than he was. It had developed a new strategy, which at first glance seemed downright chaotic. The torpedo rotated around its transverse axis, which apparently confused the laser control system. Monte copied the behavior at first. It was strange - he was actually imitating a machine. Was it smarter than he was? He would have to wait and see. Did it realize that the laser control system was also capable of learning? It would adapt to the spin of its targets.

The second torpedo actually seemed to sense this. Although it didn't stop rotating, it increased its speed of movement by briefly firing the correction engine at exactly the right moment. Very clever, especially as it used a slightly different thrust each time. Monte adopted the strategy, but had the feeling that he should come up with an idea himself. The battleship would soon be so close that someone could stand on its hull with a fly swatter and swat at them.

It was fascinating to see the mountain hurtling towards him. It looked almost unreal, like a construction drawing, because it consisted only of lines and surfaces generated by the radar's evaluation function. Some of the lines looked blurred. This was probably where important instruments were located, covered with radar-repellent coating. This had not been used on the weapons, as they gave themselves away the first time they were fired. Neomars, the only known enemy, also knew the Terran Union ships inside out. Some of them were even built on Mars in pre-war times.

Monte's body trembled. This was an internal signal to alert him to danger. A laser must have just missed him by a few centimeters. Here, so close to the source, the light beams were still extremely focused. A hit would cut the torpedo in half. Monte reacted with a few quick hooks, but the trembling didn't stop. Apparently, the weapon operators had now targeted him with crossfire. But he didn't want to hurt the battleship!

Suddenly a shadow appeared between him and the large ship. What was his companion up to? Was the second torpedo going to sacrifice itself for him? It whizzed over the battleship's hull at a distance of less than a yard. Of course! Monte immediately imitated it. The laser guns must have a certain minimum angle at which they could fire. They were mounted in small, glazed bumps on the outer hull so that he could almost look them in the shiny laser eyes, but he was safe at such close range.

His body vibrated. *Shit, no!* That thing had just fired at him at a 90-degree angle. Then why hadn't it hit the other torpedo? He called up his trajectory and extended the laser beam, which could have hit the other torpedo, into infinity. It intersected with one of the battleship's engines. That was it! It was not about the angle; it was the exterior of the ship that the lasers couldn't hit. He had to look at the big picture. Monte designed a safe path between the lasers by using the ship itself as cover. In his mind, a labyrinth was created that was crossed by two flashing dots.

The second torpedo already had a decent lead, but Monte still managed to catch up, as if it had been waiting for him. The hardest part was yet to come. They had to move away from the battleship again, which meant they would be a much better target and deprived of any cover. Monte accelerated, giving everything he had left in the tank. He could worry about braking later. They had to gain distance at all costs, because the further away they got, the more the lasers dispersed and the less accurate the guns with their hyperspeed bullets became.

His companion corrected course a little. Monte now trusted it enough to copy the maneuver without thinking. There would be a point to it. And indeed, his body no longer vibrated. Was that thanks to the other torpedo? An alarm sounded. The instruments reported a high, non-directional photon concentration on the port side. An explosion, then.

Monte didn't need to turn his head to see it. It automatically appeared as a logarithmically labeled, colorful sphere in false colors, red on the inside, blue on the outside. It posed no danger and quickly fell behind them. Unfortunately, he had no way of analyzing the light spectrally, or he would probably find carbon components that belonged to Lydia's body. Was there still enough mass left to detect traces of DNA from Tailin's body? Morris would motivate the scientists on board accordingly. After all, his position depended on it. Would the admiral forgive him for losing the physicist? But who could have guessed what role Lydia would play?

She - unlike Tailin - was now truly dead. Monte hadn't

particularly liked her, but he felt sad. The doctor had been committed to her cause, right down to the last detail. And basically, she had died because of him. It was not the first time this had happened to him. Monte hated it when his decisions had such consequences. The last time it happened, he had ended his career in the armed forces and become a freelancer.

And now? They had left the battleship far behind them. No one from there would ever encounter them again. Monte searched the memory for the position of the solar system, entered it into the launch tracker and calculated a course. He had to move away from the ecliptic of this system and fly towards the galactic center. It would take about eight hundred years to reach the solar system if he didn't manage to gain additional momentum in between. Eight hundred years was a damn long time. Everyone would think he was dead. He was especially sorry for his daughter, whom he had promised to spend a few weeks with on his next visit to the solar system. That would probably never happen now.

Maybe he would be lucky and come across a mobile tachyon receiver. Who knew how technology might develop in a hundred years' time? Maybe every ship would have the technology on board by then. But he must not delude himself; the energy requirement couldn't simply be reduced. That was a fundamental problem. Physicists knew how to make wormholes, but they couldn't put their ideas into practice.

Suddenly his body vibrated. *Alarm!* The second torpedo had come so close that a collision was imminent. Monte hadn't reacted fast enough. *Crap!* He had made it this far only to... No. The other torpedo swerved. They didn't touch, but it could only have been by a few centimeters. At the current speeds - unbelievable. Was that a coincidence? Unfortunately, he couldn't establish a connection. The torpedo could receive commands from the shuttle, but nothing more.

And yet the other torpedo wanted to tell him something. Did it perhaps have an idea of how to get to the solar system faster? Monte broke off the pre-programmed route and observed the other torpedo. It performed a kind of dance, reminiscent of a bee. *It was trying to show him the way!* Monte analyzed the dance. The center of gravity of its movements pointed in a direction that must be completely wrong, because it led to nowhere.

That couldn't be right. So why all this effort? Humans sometimes tended to make a lot of noise about nothing. Machines, on the other hand, always had a reason. He was just too dumb to understand it. The path suggested by the AI on board the other torpedo must make sense. Monte ran through the options. Was there really nothing at the location where his companion wanted to send him? The radar was very clear. What if he continued to turn back time? Of course! He was thinking about the solar system, his home, the whole time.

But he was still in another system. The outermost planet, a gas giant, intersected the orbit suggested by the second torpedo. The software wanted them to fly to the gas planet, which was slightly larger than Jupiter and about as cold as Neptune. And why? Did the torpedo expect to be searched for from Earth? That was not so unlikely if Tailin arrived there with his ship at some point. In any case, he was more likely to be found here than somewhere in interstellar space.

Thanks for the tip, friend. Monte adjusted his course so that he would reach the gas planet. He would still have to solve a problem there - he didn't have enough fuel to brake. But one thing at a time. They had to reach the planet in the first place. Monte gave a brief impulse to the correction engine, and his rear end wobbled. The second torpedo copied the gesture. Monte immediately felt much less alone.

August 8, 2802, Earth's moon

"WHAT ARE YOU ALWAYS DOING AT MIKE WILSON'S?" ASKED Kang.

Her brother had intercepted her halfway to the Miscellaneous department. He looked rather like she imagined a jealous husband catching his wife on the way to a rival might look.

"I'm doing research," Yini said.

"Oh, and why are you wearing your favorite blouse and nothing underneath? And why did you blush when I asked you about it?"

She rarely wore a bra, and she was wearing the blouse precisely because it was her favorite blouse. But that was none of Kang's business. Yini shook her head.

"Don't be like that," she said, "We're both adults."

"Sorry, it's just that I feel like we're losing touch."

She took his hand. "That's impossible, Kang. We'll be siblings for life. And I'll admit that I think Mike is nice."

"Are you sleeping with him?" asked Kang.

"Now, that's enough!"

She withdrew her hand and continued walking towards the Miscellaneous department. Kang followed her.

"Sorry, that was stupid of me," he said. "Maybe I'm a bit jealous because you hardly spend any time with me anymore."

"You're right, Kang. Why don't we take a little trip to the surface the day after tomorrow to watch the sunrise?"

"The sun won't rise at all the day after tomorrow."

"We'll do whatever you feel like. We could hire a buggy and race down the old Artemis track."

The Artemis runway was a long disused road that led from the former American moon base to the former European moon base. Its potholes were legendary. If you drove down it at high speed, the vehicle flew more than it touched the ground.

"That's boring," said Kang.

"We'll think of something. But now I really have to get back to my research."

"What are you researching? Surely it's not official? You're going to get yourself in trouble."

It was Kang who was always getting himself in trouble by doing something stupid.

"All right, then. I'll tell you."

Yini looked around. There didn't seem to be a surveillance camera within range. Still, she pulled her brother close enough to whisper in his ear.

"It's about our mother."

"Is she not well? What happened?" Kang asked back.

"I mean our real mother."

"What are you talking about? What's fake about our mother?"

Kang put his hands on her shoulders and looked straight at her face.

"Shh, not so loud," she whispered. "Apparently they're not our real parents. I found a Tsai Tailin who looks just like me. Mother, on the other hand..."

Kang pushed Yini away from him so hard that she struggled to keep her balance in the low lunar gravity. Kang was startled and grabbed her arm.

"Sorry, I didn't mean to do that," he said.

"It's okay. I understand this is shocking news for you," she said.

Actually, she didn't understand. It had seemed logical to her, as if she had always suspected that her parents were not her parents. They were simply too different. That was why she had been somewhat surprised to find out about Tsai Tailin, even puzzled, but it had seemed more like the answer to a question she had never dared to ask.

"That can't be true," Kang said. "Our parents are our parents. Period."

"But haven't you ever wondered why they're so old? Mother must have been biologically fifty years old when she had us."

"That's a perfectly normal age," Kang said.

"Did she ever show you photos of her pregnant with us?"

"No, she didn't. Father never liked taking pictures of her, you know that."

"She never took pictures of herself either."

"So what? You can't blame her for that."

"I don't blame her for anything, Kang. Father and Mother have always been kind and nice to us. But they might not be our biological parents."

"That would mean that our real parents abandoned us. Do you realize that? Who lets their babies grow up with strangers? I couldn't forgive them for that."

"Kang, you don't know what constraints they were under. It looks like our mother had to flee Neomars because of her work."

"Because of her work? She abandoned us because of her shitty work?" Kang's voice was getting louder and louder. "I can do without a mother like that. Who prefers their work to their children?"

"Shh, Kang, not so loud. This is pretty secret knowledge I'm telling you. A guy from the secret service has already asked to see me, and he wants me to report everything I find out about Tsai Tailin."

"Tsai Tailin, is that the name of our supposed mother? If she really exists, I hope she dies lonely and abandoned. Nobody abandons their children!"

Now Yini understood. Her brother had probably been having similar thoughts to hers for a long time. Was it possible that they evoked completely different emotions in him, now that they turned out to be not so unlikely? Perhaps he had always had the feeling of being let down. And now, of all times, that was about to be confirmed, if he believed her. It was a healthy reaction to question all this.

"Maybe you're right," said Yini. "It's probably all a big misunderstanding. I should do a bit more research to clear it up. I promise I'll keep you informed, okay?"

"You don't owe me anything, Yini. This Tsai Tailin is either a fraud or a damn bad mother. In either case, I don't want to know anything about her. But you have to promise me one thing."

Kang lowered his head and looked at her pleadingly.

"Of course. What is it?"

"Please don't tell our parents about your so-called research. They've really done their best to bring us up. And then their daughter comes along and denies that they are our parents at all? That would hit them hard."

"I understand, Kang. No, I won't tell Mother and Father about this. I promise."

"And then I had to promise my brother not to tell them about my research," said Yini.

They lay entwined on Mike's narrow bed. Yini was sweating. Mike stroked her cheek. His fingers, which he had used to give her an orgasm a few minutes ago, smelled of her. She liked the scent. She took his fingers in her hand and licked his index and middle finger.

"That tickles," he said.

"And what do you think of Kang's reaction?" she asked.

"You might have to give your brother some time. You've suspected this for a few days now. He only found out today."

"But he reacted so... dismissively," Yini said. "His expression was so hateful."

She recalled the moment. Kang had pulled down the corners of his mouth, and his whole body had gone stiff. He had seemed like a completely different person to her.

Mike put his arm around her and pulled her close to him. With anyone else that would have been too close for her, but with Mike she was strangely able to accept the embrace, even enjoy it. It was the closeness he was looking for, and she was glad that she could give it to him. That was all he wanted. In other circumstances, she might have felt spurned, wondering if something about her body repelled him. But Mike had a way of showing her that he cared about her as a person that Yini had never experienced before. The fact that he didn't want to have sex with her in the conventional way no longer mattered.

"He's deeply hurt," Mike said.

Yini had to think for a moment before she remembered who he meant. He was probably right. Her brother was hurt because their mother must have left them shortly after they were born. The question was why Yini didn't feel hurt. Or was she just successfully suppressing it with curiosity?

"Shouldn't I hate my mother too?" she asked.

"I don't think he hates his mother," said Mike. "No child can hate their mother. Mine used to beat me, until one day the pediatrician reported it to the authorities. I grew up in a foster home, but I still love my mom."

"I didn't know that," said Yini.

"We haven't known each other that... long."

Yini smiled. Mike had wanted to say "well" at first, but then decided on a different adverb. He was right. "Not that long" was much more fitting. They already knew each other surprisingly well.

"Have you had many girlfriends?" she asked.

"A different one every week," he said. "No, you can imagine that it was a bit... difficult for me. Most of the women who showed interest in me found it kind of offensive that I was so into closeness. But I have nothing against sex at all."

"You do it pretty well, considering."

"Because you like it, Yini."

She laid her head on his neck so that their ears were touching. It tickled and Mike laughed.

"Dear Tailin," the letter began.

Yini made herself comfortable on Mike's bed. Her boyfriend had to prepare an assignment for another department. Nevertheless, she didn't feel alone in his room.

"I started setting up a new research base today," wrote the man who might be her father. "It is located on the group of islands we have named the W Islands. I named the base after you because you always wanted to build a base on this group of islands. To make it less obvious, I've limited myself to the first letter of your name. The T-base is close to the beach, which has the advantage that it's much easier to keep it clear of vegetation. But it's a long way to the hill you always wanted to investigate. I have to save my strength, so I find it easier not to have to worry about the vegetation.

"My plan is to set up the base first with the help of our two robots, and explore the islands from there. I will also take care of the local fluctuations in the magnetic field that you pointed out to us. I'm sorry that we didn't always take you seriously. - Wait, one of the two robots has contacted me. I have to take care of whatever it needs for now and get back to you tomorrow. With love, Mark."

With love, indeed. The man had let his wife fly back alone. How much could he have loved her? She put the letter aside and reached for the next one. Mike had reorganized the pile and had clearly done a good job of it. Had he read the entirety of the letters? She would like to know his opinion.

"Dear Tailin," she continued.

"You won't believe what the robot reported yesterday. At first I thought it was a hardware error. One of its three arms wouldn't move. I turned the second robot's eyes on it - and saw a biped fiddling with the machine. A biped! Can you imagine that? It must be a new species. It's a shame you can't see it. I know you've been excited about every new species we've found.

"However, I must admit that I went a little overboard calling it a 'biped'. Yes, the animal was standing on two legs when I saw it through the eyes of the robot. It was about six and a half feet tall and vaguely reminded me of an earthly cat. The large, protruding canines indicated that it was a predator.

"I'll have to be very careful if I want to examine it on the surface. I would be very sorry to have to kill a specimen, but if it attacked me, I'd have to defend myself, wouldn't I? I already hinted that they're not really bipeds. When the animal had enough of examining our robot, it got down on all fours and ran off very rapidly.

"I hope you won't be too angry if I tell you that today, for the first time, I'm almost glad I didn't travel to Terra Nova with you. I will get to name this species. It's great! Of course, it would have been even better if we could be happy together. Until tomorrow, my love!"

A new species. Yini decided to check the catalogs later to see what else Mark Decker had found out about it. If his letters had made it this far, his discovery had certainly not been lost.

"Dear Tailin," the next letter began.

"I'm more excited than ever about my upcoming trip to the surface. During the night, one of the robots picked up noises and started the night vision camera, as I had programmed it to do. The pictures showed a large group of the cat-like bipeds. I'm calling them that because they actually moved on their hind legs most of the time. I can't show you the footage, unfortunately, but you'd be thrilled to see them doing some kind of dance, with the whole group moving around our new base. Of course, it could be some primitive instinctual reaction. Perhaps they hunt in a circle formation and our robots, completely unknown to them, have provoked them into doing so.

"It's certainly too early to go looking for them tomorrow. But I so want to, and I'm running out of patience. Especially after counting the group over and over again. There were seventeen individuals of different sizes. Can you imagine that? In comparison, our clever multifeet are loners. It takes a fair amount of communication for so many individuals to move in a synchronized manner. Unfortunately, the robots' microphones are not suitable for truly significant recordings. That's why I'm needed down there. At least that's what I tell myself, knowing full well that the base isn't complete yet. But there's no one here to talk me out of it. I don't think I would listen to them anyway, to be honest. You are my role model in this matter."

The last sentence was crossed out and the usual greeting was missing. Mark Decker must have been very excited that day. Yini put the letter on top of the smaller pile of documents she had already read and reached for the next sheet.

"T-Base, Day 1."

At the top of the letter, the writer had replaced the salutation with the day and place.

"I have arrived at the base," he continued. "The cat creatures didn't appear at first. I was afraid that the exhaust jet from the Hopper might have driven them away, but that wasn't the case. They just seem to prefer to be out and about at dusk. As soon as the sun disappeared behind the horizon, I was suddenly surrounded by them. This felt just as terrifying as it sounds because, as I said, the base isn't quite completed yet. If the animals tried to attack me, I could probably only stop them by force of arms. That would certainly not be a good start to our relationship, especially as I have the feeling that they pass on experiences to each other.

"Today there were over thirty individuals doing their circle dance around the base. This gave me plenty of opportunity to study their appearance. I really must be careful not to be too misled by the resemblance to Terran cats. Their bodies are similarly elongated and articulated, but the tail, for example, seems to serve as an additional gripping tool. I saw one of the creatures handing another what could be a primitive tool. They put it down in front of the ship. Perhaps it is supposed to be a gift? They must sense my presence in here. Given their superior numbers, I didn't dare go outside. I don't think they're aggressive, but I can't tell whether they might see me as prey. Maybe they think the robots are alive. Wait, there's a knock."

The page was only half written on. Yini put it on the pile.

"Crap, I can't find the beginning of this letter," he continued on the next page. "The noise from outside startled me so much that I dropped the page. I'll have to look for it later. What I thought was a knock was the noise of a stone hitting the outside wall of the base. My research subjects have apparently started to throw stones at the base. They use their tails to do this. One of the cameras was hit, but I still have plenty of others.

"They sit silently around the base, reminding me more of primates than cats because they sit on their hind legs. They pass stones to each other with their tails and then whirl them through the air. It doesn't seem like an attack to me, though – more like a greeting, or a test. I mean, with an estimated weight of around 330 pounds per individual, they should easily be able to tear down the outer walls. But they seem to respect this artificial structure.

"To be honest, I'm unsure how to proceed at the moment. These life forms seem to be in the process of developing intelligence. Shouldn't we as humans stay out of it? We are not necessarily a good role model, even if we have managed to get our conflicts under control to some extent. On the other hand, this is the chance I've been waiting for. The first account of an extraterrestrial intelligence!"

Yini leaned back and closed her eyes. It seemed that word of Decker's work had not spread the way he hoped. What had happened? She had a feeling his letters would tell her. She got up, went to Mike's computer and activated it with her fingerprint. The system called up her personal area. The input prompt appeared.

"Gliese 163 c, intelligent life," she said.

"No species officially recognized as intelligent exists on the planet Gliese 163 c," the computer replied.

"Can you give me more details?"

"The first and last research mission to the Gliese 163 system revealed two candidate species with potential for intelligent behavior. One of the two species, called multifeet, shows pronounced collective behavior, but is clearly pre-intelligent."

"And what about the other species?"

"The astrobiologist Dr. Mark Decker describes an intelligent species with cat-like characteristics at Stone Age level. However, his alleged findings have never been confirmed. Decker himself is considered missing. His former colleagues described him as mentally unstable due to a previous trauma."

"They didn't believe him."

"Is that a question?"

"Thank you, computer."

She pressed the power button and felt a draft. It was Mike. She recognized him by smell, but didn't turn around. The sound of his footsteps approached. He put his arms around her stomach from behind. Yini wanted to push them away at first; she didn't like her stomach. It stuck out like an old man's. But then she would have to relinquish the embrace. His chest was warming her back, and the latent headache from reading so long was receding.

"You are so beautiful," he whispered in her ear.

Yini couldn't keep tears from falling from her eyes.

August 9, 2802, Earth's moon

That night, they lay in bed together completely naked for the first time. They slept in the spoon position, with Yini in front. Even when she got up to go to the toilet, she didn't put anything on. Suddenly, her stomach no longer bothered her, nor did the stretch marks on her sides, at least when it was only Mike who could see them. It was incredible how close they had become. Yini had never thought that was possible.

She felt sorry for her brother because he was still alone, and perhaps even more so than before. He woke her up with a phone call, as if he had been waiting for her to think of him.

"Are you with him?" he asked.

"Yes," she replied.

It was none of his business. He was her twin brother, not her life. But she still felt guilty.

"But you're coming to work?"

"Of course I am. Have I ever called out?" she asked back.

"You've never gotten so angry that I haven't seen you for days on end," Kang said.

He was jealous, that much was clear. Yini could understand it, at least a little. He would always be her brother, but of course she would want to spend more time with Mike in the future.

"I'm your sister, Kang. You should find other friends too."

"I have friends. I'm just worried about you."

"You don't have to, Kang. I'm doing very well."

"So, he's fucking you good?"

"Enough, Kang!"

Yini ended the call. What had gotten into her brother? He wasn't usually such an ass! His question was completely out of line. She would have to confront him. But not now. Work was waiting for her, and she had no intention of delaying it because of Kang.

July 4, 2799, Torpedo

He would give his left leg to be able to see something at this point. Radar was useless when approaching a storm-tossed gas giant. The image was constantly changing. He only found out whether a structure was solid or transient when it moved out of the picture - or after he passed through it without difficulty.

This didn't seem to bother his companion. It must have data that Monte didn't possess. But how was that possible? The two torpedoes must have been programmed identically. Of course! It was his own fault. When he transferred himself to the memory, he had to delete its stored data. The transfer not only overwrote the control software, but also everything it knew about interpreting radar images. The other torpedo probably still had those capabilities, which was why it could distinguish between dangerous and harmless patterns. That also meant that Monte could copy the behavior of the second torpedo.

But what was it up to? It was now correcting its orbit so that it plunged deeper and deeper into the planet's gas layers. Monte's outer hull was heating up. The second torpedo was straining his confidence. Monte considered the trajectory. He couldn't hold out for more than another minute, even though his speed was slowly decreasing. What was this? A suicide mission? Rockets that were no longer needed were often sent crashing into the interior of gas giants. They couldn't do any damage there. Was that how the torpedo was programmed?

Fifty-six seconds later, it activated its correction engine. It went up again. The virtual sweat on Monte's forehead evaporated. His outer skin cooled down. What had they achieved? Monte was expecting a momentum maneuver, but they had slowed down. There was only one explanation: the second torpedo was attempting to perform a slingshot maneuver around the local sun. But in order to reach the central star, they couldn't go too fast, or their momentum would carry them out of the system on a hyperbolic trajectory.

His theory soon proved to be inadequate, as they plunged into the layers of gas again. This time Monte was not afraid. Instead he was tormented by uncertainty, because the current atmospheric density would slow them to a speed at which the gas giant could capture them. Monte had no desire to spend the rest of his almost eternal life in orbit around a little-known gas giant.

Did he have a choice? He should have developed his own ideas instead of relying on the decisions of the second torpedo. It would stay that way now. Still, it was strange. He had never voluntarily subordinated himself to control software. At least the reduced speed meant he could take a closer look at the planet. It had a thin ring system that looked on the radar like a thread of spider's webbing glistening with dew. Some small icy moon must have been torn apart by the planet's gravity here, on this side of the Roche boundary.

Further out, Monte noticed additional radar echoes, which must be moons. They blurred a little, but all moved in the same direction. Only one was behaving differently. It was orbiting in the opposite direction to the ring and the other echoes. The second torpedo seemed to be heading for this orbit, of all places, if Monte was correctly interpreting the current correction maneuver. Surely the torpedo had not identified a new target there? Though it was not uncommon for misguided missiles to attack ships that happened to come within sensor range, even decades later.

They were approaching the object moving in the opposite direction. It definitely wasn't a moon. Such an elongated celestial body would have been torn apart by gravity long ago. The approximate dumbbell shape looked familiar to Monte. He increased the scanning intensity of the radar, which was not without danger, because it gave away his presence. Captains usually didn't like it at all when their spaceship was scanned by a torpedo's radar. Something like that always triggered an alarm.

But Monte only needed to take a quick look at the 3D projection. That was not just any ship in front of them, it was his ship. His ship! *Wonderful!* The *Curious* was obviously waiting in orbit around this gas planet instead of making a quick getaway. What about Tailin? It was probably her idea. But what was the point? Monte stopped his thoughts. He would simply have to ask her, and he would have the opportunity to do so as soon as he was back on his ship.

THE *CURIOUS* TOOK OVER THE FINAL APPROACH FOR HIM. Apparently, whoever was piloting the ship had realized that there was no danger from the two torpedoes. Monte was extremely curious!

He now floated motionless next to the spaceship, which he basically considered his home. The *Curious* had accompanied him on almost all his missions. It was over two hundred years old and still in excellent condition. Its outer hull and engine were original; only the electronics had been brought up to date any time he visited a planet with a space shipyard.

Monte scanned his ship with the laser. It felt like a tender gesture. The *Curious* seemed to enjoy it, or at least, it didn't resist. He couldn't detect any new damage. During its next-to-last mission, one of the carriers connecting the control center and the engine had been shot through by a millimeter-sized asteroid.

Suddenly a rectangular frame opened. It was the airlock! Was the *Curious* trying to bring him inside that way? He measured the size of the airlock door. There was no way to get a four-yard-long torpedo into an airlock chamber measuring a maximum of two-by-two yards.

The solution approached in the form of a human being floating straight through the opening. The radar only roughly reproduced its shape: two arms, two legs and a head. But it could only be Tailin. She approached him, and Monte held very still as she docked with the torpedo. He didn't want to throw her off by making a wrong move. The torpedo was still his physical body. Tailin disappeared into the blind spot of his radar. An alarm sounded.

"Self-destruct activated," reported the safety algorithm.

Shit, what's going on? He didn't want to explode! Monte queried the status. Something had damaged the outer skin. Tailin was probably trying to access the memory somehow. If only he could warn her! But he was mute. Monte tried sending signals with the radar. The *Curious* had sensors to detect radar emissions. Monte transmitted SOS, an ancient Morse code signal, but nothing happened.

"Self-destruct in thirty seconds," said the system.

He withdrew into the torpedo's electronics, followed the connections, examined the circuits and finally came across the automatic system. But it had no optional elements and worked independently of the normal control system. That meant he couldn't abort the process once it was set in motion. To do so, Monte would have to physically sever certain conductors - but he had no physical presence. He was a spirit in a body that he did not fully control. That couldn't be happening!

"Self-destruct in ten seconds."

It was too late. Fate was so unfair. He had made it this far! Why didn't Tailin escape? He hadn't asked her to wait for him here! And only for him to kill her with his own body now!

"Self-destruct in three, two, one, ignition."

His pulse was racing. Monte expected the world to end, the universe to experience a new Big Bang. But nothing happened. He still existed, even though time had run out.

"Status?" he asked.

"Self-destruct failed," replied the security system. "Error code 44C."

The code meant nothing to him. He probably overwrote the database where it was explained when he transferred here.

"Connection failure to the self-destruct mechanism," said Tailin.

Monte was so startled that he started his correction engine.

"Hey, take it easy! Now I've lost the screwdriver," shouted Tailin.

In the radar image, a tool about twenty centimeters in size was drifting away. He needed to control himself better.

"Yes, you should," said Tailin.

"Can you read my mind?" he asked.

"I'm sorry, but there's no other way," Tailin replied. "I'm directly tapped into the torpedo's main memory. It's good to see you back!"

"I think so too. Although I could have done without the drama at the end."

"Drama? Everything went as planned. All I had to do was cut the connection to the self-destruct mechanism. That was very easy."

"Nobody told me anything about that."

"I understand. Unfortunately, I couldn't establish a connection. The torpedo's security system rejected all attempts. It must have considered me hostile on principle."

"Did you know I was in this thing?" asked Monte.

"I wasn't completely sure, but you guys were acting very strangely."

"It certainly wasn't 'us guys'," said Monte. "I just copied what the other torpedo was doing."

"That was very clever of you. It was worth sending a helper with you, then."

"Helper? What do you mean by that?"

"The second torpedo didn't behave like that for no reason. It's the *Curious*'s control AI. It's pretty smart, I must say, and it likes you, did you know that?"

The AI liked him? Was that even possible?

"Yes, it is possible," Tailin responded to his thought. "Do me a favor and be nice to it when you're both back on board."

"Okay, I'll do as you say. After all, I owe you my life."

"You're misjudging the situation, Monte. I guess that's typical of us humans. It's thanks to me that you were in this situation in the first place. You should be grateful to the control AI for the fact that you survived it."

"And your safe handling of the screwdriver."

"To be honest: I didn't know the torpedoes had an automatic self-destruct function. The AI told me, through a kind of dance. Then I looked up the exact structure of this type in a database."

"And what happens now? Are you going to bring me back on board?" he asked.

"Both of you. I'm currently connecting your torpedo to the main memory via a data cable. Then it's your turn."

"I think I'd like my body back."

"As you like, Monte. That's your decision. You can initiate the transfer yourself from the main memory."

August 9, 2802, Earth's moon

YINI TURNED RIGHT INTO THE CORRIDOR. IT WAS JUST AFTER 6 p.m. Kang should be in his room. Today she felt more exhausted than ever. She had seen - in Monte's consciousness - how people had died, and how Monte had finally reached a ship unexpectedly, on which a woman was waiting who bore her mother's name.

And now she was supposed to have a clarifying conversation with her brother? No, she really couldn't. She turned around. Kang was just as grown up as she was. She had to apologize to him before he would speak to her again? *Screw him!*

She looked at one of the clocks on the ceiling. She could be with Mike in fifteen minutes. She was looking forward to seeing him. But at the same moment, her bracelet vibrated. It was Pedersen, her boss's secretary. She accepted the call and suddenly the old man's face appeared on the wall.

"I know, Ms. Tsai, you're already off work, but someone is waiting for you here."

She sighed. Mike would have to wait. "A Mr. Smith?" she asked.

"I didn't ask him his name, since he wouldn't have told me anyway. But you've spoken to him before, and he has all the security clearances."

"I'm on my way."

Smith approached her and shook her hand. He made a sympathetic and approachable impression, perhaps because he wasn't wearing a uniform this time. The underlying anxiety she had felt at their first meeting was not present today. Smith pointed to the sofa, and she sat down while he paced up and down Ulita's office.

"I'm glad you found the time," he said.

"I didn't have much choice," she replied.

He laughed. "If you hadn't come to me, I would have visited you wherever you were spending the evening. But you probably would have minded that more than I did."

Was he alluding to Mike? She frowned.

"It's your private business who you spend time with," he said. "No one here in the archive is a security risk. We vet our employees very thoroughly. You can rest assured."

So, Mike had passed the background check, just like her. That was good.

"What can I do for you, Mr. Smith?" she asked.

"I explained what I was after on my first visit."

"I haven't finished my work yet."

"That doesn't matter," said Smith. "I need everything you have. The subject seems to be very current at the moment."

"But the peace treaty..."

"I thought you realized the consequences. Your parents ..."

"My parents? Who are you talking about? The Tsais who live in the ring? Or Tsai Tailin and Mark Decker?"

It was a gamble. If anyone knew about that, it was Smith. She would have to give him the data. But she wanted something in return.

The man hesitated, then sat down in the armchair opposite her. The scent of expensive perfume intensified. The tiny atomizer capsules in his pores were probably reacting to increased sweat production. This body must have been quite expensive.

"I was afraid you'd come across that," he said. "The admiral, on the other hand, was quite excited by the prospect. She believed you would follow the transmissions all the more closely."

"She was right about that, your admiral."

"She'll be pleased. Well, why don't you show me the timeline you created? Then I'll see what I can do for you."

"First, tell me what you know about Tsai Tailin."

"That's not how it works, Ms. Tsai. You know I have the upper hand. I promise you I'll think about your request. That's the best I can do."

"All right."

Yini stood up and walked to Ulita's computer, sitting on the real wood desk. She logged in with her details. No one else had access to this area. Yini switched to the timeline she had updated after each session.

"Here, you can read it."

She turned the screen so that Smith could see it clearly from his armchair, and let him read. His eyes scanned the text, his gaze travelling back and forth at lightning speed. It took Smith all of five minutes to run through all her work from the last few days.

"Are you a robot, Mr. Smith?" she asked.

"Hah, no one has ever asked me that," Smith replied.

"That's not an answer to my question. I hope you don't think I'm biased."

"That's true, it wasn't an answer. But I can reassure you, I don't think you're biased. It's just a question, isn't it?"

"Are you, or aren't you?"

"No, it's a Biobag, not a robot. However, the eyes have been modified so that I can absorb content quickly."

"So, you have everything you need now?"

"I haven't analyzed the data yet, but I think I have it for now."

"So, what can you tell me about Tsai Tailin?"

Smith rubbed his hands together. "It's a difficult subject," he said. "As far as I know, Mr. and Mrs. Tsai were always good parents to you and your brother, weren't they?"

"That's right. Still, I'd like to know where I come from."

"Are you sure it would not strain your relationship with your parents if you found out that they are not your biological parents?"

"How can I be sure of that? But I do know that I will cherish them both for the rest of my life. I know what they've done for us."

"That's good." Smith kneaded his hands harder. "Let me put it this way: You would presumably fail a paternity test for Mr. Tsai."

"Presumably?"

"Well, we're keeping an eye on your family, of course. Should you wish to carry out a paternity test by any means, we would arrange for confirmation."

"All that trouble just for me and my brother?" she asked.

"Neither for you nor for your brother," Smith said. "We hope that the two of you might be a motivation for your biological mother to place herself in our care. After she returned from Gliese 163, we managed to convince Tsai Tailin of the benefits of working with us for a while. Then she was unexpectedly drawn to Neomars, from where she fled again. As you can see, your mother is not making it easy for us."

"But what do you want from her?"

"While she was with us, within a year she developed a theory of tachyon physics which would have united that exotic field with the rest of physics."

"Ah, so you're looking for her to award her the Nobel Prize?"

"Haha, actually she would be a good candidate. But as you know, I come from the Admiralty. So it's about weapons. I cannot and must not go into any more detail. But clearly, Tsai Tailin must not fall into the hands of Neomars. In this respect, your observations reassure me a little. It does look as if she is now traveling alone, and Neomars must think she is dead."

"I doubt that. How would Neomars have found out that she exploded on board the shuttle?"

"I will of course pass on that part of your findings via the appropriate channels. But regardless, there were at least two other Neomars spies on board the battleship *Vanguard* in addition to the doctor."

"You let spies from the enemy fly on your ships?"

"Of course. We can't prevent it, so we leave them alone once we've found them out. At least that way we have the illusion of being able to control them. I suspect Neomars does the same thing. In any case, statistically speaking, our spies there are caught far too rarely."

"Does that also apply to the Great Archive?" she asked.

"Haha, you're funny. Why am I standing in front of you right now?"

"I mean, are there any real spies here who work permanently for one side?"

"The archive is not my area. But it would be a miracle if there weren't. They are here at the control centers. Every transmission goes through here, not just in the tachyon area."

"I thought that was precisely why Neomars and the Terran Union had agreed on a kind of neutral territory here. That benefits both of them."

"There is no such thing as neutrality, Ms. Tsai. We roasted their planet! Do you think Neomars will ever forgive us for that? No, we have to prepare for the worst. They would sink the Earth into a black hole if they could. So we need to have all the technology they have, and it would be best if we were ahead of them."

Were? That didn't fit in at all with the Terran propaganda that the Union was the haven of progress.

"Aren't we ahead of them?" she asked.

"That was once the case. The inhabitants of the Terran Union have become lazy. We are doing too well. Have you ever been to Neomars?"

"Not yet, I'm afraid."

At least, not that she could remember. Her supposed parents had fled from there when she and Kang were less than two years old.

"You should definitely visit there," Smith said. "But the conventional way. When a rocket plunges into the dense atmosphere, ah, is swallowed up by it, it's impressive. After landing, the rocket ends up in a lake. If you're lucky, there's only a light haze in the air, it's raining, Saturn emits a diffuse light, and then you realize that the yellow-brown sand all around you is made of ice grains, that the sea you can see in the distance is liquid methane, just like the raindrops, and that you'd freeze to death outside without a suit at minus one hundred and eighty degrees. Yes, and then a Neomartian picks you up at the exit, looking as if he is sweating because of the greasy film on his seemingly naked skin. You can't see his breathing mask or his oxygen supply, but the outside microphone picks up what he says anyway, and then you ask me again if we are superior to Neomars. No, we are not. They haven't realized it yet, but it's only a matter of time. So we need every weapon we can get, and that's why we need people like you to help us."

"A great speech," said Yini. "You should become a politician."

The question remained, what was true? No, the question was whether Neomars had any interest in getting back at Earth. After all, the destruction of old Mars had happened so long ago that many people alive today didn't even remember it, including the vast majority of the inhabitants of the moon formerly known as Titan – who also rejected consciousness purification. Shouldn't that prevent them from feeling the kind of hatred that Smith apparently saw as inevitable? The Neomartian spy on the ship seemed willing to do anything. Was she an exception? Yini didn't know. Maybe she was too young - or maybe she hadn't experienced enough. All she knew was that she wanted to meet her real mother.

"No, it's not really my thing," Smith said.

"What?"

"Politics."

"Ah."

"Thank you, Ms. Tsai. You've helped your homeland a lot."

"I don't really care about that."

"If I may give you one more piece of advice - don't tell your brother about your discovery."

Her body stiffened. What did Kang have to do with this?

"Leave my brother out of it," she said. "You better not let anything happen to him!"

"It's not a threat. On the contrary, I want to protect you. Your brother..."

"What about Kang?"

"We've been watching him for some time. He seems to have developed a certain... aversion to anything to do with Neomars. There are some groups that take their pride in Earth a little too far, if you know what I mean."

"He's joined up with the Terranists?"

"No, not exactly. That would make him a security risk for the archive. But he sympathizes with them, takes part in their discussions, that sort of thing. You shouldn't tell him anything that could antagonize him further."

Yini sighed. The warning almost made her sympathize with Smith. But she also suspected he'd made it all up to create a rift between her and Kang. How much was made up? She should talk to her brother. But how could she talk to him without making him suspicious of her?

"Thanks anyway," she said. "I don't know if I can do anything with it yet. Honestly, he should know what I know."

"Think about it carefully. If he goes any further in that direction, we'll have to relocate him off the moon. Good janitors are also needed in the ring."

"That would definitely throw him off balance. He's always competed with me."

"Unfortunately, I wouldn't be able to prevent it. We really can't afford a Terranist cell in the Great Archive."

SHE CAME BACK TO THE CORRIDOR THAT TURNED RIGHT AND LED to Kang's lodgings. Yini paused. He hadn't tried to contact her, which meant his apology was still pending. She had important information for him, and he was entitled to know it. Surely Smith was wrong. Kang wouldn't freak out about it, though he certainly wouldn't be happy. But she should also ask him about these Terranist ideas. She already suspected how he would react. Kang had very strict standards of truth and accuracy. For him to fall for such people was unbelievable.

The Terranist movement came from the outer areas of the ring, where the dwellings were the smallest and the view was more into black space than onto the green Earth, which was recovering so successfully from its difficult past. Yini could understand the people there feeling dissatisfied. But in a strange, twisted way, the Terranists blamed Neomars for their situation. The media helped by portraying the Neomartians as Frankenstein monsters who had given up their human forms once and for all with the help of genetic engineering. But the Terran Union's Biobags were nothing more than that, artificial vessels into which you could pour your consciousness, and which then came to life like zombies.

Yini had always resolved not to abandon her body that way. It was something her parents had taught her. They were quite old now, and they had always prepared the twins for the fact that they would die one day. Yini couldn't imagine it yet, but she was certain it would happen. How would Mike feel about the topic? She decided to broach the subject with him at some point.

She didn't turn right. Today was not the day to argue with Kang. She hadn't even read any of Decker's letters today.

"T-BASE, DAY 5," SHE READ AND FALTERED.

"Mike, do you have any idea what happened to days two through four?" she asked.

Her boyfriend, who was sitting on the bed behind her, stroked the hair behind her ear.

"I think he explains it in the text," he replied.

"Have you read the letters?"

"Only where something seemed to be missing. I have a feeling that none of this is any of my business."

"It's your business now," Yini said.

She settled herself more comfortably, put her head in the crook of his arm and continued reading.

"I went on a trip," the letter continued. "Well, it wasn't entirely voluntary. Looking back, I get goosebumps when I think about how it started - with overwhelming noise. It was the middle of the night, and I was lying on my cot. I tried to switch on the light, but the power had gone out. I just had time to grab a breathing mask and an air tank. I always keep them under the bed. That's when the walls collapsed.

"I still don't know how they did it. Maybe I'll find out more once I've looked at the security camera footage. Outside, I stumbled across a heap of multifeet that wasn't here yesterday. Were they using the multifeet as a weapon? And why? I think the Kasen themselves would have been strong enough to get me out of my nest. Kasen, that's what I'm calling the creatures from now on. For the time being, I'm gendering the word as neutral, because I don't know enough about their reproduction yet. The term is a little reminiscent of cats, but sounds completely different.

"I only realized that something was completely wrong when I saw the starry sky above me. Up until then, my reactions were purely automatic, and after that they were no longer automatic at all. Anyone who could take the roof from over my head within a minute would be impossible to stop. I glanced at the gun cabinet, but I would never have enough time to take out thirty attackers.

"At this point, I still thought that there were the same number of them as had danced around the base the day before. But a single Kasen took me out of my bed. It wrapped me in its tail. I didn't put up any resistance. The creature was two heads taller than me and had two sets of sharp claws. The tail turned out to be very muscular, but also very sensitive. It exerted just enough pressure to hold me securely, without causing me any pain.

"The Kasen laid me on its back with its tail. Or rather, it attached me to it, so to speak. The creature left my base on four legs. We encountered a second one outside. And then the ride started. The animals apparently travel across the crowns of the brine trees to get from place to place quickly. The second specimen used its tail to pull itself up the trunk of a brine tree. Mine didn't have that option, because it was using its tail to carry me. Or so I thought. In fact, it untied the knot so quickly that I fell off, pulled itself up, and caught me again just in time. It worked almost every time. But when we were just below the crowns, something must have distracted my Kasen. Maybe it was even me with one of my terrified screams. In any case, I fell and fell, and if the second Kasen hadn't caught me, I would probably have died.

"Afterwards, the two specimens exchanged noises. I can't say whether they were expressions of thanks - or something like "You'd better watch out, idiot". I was still happy, because now a window into space was opening. Did you know that there are closable hatches in the crowns of the brine trees, that the Kasen can easily crawl through? Once again, I am unsure whether this is a natural phenomenon or whether the Kasen make them themselves. In any case, they seem to know exactly where the hatches are, because they ran at high speed straight to another hatch, crawled through, jumped down the tree trunks and landed in a kind of settlement.

"Can you imagine that? The Kasen obviously have an emerging culture. The fact that we never discovered them is perhaps due to the shielding provided by the crowns of the brine trees. My radio receiver, which was supposed to connect me to the space station, didn't work there. So you, Tailin, certainly didn't stand a chance with radar scans either."

Yini winced as she read her mother's name and put the letter down on her lap. She hadn't yet spoken to Mike about what Smith had revealed to her today.

"Mike?"

Instead of an answer, she heard soft, regular breaths. Mike must have had a busy day. She could tell him the news tomorrow. Yini picked up the letter again.

"The settlement is really hard to describe. I must be careful not to introduce a Terran perspective. Otherwise, I would be talking about tents that the Kasen have erected. They seem to consist of poles piled in a cone and covered with large leaves. I don't know what's inside. I was never taken inside a hut. There was gray smoke coming out of the tops, though. So the creatures inside were probably keeping campfires going. There were pots hanging between the tents, with fires burning in them, spreading an atmospheric light.

"The creature that had abducted me put me down in an open space around which the tents were grouped. At first we were alone, but then more and more individuals came and made themselves comfortable in a large circle, settling down on all fours. Within the settlement, they mostly moved upright.

"I counted about thirty separate individuals. I was unsure if this was the group that had danced around my base the day before. I still find it hard to tell them apart. They are all about the same size. There doesn't seem to be any distinct sexual dimorphism – either that, or there are no genders at all. However, it is very unlikely that they are born at this size.

"My finder – I call him Kian because I like the name (although I wonder why I considered him male from the start despite the lack of sexual dimorphism) – nudged me with his front leg so that I rolled a few yards along the ground. I almost lost my breathing mask in the process, but didn't dare complain about the treatment. A loud discussion began. Of course, I couldn't understand a word they were saying, if they were saying anything at all. There were repeated pauses in the conversation. Because of that, I assume that part of their communication takes place in infrasound. Unfortunately, if this is true, it would be difficult for us to communicate with them. I would need my instruments to be able to determine this more precisely, and the Kasen haven't brought them to me yet.

"The discussion went on for about an hour. Almost all the Kasen had a say. My finder, Kian, replied in each case. The creatures - excuse me if I accidentally refer to them as animals in future - were mostly quiet, almost lethargic. They were probably not very interested in me. I was considerably smaller and weaker than them, so they probably didn't see me as a threat. I was glad I hadn't used a weapon.

"After the discussion, Kian took me to a tent. I was expecting to end up inside it, but the Kasen put me down next to him. He licked my face with a very rough tongue the size of a mop. When I tried to get up, Kian gently pushed me to the ground. But he didn't do anything like tying me up. To be honest, it probably wasn't necessary. I very much doubted it would be safe to leave on my own. The Kasen all went to their tents. I almost felt lonely out there on my own, but I didn't know how soundly they slept.

"In the morning, I was woken up by a shower from a water teat. I must admit that at first, I thought the liquid was urine. However, the Kasen release that from a valve in their face, which is perhaps also suitable as a weapon, as the urine is highly acidic. The water teat, on the other hand, is located on the belly. It must be connected to a water reservoir in the body. The water from it is drinkable. But I had to remove my breathing mask to find this out for myself.

"Unfortunately, I realized that I had lost my extra bottle of oxygen. I drew Kian's attention to this by showing him the half-filled bottle on my belt. He started to take it from me, but I managed to stop him. Then I grabbed my throat, which he acknowledged with a growl, only to put his clawed hand on the same spot. I lay down and played dead, whereupon he covered me with his tail.

"He didn't understand what I needed. No living creature on this planet has trouble with the low oxygen content in the air. How was he supposed to understand that it was different for me because I came from another planet? Kian had to take me back today if possible - not to my base, which was probably completely destroyed by now, but to the Hopper.

"How could I make him understand that? Maybe I could draw the Hopper. I kicked up some of the tough grass that covered the ground in front of the tent. Then, with the reinforced heels of my space boots, I drew lines in the surface, forming a flat view of the Hopper. Finally, I pulled out my lighter. It had its own oxygen tank, so it could burn anywhere. I held it so that it was roughly where the engine was. The fire jet I had landed on must have been seen by the Kasen. I pressed the button, the gas ran, the spark ignited, and a small blue flame lit up next to my thumb.

"Kian roared like a rutting stag. The sound sent a shiver down my spine. His friends came immediately. I held up the lighter, which had obviously made an impression. I only hoped that it was a favorable impression for me. Meanwhile, the Kasen looked at each other as if they were wondering who would take the valuable object from me.

"But it couldn't have been the fire that had impressed them so much. The camp was lit by many fireplaces, even though the air was so poorly oxygenated. The Kasen must have a fuel that provides enough oxygen to supplement what is in the air. I closed the lighter again and the flame went out. The Kasen were buzzing. I opened it again and the light ignited. The Kasen roared. I repeated the experiment twice more, with the same result. Maybe it was because the lighter was so small. I had not yet seen how the Kasen lit their fires. However, the creatures did not try to take the magic device from me.

"When I made no attempt to demonstrate it again, their interest waned and most of them left. Kian called out to them. He sounded disappointed, but that could be human projection. Somehow, I had the feeling that he regarded me as his personal trophy, but had hoped for more interest from his conspecifics. Only one other Kasen had remained, perhaps the one that had helped him with his raid. It looked at my drawing and commented on it with a low, babbling noise. It was only now, up close, that I noticed that the sounds did not come from the opening on the head responsible for feeding, but rather from the shoulder area. There, the Kasen have two rotatable organs, which I had initially thought were ears. Presumably they are for both talking and hearing.

"The other Kasen tore turf out of the ground with its front paws and trampled the earth underneath. Then it bumped into me so hard that I fell over. Apparently, it was startled by this, because it reacted by setting me on my feet with its tail, right in front of the area it had cleared. What did it want from me? I copied my drawing for Kian by drawing lines with my boots. I didn't get far, because the other Kasen's tail pulled me back, while Kian pushed a stick into my hand with his tail. The two of them must have colluded and wanted me to use a tool to draw. Did they think I was a bit dim because I hadn't come up with the idea myself?

"I bent over the primitive canvas and drew the outline of the Hopper. The Kasen didn't seem to agree. It wiped the image away with a paw, took the stick from my hand and sketched what I soon recognized as the base. I nodded, but of course the Kasen wouldn't understand my gestures. What was it trying to tell me? I reached for the stick the creature held in its tail. It loosened its grip and left the drawing tool to me. I left some space and drew the Hopper again, this time adding the outline of a person to represent me. The Kasen responded by wiping away the person and drawing two new figures next to the base. I crossed out the base with a large cross. The Kasen hissed at me, but Kian put his tail around its shoulders, and it calmed down again.

"Things remained complicated. The Kasen seemed to have a question I couldn't answer, and the creatures didn't understand my request. I checked my oxygen supply. If I didn't get a fresh supply by evening, I would die. You can see, Tailin, that I'm writing you this letter, so at least I haven't died today. I still don't know what I have to thank for that. Anyway, our conversation initially took a completely different direction.

"The Kasen who had started drawing was now drawing a bigger spaceship next to the Hoppers. It reminded me a little of the TransVec, but it was impossible that the Kasen could have seen our interstellar spaceship. It had never landed on the planet, and it could only be seen as a dot in the sky with the naked eye.

"At first, I could think of nothing else to do but cross out this larger spaceship. I had expected a loud reaction, but the Kasen just grabbed its chin with its right paw. It really did look like the classic thinker pose. As an astrobiologist, I should know how to avoid projection, but I was immediately drawn to the creature, as if we shared something valuable. It could still kill me if I wasn't careful, but by now I thought it would at least regret it afterwards.

"After a pause of perhaps two minutes, the Kasen took the stick from me again. It used it to draw stick figures next to and above the crossed-out spaceship. It looked as if these two-legged creatures were tumbling out of the ship, because their arms and legs were pointing in all directions. What was the creature trying to tell me? Weren't we the first visitors to its planet?

"I pointed at the Hopper again. The story the Kasen was telling me didn't help. I needed oxygen. We hadn't discovered any current signs of alien visitors anywhere, but we hadn't really looked for them. Perhaps it was an old legend that had come to the creature's mind when it saw my Hopper. In some cultures, there are stories of beings that descend from the sky. Sometimes they are gods, sometimes super beings. Perhaps the Kasen had developed something like a birth myth to explain their own origins. We hadn't found any animal species on the entire planet that looked so much like Terran cats. When the Kasen became self-aware, they must have noticed their difference, the fact that they didn't quite fit into the evolutionary diversity of their planet.

"The Kasen pointed to the spaceship he had drawn. I pointed to the Hopper. It tapped on the spaceship. I held the stick on the Hopper. The Kasen roared and opened its mouth. I admired its sharp teeth. Okay… I was frightened and dropped the stick. The Kasen picked it up and pointed it at the spaceship. I got up and stood on the Hopper. The Kasen made a quick movement with its tail. The tip was coming towards me and would have knocked me over, but it stopped just before it reached me. Kian, my captor, had blocked it with his own tail. He picked up the stick and pointed it first at the Hopper, then at the spaceship drawn by his companion.

"Was he laying out a schedule? Would we travel to the Hopper first and then consider the other visitors? That was a great development. I had managed to communicate with two alien life forms! But to be honest, at that moment, I was mainly happy that I might not suffocate."

Yini was startled when Mike suddenly slid sideways behind her. She just managed to hold him down on the bed. It was really damn narrow. Carefully, she released herself from his embrace, got off the bed and adjusted him so that he could sleep comfortably. Should she undress him? Better not – that might embarrass him. She still knew so little about him. The blanket was at the foot of the bed. She pulled it over him. Mike turned on his side without opening his eyes. His hair was pushed back over his forehead, making him look even more cute.

She checked the time. It wasn't ten o'clock yet, and she didn't feel tired at all. She picked up the pile of letters, put them on Mike's desk and sat down in the chair in front of it. It wasn't particularly comfortable, but she didn't want to stay up too long reading. Mike was now making soft breathing noises. Every now and then he smacked his lips. Yini hated smacking noises. They usually gave her a severe, physical headache. But right now they had a calming effect. It was nice not to be alone. She couldn't remember ever feeling like that before.

Yes, there was something. It had to do with Kang and her. They had begged their parents for so long to have rooms of their own that she had been delighted when they moved into a larger apartment in the Ring. But the first night without her brother had been terrible. They had been inseparable for fourteen years. Kang must have felt the same way, because he turned up in her room in the middle of the night. Yini was not at all shocked by this; on the contrary, she had been expecting him and had a second pillow all ready.

Still, it felt strange. Now that there was an alternative, it was suddenly no longer normal for them to accidentally brush against each other under the covers. Yini had turned on her side and stared into the darkness for a long time, anxiously trying not to move. Kang didn't make a sound either. They had lost their innocence overnight. That had been the last time they spent a night in the same room.

Yini sighed. Fortunately, her father - *her father?* - was waiting for her on Gliese 163c. The letter lay open on the pile. She ran her finger down the paragraphs. "I... My finder... The Kasen... I... The other Kasen... The Kasen... I... Was." She found the last paragraph she had read.

"Many hours passed before we left," Mark Decker continued. "I kept an eye on my oxygen supply the whole time. That's why I didn't pay much attention while Kian guided me through the settlement. I only now realize that he probably wanted to show me the achievements of his group. He showed me a storehouse suspended above the ground between three brine trees. The

Kasen had built it from weavers' nets. I was surprised that the nets were not dying.

"Kian must have noticed my astonishment, because he removed a piece of the net from an apparently uncritical spot and gave it to me. The threadworms that made up the net were covered in a thin, transparent substance. They were obviously dead, and the thin coating prevented them from decomposing. The storage area contained mainly plant parts, but also the remains of animals. They didn't smell good at all, and I hoped I would never have to taste the delicious food of the Kasen. I was indeed spared that fate. It seems," the first two letters were crossed out, "that the creatures don't eat every day.

"The Kasen also showed me a kind of ritual place. At least that was my initial interpretation. It was a circular area, perhaps ten yards in diameter, almost completely surrounded by prickly cherry hedges. It was home to a Kasen that was missing a front leg - or arm. Unlike Kian, it always moved on its two hind legs. Instead of an arm, it had a thin stick tied to its shoulder, which probably only had symbolic significance. The Kasen did most of its work with its tail anyway.

"Its main activity was apparently carving. There were large and small figures scattered around the area, all made of brine tree wood. I recognized the mighty growth rings immediately. The carver had skillfully worked them into the figures, giving them a more natural look. The large ones all looked very similar. The smaller ones, on the other hand, were dimorphic. Although they also had cat-like outlines, their skin was completely smooth. A third of the small sculptures had no tail at all, and another third had two, which was quite impressive. What was Kian trying to tell me? Perhaps these different shapes represented the ancestors of the Kasen. At some point, evolution must have eradicated dimorphism. Or these different Kasen were their children, for whom I had searched in vain in the settlement. It is not unusual for different generations of a species to differ significantly.

"I tried to inquire about this by pointing to one of the smaller figures. This led to the carver showing me his tools. They were not made of metal, which would have surprised me, but of bone. The carver handed me a knife. There was a handle under the cutting edge with a large hole in it - no doubt intended for the tail. The edge was very sharp and very heavy. I immediately thought of multifeet bones. I'm sure you remember how heavy the skeleton was that we recovered and brought aboard the station. Maybe it will soon be in a museum on Terra Nova. But no, you still have a few years before you reach that system.

"I wonder if the Kasen hunt multifeet? I

always thought multifeet were invincible. But perhaps the Kasen helped themselves to dead multifeet. After all, the animals weren't immortal.

"At some point, Kian got bored with the carvings. He guided me along, running ahead of me on four legs and pointing the way with his tail. This time we came to what might actually be a ritual site. The brine trees grew unusually densely here, and between them hung Kasen, arms and legs stretched out as if they had been crucified. What kind of strange custom was this?

"Kian pointed to an open space between two brine trees. Ropes hung from the trunks to the left and right. What did my kidnapper want from me? He pushed me between the trees with his tail, stood up and then raised his own arms. He wanted me to imitate him, and then what? No, thank you. I refused and just stood there until he gave up with a thud and got down on all fours again. Just then, a Kasen climbed down from its perch between the trees next to us. It had looked as if the creatures would not be able to free themselves from their position, but I had forgotten about the tail. With that, the Kasen loosened the knots connecting it to the brine trees. It stretched and stretched, then ran off on two legs without a recognizable greeting.

"This world really is very different from ours, Tailin. Will I ever find out what makes the Kasen do these strange things? Is it a kind of yoga that they do among the trees, or is it more of a service or a prayer? In any case, the Kasen who had just untied itself looked more refreshed than exhausted, as far as I could tell.

"As Kian still made no move to take me back to the Hopper after this visit, I confronted him. In other words, I stayed close to a brine tree so that he couldn't just reel me in with his tail and drag me along. He would have had to uproot the brine tree, which I really didn't think he could do. He first ran a few steps ahead, but then came back and hissed at me. Then he gave something like a speech, interrupted by short pauses. I couldn't understand a word he was saying, but I replied that I really needed air.

"'Air', I repeated several times.

"'Rrr,' suddenly came out of his ears.

"'Yes, air! I need air,' I shouted.

"I pointed to my canister. I didn't care what he called it, as long as I got what I wanted.

"'Rrr', he said.

"When I describe that he said something, I use the word 'say', although it doesn't really fit. Kian sent the words to me using his hearing and speech organs. The roaring, hissing and growling of the Kasen comes from their throats. If they want to communicate more subtly, they use the special organ on their head.

"'Yes, I need air to breathe!'

"I didn't want to confuse him by drawing his attention to the small pronunciation error. Again, I pointed to my canister, and again he thought I wanted to give it to him. Maybe I had to resort to harsher means. Kasen seemed smart enough to recognize a simple cause-and-effect relationship. I held my breath. First I held out the breathing mask to him. He sniffed and his tongue licked the mask. But he must have noticed that a slight breeze was coming out of the opening. Then I put the mask back on, took a few deep breaths and took it off again. I waited. I had to hold out for a minute or two. The Kasen had to sense that I wasn't feeling well. Then I would put the mask back on and Kian would have learned something.

"But things turned out differently. I had overestimated myself. Before I could put the mask back on, I lost consciousness. I woke up with a Kasen paw on my face. Sand trickled into my eyes from the sole. The mask was over my face. It was on backwards, but enough air was flowing from it into my mouth. I greedily sucked it in. Then I pushed the Kasen's foot aside. It was Kian who had pushed the mask onto my face. That was great! I thought less about the fact that he had saved my life and more about the fact that he must have understood the importance of the extra breathing air for me. Once again, we had managed to communicate!

"I stood up and patted off my clothes. A few bugs and worms jumped hastily to the ground. They had probably mistaken me for carrion and were now suitably disappointed. Kian pushed me forward with his tail. He apparently wanted to continue his hike through the brine forest instead of taking me to the Hopper. The creature hadn't understood anything after all.

"What could I do to convince the Kasen to take me home? I felt my suit. I hadn't really been able to prepare myself well before being abducted. But the suit had a few reserves intended for emergencies, and by now it was clearly one of those. I found a small supply of tools, a few signal rockets, an emergency medipack, a few cereal bars and the radio, which had no reception. I sat down on the ground and spread the things out around me. Kian had come closer and was looking at everything curiously. Of course, he had no idea what to do with them. I showed him the objects one by one. I cut into the trunk of a brine tree, drilled a hole in the ground, bit into a bar and rubbed my stomach and finally stuck a plaster over an abrasion on my hand.

"Kian followed what I was doing but wasn't interested in explanations and didn't make a sound. Only when I set off a signal rocket did he jump to his feet. The rocket shot high into the crowns of the brine trees. I was afraid it might start a fire, but nothing of the sort happened. Kian, however, didn't calm down at all. He must have noticed that I didn't have just one of these rockets, since two similar-looking objects were still in front of me. I held one out to him and tried to pull it back when he grabbed at it, but he was much quicker than me. It wasn't difficult to ignite the rocket. All you had to do was push through a fuse made of thin fabric with your finger and then pull on a cord. What if the Kasen managed to do that and then hurt himself with the launching rocket? It would blame me for the pain.

"But Kian couldn't manage it. He examined the rocket while holding it with his tail. The hole in the fuse was covered so he couldn't accidentally pierce it. Finally, he handed the rocket back to me and pointed into the crowns of the brine trees. He wanted me to fire it for him, that was clear. But I put the other things away again and stood up, ignoring his request. He lowered his head like a bull about to charge, but probably just wanted to aim his speaking organ in my direction.

"'Rrr,' he said.

"'Air', I replied.

"Then I drew the outline of the Hopper on the ground. But Kian wouldn't let me finish the drawing. He pulled me away with his tail and sketched the Hopper himself. The drawing was more accurate than my own. He poked his right paw at it.

"'Rrr,' he said to it.

"I guess we had an understanding. I lifted the third rocket.

"'Rocket,' I said.

"'Kit,' he repeated.

"'Roc...ket.

"'Kit.

"'Rooo...cket.'

"'Kit.'

"Kian was stubborn. Maybe I should have settled for a compromise. 'Kit' was better than nothing. After all, we now had two words in common.

"'Rrr Kit,' I said, pointing to the drawing under his paw.

"He lifted his leg briefly, as if to check that the drawing had not changed.

"'Rrr Kit,' he said.

"We reached the Hopper in less than an hour. The Kasen showed no sign of fatigue afterwards - while my legs were still shaking, as Kian had often simply skipped over large holes in the crowns of the brine trees. He released me from the protective sling of his tail at the edge of the forest. I staggered towards the rocket. Halfway there, I waved to the Kasen, but it didn't follow me. The strange building, which it probably thought the Hopper was, inspired too much awe. Unlike the base, you could probably tell that the spaceship wasn't easy to crack. Just as I stepped into the airlock, a light shower of acid began. A few drops hit my back. I treated them in the airlock with a neutralizing spray. By the time I got to the control center, there was no sign of Kian.

"A night has now passed. I have recovered quite well and now hope that the Kasen will reappear. He wouldn't have forgotten our deal, Rrr for Kit, would he? The rockets are ready. I just hope I can teach him how to launch them safely. But there's no way I can afford to renege on the deal. Kian seems to be one of the few Kasen interested in things outside his usual experience. I'll be better prepared this time - the most important equipment is already in a rucksack. It may be very optimistic, but in addition to oxygen, I've also packed an ultrasound device and an X-ray fluoroscope. It would be exciting to find out more about the biology of the creatures. I'd also really like to know how they reproduce.

"Sending hugs. Your husband."

Yini dropped the letter. Mark Decker had some interesting stories to tell. He took his work very seriously. Apart from that, she hadn't learned enough about him to form an opinion. Was he really her father? He obviously had no idea himself. What happened when a woman went into a stasis chamber at an early stage of pregnancy? Did that also put the pregnancy into a waiting state? Yini didn't know, but she didn't feel like thinking about it today. It was time to go to bed. She got up, took one last look at Mike and walked to the door. There she changed her mind, went back to the desk and drew a heart on a piece of paper, which she stuck to the computer screen. Then she left Mike's room.

July 5, 2799, Gliese 411

The light was blinding, his breath smelled bad, he urgently needed to pee, and his stomach was growling. How he had missed this! A real, biological body was something different from being inside a machine. Monte suspected that human consciousness was still specially adapted to the Biobags, even though Terrans had long been able to exist in almost any environment with sufficient storage and processing capacity.

He struggled out of the glass coffin. He had to fight against the inertia of his muscles, which had not moved for days. He was conscious of pain when he first got up, but he was glad of it, because its existence meant that he would soon be able to experience it ceasing. It was chilly in the room, giving him goosebumps. Blue overalls hung from a hanger on the wall. He pushed himself off, floated over and put the garment on. It was unusual not to be alone on board anymore.

There was also a toilet in the room with the stasis chambers. That was good. Even in stasis, the digestive system was not completely switched off. Monte floated to the seat, strapped himself in and threaded his penis into the attachment of the urine aspirator. This stiffened it, which was a little impractical at the moment. He thought about how the doctor died, which seemed to help, and he could finally empty himself. It was a great feeling. He had completely forgotten how good that felt.

"Good morning!" called Tailin, who had made herself comfortable in the pilot's chair.

"Good morning," he replied.

"It's okay if I sit here, right?" she asked.

He must have looked at her glumly. Monte nodded. "I'm just hungry."

"That's what I thought," said Tailin. "Have a look in the kitchen."

He left the control center. On the floor below, a small menu had been set up on the dining table. He pulled himself up onto the chair and strapped himself in. Tailin followed him. She hung above him from the ceiling and turned her face towards him.

"Can I keep you company?" she asked.

"Gladly," he replied and examined what Tailin had served up.

It was a classic American breakfast. The appearance was almost perfect, and the consistency was also surprisingly good. The fried bacon was crispy, the eggs were neither crumbly nor slimy. Making something like this with the food synthesizer was almost impossible.

"How did you get it like that?" he asked.

"I helped it along with the torch from the workshop," said Tailin.

That explained the excellent result. Monte had always been too lazy to go to such lengths, but perhaps he should reconsider in future. He took another spoonful of the egg and bit into the bacon strips. You could almost believe that the ship had animal products on board, but the food synthesizer had produced it all from the basic ingredients of water and carbon dioxide.

"Thank you again for saving us," he said.

"Thank you," said Tailin. "Without you, I would be on my way to Earth right now."

"Without you, I'd be dead now," he said.

Honestly, he should be annoyed that she sent a helper with him. But he had to admit that he would hardly have survived without the AI.

"Then we're actually even now," said Tailin.

Actually? What did she mean?

"What I mean is that I would like to ask you for another favor."

Could she still read his mind? He looked around. No, that was impossible. He was in his body. Monte pinched his thigh. It had happened before that a consciousness was sent into a simulation in which it was made to believe it was in a Biobag. In reality, however, it was being monitored in the memory.

Tailin laughed briefly. She must have seen his move.

"It's not a simulation," she said. "But you should also know that pinching is not a sure bet."

Monte nodded. Of course he knew that. "So, what can I do for you?"

"We have to go to Neomars," said Tailin.

Monte choked and started coughing. A piece of bacon and a few crumbs of egg flew across the room. The bacon hit the wall and wobbled back towards him. Tailin caught it.

"I know, that's a pretty... surprising request," she said.

Tailin pushed off, floated to the garbage disposal and let the piece of bacon be sucked in.

"That's the understatement of the year," said Monte. "So everything that's happened in the last few days has been for nothing?"

"No, Monte, I don't want to turn myself in. But I really need to get to Neomars. Secretly. No one must find out."

"May I at least ask why? Why are you drawn there so urgently?"

"You're entitled to an answer, of course. I don't want to put you in danger again. All you have to do is take me to the nearest tachyon station, and we'll part ways there."

What did Tailin want with a tachyon station all of a sudden? It would only help her if she underwent a consciousness purification - something she had strictly refused to do so far. What had changed her mind so radically?

"A tachyon transmitter? You know what that means?" he asked.

"Yes. Special circumstances sometimes require extreme decisions."

"What is so extraordinary as to bring you to that decision?"

"It could be the end of the universe, Monte."

"That's still a few million billion years away."

"If nothing happens before then, yes."

"So, something could come up? What could be so powerful that it threatens the entire universe?"

"That's what I want to find out," Tailin replied as a deep crease formed on her forehead. "That's what I *must* find out."

"But what makes you think that?" asked Monte.

"When you left on the battleship, I used the time to investigate my own ship. The one you rescued me from."

Monte remembered. It was damaged in a very strange way.

"And what did you find?" he asked.

"I don't know," replied Tailin. "I'm at the end of my abilities. Unfortunately, all the options out there are terrifying. So terrifying, in fact, that a clandestine return to Neomars seems like child's play by comparison."

"Okay, so you think we're in for something terrible," Monte said. "But can't you at least explain it in a little more detail? What exactly is this danger?"

"My guess is that someone has constructed a weapon that threatens the very foundations of the universe."

"But we're a long way from any inhabited system here. Were you followed by another ship that had this weapon on board?"

"Of course I was pursued, but my pursuers did not have such a weapon."

"How did they hit you, then?"

"Perhaps from the moon, or from Neomars? The weapon could be used in a similar way to tachyon communication, that is, in real time over huge distances. That would be every military man's dream. Hitting the enemy where they feel safe."

"And you think Neomars has built such a weapon?"

"I can't imagine that. But all my instruments are on Neomars, the devices I could use to get to the bottom of the problem."

"Couldn't we procure instruments in the Terran Union? That seems safer than returning to Neomars."

"No. This concerns tachyon technology. Do you know of any Terran company that can produce such technology that isn't controlled by the military? We would stand out. The instrumentation is probably sitting around unused on Neomars."

"Are you sure? Maybe they're already using it to construct this ominous weapon."

"That's unlikely. The instruments are purely diagnostic tools.

I can use them to examine the condition of tachyons. It basically works like a tachyon receiver, only on a smaller scale. It couldn't be used to build a weapon."

Monte sighed. He didn't like the idea at all. Tailin had a right to her own life. She didn't belong to Neomars or the Terran Union. She should retire to some colonial planet, start a family... She was still young and didn't have to make the mistakes he had made.

"If Neomars catches you, they won't let you go," he said.

"I realize that."

Monte sighed again. He would most likely regret this, but he had no choice.

"If it's really that serious, I could retrieve the instruments for you. You've been hiding in the asteroid belt for so long."

"That really is a generous offer, but I can't let you do that, Monte. You've already put yourself in danger for me once. Besides, you don't know your way around Neomars."

"Oh, I've visited there twice, on missions. I know a few people who still owe me a favor or two."

"That wouldn't help you, because I secured the instruments before I left. You don't have a prayer of getting them out of there."

Monte looked at Tailin. What she was saying sounded like a lie. Why would she secure a few simple diagnostic instruments against access by third parties? When she escaped, she hadn't even known she would return. But what if it was true?

"You don't want help. I'll have to accept that."

Monte was both disappointed and relieved, which annoyed him. Neomars had difficult terrain: negative 292 degrees Fahrenheit on the surface, a toxic atmosphere and omnipresent surveillance. He always wondered why the people there put up with it. It must be their shared anger at the Terran Union that united them. After all, Earth had destroyed their homeland - even if that had been centuries ago.

"Don't be angry, Monte. This is really something I have to do on my own."

"And you'll even have your consciousness uploaded for this?"

"It's not like I have any other choice," said Tailin. "If I travel in a stasis chamber, I might get there much too late."

"Is there such a rush? It often takes years of testing before a new type of weapon is put into service."

"It could be the tests we should be most afraid of."

August 10, 2802, Earth's moon

Yini came to. The reading bowl beeped, complaining that it had lost contact. Yini switched off the beeping and sat up. Tsai Tailin was still alive, and she was on her way to Neomars, maybe even arrived there already. Who could she ask about that? She slapped her forehead with the flat of her hand. Who was the chronoscribe here? It was her job to determine the exact timeline.

However, she only had the data from the tachyon station. Yini stood up and put on her wig. There must be more data she could use to classify the events more precisely. She already knew who would help her: her brother. As the maintenance supervisor's assistant, he knew people everywhere, and he certainly had acquaintances who owed him favors. Kang was different from her; he was good at making conversation with strangers. Which made it all the stranger that he had never found anyone to have a relationship with. Perhaps he expected too much. People were one thing above all: different. Yini was always amazed at the astonishing diversity within a single species. Was it the same with snails or hedgehogs?

So, off to Kang. There was only one problem: the working day wasn't over yet, and Kang's boss, Zahir, attached great importance to working hours. Kang often complained to her how fussy Zahir was about that. She would need an excuse. Yini looked at the reader. For now, it had given her all the information she needed. She yanked the cable that connected the reading bowl and the evaluation computer out of its socket. The reading bowl beeped angrily, but this time the noise could not be deactivated.

"Computer? Give me the janitor, please," she ordered.

"This is Zahir. What can I do for you, Yini?"

"I wanted to thank you for the valuable tips you gave me the other day."

"You're welcome. Did you have any luck with Szymanski and Dubois?"

"They both helped me a lot."

She'd had the best luck with the one she hadn't wanted to visit. But what was going on with Mike was none of Zahir's business. She herself had no idea what they were exactly. Yini pushed the thought aside.

"But that's not why you're getting in touch," Zahir said.

"How do you know? Can you read minds?"

"I hear the reading bowl beeping. It's no longer connected to the computer. Let me guess; you tripped over the cable when you got up."

"Yes, that's exactly what happened! You're clairvoyant!"

"No, I've been fighting with the manufacturer of those devices since the latest generation was introduced here. The stupid cables just hang there, because they've done away with the spring mechanism that used to automatically pull them back into the housing. Now eavesdroppers keep tripping over them all the time. The manufacturer claims it's cheaper, and they say everything is so light in lunar gravity that there's no risk of damage or injury."

"Unfortunately, that's not true," said Yini.

In fact, it wasn't the first time this had happened to her. She was reassured that her actions would not stand out.

"I know," Zahir said. "I'll send Kang over there, if you don't mind."

"Yes, that would be perfect."

"Yini?"

"Yes?"

It was strange for the janitor to follow up like that. It sounded like he had something on his mind.

"Please talk to Kang. I'm worried about him. As soon as the

conversation turns to you, he becomes... different. He's tight-lipped. He wasn't like that before."

"Thank you, Zahir, for bringing this to my attention. I was planning to talk to him anyway."

"Thank you."

Now she felt bad. She had tricked Zahir, even though he only wanted the best for her brother.

KANG ARRIVED EXACTLY 31 MINUTES LATER. HE MUST HAVE BEEN busy elsewhere, because it took fifteen minutes to get to her room from the janitor's office. Her brother was carrying a backpack containing tools and had a replacement cable in his hand.

"Zahir sent me," he said.

"Hey, is that any way to greet your sister? Glad you're here, and thanks for taking the time."

Sometimes, when Kang's mood wasn't too bad, showering him with kindness worked. At some point, he could no longer defend himself and gave up his grumpy attitude.

"I'm only here because my boss ordered me to," said Kang.

Today was probably not one of those days. But she wouldn't stoop to his level. Another argument wouldn't help anyone.

"I'm happy to see you anyway," she said.

"Here, the cable," Kang said. "Step aside."

He didn't even try to ask nicely.

"Of course," Yini said. "I broke the cable on purpose."

"Are you crazy?"

"I wanted a chance to talk to you, Kang. Look, we're siblings. We should stick together."

"Is that so?"

He didn't look at her, just put his backpack on the ground and unpacked his tools.

"Yes, it's true. Kang, I need you."

Maybe it would help that he was needed. Wasn't that the strongest motive of most people?

"Oh, but you've got your Mike now. He's much more experienced and smarter than me, and I'm sure... never mind."

Was he really jealous? Then there could be no compromise.

Her love life was none of her brother's business. She bit her lower lip. Kang wasn't making it easy for her.

"That doesn't mean I don't need you anymore," she said. "After all, you're in the janitor's office."

"Aha, you want to spy on Zahir? Is that what you want? I'm definitely not going to say anything bad about him."

"Nor should you, Kang. It's about something completely different."

"And what's that?" He opened the cover of the computer.

"It's about our mother, Tsai Tailin. Apparently, she made it back to the solar system."

"That again? I already told you who our parents are. That woman is a fraud. She *must* be a fraud."

"And if she's not? I saw her through the eyes of a man who works as a detective, so to speak. She looks just like me."

"Because that's how you wanted to see her. It's a known effect of eavesdropping. The images you see blend with your own thoughts and images. You should discuss it with your supervisor, not with me."

"Kang, I can tell the difference perfectly well. I've been able to observe them for several days. Those blended effects usually disappear quickly when the consciousness realizes it is seeing something else."

"You're welcome to believe whatever you want. But leave me out of it. I never want to hear about this so-called mother again."

"And if she is? Wouldn't you want to see her at least once?"

"If she was our mother, I'd wish her dead. If she was our mother, then she abandoned us at the age of two! Nobody needs a mother like that!"

Kang spat, but quickly wiped the stain away with a handkerchief.

"So you don't want to help me look for her?"

He shook his head. "You know where she is. What's the point of looking for her? Let her freeze to death in that icy hell."

Icy hell? Was he talking about Neomars? She had never mentioned Tsai Tailin's whereabouts.

"What made you think of Neomars of all places?" she asked.

"They were looking for her, weren't they? They must have caught her. What Neomars wants, they get. Like my sister.

That's how it's always been. But this time you'll have to help yourself."

Kang pushed the side panel back onto the computer and locked it. The scratchy clicking sound hurt her ears.

"Done," he said. "But please don't trip again anytime soon. And never, ever, ever ask me for help with some pretend mother."

IT HAD BEEN A MISTAKE TO ASK KANG. YINI TOOK A WET WIPE from the container and used it to clean herself.

How had Kang known that their mother was on her way to Neomars? He hadn't batted an eyelid when she'd asked, but his answer hadn't been logical. Neomars didn't always get what they wanted. The universe, even the area colonized by humanity, was big enough to hide for a lifetime. On Terra Nova, for example, Tsai Tailin would definitely have been out of Neomars's reach.

The rumpled blanket and the displaced reading bowl the other day... Kang had at least basic training as an eavesdropper. Had he been spying on the transmissions? But why? He could have just asked her, couldn't he? She would much rather have told her brother about the adventures of Claudio Pedramonte than that shady guy, Smith. But Kang was supposedly not interested in their mother at all. She didn't believe him, but why was he so keen to hide that from her?

Yini pressed the green button, and the toilet started its self-cleaning process. The bracelet on her wrist vibrated. A message appeared on the tiny display: "You have a slight vitamin A deficiency." Ah, indeed.

"Toilet, do you have any idea what Kang is up to?" she asked.

Yini knew what would happen. One of the ubiquitous microphones picked up her request. The system realized that she was alone in the room, so it interpreted itself as the addressee of the message and searched for the answer.

"Your brother, Tsai Kang, is currently planning to repair a malfunction in the AR system in Sector 7C. This information is seven minutes old."

"Thank you, toilet. You're obviously just as smart as I am."

"I'm sorry, Tsai Yini, but your speech intonation was not clear. Should I interpret your sentence as a statement or a question? Here's a tip: If you add the keyword 'question' to the sentence, you will avoid such queries."

The computer system of the Great Archive liked to give such advice, which seemed a little passive-aggressive. Yini just smiled. Let the system see how it coped with her sentence. But her smile felt stale. Her brother should be there for what she was about to do. It was their joint task. Of course, she would solve it anyway. She was not alone.

●

"He definitely doesn't want to help you?" asked Mike. "I don't understand that. But I don't have any siblings."

They sat opposite each other at his desk. When someone entered the office, it looked like Yini was just a normal client, looking for some object from Dr. Wilson's inventory.

"I think he's deeply hurt," Yini said. "I kind of understand. What kind of mother abandons her two-year-old twins? But I think it's unfair to judge her without knowing the circumstances."

"Maybe he's a bit jealous, too. You've always been very close, haven't you?"

Yini nodded.

"Now he thinks he's losing you. You're spending time with me instead of him, and you're also looking for a mother who's a stranger to him."

"Maybe that's it," Yini said, kneading her hands. "I just don't know how to convince him that his fears are unfounded."

"They're not. What he's afraid of is real. What if you decide to fly to Neomars?"

Yini felt her cheeks grow warm. She hadn't mentioned that to Mike yet. Somehow, she had hoped he would offer to help her of his own accord, but he made no move. He seemed to have no idea what step to take next.

"Actually, I have thought of that," she said quietly.

She didn't look at Mike. She didn't want to see the rejection on his face right away. It was enough for him to say it.

But he only exclaimed "Oh!"

Oh? What kind of answer was that? Now she had to raise her eyes. Mike was pale and had reddish spots on his forehead and cheeks.

"You look like you've just witnessed a murder," she said.

"I... yes. Well. Just some rather unpleasant memories."

"Have you been to Neomars?"

"Yes, and it was terrible. My first girlfriend got it into her head to emigrate to Neomars."

"Because of the beautiful landscape?" she asked sarcastically.

"No, because of their genetic engineering. She wasn't happy with her body. Too slow, too sensitive, too weak..."

"She could have bought a fancy robot body."

"She didn't want that. It had to be her own body, and that was only possible on Neomars. We flew there once, and it was terrible. The cold, the confinement... As a normal human, you are confined to the tunnels."

"But isn't it exactly the same on the moon?"

"No, the whole universe awaits me on the surface of the moon. Billions of light years! On Neomars, you can maybe see a hundred yards at best."

"I understand."

"And then there's the fact that standard humans are always a bit looked down upon. That didn't bother my girlfriend, but I wanted to stay the way I was."

"I'm glad you didn't let yourself change."

"Thank you, Yini. Unfortunately, my stay did change me a little - I've had enough of Neomars."

Her chest constricted. Yini looked at the tabletop. That was it, then. They had only known each other for a few days. She could hardly ask Mike to overcome old traumas for her. Her brother should be her helper on this mission, not a friend who had nothing to do with the affair. *Kang, how could you leave me like this? Damn it, you have a duty to...*

"That being said... if you have to go there to look for your mother, I'll go with you," Mike said. "That is, assuming you want me with you."

"Really?"

Yini studied his face. He still looked shaken, but nodded.

"It could be that you'd rather find your mother alone," he said.

She shook her head vigorously. "No, I can't do it alone. I really hoped my brother would help me. But I hope you don't feel like a substitute. I'd be happy if you came with me."

"Then so be it," said Mike.

Yini jumped up, ran around the desk, threw her arms around his neck and kissed him.

"Do you have any idea how you want to proceed?" Mike asked.

Yini was sitting in front of the desk again. She looked at his face and noticed a reddish streak on his temple.

"Wipe your right temple," she said. "I think I left some lipstick there."

She had put on her make-up before work today because she wanted to visit Mike afterwards. He moistened his finger and rubbed his temple.

"You got it," she said, "and no, I have no idea yet."

"Then we need to talk about transportation first," Mike said.

"Definitely not a tachyon transmission," Yini said.

"I'm not a fan of that either. But in that case... even with the fastest courier ship, we'd have to travel for at least two months."

"We'll arrive in our own bodies that way," Yini stated.

"There are good Biobags for hire," said Mike. "They're adapted to the extreme conditions, and the first three days are included in the price of the transfer. That's how it was back then, anyway."

"I can't face my mother in a rented body! Imagine a random woman coming up to you and claiming to be your daughter."

"Don't you think she would still recognize you? Surely you have some kind of connection?"

"I don't believe that. If anything, she'll recognize me by my appearance. That's how it happened with me. I saw her through Claudio Pedramonte's eyes and truly thought I was seeing myself."

"But the last time she saw you was over twenty years ago."

"That doesn't matter. She looks at herself in the mirror every day, and I'm sure she remembers what she used to look like."

"And what if you don't recognize her? She must be getting pretty old, over fifty now, right?"

"We still have to work that out," said Yini. "I need some data from other departments. Would you help me find it?"

"Look, here," said Yini. "The transmissions from Pedramonte only just arrived."

"How do you know that?" asked Mike.

"That's accessible information for me as an eavesdropper. I'm supposed to chronicle the times, after all."

"I see."

"The sender is a mobile tachyon station in interstellar space that the Terran Union placed there to shorten the signal paths. It took him and my mother a little over three years to get to that station from Gliese 411, where Pedramonte's experiences took place. So, my mother would have arrived in the Gliese 411 system by 2799 at the latest – probably earlier, because her distress signal took two years to reach the tachyon station."

"The question is, where from?"

"I think she answered that: she came as a refugee from Neomars. At Gliese 411, which is eight light years away from the solar system, she still had her own body, so she must have escaped from Neomars at least fourteen years ago. That's as quick as it gets."

"How old are you, Yini?"

Hadn't she told him that already?

"Twenty-four. I was born in 2778," she replied. "My parents supposedly escaped from Neomars when we were two years old, in 2780. If my real mother arrived at Gliese 411 in 2796, she must have left Neomars in 2782 at the latest."

"But an earlier date could also be possible, for example 2780. She might not have traveled directly to Gliese 411, and not at top speed."

"That's true. Everything fits so far. She could have handed us over to my parents in 2780 and then fled. Or they met on the run, and my parents offered to look after us. I wouldn't put it past them – they're very nice people. They always looked after any cat that wandered into our house."

"And what about your father, Mark Decker?" Mike asked. "Could he even be your father?"

"You mean there could be a third party? How long have those letters been in your collection?"

"Wait, let me check." Mike leaned over the desk. A screen popped up, and he typed something. "I've got it," he said. "Artifact BC32X, a collection of digitized letters. They were captured six years ago by a Dr. Michael Koslowski from the Department of Tachyon Transmissions."

"The name means nothing to me. Maybe it was my predecessor."

"Koslowski had the letters printed out to get closer to the original state. He was probably expecting some secret codes in them."

"What made him think that?"

"It was probably because of the strange way the letters turned up on Terra Nova."

"Now it's getting interesting."

"The letters were in a Hopper, but the ship was otherwise empty. Mark Decker must have sent it towards Terra Nova sometime after the rest of the crew left. The letters are supposed to be a warning, but that seemed implausible to those in charge."

"So far, Decker has only described his research work. It's excitingly written, but there's no mention of any danger."

"Maybe there will be. You should read them to the end."

"That's my plan. Still, my mother is taking the lead at the moment."

"But your mother also seems to be connected to Decker's story."

"I don't think so. Look, Mike. Decker must have sent the letters he wrote to a Tsai Tailin in the Hopper towards Terra Nova over thirty years ago. They were sent from there to the solar system six years ago via tachyon transmission. This Tsai Tailin presumably left Gliese 163 c a few months before the Hopper, and she was on a faster ship, a TransVec. Nevertheless, it would take her at least a few years to reach Terra Nova. From Terra Nova to Neomars, however, it would take at least seventy years. In that case, the TransVec wouldn't have arrived in the solar system yet. So, the Tailin from Pedramonte's transmission could be my mother, but not the one from the letters. Then of course Decker can't be my father either."

Yini took a deep breath. Two Tsai Tailins who were both physicists? That would be a very strange coincidence. Or had she miscalculated? She was an experienced chronoscribe, but dealing with dates still left her breathless. The universe, with its overwhelming size, was merciless about stealing many years of a traveler's life. The deal was a particularly nasty one: those who roamed the cosmos got to keep their own years, but lost the life they could have led.

"You're forgetting one thing," said Mike. "There's a tachyon station in orbit around Terra Nova. Tsai Tailin could have gone directly to Neomars from there. Then she would have had enough time to get pregnant with you two and give birth to twins."

"I've gotten to know Tsai Tailin quite well," said Yini. "At least through someone else's eyes. For a tachyon transfer, she would have had to allow a consciousness purification. She stoutly refused."

Technically that wasn't true, because at the end of the last transmission, Tailin had seen no other solution. But that had been a clearly recognizable development.

"And apart from that," Yini continued, "there's a practical reason against it: pregnancies aren't transmitted by tachyon, only the information that forms your consciousness."

Mike smacked his forehead. "Of course, you're absolutely right. Then Tsai Tailin is either not the same person - or she's not your mother."

Yini had to swallow. She had already decided that her father and mother were not her biological parents - and had deliberately kept this secret. Had she done them an injustice? And what about Kang? Was he right to be angry with her? But the image was still there. The woman Claudio Pedramonte had seen was herself, only slightly older. She had never seen the other Tailin.

But it was not yet time to conclude the story and go back to work. This Tsai Tailin could still be her mother. She would not be Mark Decker's wife, the geophysicist who had explored Gliese 163c, but a tachyon physicist from Neomars who had escaped from there 22 years ago. This Tailin would have slept for about fifteen years on the way to Gliese 411 in the stasis tank, plus another three years on the way to the tachyon station. That would make her only four years older today than on the day her twins last saw her. It would be easy to explain why Yini had recognized herself in her.

"There's no way around it," said Yini. "We have to go to Neomars. I want to sort this out now."

"I've got an idea," said Mike.

"That's good, what is it?" asked Yini.

"I can't tell you. You have to trust me. I'm going to see someone now who might be able to help me."

"Would you like me to go with you?"

"No, that wouldn't be helpful – on the contrary. This person only trusts me."

"Suit yourself."

"It will take a while. Will you wait for me here?"

"All right, I'll wait. There are still plenty of letters left."

He stood up, took off his coat, gave her a kiss on the lips and left the office.

"Dear Tailin," Decker had begun his next letter. "The T-base no longer exists. The two Kasen really did a great job. I used the day yesterday to carry everything that was still usable to the Hopper. It wasn't much. That wasn't directly due to the Kasen attack, but to the other flora and fauna on the planet, which was able to stroll right in for two days. Fortunately, the most important measuring instruments were stored in the Hopper.

"Today I ask myself why I was stupid enough to set up the T-camp in the first place. The Hopper has plenty of space for me. It's a bit further away, but hopefully that won't be a problem. When the Kasen come back, I expect them to take me back to their settlement. I already have a rucksack with the most important—"

The letter ended in mid-sentence. Yini feared there might have been another attack.

"Dear Tailin," it continued. "You wouldn't believe it, but yesterday I fell asleep while writing. Unbelievable! My stay down here must be wearing me out more than I thought. Unfortunately, the Kasen still haven't come back. I'm thinking about firing off a signal rocket to remind them of their 'Kit' deal.

"Wait, now there's a knock. That can only mean one thing.

"I was right. The outside cameras show two Kasen. They're probably the same ones who kidnapped me the first time. This time they apparently just knocked on the outside wall and then politely withdrew. They're hiding at the edge of the forest. At least that's what they think, but the infrared camera can still see them. I hope that's not a bad sign. But now I have to go. Keep your fingers crossed for me!"

Yini imagined Mark Decker getting out of the Hopper. He would probably make himself as tall as possible so that his visitors would recognize him. Had he given them their gifts straight away? She pulled the next letter from the pile.

"Dear Tailin," Decker wrote. "You won't believe what I was able to experience today. I'm writing you this letter while lying in one of the tents that I only saw from the outside last time. The broken ends of the wooden poles reveal that it must be newly built. The Kasen probably built it especially for me. I don't have to share it with anyone, either. That's practical, because it means I can seal the inside for the night. It's ten times more pleasant to be able to sleep without a mask.

"I was also able to dissuade them from lighting a fire in the tent, as they seem to do in all the others. I simply showed them the electric heater in my suit. I should have enough breathing air with me this time. I'm sure I'll have enough for a week, plus I have an oxygen separator. The only problem is the electricity. You know the separator - it needs as much direct sunlight as possible. If the worst comes to the worst, I will have to persuade the Kasen to take me to the top of the brine trees.

"But back to my experience today. Kian and his friend, partner, spouse, whatever, took me to an area I dubbed the 'black swamp'. You can probably already imagine what it looks like. It's a large clearing in the brine forest. It could not have been created naturally. All that remains of the brine trees that once stood here are a few stumps that are broken off in a bizarre way. Incredible forces must have been at work here. Not even a space station crash could have caused something like this.

"The trees are not burned, they have been mechanically chopped to pieces. The ground is soft and becomes increasingly muddy towards the middle of the clearing. It is slightly lower than the surrounding area. That is probably why the acidic precipitation collects there. I walked a little way into the swamp, which Kian and his friend protested for a long time. But my boots are not bothered by a bit of acid. What I hadn't calculated was the sticking power of the mud. By the end, I could no longer lift my feet. Of course, I could have taken my boots off, but that wouldn't have been good for my feet. Luckily, Kian was able to pull me out of the swamp with his long tail.

"'Then you weren't very far in', you would say now. But you're wrong. Due to my experiment, I witnessed another incredible event: because Kian's tail wasn't long enough to rescue me, the Kasen borrowed his friend's tail. The two body parts joined together at their ends and pulled me out of the swamp like a single tail twice as long. Can you imagine that? The creatures can borrow each other's body parts! I've only seen it happen with the tail, but why wouldn't it work with the other limbs?

"It's a real shame that the rest of you are no longer here. Especially that *you* are no longer here. There's so much to discover!"

That sounded exciting. Yini envied the man a little. Everything she saw all day was second-hand, even these letters. Mark Decker, on the other hand, was exploring what no one had ever seen before. Or had explored? Was he still alive? Maybe Mike could find out for her. Even if Decker wasn't her father, he was an interesting person who was passionate about his research.

"Kasen settlement, day 2.

"I refused to leave the tent today. Who knows what Kian and his friend think of me now? But I couldn't help myself. I took samples at the black swamp, of course. The viscous, dark mass seemed strange to me from the first moment. And I was right. It consists of complex silicon compounds.

"Yes, silicon - the basic element of sand and rock. Nevertheless, the mass is elastic. This is because the silicon in it does not form crystals, but chains, molecules reminiscent of organic compounds. The only difference is that the compounds do not contain carbon, but silicon, which is also tetravalent. This apparently makes the mass particularly durable. Most astrobiologists, and I am not the only one, consider such compounds to be energetically improbable. After all, two hydrogen atoms and one oxygen atom form water, nothing more complicated. But hydrogen peroxide does still exist. And there must be circumstances under which these silicon compounds were formed.

"So, there's a knock. They're probably trying to get me to come out of my tent again. They're right. I should keep them company for a while. Maybe there are more exciting things to discover."

Hopefully, Mark Decker, hopefully! Yini looked at her watch. Mike had been gone for half an hour and she hadn't missed him yet.

"Kasen settlement, day 3.

"Something terrible happened yesterday, and I'm somehow to blame. It upsets me so much that I'd rather not write about it, especially because I've made this kind of mistake before. But I owe you the truth.

"So... The two Kasen picked me up at my tent. They brought the signal rockets I had given them as part of the deal. It was obvious what they wanted: They wanted me to show them how to use the rockets. I was unsure at first. But Kian kept showing me the rockets and nudging me with the tip of his tail.

"When I didn't react, the nudges got stronger and stronger, and by the end they were really painful. I complained about it, of course, but he pretended not to understand me. But I understood him. I had shown him what the things could do, and now I was denying him the chance to try it out for himself. That wasn't fair from his point of view. I finally let myself be convinced. To be honest, I was also a bit scared because I didn't know how brutal he might become towards me.

"We moved away from the settlement so as not to accidentally set fire to a tent. Kian's still nameless friend accompanied us. I first showed Kian how to remove the safety catch from the rocket. Then I pointed it in a safe direction and pulled the cord. With a hiss, the projectile shot out of the narrow tube, flew into the air, crashed into the crowns of the brine trees and disappeared in a spray of red sparks. The two Kasen roared loudly.

"'Kit,' said Kian.

"'Yes, exactly,' I said. 'That was a good start.'

"The Kasen nodded, probably because it had seen me do the head movement before. We had probably started imitating each other - a sign of empathy.

"Kian, who stood next to me on two legs and towered over

me, picked up a rocket. One of his claws sank into the hole in the fuse as if of its own accord. With the other, he pulled the cord, just as I had done. The rocket was already fizzing. However, he wasn't aiming at the crowns of the brine trees, but at his friend, who was laughing. What were they both thinking? Should I throw myself in between them? The Kasen were big and strong, but certainly still vulnerable. I shouted 'No' and 'Stop it' and 'Aim somewhere else', but he didn't understand me, probably mistaking my sounds for pure enthusiasm, because he roared in response. The bullet came out of the barrel and flew straight into Kian's friend's face. The Kasen fell over backwards like a felled log.

"I immediately ran to him and threw myself over his face to put out the flames. His fur had caught fire. A paw grabbed me from behind and flung me away. I assumed that my last hour had come. Kian would blame me for his friend's injury and kill me. But he just left me lying there. I pulled myself up and saw him grab his friend by the back and run with him towards the settlement.

"*Shit, shit, shit*. Where was I supposed to go? The Hopper was probably twelve miles away, and I wouldn't be able to find it without my equipment. The settlement, on the other hand, was almost within shouting distance. If the Kasen wanted to kill me, I had no way to stop them. I followed Kian's tracks to the settlement.

"The Kasen had halted in a clearing in the middle of the settlement. Kian's injured friend was lying on his back in front of him. He had his arms and legs stretched out to the side. His eyes were closed. How was he? I wanted to examine him, but the tip of a tail held me back. It belonged to Kian, who I could now easily distinguish from his fellow Kasen.

"A particularly large Kasen approached the injured creature. If I am not mistaken, it was the carver. He had brought his tools with him. How was he going to heal the injured Kasen with those? I tried to reach him again. Kian's friend had probably suffered an eye injury, but surely it could be healed. I had medical supplies. I wasn't sure how well they would work on alien life forms, but surely that was better than letting him die?

"But the Kasen weren't going to do that. The carver pulled out a particularly large drill. The spiral-shaped cutting edge shone. It was made of a white material, probably multifeet bone. The carver raised the drill high above his head, let out a blood-curdling scream and sank the drill into the injured creature's throat. I felt sick and had to vomit. Another intelligent creature had died because of me.

"After I spilled the contents of my stomach on the ground, I turned to Kian and spoke to him. 'Why is he killing your friend? Why wasn't I allowed to save him?' I had many other questions. Kian looked at me. I thought I saw a certain curiosity on his face. I'm sure he didn't understand a word I said. I didn't perceive any sadness. When I had finished, he licked at the stain from the contents of my stomach.

"There was more between us than I had imagined."

Whew, that was exhausting. Why hadn't these letters been previously published? Surely they couldn't be the fever dreams of a desperate man. Or was it simply because it was not yet possible to ask the author for permission? It was time for Mark Decker to arrive on Terra Nova. Yini also had a few questions for him.

"Kasen settlement, day 4.

"Every cloud has a silver lining. God, I hate that saying. But there is a bit of truth in it. It's still quite early in the morning. I got up before the crack of dawn to find out more about the Kasen. With the X-ray and ultrasound scanner and a few sample tubes, I walked to the place where the carver killed his injured conspecific. The corpse was still there but was already being visited by a variety of scavengers, which I first had to scare away. Then I was finally able to scan the creature.

"The results were quite surprising. Its body does not consist of separate organs, as I expected. Rather, all vital functions seem to be distributed. The only things clearly recognizable are channels for water, food and breathing air. They become narrower and narrower towards the inside of the body until they are microscopic in size. This is how they supply all their cells with everything they need. As the creature has no heart to set the pace, I couldn't find any definitive sign that the corpse was any more or less alive than before. There was certainly less life in it, but the majority of its cells were still functioning at the time of my examination. There must be some kind of control mechanism at or below the throat that the carver had overridden, because Kian's friend was clearly dead, even if his cells didn't realize it. Unfortunately, the carver must have destroyed this organ with his tools. In any case, I found no trace of it.

"Nor could I make out any reproductive organs. Perhaps the creatures reproduce by parthenogenesis, i.e. by simple cell division? My search for a brain was of course also unsuccessful. It is impressive to see the different paths evolution can take.

"But even more exciting, not to say frightening, were the analyses of the cell material that I have just completed. You remember the silicon compounds I found in the black swamp? They also occur in these creatures, whose biochemistry is nevertheless based on hydrocarbons. I can't yet say definitively whether the silicon compounds help or harm them, but they are definitely foreign to the body, and I haven't found any of them in the other, less gifted species on this planet.

"What was striking, however, was that in the cells of the dead body which were still going about their daily business, the silicon compound content was higher than the average. So perhaps they have a life-prolonging or at least stabilizing effect. I had a crazy idea earlier, when I went outside for a moment: maybe I can develop a substance that neutralizes the silicon compounds. It would be interesting to see what effect it has on the casings.

"Ah, I have to stop here. I hear footsteps outside."

Yini yawned, which was not due to the content of the letters. It had been a busy day. Mike still hadn't returned. She could lie in his bed and wait for him. Yini got up and stripped down to her underpants. She was shivering. It was chilly in Mike's room. She took two more letters from the pile and lay down in Mike's bed. The blanket was thin. When she pulled it over her, her nipples stiffened. Too bad Mike wasn't here now. She lay down on her side and continued reading.

"Kasen settlement, day 5.

"Unfortunately, I didn't have time to finish my letter to you yesterday. Something terrible has happened! I regret more and more that I allowed you to leave. I should have prevented it. You should have been there when I saw what the Kasen showed me today.

"I don't know if it was planned. Maybe it was carelessness. When Kian came to my tent yesterday, he clearly invited me to accompany him. We walked to the place where the carver had treated his friend to death. Kian showed no distress, nor did the other Kasen. Perhaps it is not customary in their culture, or perhaps I simply don't understand their expressions. We must not forget how subtle non-linguistic communication can sometimes be. Among the Kasen, I am something akin to autistic.

"But Kian picked up the body. He got down on all fours and placed the dead body on his back with the help of his tail. It looked as if the dead body was clinging to Kian's fur. Perhaps it was an instinctive reaction of the still living cells. Or maybe there was still some residual consciousness in him. If thinking is distributed throughout the body like all the other functions, this could generate tremendous resilience. We should instead ask ourselves why evolution has made us so vulnerable.

"I realized on the way that our destination must be the black swamp. The group consisted of seven Kasen and me. I brought up the rear. The carver led the way. If the body on Kian's back started to slide, he straightened it out with his tail. He didn't need to look behind him. I don't know how he managed that. Three of the Kasen in the procession carried something like shovels, probably made of bone.

"When they arrived at the black swamp, they used the tools to dig a hole. It was obviously hard work, because they took turns. Three Kasen dug at a time, while the other three rested. The carver also took part. Only Kian had to stand there with the body on his back. The swamp evidently served as a graveyard for the Kasen. I watched them from a distance as the black mass splashed about. Every now and then a muffled sound could be heard, presumably when their shovels collided.

"When the hole was big enough for the dead body, the Kasen halted their work. They gathered around the hole. I joined them. At that moment I saw it: at the end where I was standing, something metallic shone. Or had I made a mistake? It was far too cloudy to see anything. I took out my flashlight and shone it into the grave. The Kasen - except Kian - made threatening noises, but I didn't care. There was clearly an artificial structure down there. It was made of machined metal, which the Kasen didn't have yet. I saw a triangular surface that jutted upwards at an angle, then bent at an angle of about a hundred degrees and ended in another triangle. I couldn't make out what was behind it. But it was nothing that could have formed naturally.

"A spaceship! I think I even shouted the word out loud. An

unknown, space-faring civilization! What mankind has always sought and feared! And their relics were buried here. I wanted to jump down, but Kian, even though he was still carrying his dead friend, must have recognized my intention and held me down with his tail. I protested, but he didn't understand me, or didn't want to understand me. Perhaps he saved my life, because the other Kasen were already all shouting in confusion.

"When the carver joined in, I was almost deafened. The others immediately quieted down. The carver himself then took the body from Kian's back and placed it in the grave. Without any further ceremony, the Kasen filled it up again. Kian didn't take part this time either, even though he was free again. Perhaps they wanted to compensate him for his loss. It's a shame I'll probably never know what the dead Kasen meant to Kian.

"As for the artificial structure, I had a plan. I already knew the way from the settlement to the swamp. I would go there at night, and take a closer look at what I had spotted. The Kasen were obviously not interested in the object. It couldn't be the first time they'd seen it. Presumably, since they didn't know what to do with metal, they left it alone, just as we would ignore a randomly unearthed stone.

"I got ready for bed and was just about to finish the letter to you when Kian came and stood outside the tent. I immediately realized what it was about. He must have recognized my great interest. I packed up my measuring instruments, put on my breathing mask and left the tent. Kian put the tip of his tail on my mouth. He was telling me to be quiet. He had one of the white shovels on his back. Was he really going to open his dead friend's grave with me?

"No. Kian led me to the clearing with the swamp from another direction, a side away from the settlement. It wasn't completely dark; the night was lit up by some bioluminescent floating creatures. They stayed within the clearing, perhaps because there were no weaver nets there. This gave me a good view of the piece of debris that must have landed here a long time ago. My impression was that it had dug deep into the ground. Nevertheless, what was visible was still impressive.

"It was clearly not human technology. Neither Neomars nor the Terran Union construct spaceships in such a perfect crystalline form. The part visible above the swamp consisted of three octahedrons stuck together, eight-sided, regular bodies that looked like two pyramids glued together at the base. The foremost body, however, looked as if it had been cut off, as if an unknown force had simply removed a third of its shape from the universe. I stepped closer. Kian didn't hold me back, but he didn't follow me either. The accident, or whatever it was, had opened the octahedron. However, I couldn't see the contents from my perspective. I knew the flora and fauna of the planet wouldn't have left much.

"Nevertheless, I was shocked when I was finally able to see inside the octahedron. I had expected something like a cabin, a few chairs on which more-or-less humanoid astronauts had sat and explored their surroundings on screens. Perhaps, if they were wearing sturdy spacesuits, even their skeletons were still intact so that I could examine them.

"But I found nothing like that. The octahedron contained smaller octahedra, and these in turn contained even smaller octahedra. With a microscope, I could have probably found another generation of octahedrons. Otherwise, the object was empty. If the octahedrons had ever been filled with any mass, it had evaporated. There were no aliens here, just the viscous mass that made up the swamp and had somehow diffused into my Kasen. Yes, I already think of the beings here as my Kasen, and yes, that is arrogant. Kian probably sees me as his 'whatever' as well, and he's more right about that than I am, because I've never saved his life - he's saved mine several times.

"Of course, I didn't want to accept the find just like that. An alien spaceship wasn't enough for me – typical Mark – I also wanted to find the aliens. I used ultrasound and X-ray scanners on the externally intact octahedrons. The images the devices gave me were beautiful and regular, showing octahedrons of all sizes. I asked Kian for the shovel and removed some of the black sludge that covered the ship at ground level. At a depth of one yard, I came across another smooth surface. The X-ray scanner told me that it was an octahedron.

"What had I seen in the grave? A metal plate that bent about a hundred degrees. The sides of an octahedron are at an angle of just under 110 degrees to each other. I wouldn't find anything different in the grave than here. Maybe I was just unlucky? The octahedrons could be something like cargo holds, while the actual spaceship in which its pilots were sitting was underground. But this was the Kasen graveyard. They wouldn't let me dig it up so easily. I needed the space station. There was a neutron scanner there that could reach several yards below the surface. I could have used its data to search specifically for a shape that wasn't an octahedron.

"Could have, should have. I had to work with what I had. I climbed out of my hole, pulled out my laser cutter and used it to remove a small piece of the material from the cut octahedron. The cut edges left by my cutter were far rougher than the edges caused by the accident."

"Settlement of the Kasen, day 6.

"I'm still processing my findings from the last few days. I'm not making much progress in analyzing the silicon compounds. They are amazingly varied and constantly changing, even though they are based on simple principles. In this respect, they remind me of the building blocks popular with children. This gave me an idea: if I can block the connectors, for example by using a different connection, then the silicon connections should dissolve - at least they could no longer change. However, I need the Hopper to synthesize a suitable molecule, which means I'm not making any progress in this direction. It's probably time for Kian to take me back to the Hopper. I hope it will be easier to teach him each time.

"We went on a trip this morning. It was unplanned, or rather, prompted by me. I had already noticed that the Kasen avoided a certain direction when leaving their settlement. That struck me as odd, because they don't really seem to be afraid of anything. When I had to set up the solar cells for the oxygen exchanger, I deliberately moved in that direction. Please don't call me careless, Tailin - I was almost one hundred percent sure that Kian was watching me almost around the clock. In fact, after a short time he was at my side, trying to push me in a different direction with his tail.

"I didn't protest, but I wasn't impressed either and kept walking in the unwanted direction with my solar cells. If there was something there that the Kasen were trying to avoid, it had to be interesting for me as a researcher. After a while, Kian relented. He was probably already aware of my curiosity and was perhaps afraid that I would secretly pursue it at night. It touched me how concerned he was about me. But you're right, I can hear you now, Tailin. I mustn't anthropomorphize him. Maybe I was just his collector's item, his trophy that he was saving to eat at some point. I had seen how the carver rammed the drill into Kian's friend's neck, even though he could certainly have recovered with proper treatment. And it was my fault.

"Nevertheless, I couldn't hold back. Kian took me on his back and climbed to the top of the brine trees. It wasn't far to our destination, a few miles, I guess. He didn't get down on the ground, but carefully lowered me from his back. The canopy swayed under my weight. It consisted of branches tangled together. Wherever a ray of sunlight could be caught, they had grown leaves. Nevertheless, there were always gaps where you could see the ground, or through which you could fall.

"Kian placed himself and me in front of a particularly large hole. The sun was burning down on our backs and at the same time illuminating the clearing below us. I saw - a nest. It looked like a huge bird's nest. We had not discovered any birds on Gliese 163 c that could inhabit such a nest. But the nest didn't stay empty for long. A Kasen trotted in from the right. Its tail was considerably shorter than that of Kian and his neighbors, but its head and paws seemed larger to me. The whole creature would tower over even the carver.

"A second specimen came from the other side. It was much smaller. The two greeted each other with grunts and growls. I couldn't make out whether they sounded hostile or friendly. Kian pushed my head down when the larger one suddenly sniffed in our direction. They probably wouldn't be peaceful towards us. At least the first individual seemed not only bigger and stronger than the Kasen, but also faster.

"The two met in the nest. They twined their tails together and seemed to be sniffing at each other. Then the larger one lay down on its back so that its belly was unprotected. The smaller one sank its fangs into it, roaring. It paused for a moment and then tore a large chunk out of the bigger animal's belly. I froze, then felt sick, but this time I didn't lose the contents of my stomach. The larger specimen didn't seem to mind the treatment. It was strong enough to fight back, yet refrained from doing so.

"Had I misjudged the situation completely? That wasn't an attack, that was sex! What is the function of bisexual mating?

The exchange of genetic information. The smaller animal got its genetic information from the larger specimen by gutting its stomach. The act seemed complete after three bites. The small animal lay down in the nest while the large one dragged itself away. It left behind a trail of crumbs from its injured belly. Would it survive? Why not? If these animals were as similar to Kasen as they looked, then they too had no organs that could be dangerously injured.

"It was a shame I couldn't ask Kian any questions about this. Had we been watching a related, less highly developed species? Or could it be a group of the same species? Is it even possible that the intelligence undeniably present in the Kasen could have developed in such a small group? It would have to start somewhere. Perhaps their settlement represents the nucleus of a future, planet-spanning civilization. If so, I mustn't interfere with it under any circumstances. But isn't it already too late for that?

"At least I now know why the Kasen never leave their settlement in that one direction. They have too much respect for their cousins. They can probably keep them in check collectively, but no one can predict what a solitary encounter in the brine forest would look like."

There was a crack. Yini was startled, fearing an attack by the wild Kasen cousins. But it was only Mike. His expression was unreadable.

"Thank you for waiting for me," he said.

"That wasn't difficult at all. I had some interesting reading. Did you know how the Kasen have sex...?"

"I got a ticket to Neomars," Mike said.

His poker face slowly dissolved. Yini had expected a smile, but the corners of his mouth pulled down too far for that. He had one ticket, of course, not two.

"Oh, that sucks..." she said.

She was actually relieved. She could hardly believe it herself. Shouldn't she be sad that the person she had grown so fond of couldn't accompany her? If she traveled alone, there was one huge advantage: she wouldn't have to worry about him.

"Yes, I'm very sorry," he said. "Should I cancel with my... acquaintance then?"

"No, absolutely not. I have to go to Neomars, whatever the cost."

"Really? It could be dangerous. Especially if they know who you are."

He was right. If Tsai Tailin really was her mother, they could blackmail her with her daughter. She couldn't allow herself to fall into the hands of the wrong people. On the other hand, who would tell Neomars who her mother was? So far, no one knew except Kang and Mike. She trusted both of them. And the Admiralty? She couldn't assess them at all.

"How would they find out?" she asked.

"They might have drawn similar conclusions from the transmissions."

"The family name is common. I only thought of it because of the external similarity."

"Which may still exist."

"That's unlikely. Remember that Tailin intended to go to Neomars via tachyon transmission. The Biobag she's using is certainly not similar to her biological body."

"You're probably right about that."

Yini wasn't all that sure. Most people deliberately chose a Biobag that was at least visually similar for such a transfer. With a little advance notice, it was possible to click the exterior together in a modular system. Many even had Biobags grown from their own DNA. It was strange. Anyone could be whoever they wanted to be, and yet most of them remained themselves - the way a random mix of DNA had determined when they were conceived.

But Tailin certainly wouldn't want to be recognized on Neomars. So surely she wouldn't choose a Biobag that looked like her. The only question was how Yini was supposed to recognize her mother. It would have to work the other way around. Yini had to be recognized. She decided to take a tour of Neomars.

"I don't know if I can let you go," Mike said.

"Excuse me? You don't have a choice."

"I'm thinking about the story you told me about Mark Decker. He felt guilty because he hadn't forbidden his friend to look for his wife."

"I remember it very well. But that's something completely different. I'm not your subordinate, and I'm not running out into a storm of acid."

"Negative two hundred and ninety degrees and a methane atmosphere are similarly deadly."

"I'll be careful, I promise," Yini said. "How did you manage to get the ticket?"

Mike sighed. "It was a mistake."

"Not at all."

Yini pulled the blanket away, stood up and hugged him. Mike was all tense. Only when she gently massaged the back of his neck did he loosen up.

"I talked to people it's better to stay away from," he said. "People from Neomars."

"Spies?" she asked.

Yini thought back to what Smith had told her. Since then, she'd been expecting spies everywhere. Maybe Mike was one, too. She didn't care, as long as he didn't just see her as a means to an end.

"Smugglers," he said.

"Smugglers?"

"Where do you think all the stuff comes from that isn't allowed on the moon or made here?"

"Is that legal?"

Mike laughed. "Of course not. That's exactly why it's so profitable."

"And how do you know these people?"

"I was afraid you'd ask that. I went through a phase where I was really bored, and I tried all sorts of things. Illegal substances."

"I see. I was always too scared to do that."

"Well, that was very sensible."

"But at least you know the right people now."

Yini shivered. She let go of Mike and slipped back under the covers, where her own body heat was waiting.

"Why don't you come to bed too?" she said.

"I have to brush my teeth and go to the toilet first," he said.

Yini nodded and Mike disappeared into the bathroom. She heard his stream of urine splashing into the bowl. It always sounded particularly loud in the low gravity here. He hummed something while brushing his teeth. It certainly wasn't a song, more like the bellowing of a rutting stag.

"And how exactly will this work?" she asked as he lay next to her in bed.

"I'll take you to the rendezvous point. We have to be there on time. The start is at ten o'clock standard time."

"How far is it?"

"A small but deep crater about twelve miles from here, that's not on any map. We'll need an all-terrain rover. I've already booked one at the tourist office."

Yini was reassured. The fact that she was skipping work would only become apparent after two or three days. Her boss didn't check her progress every day. Ulita would still be disappointed. Yini could forget about succeeding her as head of department. That had never been her plan anyway. The work was interesting, but in the long run it was annoying that everything was second-hand. She wanted to experience something for herself.

"Thank you, Mike," she said, "you really are a good friend."

"I hope so," he said.

"How long will we not see each other, then?" asked Yini.

"I'll give you a contact you can use to arrange for the flight back. I can't do that for you. So, you won't be away any less than eight weeks."

"So we won't see each other for at least two months," said Yini, turning onto her side.

"Yeah."

Mike, who was lying behind her, pulled her close and breathed deeply. It was as if he wanted to take in her scent and store it deep inside him, to have a supply. She indulged him.

"Mike?"

"Yes?"

"Would you lend me your fingers, please?" she asked.

His arm moved forward. She grabbed his hand and pulled it between her legs. Then she used his middle finger to pleasure herself. It was the best therapy when she couldn't fall asleep because of difficult decisions.

August 11, 2802, Earth's moon

The smugglers' spaceship was cramped and cold. The captain took a genetic sample from all the passengers, using a mobile analyzer, in order to compare it with the central DNA database that both the Terran Union and Neomars maintained. They probably wanted to make sure no one was traveling under a false name. She really would have liked the smugglers to be... more flexible. The ticket Mike had given her was not for a cabin, but for the last free stasis chamber - in the cargo hold. Yini was already in it. However, she was still dressed, since the liquid was missing. Instead, the chamber was padded. The captain of the ship had explained this to her after the welcome. The ship started its engine under the protection of the crater walls until it launched. Then it drifted for a while with its engines switched off, so that space surveillance could not distinguish it from an asteroid. Only at the end of this phase, when it was almost impossible to catch up, would everyone on board have to climb into the stasis chambers, because that was when the acceleration began.

Yini still had half a day until then. She wiped the lingering tears from her face from saying goodbye. The captain was probably still waiting for a piece of luggage. The hold, in which she was packed like cargo, was almost full. Smuggling must be a lucrative business. The parcels were well tied up and secured to the walls and ceiling. She could have stood up and looked around, but she didn't want to know what illegal goods were traveling along with her.

She pulled a small package from her waterproof belt pouch, which contained her most important belongings. Neither Mike nor she trusted the smugglers, so she wanted to have the bag with her in stasis. No one would be able to steal from her during the hellish acceleration, but once it ended, she would lie relatively unprotected in the chamber until she was freed from it.

The package bore a hand-drawn heart. Mike must have added it before he left. Yini smiled, and despite the cold, she felt warm. Mike was... She couldn't describe it. The package contained the portion of Mark Decker's letters that she hadn't read yet. Mike had made her fresh copies that smelled of his office. Yini missed him already. She opened the bundle and began to read.

"Kasen settlement, day 8.

"If you're paying attention, Tailin, you must have noticed the missing day. I managed to persuade Kian to take a trip to the Hopper. He immediately granted my wish when I started playing the Rrr/Kit game. This time he must have understood that I wasn't trying to make a deal. He took me to the Hopper and disappeared into the woods.

"The rest of the time up to this point consisted of work. I didn't know when he would return, so I had to make the most of every minute. In the chemistry lab, I formulated the compound to break down the building block principle of the silicon compounds. That alone took me seven hours. Then I checked my measurements from the forest. The material I recovered from the spaceship really takes the principle of the octahedron to the extreme. Right down to the resolution limit of my electron microscope, the shape was repeated.

"I suspect that this also applies to all smaller scales down to the Planck length. But that is speculation. You would need very advanced technology to take the principle that far. It would be easier to stop at the crystal lattice. Octahedral crystals are not uncommon in atomic or ionic bonding, as long as six ligands are available. Do you understand? I don't know if I will find the time to write a scientific article on this topic. On the one hand, I should have all the time I need, because it will be years before the next research crew arrives. Though I sometimes have the feeling I might run out of time. I hope that's not a bad omen. I'm sure you would reassure me now and call me an old pessimist, but I'm just a realist.

"Because I think I have a real problem. I'm not a qualified, practicing doctor, unfortunately, so I can only describe the symptoms to you. Sometimes my field of vision suddenly narrows. A tremendous pain throbs in my temples, making me want to bang my head against the wall to drown out the screaming pain. But it doesn't stop at screaming, because synesthetic sensations are also occurring. I see lights and hear sounds that aren't there, and sometimes a horrible voice speaks to me that I don't understand, but which sounds familiar. This always stops after a certain interval. Could it be a brain tumor? I need to consult the database in the space station. If I die, then I die. That's okay. I'm just afraid that I might start understanding the voice at some point.

"I'm really glad that my mistake didn't have such negative consequences this time. But if the silicon compounds have such effects, it might not be a good idea to try to clear them out of the system. Perhaps they could even serve as a cure for all earthly diseases? I'd better postpone the test of my substance."

"All passengers," announced the captain of the ship. "Please prepare for take-off. We'll be taking off in twenty seconds. It will be unpleasant, very unpleasant, but please don't panic. Or do panic – it won't change anything. The stress will subside after a few seconds. You probably won't die unless a piece of cargo happens to fall on your head, ha-ha."

Thank you, Captain, you're a real comedian. Yini put the letter aside and checked that all her limbs were well cushioned. Then the countdown began.

"Three - two - one - start."

The button of her pants dug into her stomach. Her eyeballs tried to disappear into their sockets. Her larynx blocked her airway. She was leaking. Luckily, she was wearing a diaper. How long could a few seconds be?

The strain disappeared. She was floating. Her muscles ached as if a giant had been sitting on her. It was sticky between her legs. Yini pulled herself out of her chamber. There was a toilet at the entrance to the cargo hold. A man and a woman were already waiting in front of it. They greeted each other with a nod. Were they smugglers, or paying passengers like her?

"Welcome to interplanetary space," said the loudspeaker in

the captain's voice. "We will now be in slow flight for four to five hours. Remember the smoking ban and please don't do it in the corridors. Don't loiter in the corridors, but stay in your chambers. Half an hour before the end of this sneak flight, we will ask you to prepare for stasis. I'll say it right now: you won't have more than half an hour. If you don't initiate stasis in time, I hope you enjoy weeks of pain. No one will be able to help you. Thank you for your attention."

The door of the restroom opened and the woman who had been waiting in line in front of her came out and smiled at her. The cramped room stank, even though the ventilation was roaring. Yini involuntarily held her breath, but soon had to give up the fight against the odors. After cleaning herself in the toilet, she floated back to her chamber. The letter from Day 9 had fallen to the floor next to the stasis chamber. Yini picked it up and checked the time. She still had at least three hours. She settled into the glass coffin and read.

"I have to admit, I'm a bit short of breath today," Decker continued to write. His handwriting was much more scrawly than usual, as if the astrobiologist had pressed hard while writing. "After the cleaning operation, I was again overcome by this intense pain. It clearly has its source in my head and radiates throughout my body. It's as if an octopus is sitting in my skull and extending its tentacles into all my limbs. Fortunately, the pain comes and goes in waves. When it's there, I can barely stand on my feet, and perceive my surroundings as if through a fog. When it recedes, all that remains is a dull thud that warns me to prepare for the next wave.

"Hold on, there's a knock.

"Kian has come to see me. At first, I assumed he wanted to pick me up for a hike. But he must have noticed my condition, because he headed in the direction of the swamp. I feared that he wanted me to heal there, just as his friend had recovered from his injury there. I protested loudly under my breathing mask and he finally let me slide off his back.

"'Kit,' I said.

"He must take me back to the Hopper. There were stronger painkillers in the medicine cabinet, which would hopefully deal with the octopus in my head.

"'Rocket,' Kian corrected me.

"'Rocket,' I repeated, 'I want to go back to the rocket.'

"'Back rocket,' he said. 'Help. Sleep.'

"I was thunderstruck. Kian had made huge progress! No, that wasn't possible. He must have been listening to me the whole time. I have often thought out loud and talked to myself. The Kasen must have deduced the meaning of some words from context. How advanced were his skills? I absolutely had to subject him to a few intelligence tests.

"But now, of all times, the octopus woke up again.

"'Shit,' I said.

"'Shit,' said Kian.

"I looked for a brine tree, sat down on the ground and leaned against the trunk. The tree gave me security. The octopus slid into my limbs, which began to twitch uncontrollably, but didn't gain control over them. Kian sat down in front of me. Now he really did look like a very big cat. All that was missing was for him to start purring. He had a clear, steady gaze that rested tirelessly on me, which was probably so striking because his eyes had no lids. The octopus shook me, while Kian's gaze riveted me to the brine tree. It was also thanks to him that the octopus didn't start talking again. At least that was how it felt.

"When the seizure was over, Kasen's tail helped me to stand up. I walked a few steps towards the settlement, then I remembered what I had been planning to do. The painkiller!

"'Back to the rocket, please,' I said.

"'Please,' Kian said and settled me on his back with the help of his tail.

"I'm not sure how long it took us to get to the Hopper this time because I suffered another seizure in between. I woke up in the airlock. Kian must have opened the airlock door for me. I switched on the light and looked around. There was hair on the floor that looked like a Kasen's. Had he come into the airlock with me? I had always felt safe in the Hopper, but Kian had probably learned how to open the outside door of the airlock by watching me.

"I stuck my head out of the outer door, which was still open. There was no Kasen to be seen in the area. Kian had probably headed back to the settlement. Of course, his friend was waiting for him there. Or was he inside the ship? I closed the outer door, waited for the pressure to equalize and pulled the mask off my face. The octopus stirred again. This time I had the feeling that it was looking for a conversation, and that scared me so much that cold sweat ran down my back. I opened the inner door.

"'Hello, are you here?' I called out.

"There was no reply. I left the airlock and climbed up to the control room. The whole time I was expecting the octopus to attack, but it took its time. Or was it giving me time? Time for what? I had to find out what the disease was. If it was incurable, I wanted to determine my own end. I climbed back down one floor and opened the small medicine cabinet. There was the painkiller. It really could make anyone happy. I read the package leaflet. It recommended a thorough diagnosis before use, especially a blood count. The necessary equipment was available here.

"But there was also the octopus. It was pounding on the inside of my skull as if it wanted to be let out. I thought of the carver's drill. If used correctly, it would certainly give me relief. The octopus simply needed fresh air. Who could blame it? But what kind of strange ideas were these? I couldn't just drill a hole in my skull! Was that something the octopus had whispered to me? It hadn't even started talking yet. I had to silence it. I took a tablet from the packet, swallowed it and washed it down with water. Then I sat down on the floor to wait for it to take effect.

"It was phenomenal. I felt reborn after just ten minutes. I was bold, full of vigor, invulnerable and immortal. I would get the octopus under control. I got up and rummaged in the medicine cabinet. The device for determining my blood count was on the bottom shelf. The batteries were dead, so I had to plug it into a socket first.

"I used the waiting time to make myself a peanut butter sandwich. It was delicious, the best I'd ever eaten. I tried some dry toast, and it was unique. I tasted every grain. I saw the sun of Terra Nova, which had filled this grain with its energy. The package featured a farmer's wife, a woman in typical colonist garb, holding a sheaf of corn. She looked hot, so much so that I had to go to the toilet to relieve myself. Afterwards, I drank cold water from the tap, and it was like drinking from a cheerfully bubbling mountain stream.

"But afterwards I was still thirsty and hungry and sexually aroused. Although the tablets were very effective, they were also exhausting. I threw myself into work. The blood analysis machine was now powered up. I drew some blood from myself. All I had to do was put a cuff around my elbow. A needle automatically came out of it and dug into my skin. I didn't perceive the puncture as pain, but as a tickling sensation.

"The machine hummed loudly at first. Presumably it was breaking my blood down into its components. Then it spat out the first values. My blood sugar was below the limit values. But the inflammation values were okay. The display recommended reducing my intake of saturated fatty acids. The concentration of white and red blood cells and the coagulation factor were completely within limits. But my immune system was going crazy. It was as if I was suffering from severe flu. But strangely, I didn't have an elevated temperature. Was this my immune system's special way of fighting the octopus in my head?

"'End of standard program' appeared on the display. 'Follow-up check of blood lipid values required in 8 weeks'

"Standard program? I wanted to know everything. The instructions on the device told me that there was also a special program. It was intended to determine not only the usual health values, but also to record the entire composition of the blood. It was designed, among other things, to search for cells that a cancer had introduced into the bloodstream - or to identify pathogens circulating in the bloodstream.

"I followed the description and started the special program. When the needle went into the bend of my elbow again, I suddenly had to laugh. The device complained because I wasn't holding still enough. It repeated the process. This time I bit my lips. The loud humming noise lasted much longer than before. According to the description, the device first separated the blood into several samples and then analyzed them differently.

"I got the jar of peanut butter from the food cupboard and ate while the device did the math. I also drank water from the tap until I felt sick. After I had relieved myself in the toilet and returned, the appliance was quiet, with the display lit up, as if it had something to tell me. But it didn't.

"'No known substances found'.

"The result was disappointing. An asterisk flashed next to it. According to the instructions, this should be an error message. I tapped on it and was shown a number: 'E174'.

"All the error numbers were listed in the appendix to the instructions. E174 stood for 'Error when entering a molecule: structural formula not in the directory. Unknown molecule'. What did that mean? Apparently, the device had detected something in my blood that was not in its internal directory. Until I knew more, this spoke against the quality of this directory. Unfortunately, I didn't have a test subject on whom I could check this hypothesis - apart from myself. I started the experiment again. This time I used the crook of my left arm. Perhaps the algorithm had stumbled upon a damaged molecule by chance. In that case, the chances of the same thing happening again were slim.

"I won't tell you how I passed the waiting time. This super pill from the medicine cabinet is really awesome. I was able to do fifty squats in a row! I was all the more pleased when the device no longer gave me an error message after the analysis. Nevertheless, I asked to see the list of substances it had found in my blood. At the top of the list was dihydrogen oxide, i.e. water. This was followed by various proteins, electrolytes such as sodium and calcium ions, lipids - i.e. fats - glucose - sugar - and urea. The table row below the urea was labeled something I had never seen before: 'U1'. What was U1? Unfortunately, the instructions for the device didn't include a complete list of possible blood components. I scratched my head. U, that sounded like urine, uranium, U ... u as in unknown?

"The concentration of the substance was high. I'm not a doctor, but I am an astrobiologist. I imagine I know every substance that might appear in human blood. I scrolled to the main menu. The device still had remnants of the first measurement, which ended with the E174 message, saved so that additional analyses could be carried out if necessary. I let it search for known substances in these remnants again. This time it did not find an error. Instead, it also found a significant concentration of U1.

"I read the instructions again from the beginning. The first chapter read like an advertisement. I was about to turn the page when I came across the possible explanation: 'This system is self-learning. You only need to enter new ingredients once; then they are stored in the directory and reliably recognized in subsequent analyses.'

"So that's why the error message didn't appear on the second attempt. But I did have an unknown substance in my blood. Maybe it really was cancer cells. Did the system know all the mutated cells a cancer could cause? That was rather unlikely. However, their concentration was unusually high. Therefore, I must have long since reached the final stage of the disease. The pain felt like that too if I allowed it to happen. But I didn't feel deathly ill at the moment. Was it just the happy pills?

"In any case, I had to find out for myself what was in my bloodstream. If it really was cancer cells, I had to find a way to stay in control of my life and death. Maybe an overdose of happy pills would be the perfect way to nirvana. My only fear was that the octopus in my head would no longer allow me to escape its influence that way.

"I unpacked the medicine cabinet until I found a slightly thicker needle for drawing blood. I pushed it into the crook of my arm where the device had drawn blood, hoping it had chosen the optimal spot. Blood soon flowed into the chamber of the syringe. I didn't mind watching, the way I usually do. I pulled the needle out again, sat down at the light microscope and prepared an initial sample, hoping that the unknown molecule would be large enough to identify at the limited resolution.

"With my eye on the eyepiece, I worked my way through the sample's field of view using the adjusting screws. The blood cells looked fresh and healthy, which gave me hope. I was about to increase the resolution when I came across a diamond-shaped shadow. I varied the distance very gently and realized that the shadow was a flat projection of what was actually a three-dimensional structure, which I identified as a tiny octahedron. The same material the spaceship was made of had made its way into my bloodstream.

"It couldn't be. I pushed my chair back, rubbed my eyes and tried again. It was probably just my imagination. But no. When I shifted my field of vision, a much larger structure made up of several octahedrons slipped into view. How had this stuff gotten into my body? But above all, why was it there? In my mind's eye, I saw the alien spaceship and the swamp covered in the material. I remembered how we had buried Kian's friend and cleaned him up later. It must all be connected. And what about the wild relatives Kian showed me?

Why are the two species so similar, and why do they behave so differently?

"But the much more important questions are: Why me? How did the structures find their way into my bloodstream? What do they want there? What influence are they having on my body? Are they the source of the pain - or are they the antidote? After all, they seem to be able to heal injuries. I saw that clearly in Kian's friend.

"I made a printout of the structures to show Kian. Perhaps he can do something with it."

The letter broke off without a farewell. Yini put it aside. It didn't stay there, but went drifting through the cargo hold. There was a draft from somewhere. She caught the letter and put it in her belt pouch. Then she looked at her watch. They had only been in flight for an hour. She took out the next letter.

"Kasen settlement, day 11."

Apparently, he had skipped another day. Was Mark Decker really terminally ill? She counted the remaining letters. He had written three more. Only three? It didn't look good for him. She wished so much that he would see his wife again, but the chances of that were close to zero.

"Kian kept me waiting for a whole day. The ship's security system told me that he had returned. Someone was fiddling with the airlock. After I recognized my visitor, I opened the outer door using the remote control and climbed down.

"Kian was waiting in the medical station. He must have understood how the inner door worked, because it only opened when the outer door was closed. I saw the Kasen nimbly climbing up the ladder.

"I was surprised, but not angry. After all, this was where I had stored the sketches of the structures in my bloodstream. We greeted each other by bowing. I performed the movement first and Kian copied it. Then I showed him the sheets. He reacted very dismissively. But it wasn't clear what his aversion was directed at. Perhaps it wasn't proper to draw the objects. Or perhaps he was afraid of them. I showed him the contents of some of the cupboards.

"We then explored the control center. He was particularly excited by the camera images on the screens. He kept trying to reach for the objects in them. When I showed him the recording of his arrival today, he jumped towards himself, snarling, but immediately retreated when the other Kasen didn't react. I watched him. At first, he was still annoyed that a stranger had entered what he considered to be his territory. But then he obviously noticed details that he knew about himself. He tried to look behind the screen, raised his arms in the same way as in the video and also put his ears up. Finally, he was apparently satisfied and lay down on all fours until the video was over.

"I fetched the analyzer from the floor below us. Kian accompanied me. Although he was so big, he proved to be surprisingly dexterous and never knocked anything over even with his tail. Most of the time he moved on two legs. The cuff of the measuring device was just big enough to fit the Kasen. I slipped it over his left forearm. I realized that the needle wouldn't encounter blood. But the device should be able to cope with any material. I was less sure whether Kian would accept the pain of the puncture. He did not. But as I was three yards away from him at that moment, he didn't hold me responsible. He simply ripped the cuff off. The device started working anyway.

"Ten minutes later I got the result. It consisted of 136 error messages about molecules that were unknown to the unit. Only one substance was mentioned by name: U1. Its percentage was even higher than the amount in my bloodstream. I absolutely had to investigate the swamp again. The spaceship that had crashed on this planet might still contain the secret of the substance U1.

"Kian was quickly persuaded to leave. He was probably already bored in the Hopper. He took me back to the settlement, but refused to go directly to the spaceship. I set off on my own. Just before I reached the swamp, the pain returned. Unfortunately, I hadn't packed the pain pills. How could I be so forgetful? I tried to pull myself together at first. But the octopus tugged at my limbs. I fell to my knees, bruising them, but the pain was nothing compared to that caused by the octopus. I threw myself onto my face and shoved my arms underneath me when they wouldn't stop shaking and wriggling. It was as if the octopus was trying to take control of me. I couldn't let that happen. I rolled on the ground, screaming in pain, biting my tongue until it bled, tasting the dirt and leaves beneath me, wetting my pants, sweating and crying until someone picked me up and took me to my tent.

"My savior was once again Kian. At least that's what I assume, because he was standing in front of me when I woke up. I was lying naked on my back on my bed in the tent. I looked down at myself. Everything was clean. Kian must have cleaned me too. At that moment, a second Kasen entered the cone-shaped room. It was Kian's friend. I remembered how we had cleaned him. He carried two brine tree leaves in his hand, cut lengthwise into many strips. A viscous sap dripped from them. He placed the two leaves on me. They enveloped me in an intense honey scent that made my senses fade.

"When I woke up again, only Kian was there. The pain had disappeared. But I knew it wouldn't stay away forever. I had maybe half an hour of full consciousness. My first idea was to send Kian to the Hopper to get the happy pills. My second idea was to make myself the subject of a scientific experiment while he was away. After all, I had produced that substance that suppressed the activity of the silicon compounds. I would try it out on myself instead of a Kasen. That was much less ethically problematic anyway.

"I drew Kian the cupboard where the pills were.

"'Rocket. Pills. Happy,' I said and gave him the sketch.

"Kian looked at it first, then tore it into shreds. 'Happy, pills, rocket,' he said.

"I was very excited to see what he would bring me. I was even more excited about the effect of the antidote. The Kasen had probably been under the influence of the silicon structures for many years. They were still new in my body. If the remedy could be successful, it would be with me. Kian took his leave with a bow.

"I had put the antidote in a small box under my bed. I pulled it out. The syringe or the spray? As soon as I formulated the question in my mind, the pain started again, as if it had been waiting for this. The protective curtain of fog that the honey scent of the brine tree leaves had spread around me disappeared in one fell swoop.

"I collapsed, but fell onto my bed in such a way that I could still reach my antidote. I stretched, moved my hands, but immediately withdrew them because I had burned myself. But there was no flame. Nevertheless, I was burning brightly. I smelled burnt skin, saw how it blistered and felt the inhuman pain.

"It was the octopus in my head. It laughed derisively.

"'I wouldn't do that, if I were you', it said.

"Now I even understood what the voice was saying. I must have lost my mind. There was no way I could answer it. I would be admitting that I was no longer in control of myself. But wasn't that already the case? I was burning even though there was no fire, I moved my hands towards the syringe without reaching it, I heard voices even though I was alone.

"I would have liked to imagine that I could hear you too, Tailin. You would be cheering me on, spurring on my ambition to take on this many-legged thing in my head. But I hadn't lost my mind that much. I knew you were many light hours away and couldn't hear me, even if my pain seemed great enough to extend into the cosmic background radiation.

"The human body has a few fascinating properties. One of them is that it can get used to anything. The terrible pain did not stop, but it did decrease. The octopus had given all it could. I didn't regain control of myself. But if I concentrated all my willpower on my hand, it could feel through the fire. I moved it off the bed on four fingers, but it fell to the floor, where it plunged into a new pit of flames. I didn't let it surprise me. I grasped the syringe.

"Just when I thought I had won, the octopus changed tactics. It tried to take over my index finger and make it empty the syringe before I could press it into my flesh. But that was its downfall, because now I knew I had found a strategy against it. The octopus was scared! My remedy would finish it off. I lifted the syringe. I just had to manage to plunge it into my body. My index finger was rigid. The pointed needle moved towards my body in slow motion. It was an efficient movement that had the support of gravity, a most welcome aid that I hadn't even planned for. I gave it all my willpower. I put all my weight onto the elbow joint that was performing the movement. The syringe stung as it buried itself in my stomach. I didn't know what I was hitting, but it didn't matter. I was between life and death. No, I realized. It was my life and Kian's life.

"My life. The index finger bent, pressed down on the syringe from above, pressed its contents into me. The other hand suddenly appeared from the side without my control and struck, but it was too late. The cannula broke off. Its tip was stuck in my stomach while the rest of the liquid ran over me.

"There was silence for a moment. I was just as anxious as the octopus to find out who had won this duel. Then I heard it scream. They were children's screams, excruciating, but at the same time I was happy about them. I knew they weren't children, not at all. They were old, ancient, and they had a hope concerning me that they wouldn't relinquish. They had a mission. The thoughts flowed through my head like a clear stream and dripped out of my ears, deafening and immobilizing me and obscuring my vision and closing my nose and shutting my mouth and night fell."

The text ended there. Yini's heart pounded, and she was sweating. It was as if she had witnessed Mark Decker's death. Her chest ached. The octopus seemed to have taken hold of her too. She consoled herself with the fact that this wasn't the last letter. In any case, Decker couldn't have written it while he was struggling with death and the fantasies in his head. He must have survived. But the dramatic effect was undeniable. Especially because someone had written something under Decker's handwriting in awkward children's scrawls. Yini had an idea who might have added it.

"Happy, pills, rocket," it said.

She imagined Kian finding the dead Decker. How he shed Kasen tears for him and read his letters, understanding them better and better as his intelligence grew, before finally adding his own signature.

"Ladies and gentlemen, I have the good fortune to be able to inform you that we can switch to the acceleration phase sooner than expected," the captain interrupted them. "I would ask you to get ready now. Remember that you can only fill the capsules once they are closed, due to weightlessness. You will find instructions on the inside of the lid. If you need help, don't ask me, and you'd better not ask your fellow travelers either, because they should also be floating in their chambers by then. See you in Saturn's orbit. Captain out."

What a pity. She wouldn't find out today how Decker had fared. Yini carefully folded the letter and put it in her belt pouch. She floated out of the chamber and... hesitated. Should she really go through with this? She felt completely out of place. But by now it was too late. She undressed. She had to go into the stasis chamber naked. She shoved her clothes and wig into a compartment underneath the chamber. There was a towel ready for her arrival. It looked old but smelled fresh. Just as she was bending down, a man approached from the corridor. She recognized him by his scent. He was dressed like a member of the crew.

"You better stay the hell away!" she shouted.

The man grinned and pointed to his name badge. "Excuse me, young lady, but I need to check that everything is secure."

"Get out!" she shouted.

The man swallowed hard. He was probably not used to being yelled at. He disappeared back into the corridor. Yini took a deep breath. This wouldn't have happened to her on a regular passenger flight. But she would never have received permission for this trip. Hopefully Kang wouldn't suffer any repercussions because of her, but she didn't think he would. Ulita and Zahir were fair bosses. They would only be angry with Yini. And Kang? He had to understand how important it was for her to get to know her mother.

Yini took the blanket and pillow from the glass coffin and stuffed them into a space behind it. Then she wriggled back into the chamber. She fastened her belt pouch to the handle on the side. She pulled the lid shut. She panicked briefly, but breathed it away. The promised instructions on the inside were simple: close the lid, press the start button, stretch out, don't fight the liquid.

She took another deep breath. But she couldn't wait too long. It would take a few minutes to fill the tank and the captain would take off exactly on time. She pressed the button. A cool liquid poured out of the bottom of the tank. Yini didn't move. She got goose bumps all over her body. The liquid lifted her body. It weighed nothing, so the slightest buoyancy was enough to carry it. After a few minutes, the liquid pressed her against the glass lid. Suddenly she saw a man directly above her, pointing a camera lens at her. What a pig! The man grinned. Why wasn't he in his coffin? He was probably working with the captain. Yini memorized the face. When she woke up, she would punch his damn nose in. She knew a thing or two. She had taken several self-defense courses. This guy would experience the results first-hand. She was so angry!

The liquid sloshed over her face. In her excitement, she hadn't noticed how high it already was. *Don't fight the liquid.* It was certainly no coincidence that this sentence was written directly above her face on the inside of the lid. She had to suffocate first so that the stasis chamber could preserve her life. As soon as she passed out, the tubes and cables would automatically take over all her orifices.

She started getting sleepy. The air she breathed contained a sleeping aid. It was a process that was better to go through unconscious. Allegedly, the medication had once failed on a passenger, and he had had to witness the tubes penetrating him. Unfortunately, he had resisted, which the control system of his chamber had not expected. Horror stories told by the popular media. Yini held her breath and closed her mouth. Fluid ran into her ears, nose and eyes. *Don't fight the liquid.* She had to force herself to open her mouth again and breathe. At first she choked, but then the darkness came to save her.

October 8, 2802, Neomars

THE FIRST THING YINI SAW WAS THE GRINNING FACE OF THE OLD man who had been filming her. He was hovering directly above the transparent lid. Now he was also sticking out his tongue and pretending to lick the glass, or whatever it was that stasis chambers were made of. Yini realized that she could move her feet again and kicked the glass from below. The man startled and disappeared. *Just you wait, you asshole! I swear, if I catch you—!*

Where was she anyway? And more importantly - when? She focused her gaze on the inside of the lid. The calendar entry on the transparent screen showed the eighth of October. Below it, a streaming message congratulated her on her arrival in Saturn's orbit. Yini felt hot, although the liquid in which she was still floating had already cooled considerably. *Saturn!* She had never seen the ringed planet up close, at least not that she could remember. Her parents had never spoken highly of it. From the surface of Neomars, Saturn's former moon Titan, they had probably never been able to see it in all its glory because of the moon's dense atmosphere and bound rotation.

She had to get out of here as quickly as possible. Yini spat out the tube that had already retracted from her esophagus and pulled the breathing tube out of her nose. It was uncomfortable because the tube was resisting. She immediately realized why: the residual air in the stasis chamber was filled with a terrible smell of decay. Yini breathed as shallowly as possible. She felt around, but all the other tubes had already left her orifices. She pressed the "Begin Exit" button directly below the greeting.

The liquid drained out with gurgling noises. Ventilation blew fresh air into the chamber. Two minutes later, she was lying on the bottom of the chamber. The ventilation turned up with a roar so that a stream of warm air enveloped her from all sides, drying and warming her. The contrast was all the greater when, after a countdown, the lid lifted. It was freezing cold in the cargo hold, where her stasis chamber was located, and the ventilation was no match for it. Yini pushed herself off. The smugglers' freighter was apparently drifting motionless through space, presumably to avoid the attention of the authorities. Yini reached the ceiling of the cargo hold and pushed herself off towards the floor. There she held on to the stasis chamber and opened the compartment underneath where her things were.

Dressed, she felt much better. She emptied her belt pouch, putting the letters she had already read into her rucksack. She didn't need them anymore. Strangely enough, after the long flight, she wasn't hungry, thirsty or in need of anything else - apart from giving the dreadful peeping Tom a few punches. She really wanted to see his face when he realized how painful a boot in his privates could be. She had never experienced such a desire for violence before.

Her wish was not granted. The man was nowhere to be found, neither in the galley nor in the control room, and she had no access to the technical rooms. She angrily kicked a garbage can and had to quickly catch it before it could move through the ship and scatter its contents. The object of her hatred was probably busy preparing the cargo holds for landing.

Yini was surprised at how many passengers were on board. The crew, recognizable by their dirty uniforms, were outnumbered. Most of the guests were genetically adapted Neomartians. They had a compact, broad but slender build and oily, dark skin that protected them from the environmental conditions on the surface. One disadvantage of this change was the mask-like appearance of their faces, since their enormously thick skin made facial expressions impossible. A second disadvantage was that you never knew exactly where their voices were coming from, as the face - like all body orifices - was protected by a semi-permeable membrane.

The second largest group consisted of people who were sometimes disparagingly referred to as "primitive people". Yini didn't like the term. They were people who for some reason rejected genetic engineering - or, like her, had simply never had the need for it. There were more of them on the Earth rings and the moon than on Neomars, but they had long been a minority. The majority in the Terran Union were humans who switched freely between different bodies, both biological and technical. In a humanoid body, they were at most recognizable by their custom-crafted beauty or special abilities. There were no passengers of that kind here. Those who could afford custom-made Biobags also had their own spaceships.

But the second variant, the technical bodies, was also popular. Yini met at least two of them. One had taken the form of a many-legged spider. She struck up a brief conversation with him, and learned he was planning to go into the mining business. The other was in the form of an android. Yini might have overlooked other members of this group. Normally, people in technical Biobags had to identify themselves with a special holographic tag at chest height, but of course nobody checked that here. An inconspicuous container such as a toaster or an electronic toy were common ways of evading detection. It was possible that the coffee machine she had used to make herself a cappuccino was actually a person on the run.

Her stroll ended in the cupola, a small bulge between the galley and the control center. From the outside, it must look like an Adam's apple. Perhaps the smugglers' freighter had once been an excursion ship. Strangely, the dome was almost empty. Was Yini the only one flying to Neomars for the first time? Saturn was just coming in sight, in all its splendor. They flew over the famous hexagon at its north pole, which looked like a painting from this distance. It was hard to imagine that huge storms were raging in it. Nothing could be seen of the rings; the ship would have had to turn on its axis to bring them into view. But a sparkling diamond caught her eye, which seemed to focus the little light from the sun. That must be Enceladus, an ice world with no atmosphere to speak of, in whose belly lay an ocean that had apparently given rise to a completely different kind of being.

"That's Enceladus," said a melodic-sounding voice beside her.

Yini instinctively moved a little to the side.

"Don't worry, I'm one of the good ones," said the voice.

"I know," said Yini. "I mean, about Enceladus."

Hovering next to her was a female android she had seen earlier. Or was it actually female? The technical body had no sexual characteristics whatsoever. The voice, however, sounded female.

"Unfortunately, it is blocked to all visitors," the voice said. "I would love to wander through its icy wastes."

"That would be amazing," Yini replied. "I'm Yini, by the way."

"I'm Ari," said the voice.

"Nice to meet you. What brings you here?"

"I'm on a quest," Ari said. "That's my job. I track down people who have gone missing."

"What a coincidence," said Yini. "I'm looking for someone too. Do you have any tips?"

"Ask those who are usually overlooked and have a lot of time to look at the world: Old people, homeless people ..."

"There are homeless people in Neomars?"

"Of course there are. It's the old cycle, unemployment, drugs, loss of housing... Neomars is no paradise."

"I see. I thought society here was somehow more... cohesive. You know, a common enemy..."

"That was a long time ago," Ari said. "In the end, it always comes down to people, no matter what body they're in, with the same familiar weaknesses and strengths."

Yini nodded. She looked at Enceladus, the icy moon, and sensed Ari's departure.

SHE FIRST NOTICED THAT SOMETHING THREATENING WAS ABOUT to happen when she heard a wave of noise sweeping from the control center into the dome. People were relaying something they had overheard. The captain put an end to the rumors with an announcement.

"Dear fellow travelers, I regret to inform you that we have a visitor. A patrol from the Neomars border police has hailed us and set course for our location."

Tachyon: The Weapon

It became noisy in the spaceship. Many passengers floated past her, presumably on their way to the cargo holds where they were hiding smuggled goods.

"I ask you all to remain calm. It should only be a routine check. I happen to know the head of the border police well. You have nothing to fear."

Most of the passengers didn't seem to believe the reassurance. Yini fumbled for the fanny pack she was wearing under her trousers. Apart from a few changes of clothes in a rucksack, she had nothing else with her. So she should be safe, unless the visitor had come for her. That was unlikely. On the other hand, weeks had passed since she left. A lot could have gone wrong. She would prefer to contact Mike to clarify this, but a conversation with a Terran facility on the moon might arouse suspicion.

When the police ship docked, the shock was felt throughout the smuggler's ship. This was certainly not just any patrol. Yini exited the dome and floated into her cargo hold. Her backpack was gone. Crap. Who would steal a bag of clothes on board ship, where the thief couldn't even get away? She fumbled for her belt pouch again. It also contained her credit card. With 10,000 universal credits, she could afford new clothes. It was a pity about the pretty dress she had packed for official occasions, made by her mother.

Or rather, her possibly adopted mother.

It became quiet in the ship. A few people in uniform – she recognized two men and four women – floated in from below. One of the men nodded to her without saying anything. They moved in formation to the control center. What was being discussed there? Yini would have loved to listen in. But she wasn't kept in suspense for long. The uniformed men returned. The person with the most shoulder stripes, a woman, was holding a tablet. She approached her. Yini pressed herself against the inside of the dome. There was no escape route.

"Are you Tsai Yini?" the woman asked.

Yini shook her head. "There must be some mistake."

The woman smiled and held the tablet out to her. The photo was clear. Crap. What did they want from her, and who had revealed that she was coming?

"I have to ask you again: are you Tsai Yini?"

Yini nodded. There was no point in lying. They certainly had her DNA and perhaps her consciousness imprint as well. She had never done a consciousness purification, but storing an imprint was mandatory for eavesdroppers like her, if only in case there was a convergence.

"Then I must ask you to accompany me," the woman said.

"What am I being accused of?"

"You'll find out soon enough. I'm not authorized to give you any information. You can see the official instructions here."

She held the tablet out to her again. Yini read the text, but all it said was that she was to be arrested. She sighed. At least she had made it to Neomars.

Unfortunately, that also proved to be wrong. The police cruiser was not heading for Neomars, but for the sparkling diamond whose icy deserts Ari had dreamed of. Her dream would now come true for Yini. But she had neither a machine body nor a spacesuit, or anything else that could protect her from the cold and the deadly vacuum.

At least she had a good view from the porthole next to the seat she was strapped into. The ship touched down on a vast plain. The horizon was unusually close, and it was far darker than she had expected on a glittering gem. There was no sign of Saturn either, and it would probably stay that way, because Enceladus always kept the same side turned towards it. From this perspective, the moon seemed more gloomy than promising.

Despite this, the crew of perhaps thirty people was in a cheerful mood. Apparently they had a few days of shore leave ahead of them, and Enceladus probably had the perfect infrastructure with pubs, a casino and a brothel. They exchanged tips on where to find the best beer and the best gambling partners of any gender. Both the casino and the brothel advertised themselves as the last such establishments before interstellar space. Yini had a computer at her disposal and was trying to get as much useful information as possible. She had to make it from this icy moon to Neomars.

It took a while before the exit could begin. When Yini stepped out of the airlock, she realized why: a tube with atmosphere had been docked to the ship. This meant that no one needed to wear a suit to disembark. She would have preferred the suit. How else was she supposed to escape from the station? And she definitely had to if she was going to find her mother.

Together with the crew, she reached a kind of reception room that looked like a big tent. A man in uniform was waiting for the crew, handing out room keys. Yini, on the other hand, was approached by two uniformed women who did not introduce themselves by name.

"We'll take you to your destination," said the one with an extra star on her shoulder stripe.

Yini merely nodded. She wasn't familiar with military ranks. She couldn't even tell which branch of the military they belonged to. They marched through semi-dark corridors for about fifteen minutes. Getting around took some getting used to. Yini was glad that she had already developed a technique for dealing with low gravity on the moon. The smell of sweat from the reception room mixed with the smell of machine oil emitted by life support. At first the walls were made of ice, but then they were covered with a plastic material. There were handles on the walls and ceiling that could be used to give yourself a boost.

The corridor ended in a much larger room with no supporting pillars, which seemed oppressive due to its low ceiling. Yini felt as if many yards of ice were about to fall on her. A door was open on the left-hand side.

A woman came towards them. She had no visible genetic changes, was small and round and made a motherly impression. But when she stood in front of Yini, she automatically took a step back.

"I am Andrea Karpati," said the woman. "I run this facility. You can call me Andrea."

She held out her hand and Yini squeezed it. It was a warm and firm touch.

"I am Yini. And what kind of facility is this?" she asked.

"Officially, it's called a 'sheltered accommodation facility for persons defining themselves as female with legally restricted mobility', but in reality, it's a prison."

"I'm not sure what I'm doing here," said Yini.

"That's not unusual. Whoever had you brought here will discuss it with you. All I care about is that you stay here until I see your release papers, and that you're as comfortable as you can be in a prison during that time. We're well populated with seventy-seven inmates, so it only works if we each do our jobs. Yours is to do as you're told and not start a fight."

"That sounds simple."

Andrea Karpati knew what she wanted. Yini trusted her to keep order here, even without any other guards.

"If you can manage that, we'll get on well," said the prison warden. "There are nineteen guards, yes, men too. Only they have anything to say to you. If any of your fellow inmates here try to tell you what to do, please come see me first."

"Okay."

"We have mandatory exercise twice a day for two hours. It's not harassment, it's vital because of the low gravity. To be honest, four hours is not enough, so feel free to use the exercise equipment whenever you feel like it. You'll thank yourself if you ever get out of here."

Karpati was right. Even on the moon, it was important to exercise every day. But Yini didn't like the *"if"*. It sounded like it wasn't very often that someone got out of here.

"May I ask what your background is, Andrea? How did you end up in a prison on Enceladus?"

"I was a teacher in the Earth Ring and was talked into smuggling by some fake friends. They caught me, I did four years here, and then the post happened to be vacant. It's not that easy to find someone for a job 200 yards below the surface of the ice."

She shared a cell with two other women. Three cubicles, each about a yard high, had been dug into the wall at the back of the room, one above the other, in which the beds were hidden. Yini had the top bed. In the low gravity, she could get in without a ladder; all she had to do was jump.

Her two fellow inmates were good friends, although they were nothing alike. One, Maria Steinmetz, was a Neomartian and always had to lie at an angle in her alcove. The other was an outwardly delicate young girl who only revealed her first name, Brinja. Yini thought she herself was pretty young, but at first she couldn't believe that Brinja was only eighteen. Maria, whose age Yini couldn't guess at all, and Brinja were always giggling together about everything and everyone. Unfortunately, Yini lacked their sense of humor. Perhaps it was because she had a job to do.

That same day, she was called into the interrogation room by a female guard. A man in civilian clothes was waiting for her there, who introduced himself as Ulf Klose. They shook hands.

"I'm your lawyer," he said.

"My lawyer?"

"Yes. I have been appointed by the Great Archive on the Moon to represent you, Ms. Tsai."

"Represent me?"

She was incapable of any rational thought. Wouldn't some policeman or prosecutor have to speak to her first?

"Yes, as your lawyer. You are a citizen of the Terran Union. You can't just be held here like this. I represent your rights."

"But what am I being accused of? Can I speak freely here?"

"Yes, you can. Wiretaps are not allowed when talking to lawyers. Even if there was one, your words could not be used against you."

"Fine, I was on board a smuggler's ship. But I didn't break any law by doing that."

"That's absolutely correct. You didn't even enter Neomars territory illegally. I assume that's what you intended to do, but it didn't happen because you were brought here."

"Exactly."

"Which, by the way, is due to my timely intervention. While you were still unconscious in the smuggler's ship, I insisted on having you brought to Enceladus in time to save you from entering illegally."

"Otherwise they would have let me land on Neomars?"

"Absolutely, Ms. Tsai. The trap would have been sprung. So the problem is no longer that you're being accused of illegal entry, but of being a spy for the Terran Union. Allegedly, you wanted to visit a famous physicist and persuade her to return to Earth. That's no laughing matter in Neomars. Or to put it another way: even the attempt is punishable."

The 'physicist' was her mother. Someone must have betrayed her. Someone who knew her plan. There were only two people who could have done that: Kang and Mike. Suddenly she froze. She didn't want to have to think of her brother or her boyfriend as traitors. But there had been the rumpled blanket on the couch and the strange smell in her study.

"I'm not a spy, you have to believe me," Yini said.

"I believe you, but that's not the point. Someone informed the Neomars authorities about your alleged plan weeks ago. They also knew exactly which ship you would arrive here on. So far, everything this source has reported about you has been confirmed. In addition, letters to a Tsai Tailin were found in your luggage. We should think carefully about why you had those letters."

"When did you actually start representing me?" asked Yini.

"About two weeks after the launch, your boss Ulita Kuznetsova received an anonymous tip about your plans. She instructed me to exercise your rights proactively. This is legal, as you were unresponsive at the time. I requested all the information from Neomars and then traveled here by tachyon transmission. That's a pretty expensive affair."

"And who's paying for all this? The archive?"

"Mrs. Kuznetsova privately, as far as I know."

Someone, Kang or Mike, had betrayed her and then gotten a guilty conscience. Or both had reported her, independently of each other, for different motives. Or one had gotten wind of the other's betrayal and sent her help through her boss. Yini sighed. Unfortunately, this help had completely failed to achieve its purpose. Now she not only had to escape from prison, she had to fly to another moon of Saturn.

"Thank you, Mr. Klose. This physicist - I believe she's my mother. I just wanted to see her. Surely the Neomars court must understand that?"

"Well, unfortunately it's not that simple. The report about you also mentions that you would use this as an excuse. Your parents, who have already been questioned, have stated on the record that they are your biological parents."

Crap. How could she get out of this?

"And what would be your strategy, Mr. Klose?"

"I would plead insanity. You had a delusion that you were pursuing, but now, after the long journey, you've woken up and realized that you've gotten yourself into something that has no factual basis whatsoever."

"And the letters?" asked Yini.

"They were written many years ago by a confused, lonely researcher after he broke away from his crew in violation of the rules. They seem to be a colorful mix of facts and madness."

"So what should I do?"

"I'll organize an official interrogation. In it, you state that you were in a state of emotional imbalance. Apparently, you also entered into a new relationship at the same time."

"How do you know that?"

"It's in the documents. There's no mention of a source. But we all know how emotions can throw you off course. You're a young woman, in love and a little confused, who only wants one thing - to get back to her boyfriend. We'll forget the story about Tsai Tailin."

"Okay."

"That means you agree?"

The lawyer raised his eyebrows. He must have expected more resistance.

"Yes, I agree. It's the best solution. When will the interrogation take place?"

"Someone from Neomars will have to fly here. I think that should be possible within three days, four at the most. Then I'll obtain a return ticket for you."

"And you think it will all go smoothly?"

"I'm fairly sure it will. From what I understand, there have been discussions about this at higher levels. Neomars doesn't necessarily want to have to condemn you as a spy. That might lead to a few of their spies being exposed, which would provoke a backlash and so on. It would put stress on the secret services. All you have to do is stick to what we agreed and everything will be fine."

Everything will be fine, sure. So, she had three days to plan and implement her escape. If everyone here assumed she would soon be allowed to fly home anyway, no one would suspect her of having other plans.

"Will you explain this to the prison warden, Ms. Karpati?" she asked.

"Of course. I'll let her know when our conversation is over."

"That's great. Then thank you very much for your help, Mr. Klose."

Yini stood up. The lawyer also stood up. He still seemed a

little indecisive, took his computer out of his bag and put it back in his pocket. He had probably been told what a stubborn person she was. She felt a little sorry for Klose. This job would probably not be easy money after all.

At 10 p.m. standard time, the lights went out in the prison. Yini heard Maria and Brinja giggling from the bottom sleeping alcove. She fumbled for her belt pouch. Now would be a good time to finish reading Mark Decker's letters. The rest of the paper was still in her pocket, which had been left in her possession after a cursory check. But she had no light. Yini fumbled for the nightlight switch and flicked it, but nothing happened.

Crap. "Lights out" was obviously taken very seriously here.

"Can I ask you something?" she whispered.

"Sure," one of the young women whispered back.

"What do you do if you have to go out at night?"

"There's a bucket on the left outside the door. No one will see you in the dark."

"And for bigger needs?"

"You have to ring a guard. They'll take you there. But they don't like to do that."

"I see. Thank you, Brinja."

She had taken a wild guess.

"Of course," the voice replied.

October 9, 2802, Enceladus

"Shall we go to the gym together?" Brinja asked after breakfast, which consisted of a sticky, slightly sweet porridge with pieces of apple in it, or something else of the same consistency.

"No, thank you, I'd rather be alone," said Yini.

"Suit yourself," said the young girl.

Yini wanted to check the prison for possible escape routes. The company of her cellmates was rather a hindrance.

"She doesn't mean it, Brinja," said Maria. "You know newcomers always look for the secret back exit first." Yini laughed. But it was probably true. Nobody liked being locked up.

"But isn't she getting out again soon?" asked Brinja.

Apparently, people were already talking about her. News traveled fast here.

"So what?" Maria asked back. "The flight instinct is universal."

"That's true," said Brinja. "It was the same for me ten years ago, when I was here the first time."

"Wait, what? Did you do time as a child? Is that legal on Neomars?" asked Yini.

Brinja laughed. "That's very kind of you, my dear, but I've been in more prisons than you've shagged men. I'm one hundred and thirty-six!"

Oh. She had a Biobag. Brinja didn't seem to mind the time she spent here, but that was probably how it was when you were basically immortal.

"Sorry about that. I didn't know," said Yini.

"No problem. It's no wonder with this body. I took it from a perverted criminal, by the way. I could never buy a little cutie like this."

"Well then, congratulations."

"Thank you."

She left the cell. The doors were open during the day. Anyone who wanted to and reported early enough could work in the kitchen or laundry. The jobs were coveted. You earned next to nothing, but the time went by faster. Yini pretended to want to see everything first, and explored every nook and cranny, but of course there was only one exit - the one she had come in through.

At ten o'clock, an alarm sounded. It was time for official exercise. Everyone, including the guards, joined in. There was a sports room full of equipment. Due to the lack of gravity, they couldn't use weights, but they could use springs.

Sweating profusely, Yini walked to the shower afterwards. The others didn't bother, and instead flocked to the food counter. But she couldn't stand the sweat drying on her skin. When she was dressed again, she heard a noise, a dull hammering. It seemed to be coming from the wall behind her. She stepped out of the shower. Behind the wall was a storage room. "No trespassing" was written in large letters on the door. There were several of these doors inside the prison. Most of them could only be opened by looking into a retina scanner, which could apparently distinguish between authorized and unauthorized persons.

This door was different. To the left of it, a scanning eye offered its services. But the door seemed to be open! If Yini wasn't mistaken, the thin cloth coming from of the crack and tied tightly to the handle gave that away. She pulled on it, and sure enough, the door opened. The cloth prevented the latch from engaging.

The room behind the door was brightly lit. It was full of cupboards. Yini slipped inside, aided greatly by the low Enceladus gravity, and pulled the door shut behind her. The cabinets were set up in such a way that they left a passage open to the back of the room. Yini tiptoed to the gap, which was wide enough to squeeze through. She gave it a cautious glance - and discovered a person in a guard's uniform working on a cupboard

Tachyon: The Weapon

with their back to her, making the loud noises she had heard. Yini crept through the gap, which meant she was close enough to touch the person. He had short hair ringing a mirror-like bald head and was about fifty years old.

"What are you doing?" she asked.

The person turned around jerkily and raised the tool he had been handling as if he was about to attack Yini with it.

"Tai... That's none of your business," the man said, his eyes wide.

"Prying open a cupboard is exhausting, isn't it?"

Yini pointed to his armpits, where sweat showed darkly. A tag on his lapel bore his name: Andy Boxleitner.

"Get out of here," the man said. "This room is off-limits to prisoners. Or do you want solitary confinement?"

"Only with you, Andy. Don't tell me you're opening the cupboard on behalf of your boss. What's in there, anyway?"

She pushed all the way through the gap. There were letter symbols on the cupboards. S, M, L, XL ... they were sizes! This must be some kind of wardrobe.

"Spacesuits," the man said. "This is the emergency supply. If the station has to be evacuated, there are suits for everyone here."

Yini pushed him a little to one side. The wardrobe he had been working on bore an S.

"That's perfect. I'd like one of those," she said.

"Are you crazy? My colleagues will discover it and then everything will have been for nothing."

"Everything? Everything what?"

The man huffed. He was twice Yini's age, but she seemed to scare him. Maybe it was just the situation. If she raised the alarm, he would be in trouble. Who wanted that? No. That was too short-sighted. He could always talk his way out of it, claim he was the one who caught her. People would be more likely to believe him than her. There must be more at stake.

"Well, Andy, shall we have a word with Andrea?" she asked.

"That won't be necessary," said the man. "There is... Well, there's a plan."

"A meal plan, or what?"

"An escape plan. Not for me, but for a prisoner."

"Very good. Take me with you. I need to get out of here urgently."

"That's out of the question. The plan is too important."

"All the more reason you should take me with you. If I talk to Andrea, you can forget the plan."

The man's face worked.

"I won't be a drag," Yini said. "I have influential friends. Once we're on Neomars..."

The man laughed. "Neomars? You must be crazy. We're not escaping to the nearest prison. We're going to Earth. There's a spaceship out there waiting for us."

"You have to drop me off on Neomars."

"How do you imagine that would happen? It's impossible. As soon as you approach Neomars, they'll snatch you."

"But I have to take my... Never mind. Yes, I admit, it might be a bit much to ask to be taken to Neomars. But just take me out with you. You must have found a way to the surface, right?"

"Yes, I have. It's a ventilation shaft. With the right tools, we can get through."

"Very good. You get me a size S spacesuit, too, and you take me to the surface with you. In return, I won't betray you. Do we have a deal?"

The man nodded. Yini shook his hand.

"Thank you, Andy. You're a lifesaver."

"Don't thank me too soon. The surface of Enceladus is no paradise. Are you sure this will help you?"

Yini nodded. Every step closer to Neomars helped her. Maybe she could hijack a ship, or maybe she could turn herself in and claim to really be a spy. Then she would have to be taken to Neomars. One step at a time.

"When and where are we meeting?" she asked.

"The day after tomorrow, nineteen hundred hours standard time, in life support. I'll have the door ready."

So again, during mandatory exercise. Well, if it was noticed then, it was too late anyway. The man turned away. But there was something about the way he moved that seemed strange to her. He had turned too quickly, so quickly that he had to compensate for the excess momentum. Something was wrong. He had a guilty conscience and therefore couldn't look her in the face!

"Tell me, Andy, about the day after tomorrow, are you sure about that? Why are you getting the suit today?" she asked.

"All right," he said. "I lied to you. I'm sorry. It was a reflex."

"And what's the truth?"

"Tomorrow, nineteen hundred standard time."

"WHERE WERE YOU AT THE GYM EARLIER?" ASKED BRINJA when Yini joined the other two in the canteen with her tray.

"I had a terrible stomachache today because of my period," she said.

"Oh, you poor thing," said Maria.

Yini wondered how the period went for Neomartians with their enhanced skin, but didn't dare ask the question.

"Go ahead and ask," said Brinja.

"Ask what?" Yini asked back.

"I can see it on the tip of your tongue. I dare you! Maria doesn't bite."

"Don't let it bother you," said Maria. "Almost all body-typical people ask me at some point how my period works."

"I admit, I'm interested too," said Yini.

"See, there you go," said Brinja.

Her soft voice still didn't seem to match this woman's true age.

"It's very simple," Maria explained. "Some of my cells produce a natural contraceptive, so I don't have a period at all. If I ever want to have a child, I can do it with artificial insemination."

"I see."

"But as far as exercise is concerned, you should excuse yourself next time," said Brinja. "Karpati can't take a joke. If you don't join in twice in a row, you'll quickly end up in solitary confinement."

"Is there such a thing?" she asked.

Yini was glad that she would be leaving this place tomorrow.

"What else can you take away from people who have already lost everything?" asked Maria. "Social interaction, that's the only thing."

"But I understand that Karpati needs to use some kind of

consequences," said Brinja. "We're not all gentle sheep here. By the time you get to the icy desert of Enceladus, you must have done something serious. What was it with you?"

"I'm innocent."

Brinja laughed. "That's what everyone here says. I killed both my ex-husbands. They deserved it, that's all I'm saying."

It became quiet at the table. Most of the other prisoners had already left the canteen. This time, Brinja didn't ask her to ask Maria. She decided not to. The Neomartian seemed like a very tragic character to her.

"Could you show me around a bit?" Yini asked. She still had to find out where life support was, because that was where Andy wanted to meet her.

"Oh, you didn't find an exit this morning after all?" asked Brinja. "Very sensible of you to face up to reality. Not everyone can do that in one day."

THEY CAME TO A SLIGHTLY WIDER STEEL DOOR, ALMOST A GATE.

"And where does that go?" asked Yini. "Is that the emergency exit?"

"I wish," said Brinja. "Have a guess."

"That's the castle of the Queen of Enceladus, Andrea the First," said Yini.

"Haha! You're pretty funny. Maybe it will be fun with you after all."

"Thank you."

"If you want, you can sleep with us in the bottom bunk," said Maria. "You won't feel so lonely there. There's still a bit of room. We sometimes chat and gossip until after midnight."

"Maybe," said Yini. "But what's behind that gate?"

"That's the wing with the solitary cells," said Maria.

"Is anyone in there at the moment?"

"No, none of us have upset Queen Andrea," Maria replied.

"You're forgetting the federal prisoner," said Brinja.

"That's just a rumor."

"No, it's true. Katharina told me. She took food back there from the canteen herself."

"Did she see the woman?"

"No."

"There you go, Brinja. You're so old, but you still believe any nonsense you hear."

"What state prisoner is that?" asked Yini.

"Don't listen to her," said Maria.

"Supposedly a woman with superpowers lives there," said Brinja. "They had to bring her here, under two hundred yards of thick ice, because otherwise she can teleport out of anywhere."

"You see, Yini, I warned you. So why is she staying in her cell, this superheroine?"

"She's not a hero, she's a criminal," said Brinja. "She stays in her cell because that's where she's best looked after, and she won't come to the surface anyway."

"But she could teleport into the elevator and then ride it up?"

"Exactly. That's why there's now a soldier in the cabin around the clock to keep an eye on her."

"Did Katharina tell you that too?"

"Yes, she brought him food."

Maria laughed. "That Katharina really has a vivid imagination."

Brinja elbowed Maria in the side, but the skin didn't bend a bit. Brinja, on the other hand, rubbed her aching elbow.

"I think I've seen enough for today," said Yini.

"Kasen settlement, day 14."

Decker's handwriting was much less legible than in the previous letters. At least that was how it seemed to Yini. The letters from her backpack had not yet been returned to her. If she really did escape with that guard tomorrow, she would lose them forever. But they were only copies that Mike had made for her anyway. She would see Mike again one day. Yini heard the two friends giggling and talking below her. There were only ten minutes to go until lights out. She'd better hurry with the letter.

"I owe it entirely to my friend Kian that I can write the following at all. After I had injected myself, I lost consciousness. Kian told me today what happened next after I questioned him for a long time, as best I could with sign language. He used the perfect means for this - he simply demonstrated it to me.

"I lay down in the same place he had found me, next to my bed on the floor. Kian corrected my posture and my limbs until he was satisfied. I felt completely bent out of shape. I probably suffered from severe spasms three days ago – that's how long it had been.

"Then he fastened me to his back with his tail. We walked through the forest. I was able to look into their mighty crowns until Kian closed my eyes. It was probably more authentic that way. The Kasen put me down where we had temporarily stored his friend. I suspected what was about to happen, but hoped that Kian wouldn't overdo the accuracy of the demonstration. Kasen towered over me like the carver. Unlike him, he didn't have the presumably sacred drill in his hand, but a pointed stick.

"Kian brought it down on me, just like the carver had done to his friend, but stopped the stick millimeters from my larynx. I was breathing heavily. Kian closed my eyes again. He was so wonderfully patient with me! He probably thought I was the stupidest creature in the forest, that he had to protect from the local hardships.

"He carried me to a shallow pit and began to shovel some mud over me. I quickly understood what he wanted to show me - he had buried me, just as his friend had been buried. Kian lifted me out of the pit and cleaned me off. I just managed to stop him from using his urine stream by quickly jumping aside. He made sounds reminiscent of human laughter. Was he imitating me? He was a quick learner.

"I guess that solved the mystery of my recovery. Except that I wasn't actually healed. No, that was wrong. Nothing was wrong with me. I no longer had a headache. But the octopus was still there, and now I could hear its voice clearly and distinctly. Not only that: I felt the need to follow its instructions. It wasn't a compulsion. The octopus wasn't forcing me to destroy the spray with the antidote that was still waiting for me. I simply had a desire in my heart to get rid of it. The octopus wasn't forcing me to eat something distasteful. It simply made what I was supposed to eat so tasty that I couldn't help myself. And it made me feel good, too!

"Nevertheless, it allowed me my own thoughts. For example, I thought long and hard about what had caused the change. It was probably a matter of the concentration of silicon structures in my body. Before the injection, it was low enough that I could still defend myself. But fighting back was painful. The injection had killed me, just as I wished. Kian had brought me back to life - with the help of an even larger dose of silicon structures, though he didn't know that.

"The crucial question for me was why the octopus allowed me my own thoughts. Was it simply too lazy to control them all, did it just not care, or was it incapable of doing so? I tested all those theories during a trip to the Hopper. Kian now perfectly understands a request to visit the Hopper. In the medical department, I checked my blood values again. As I suspected, the proportion of U1 had risen to almost twenty percent. This was already having some negative effects. My blood was clotting faster. If the octopus continued to increase its influence, I would eventually die of a thrombosis. I took an anticoagulant to be on the safe side.

"Then I picked up my lab diary with the formula for the antidote in it. As long as the notebook was closed, the octopus didn't complain. When I opened it in the right place, I suddenly had an incredible appetite, even a ravenous appetite for paper. I buried my face in the book, but at the same time used my hands to throw it far away from me. As soon as the formula was no longer in front of my eyes, my ravenous appetite disappeared.

"I had become a danger. What if the octopus saw another person as a danger? Would I then try to eat them? Would I kill them some other way? Which of my abilities did the octopus have access to? I let Kian take me back to the settlement for the time being. There I tested various scenarios. They all had the same terrifying ending: the octopus in my head could access all my abilities if it needed them. And not only that – I would also use any ability to its full potential. Of course, I didn't develop any superhuman abilities. But I did manage to run as fast as Kian for a brief moment, climb a brine tree all by myself, and solve integral equations in my head. I had always hated math.

"That evening, Kian came to see me again. The Kasen stretched out in front of me. Suddenly he dropped his prey in front of me. It resembled a six-legged rodent that quickly fled towards the exit. The animal was almost as big as I was. Kian promptly tore it in half. Material similar to what I had found inside the Kasen emerged from the rupture. I was shocked. My heart was racing, and not because of my friend's cruelty.

"I realized that I myself was potential prey for him. The fact that he had spared me might not be because he considered me a friend or protector: the silicon structures inside him made him do so. The Kasen of this settlement may have been no different from their wild siblings at some point. Then they came across the crash site, and all at once they had been able to realize their potential. They developed a primitive society because that was what the octopuses in their bodies wanted.

"But what was the point? I was an astrobiologist. I slapped my forehead. How could I ask such a stupid question? It was about growth, about expansion, about development, as always in life. When Kian and his friend first came across us, perhaps even before then, the structures must have realized that I offered the higher potential for expansion. I had technology. Maybe they didn't understand it, but they must have realized that I came from another planet. That I could go back there.

"At that moment, I came to the only correct conclusion: I had to kill myself."

It suddenly went dark. It couldn't have come at a more suspenseful moment. Yini shuddered. These letters were stored in the archive. Their contents must be known. Nevertheless, everyone seemed to think Mark Decker was a lunatic. But what if his report was true?

Yini was freezing. She pushed herself out of her bunk and let herself slide down.

"There you are at last," Brinja said.

"Is the invitation still open?" asked Yini.

"Of course," said Maria.

Yini crawled under the blanket that the two of them shared.

"You're freezing," said Maria. "Come into the middle."

Yini felt someone climbing over her.

"Here, put your arms around me," said Brinja.

She put her arms around the old woman in the body of a young girl. Behind her, she felt the hard but warm skin of the Neomartian. It felt like family. Yini felt sad. She would have to leave them again tomorrow.

October 10, 2802, Enceladus

YINI UNCURLED HERSELF AND STRETCHED. SHE HADN'T SLEPT THIS well for a long time. Maria had her hand on Yini's hip. Yini carefully slipped it off. Her left arm had fallen asleep. Brinja's head was resting on it. Yini pulled it away as gently as possible but couldn't keep Brinja from waking up.

"Shit," Brinja said.

Immediately afterwards, it became light in their cell. Yini couldn't see what was happening because the light was blinding her. She smelled uniform boots.

"Get up now, ladies!" ordered Andrea Karpati.

Brinja jumped out of the bunk. Yini followed her and bumped her head. Maria was the last to stand next to her.

"They must have let us oversleep just so they could punish us," Maria whispered in Yini's ear.

Karpati scrutinized them. They must look like they'd had an exhausting night, but they'd just slept blissfully. Yini was in her underwear. Brinja was wearing a shirt with spaghetti straps that came down to her hips. Maria was naked.

"It's half past nine!" shouted Karpati. "You're way past your alarms. You know what that means?"

"The usual twenty lashes on our bare asses?" asked Brinja.

Yini was startled. What kind of conditions were these?

"Haha, always ready with a wisecrack, eh, Brinja?" asked Karpati. "You will clean latrines from eighteen hundred to twenty-two standard time, understand?"

"Understood," said Brinja and Maria.

"This also applies to new arrivals," said the headmistress.

"Understood," said Yini.

Shit. She had to meet Andy, the guard, at 19:00. Otherwise, she would never get out of here. She had been so lucky! And now she'd ruined it by oversleeping. Yini only now realized that Karpati had left the cell and that there was only a curious guard staring at her breasts. She turned around and put something on.

She usually felt better after a shower. Not today.

She usually felt better after exercise. Not today.

She usually felt better after eating. Not today.

What was she supposed to do? If she wasn't at the latrines by six, people would be looking for her. Everywhere. Andy's plan might fail. If she started work at six, she couldn't just disappear at seven. People would be looking for her. Everywhere. Andy's plan might fail, and she was in the middle of it. She would be stuck on Enceladus for a long time. There was only one other option: she would go to work at six and stay until ten. Then at least Andy and the person he had organized all this for could leave the icy moon.

That was only fair. Why had she overslept? But who could it be that Andy had organized this for? She didn't suspect Brinja or Maria. They had accepted the order to clean latrines without complaint. It was the only job for which there were never enough volunteers. That was why Karpati tended to seek out candidates who had done something wrong.

What if Yini let Brinja and Maria in on the plan? They didn't seem like spies to her, or the kind of people who would betray her to the prison authorities. All they had to do was keep quiet until their special shift was over. Without a search, no one would miss Yini.

That was one solution. It still took Yini until just before six to decide. Brinja brought the cleaning supplies to their cell. Maria was still changing her clothes.

Yini pointed to the alcove in the wall. "Just for a moment," she said.

The two friends nodded. They sat down in the alcove. Maria had to really squeeze herself in.

"What's the big deal?" she asked.

"I need your help," said Yini.

Tachyon: The Weapon

"If you could tell us what it's about..." said Brinja.

"About an escape."

"You're crazy," said Brinja.

"Let her finish," said Maria.

Yini explained how she had caught the guard Andy and got him to tell her about the escape plans.

"He's really okay with taking you with him?" asked Maria.

"I don't want to go with him. I have to get to Neomars," said Yini.

"Have you taken leave of your senses?" asked Brinja. "I definitely want to go."

"Me too," said Maria. "Never again to Neomars."

"But I can't..."

"Either you take us with you or you'll miss your date," said Brinja.

"I don't even know if the ship has that many seats," said Yini.

"All right," said Maria. "A compromise: you take us with you, and if there's no possible way, we'll stay here and cover for you."

"That sounds fair," said Brinja.

Yini sighed. "Okay. I'm sure the guard won't be thrilled."

"Let's go," whispered Brinja.

They were alone in the toilet block. Yini picked up her cleaning bucket, closed the lid so that nothing spilled out and ran to the exit. The other two followed her. No one said anything. Yini was shaking. Everyone was doing exercise at the moment, including the guards. At least the cleaning job had the advantage of explaining her absence.

"I hope you know where life support is, because that's where we need to go," Yini said.

"Follow me," Brinja replied and took the lead.

They had to cross the cafeteria. Something rattled. Apparently one of the assistants was still cleaning up. It was a Neomartian woman. She stood tall and stiff in front of a sink and had the entire room in view.

"Let's go," Brinja said.

They had no choice. They crossed the canteen in single file.

Women with cleaning utensils were not an unusual sight. The Neomartian greeted them with a gesture.

"Hey, Susanna," said Maria.

"See you tomorrow at the Neomars group?" asked the Neomartian.

"Of course."

They had made it through. Brinja led them to the right. Then they were standing in front of a door with a sign reading "Life support. No unauthorized access".

"It's closed," said Brinja. "That guy was fucking with you."

Yini pushed past her. Something shiny was covering the door lock. This time Andy hadn't used cloth, but clear tape, which was less conspicuous. Yini pulled the handle and the door swung open. Booming and whistling noises came from the life support system. Yini quickly pulled the door shut again. Then she changed her mind, opened the door again and pulled off the tape. That way, no one could follow them easily, such as a curious Neomartian from the cafeteria.

"It's a bit twisty in here," said Brinja.

"Shh," said Maria.

There were a number of small branches, but only one main corridor. However, it led downwards, not upwards. After perhaps eight or ten minutes, they reached a larger room containing a kind of cooling tower. There was only one way in - the one they had come through. They were alone.

"That guy screwed you," Brinja said.

"Quiet," said Andy.

Yini jerked around. The guard must have been hiding somewhere. Now he was pointing a gun at her.

"You can't shoot us all at once," Brinja said. "Come on, let's get him."

"Take it easy," Yini said. "Andy, we had a deal."

"Not like this. You said you were alone," the guard said.

"It was the only way." Yini explained to him the dilemma she had been in.

"Then you shouldn't have come at all. This is far too important. This isn't a game for a spoiled brat, it's interstellar politics."

"You're such a show-off, Andy. Couldn't be any smaller?" asked Brinja.

Yini noticed that Maria was no longer standing next to her.

She was probably preparing an attack. Andy would shoot and then... It was all her fault.

"Please, Maria and Brinja, please leave him alone. For my sake."

"I can take care of myself," Andy said.

Suddenly someone appeared beside him and pushed his gun down.

"I told you to...!" shouted Andy.

"Don't, Maria!" shouted Yini, who saw the Neomartian coming at him from behind.

Andy tried to raise the hand with the gun, but a new arrival, a woman, prevented him from doing so. At the same moment, Maria struck, but realized just in time that the guard had stopped resisting. Her blow still landed on his back. He was thrown forward. Yini jumped towards him and caught him.

"Shit," Andy said, panting.

"I'm sorry," Maria said.

"Is that you, Yini?" the stranger asked.

"What, you two know each other?" asked Brinja.

Yini shook her head. She had never seen this person before.

"It's me, Tailin."

She knew the name, though. Her eyes widened. This couldn't be her mother. The way she looked - blonde, pale, curly hair, a mouth far too wide... Yini had seen Tsai Tailin in her savior's consciousness. Yini shook her head, but could find no words.

"I am your mother, Yini. I had to leave my body behind, that's why you don't recognize me. But I would recognize you anywhere. You have a birthmark behind your right ear."

Yini reached behind her right ear. There had always been a raised spot there, covered by her wig. A doctor had once offered to remove it, but she had refused.

"That's your mother?" Brinja asked. "Did you know this?"

Yini shook her head again. There was a lump in her throat.

"Why did you leave us, then?" she asked.

"Because I loved you so much, and I didn't want you to have to live a life on the run. I hope you can understand that."

They fell into each other's arms. The explanation wasn't enough for Yini, but it would have to do for the moment. It seemed she had finally found her mother.

The guard pulled Tailin away from her.

"I'm sorry, but you have to keep going," he said. "The ship will only wait until eight o'clock. That's the deal."

"We have to get to Terra Nova," said Yini.

"Excuse me?" asked Tailin. "We have to get to Neomars. I need my instruments."

"It has to be Terra Nova," said Yini. "I'm convinced Mark Decker will arrive there soon. I'm sure of it. There's only the one place he can go. And he's dangerous. I'll explain it to you on the way."

"Well, I'll see you on Terra Nova," said Andy, the guard. "After I fetch Tailin's instruments."

"No, Monte, of course you're coming with me," said Tailin.

Wait, what? Monte? The man whose consciousness Yini had been in for days?

"You're not Andy Boxleitner?" she asked.

"No. I snuck in here under a false name so I could help Tailin."

Why hadn't she recognized him? Because she had never seen him. Monte wasn't someone who constantly looked at himself in the mirror. Or was he using a different Biobag?

"You're coming with me, Monte," Tailin repeated.

"I'm afraid I can't," said Monte. "The ship only has four stasis chambers. One of us has to stay here. I'm sure nobody suspects me. I'll ask for special permission to go to Neomars. I'll get the instruments there. Then I'll look for a ship to Terra Nova."

Tailin sighed. "I secured them. I've already explained that to you."

"Then figure out how I can bypass the security," Monte said. "You can tell me the conventional way. It'll take me a few days to get to Neomars."

Tailin and Monte hugged each other. They looked almost like lovers. Something pricked Yini's heart.

"I don't mean to interrupt, but do we have enough spacesuits?" she asked.

"Yes. Your friend from Neomars doesn't need one, you have one, and the young lady here can have mine. It'll be a bit too big, but that's better than too small."

"My name is Maria," said Maria.

"I'm a hundred and thirty-six," said Brinja.

"And I am the King of England," said Monte.

"You're Claudio Pedramonte," said Yini.

"Where did you get that from? Never mind. You really have to go now!"

They put on the spacesuits, which adjusted themselves to their figures and were comfortable to wear. Only Brinja's had a few wrinkles. Monte led them up a ladder to the ceiling. From there, they could see a shaft right above the cooling tower. It was open. They would have to jump to reach it. But in the low gravity, it looked doable.

It was quiet. The cooling tower was apparently not in operation. Yini was second in line, right after her mother. She jumped. The suit increased her jumping power, so that she almost sailed past the opening. But her mother reached for her and caught her. Yini climbed after her to make room for the other two.

Monte stayed behind, as agreed. They hadn't even said goodbye to each other. Hopefully he wouldn't get into trouble.

"We're all here," said Maria, who had jumped in last.

They climbed up the ladder. It got darker with every step until the blackness finally enveloped them completely. Brinja hummed a song whose melody sounded familiar to Yini.

"How many times have prisoners escaped from Enceladus?" asked Yini.

"None in my lifetime," said Brinja.

The shaft ended in a slightly larger room. Yini only heard it at first because the sound of their footsteps changed. Then Tailin switched on her helmet light. The room had been hewn out of the bare ice. The skeleton of an animal lay in one corner. How had it gotten here? Brinja felt the bones. Yini pulled her away.

"Leave it alone," she said.

"The exit is up there." Tailin shone a light at the ceiling.

There was a circular lock with a rotating wheel. Everyone put on their helmets and secured them. Yini heard the breathing of the others over the shared radio channel. Only Maria would not be able to hear them. Tailin gave her a signal and Maria, the strongest among them, opened the mechanical lock and pushed the lid up. Yini expected a gust of wind, cold blowing in from outside, snowflakes and ice crystals, but that was naïve, of course. There was no wind on Enceladus, and if there was, pressure equalized from the inside out.

"We have to hurry," said Tailin, "or someone will notice the loss of pressure."

Yini was the last one on the surface. She closed the hatch again and locked it in place. Then she looked around. The image was similar to the one she had seen from the porthole of the police cruiser. It hadn't gotten any brighter. Between the plain, which only ended at the horizon, and the blackness above her, she felt tiny.

"Our spaceship is waiting in a crevasse to the north," Tailin explained. "It's ten minutes from here at most." Yini remembered Ari, the woman in the android body. She would realize her dream for her. The strategy of leaving from a hollow sounded familiar to Yini. On the moon, the smugglers had also taken off from a crater.

The small troop moved across the ice. It was child's play; Yini just had to be careful not to jump too high. The crevasse came into view in a few minutes. It looked like a lightning bolt that had struck the ice. It branched out directly in front of them. It was widest there, enough that a small spaceship could fit inside.

They found a yacht, a private spaceship, the kind only rich people could afford. Its elegant, bird-like winged shape allowed it to fly even in the atmosphere of a planet.

"The entrance is at the bottom," her mother explained.

That was a bit impractical. Normally the yacht would stand on landing legs, leaving enough space to use the exit at the bottom. Here it was stuck horizontally in the shaft. Below her, it went further into the depths. Tailin handed out two safety lines to each of them. Maria wrapped one of them around her wrist. They attached the others to their suits. Then they tied them together.

"Are you all right, Maria?" asked Yini.

The Neomartian nodded. Her skin had turned white. This time, Tailin climbed forward. She knew the code that would open the entrance. She skillfully shimmied along the stubby wings.

"You'll have to attach the free end of your line to the hooks down here," Tailin explained. "Then you swing from hook to hook."

The yacht's wings concealed the way Tailin moved towards the entrance. Yini only heard her breath quicken.

"It's open," Tailin said. "You can come."

They followed. Yini was last in line. She followed her mother's lead. As she hovered just above the depths of the crevasse, held securely by the line, she paused for a moment. She wanted to take in the situation fully. Vertical walls of ice extended into the depths. It was so clean that it shimmered blue. If she fell into this crevasse, she would never make it back to the surface despite the low gravity. Her heart reacted and beat faster. Yini pulled herself into the opening in the belly of the yacht.

It seemed they had the ship to themselves; no horny old man to ogle them in the stasis chamber. The yacht was as small as it looked from the outside. There was a control center with four seats, and behind it was a small room that served as a kitchen and workshop. The stasis chambers were built into the floor and ceiling in pairs. They had probably been installed later, as the arrangement was impractical: the ones in the ceiling could only be entered and exited in zero gravity.

Otherwise, the ship was equipped with the best of the best. All the equipment bore well-known logos and brand names. The food supplies were luxurious - there was shrimp, Martian wine and supposedly Terran caviar, among other things - but their quantity was reasonable, especially as there were now four of them. They would be spending most of their time in the stasis chambers anyway.

"Launch in one minute," the ship's control system announced.

They entered the control center. Yini was once again the last to arrive. Maria and Brinja had sat down in the two chairs at the back. The front left was still empty, next to her mother, who was the pilot. It was strange. Yini no longer flinched when she thought of this woman, who had been unknown to her until an hour ago, as her mother. But it didn't hurt to think of the woman in the Ring as her mother as well. She had two mothers. And why not?

Yini fastened her seatbelt as the countdown began. When it was over, the engine pressed her gently into her seat. Enceladus' escape velocity was low, so the yacht was able to take them into orbit very slowly. No one was looking out for them. There was also no one there to discover them. Why should there be? No one had ever been able to escape from the prison. That was strange, since Monte had found a way. Perhaps it was because of the myth that no one ever tried to break out. Not even Brinja with her accumulated prison experience.

"What about Terra Nova now?" her mother asked.

"It's a long story," said Yini. "How much time do we have?"

"We have about five hours to determine our final destination. That's how long we'll be drifting out of the system without power."

"Good, that should do. I have to tell you everything from memory, so I can't guarantee the details. Unfortunately, they took most of the letters away from me."

"I see," said Tailin.

Yini summarized Mark Decker's story as best she could. Her mother reacted very emotionally to it, almost as if she were the Tsai Tailin to whom the letters were addressed. She was terrified when Decker was abducted, held her breath when it looked like he was going to die.

"That was the moment when Mark concluded that he had to kill himself," said Yini, leaning back.

"What happened next?" asked Tailin. "You can't stop there!"

"I don't know what's going to happen next. The last letter - I haven't read it yet."

"Do you have it with you? Please tell me you brought it with you."

Yini fumbled for her belt pouch. The letter was still there. She took it out.

"Yes, here it is."

"May I see it?" her mother asked.

Yini gave it a push and the letter drifted in her direction. Tailin caught it and examined it carefully.

"That really is his handwriting. There's no way," she said.

She smelled it.

"They're copies of copies of scans," Yini said. "They smell like me at best."

"I know," Tailin said, "You smell the way you did when you were a baby."

Yini had to swallow.

Tachyon: The Weapon

"Can I read the letter to you?" her mother asked.

"Please do," said Yini.

That was all she could get out. This was unbelievable. It was too much. She had found her biological mother. And her mother, in turn, had rediscovered her old love. At least that was her reaction, even though all the circumstances were against it. The facts of time were irrefutable. Yini knew it. She was a chronoscribe. Who, if not she, should know that? Nevertheless, she wasn't brave enough to mention it to her mother.

"Research station Albatross-1, day unknown," Tailin began.

Yini felt like a little girl again, listening to her mother read a story. She would have loved to snuggle up in a blanket. But this wasn't a children's fairy tale. The story couldn't have a happy ending. Yini was afraid of that. She wanted Tailin to read as slowly as possible.

"I don't even know what day it is anymore, dear Tailin."

Her mother let out a short sob.

"Something bad has happened, or rather: something bad will have happened. I told you about my decision. I swear I tried everything to make it happen, but I was unsuccessful. Please don't be angry with me. I just didn't have the strength. Even though I might be putting the whole of humanity in danger.

"I tried drinking acid. I threw myself off a brine tree. I provoked the wild Kasen until they attacked me. Which didn't take much effort. I let the weavers' nets catch me. I even asked my friend Kian to kill me. Which was also surprisingly easy, because he understands me pretty well by now and has a relaxed attitude toward dying, which is of course no surprise given that he can be revived at any time in the swamp. To cut a long story short: I was either saved or had a powerful opposite impulse at the last second. The octopus in my head seems to decide this based on efficiency. When I fell from the brine tree, it probably couldn't think of what to whisper to me quickly enough. How happy I was when I fell towards death!

"Now I no longer believe in it. I am condemned to live. Nevertheless, I can still think freely. Unfortunately! At first, I thought it was a mercy. Now I think it's a punishment. Even while I'm doing something that will end up harming humanity, I can think freely about the consequences. I certainly deserve this punishment. Roger should not have died. It was and is my mistake. But humanity shouldn't have to suffer because of me.

"Yesterday, for example, I suddenly had an urgent desire to go back on board the Albatross. I am now back in our shared cabin, having joyfully - and at the same time hating myself - programmed the flight destination: the Gliese 167 system, where the agricultural colony Terra Nova is located.

"The space station is relatively slow. It will take many years for it to reach Gliese 167. But when it does, no one must approach it. Absolutely not! The best thing to do is to have it shot down. I'll probably contact you personally and ask to be allowed to stay alive. Don't listen to me!"

Tailin sobbed again. Yini fished a handkerchief out of a dispenser and handed it to her.

"Because if you believe me, the silicon structures will find a way to influence you too. They're just waiting to do it. I can't even blame them. It's the way of evolution. Humans clearly offer more potential as a substrate for their development than the Kasen. But you have the power to prevent that. Please do me one last favor and take me out of the sky in a ball of fire. It would be a comforting thought to be allowed to die in a ball of light and heat.

"To give you the chance, I have a plan. This is the last letter I will write. I will ask Kian to deposit it in the Hopper with the others. Yesterday I programmed the Hopper for the destination Terra Nova. As it will have no crew and is small and light, it can accelerate much faster than the cumbersome Albatross. That will give it a head start. My letters will reach the colony well before the danger. I hope you draw the right conclusions! Once again, you must destroy the Albatross. Do not come on board. Shoot first, ask questions later. Don't let me get a word in edgewise. Who knows what clever arguments the octopus in my head will whisper to me? I. Must. Die. Understand?

"I do feel sorry for Kian. The Kasen can't be dissuaded from accompanying me. I showed him the stasis chambers, which are far too small for him. There's no way he'll survive a flight lasting over a hundred years with the food and air supplies on board, so he will die in a few months and his sacrifice will be completely in vain. Still, I can't talk him out of it. Think about him in silence for a few minutes.

Tachyon: The Weapon

"Kian is standing next to me right now. He's waiting for me to finish the letter. I've taught him his name. He'll sign it. I want to tell you, Tailin, that I have always loved you and always will. Perhaps you will never read these lines. The..."

Tailin fell silent, tears streaming down her cheeks. Yini gave her time. It was heartbreaking, though.

"Will you read on, please?" her mother asked, sniffling.

"Okay."

The letter sailed from one seat to the other. Yini smoothed it out. It had damp patches. It was only a copy. The ink would surely have run all over the original.

Yini swallowed. "The chances of that are minimal. But if you do - I'm so sorry I never got to show you what you're worth to me. I'm even more sorry for my selfishness. I shouldn't have gotten back out of the TransVec. I was so obsessed with my own guilt over Roger's death that I completely lost sight of everyone else."

"And yet I had him on my own conscience," Tailin said, choked up with tears.

"But still, and this is important: you have to let me go. The man you knew is dead. I am a zombie. I have died several times and I still exist without being the master of my own fate. If I reach Terra Nova, you will have to kill me. The same goes for anyone else who reads this message, of course.

"That's it from me. Please give my regards to the sun. With love, your husband."

Tailin was crying loudly now. Yini looked at the letter. "Kian" was written underneath in awkward letters. Next to it, the same hand had drawn a symbol reminiscent of a nest of snakes. Yini wiped the tears from her face. They still had time. Her mother could cry until she no longer needed to cry. When she had read the word "love", she had thought of Mike. She owed him a letter too. However, so much had happened that she couldn't possibly summarize it in a few minutes.

Yini pulled the computer towards her. She programmed a message for the yacht to send when it was safe to do so. She herself would be slumbering in the stasis chamber by then.

"Dear Mike," she wrote, "The days I spent with you were so wonderful. I would have loved to experience many more of them with you. But something came up. I have found my mother and am now flying with her to Terra Nova. I have a suspicion that the search for my mother has turned into a mission to save the world. You know I don't bother about small things. But I could certainly use the help of a brave archivist. That's an offer, not a promise. Maybe I won't even like you anymore when I see you on Terra Nova, but you would still have the option of helping to save the world. You could go down in history with me. That's something too, isn't it? The stasis chamber is already waiting for me. When I leave it again, many years will have passed on the moon. You'll be an old man if you haven't also boarded a spaceship to Terra Nova. I would be delighted to be able to tell you my whole story there. Your Tsai Yini."

Yini sighed, read the message again, corrected a comma error and pushed it into the pipeline. There was no way Mike would follow her. It was a de facto suicide note. She sniffled.

"Where did you get those letters again?" asked Tailin.

"From the Great Archive."

"So the Hopper did arrive at Terra Nova."

"Yes. They were scanned there and forwarded by tachyon transmission."

"But they're not being taken seriously."

"No. Supposedly, experts analyzed the contents and diagnosed your husband with psychosis. There were no traces of any foreign cells, but there were molecules of psychotropic substances on the original paper."

"They think he was on drugs?"

"Drugs, alcohol, depression and finally a full-blown psychosis. They obviously never found any traces of these Kasen."

"That's right. Your father was not averse to alcohol and soft drugs either. But he was still a good astrobiologist. The best. You must take him seriously."

"Tailin?"

"Yes?"

"Mark Decker cannot be my father."

At last it was out. Yini was relieved.

"Mark is your father, Yini."

"But how can that be? You can't be the same person who explored Gliese 163c with him back then. That doesn't work chronologically."

"Yes, it does work. I made the big mistake of separating

myself from my biological body on Terra Nova, even though I hate the whole uploading technique. After that, I swore I would never leave my body again. But at the time, I just wanted to get away, and a tachyon transfer worked the fastest. The technicians promised to clone a new body from my own DNA, but it's still not the same. I even changed my research focus and went into tachyons because that was in high demand on Neomars at the time."

"You see? Decker can't be my father. Even if you were pregnant by him! Only your consciousness is recorded during the transfer. Everything organic, including embryos, remains in the old body."

Tailin sobbed. Yini felt horrible for making her mother cry.

"I'm sorry, I..." She paused. "You can go on saying that he was my father."

"He really is!" exclaimed Tailin. "After I arrived on Neomars and transferred into a Biobag, I was told that my real body had been pregnant. That was extremely stressful for me. I had failed the babies, even if they were just clumps of cells, too small for the scanner to detect. But then I had the idea of using Neomars's excellent reproductive medicine. You know that the genetically modified Neomartians can't get pregnant naturally?"

Yini nodded.

"We prefer to call it 'the old way'," Maria disagreed from the back row.

Yini had completely forgotten about her two friends.

"Sorry. I was still officially married to your father. So I had a pair of twins made legally from his DNA and mine, with the help of the DNA database. They were implanted in me and nine months later you were born. I loved you so much, both of you! How is Aunt Hao doing?"

"You mean... Mother? Sorry, that slipped out... And she's also ..."

"Hao is my mother's sister. She and her husband didn't have any children of their own because she was infertile, and she agreed to take you to Earth with her. She was the best mother I could have given you."

Yini wiped her cheek.

"I'd be happy if you kept calling her Mother," Tailin said. "And what about Kang? How is he doing?"

August 13, 2802, Neomars

"Are you Claudio Pedramonte?" asked the officer at immigration control.

Monte looked at his face but couldn't read any emotion. The Neomartians must be perfect poker players.

"Yes, that's me," he said.

There was no reason to conceal his identity. Another officer approached him from the side, put on a scanner and checked his DNA.

"It's true," he said.

"Very good, sir. You are expected."

On Neomars, one building looked like the next, and the only difference between the corridors was the color of the digital information strips on the walls. Monte was glad that a Neomartian was showing him around. He liked it even better that his companion - or guard - didn't try to start a conversation with him.

They finally reached a briefing room that looked hideously generic. There was nothing here that could be remembered later, but perhaps that was the goal.

A woman in a Neomars uniform was waiting in the room, though she did not show the typical genetic manipulations. As she was, she could have come from the Terran Union. Her skin was unusually dark. She wore her hair short in military style. The woman stood up and shook his hand.

"I'm Anastasia Moshchenka from the Neomars Intelligence Service."

"Claudio Pedramonte."

She gave him a broad smile and he returned it.

"Come, the admiral is waiting."

The woman sat down at the front of an oval office table. He took a seat to her left. Monte heard the hum of a hologram, and then he saw her.

"Great that you were able to make it possible," Moshchenka said.

Monte was impressed. The signal travel time from Earth to Neomars was far too long for a live holo. So the admiral was connected via tachyon transmitter. At what cost! You could buy a space freighter for the price of ten minutes of conversation.

"I don't want to beat around the bush," said the Admiral. "As promised, I've sent you the best horse in our stable. Please don't make it unnecessarily difficult for him."

She was obviously talking about him. It was only now that Monte realized how old she had grown. She looked well over 70, even though they had once been in the same class at school.

"I'm still wondering how I know I can really trust you and your horse completely," said Moshchenka.

She grinned at him as if she wanted to examine his bit next.

"Well, I'll figure out the location of the weapon in a few days," Monte said.

"The weapon you claim never to have developed," said the Admiral.

"Of course, we would have liked to have developed it, I admit that," said Moshchenka. "But in fact, this Ms. Tsai seems to have been working on her own account. Of course, we couldn't tolerate something like that."

It was funny to watch the two highly decorated women mistrust each other. They had every reason to do so, as they were dealing with a weapon that could thoroughly shift the balance of power in favor of whoever got their hands on it first.

"What is his interest in this game?" asked Moshchenka.

"He has personal motives," said the admiral, as if he wasn't even present. "The woman belongs to him. We will guarantee her safety together."

"And then together we'll destroy the weapon he's going to obtain for us."

"That's the plan," said the Admiral.

"I have recorded our agreement," Moshchenka said.

"So have I."

Monte knew what the agreement would be worth once he had the weapon in his hands. They considered him a mere tool. But he would be able to use it to force the Terran Union and Neomars to reunite. He could go down in history if he wanted to. Hadn't he already secretly done enough for that, risked his life often enough for a higher purpose? Or he would simply retire with Tailin somewhere where she could pursue her research undisturbed. It would be his decision, and that felt amazing.

Afterword by the chronoscribe

DEAR READERS,

What is the truth? Although it is my job to find out the truth over the course of time, I cannot answer that simple question. I have tried very hard to find an objectively correct sequence. That is all I can promise you.

Have you ever listened to a tachyon transmission? Then you understand me. If not, think of it like the stories children tell when they are still in the magical phase. They are full of truth, even if not all the facts and events would be interpreted in the same way by other people. The people into whose consciousness I slip have their own wishes, fears and desires, which naturally affect their experience of reality.

Needless to say, I also used secondary sources in my research. Mark Decker's original letters are stored in the Great Archive. I initially took his experiences in orbit around and on Adad - Gliese 163 c - from my mother's reports, which she shared with me in vivid detail on our long journey to Terra Nova. Please forgive me for the poetic license of formulating them from my father's perspective for the sake of atmosphere. Perhaps I have added something at one point or another that my mother could not have known. But I guarantee that I have left out far more: private, intimate, unsafe things. You know what I mean. My mother's narrative style is incredibly detailed. I admit that I was unsure at this point, because obviously my father's consent could not be obtained. However, I believe that this publication is also in

Mark's interest. In my father's interest. I still have to get used to having two fathers and two mothers.

As far as I know, my brother Kang still doesn't accept this. I feel so sorry for him. For a long time, I deluded myself into thinking that I was only putting this compilation together for him so that he could find out where he came from, because that's important in order to have a position in space. But that's not true, at least not entirely. Above all, I compiled this volume for myself. In that respect, I must thank the Admiralty Intelligence Service for the impetus.

Mr. Smith, I still don't know your real name, but I'm sure someone will submit my thoughts to you. I could not comply with your request for secrecy, and I am glad that we live in a society where nothing can force me to do so. Even though I understand that you and your department have an important role to play.

I have placed Mark's experiences before his letters because that corresponds to the chronological sequence. Some things would have been easier for me if I had also received the letters as a second step. But in this respect, I cannot and will not blame Dr. Mike Wilson. No, I don't want to blame him at all. Mike, you have been a great help to me, and I very much hope that you will continue to play this role for a long time to come. I could say a lot more about you, but that doesn't belong here. I've probably - *hopefully* - told you in person before this compilation gets the publicity it deserves.

The historical events on Neomars, on Terra Nova or within the Terran Union, which I have mentioned for the purposes of classification, are in many cases established common knowledge. I have stuck to the versions shared by the majority of archaeologists. The Admiralty has extensive documentation on Claudio Pedramonte. Unfortunately, I was unable to view even a fraction of the material here because almost everything is classified as top secret. I hope that this will change once certain deadlines have passed.

Will I have to rewrite history as a result? I don't think so. This story is true. Perhaps there is a second story that another tachyon eavesdropper could write. You might not even recognize this story in it. If you come across something like this, please don't accuse my colleague of anything. They will only have told their story, as I have told mine.

But we are all equal before one power: the future. Kian, the cat creature, probably doesn't have one. Mark Decker - is he asleep or dead? Terra Nova is undoubtedly facing decisions that could change its future. The strange attacks are keeping the physicists busy. Pedramonte - did he manage to escape from Enceladus? Will I still be able to work in the Great Archive after this book is published? No one knows. The only thing that can be said with certainty about the future is that it is unattainable. The four of us are sitting in a space yacht approaching the Gliese-167 system. As soon as we have established a direct radio link, everything I have gathered here will be circulating on the interplanetary web. We need to prepare for what's coming. Wish me a safe journey.

Thank you.

Sincerely yours,

Tsai Yini

PS: If you find tachyon physics as exciting as I do, I recommend the essay that I have attached to this volume. Kang sent it to me after he showed me the transmitter on the moon. I remember well how enthusiastic he was. Perhaps some of this enthusiasm will be passed on to you. That would really make me happy. Unfortunately, Kang didn't tell me who wrote the essay, and now I can't ask him. But I have a sneaking suspicion that it was him. It would be just like him.

Around the Campfire

Dear readers,

We have come to the end of a long journey that has really shaken its protagonists. But this story is far from over.

By the time you read these lines, I will have already written the next steps in the lives of Monte, Yini, Mike, Tailin, Mark and Kian. At the moment, I freely admit, I only know it very roughly, because I belong to the category of "discovery writers" - authors who discover a story together with the protagonists instead of thinking up the exact course of events in advance. Both strategies work for creativity. Discovery writing usually involves more reworking after writing than plotting does. I had excellent support from the publisher and from the editor Heide Franck. Many thanks for that!

But I would also like to thank you, dear readers, for your trust. "Tachyon" is designed as a trilogy, and you had the courage to partake of the first part. I truly hope you enjoyed it. Please feel free to email me at brandon@hard-sf.com with your impressions. If you want to make an author happy, please write a review on the website of your favorite bookstore, or simply recommend the book to others. I'll see you again in the second volume. I'm looking forward to it. This time my epilogue is not a "farewell", but a "see you soon".

In closing, may I ask for a short review? Nobody likes to buy a book they know nothing about. You're familiar with my books now, so it would be greatly appreciated if you could write a few words here:

hard-sf.com/links/4238962

Tip: As always, you will receive an illustrated PDF version of the essay on tachyons if you register at hard-sf.com/subscribe.

Once again, thank you so much for reading my books!

Warm regards,
Brandon Q. Morris

Here is the link to "Tachyon 2: The Ship": hard-sf.com/links/4299930

- facebook.com/BrandonQMorris
- amazon.com/author/brandonqmorris
- bookbub.com/authors/brandon-q-morris
- goodreads.com/brandonqmorris
- youtube.com/HardSF
- instagram.com/brandonqmorris

Also by Brandon Q. Morris

The Portal

Tyler's wealth bought him adventures…

…but this time he was in over his head.

Could the legendary underworld be found?

After years of hard work, Tyler built his IT Security company into a massive success. He trusted his people and now it was time to enjoy the fruits of that labor. Everything was perfect until an unexpected discovery. Should they go through the Maya portal?

Adriana's small diving instruction shop is popular enough with the tourists for her to scrape out a living, but it's not the life she expected. When she got the call, it seemed impossible. Wasn't Xibalbá a myth?

In a fantastic world of danger and possibility, two people want to discover the truth, but for entirely different reasons.

Have they opened Pandora's box?

You'll love this Portal Science Fiction thriller because the story pulls you in and leaves you guessing about what might happen next.

Get it now.

Portal Science Fiction – an underwater star gate.

hard-sf.com/links/4104350

The Disturbance

25 years of effort…

…and the first images are a disaster.

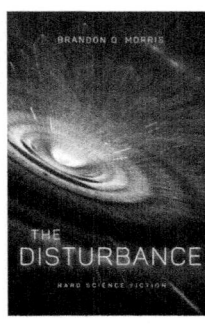

Was the entire experiment a failure?

For astronomer Christine, the results didn't make sense. Everything worked and they should be able to see the beginning of time, but a veil blocks the past. There must be a solution. What could be causing the obstruction?

The data point to the discovery of a black hole.

And it might be moving…

…directly toward earth.

As the stakes grow and with every step forward, more questions that never seemed possible in the world of physics present themselves, Christine has to make a life or death choice.

What will stop the Disturbance?

You'll love this hard science brain twister, because the suspense and other odd happenings, are brilliantly crafted by physicist/author Brandon Q. Morris.

hard-sf.com/links/2414404

Mobius

Tomorrow is yesterday.

It is 2056. Mathematics professor Elisabeth Gabai is fascinated by multi-dimensional forms that have no equivalent in reality. Then, her boss sends her to the site of an artifact that might have come straight from her theories—or from the technology of an advanced civilization.

Twenty-eight years earlier, physicist Max Webber is hell-bent on improving Einstein's theories of relativity. His latest concept seems flawless, except it predicts the end of humanity. The extinction of Earth can only be prevented if Max can locate a multi-dimensional object. He's in a hurry; tomorrow will inevitably be too late.

But how is he supposed to accomplish this goal when physics tells us the artifact he seeks cannot possibly exist?

hard-sf.com/links/2526669

The Beacon

Peter Kraemer, a physics teacher with a passion for astronomy, makes a discovery that he himself can hardly believe: Stars disappear from one day to the next, with nothing left of them. The researchers he contacts provide reassuring and logical explanations for every single case. But when Peter determines that the mysterious process is approaching our home system, he becomes more and more anxious. He alone perceives the looming catastrophe. When he believes he has found a way to avert the impending disaster, he choses to pull out all the stops, even if it costs his job, his marriage, his friends, and his life.

hard-sf.com/links/1731041

Helium 3: Fight for the Future

The star system is perfect. The arrivals have undertaken a long and dangerous journey—an expedition of no return—seeking helium-3, essential for the survival of their species. The discovery of this extraordinary solar system with its four gas giants offers a unique opportunity to harvest the rare isotope.

Then comes a disturbing discovery: They are not alone! Another fleet is here, and just as dependent on helium-3. And the two species are so fundamentally different that communication and compromise appear hopeless. All that remains is a fight to the death—and for the future…

hard-sf.com/links/1691018

The Triton Disaster

Nick Abrahams holds the official world record for the number of space launches, but he's bored stiff with his job hosting space tours. Only when his wife leaves him does he try to change his life.

He accepts a tempting offer from a Russian billionaire. In exchange for making a simple repair on Neptune's moon Triton, he will return to Earth a multi-millionaire, enabling him to achieve his 'impossible dream' of buying his own California vineyard.

The fact that Nick must travel alone during the four-year roundtrip doesn't bother him at all, as he doesn't particularly like people anyway. Once en route he learns his new boss left out some critical details in his job description—details that could cost him his life, and humankind its existence...

hard-sf.com/links/1086200

The Dark Spring

When a space probe returns from the dead, you better not expect good news.

In 2014, the ESA spacecraft *Rosetta* lands a small probe named *Philae* on 67P, a Jupiter-family comet. The lander goes radio silent two years later. Suddenly, in 2026, scientists receive new transmissions from the comet. Motivated by findings that are initially sensational but soon turn frightening, NASA dispatches a crewed spacecraft to the comet. But as the ship approaches the mysterious celestial body, the connection to the astronauts soon breaks. Now it seems nothing can be done anymore to stop the looming dark danger that threatens Earth...

hard-sf.com/links/1358224

The Death of the Universe

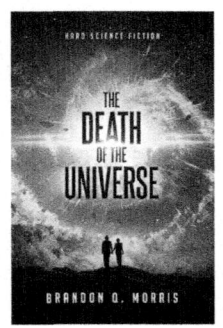

For many billions of years, humans spread throughout the entire Milky Way. They are able to live all their dreams, but to their great disappointment, no other intelligent species has ever been encountered. Now, humanity itself is on the brink of extinction.

They have only one hope: The 'Rescue Project' was designed to feed the black hole in the center of the galaxy until it becomes a quasar, delivering much-needed energy to humankind during its last breaths. But then something happens that no one ever expected —and humanity is forced to look at itself and its existence in an entirely new way.

hard-sf.com/links/835415

The Enceladus Mission (Ice Moon 1)

In the year 2031, a robot probe detects traces of biological activity on Enceladus, one of Saturn's moons. This sensational discovery shows that there is indeed evidence of extraterrestrial life. Fifteen years later, a hurriedly built spacecraft sets out on the long journey to the ringed planet and its moon.

The international crew is not just facing a difficult twenty-seven months: if the spacecraft manages to make it to Enceladus without incident it must use a drillship to penetrate the kilometer-thick sheet of ice that entombs the moon. If life does indeed exist on Enceladus, it could only be at the bottom of the salty, ice covered ocean, which formed billions of years ago.

However, shortly after takeoff disaster strikes the mission, and the chances of the crew making it to Enceladus, let alone back home, look grim.

hard-sf.com/links/526999

Ice Moon - The Boxset

All four bestselling books of the Ice Moon series are now offered as a set, available only in e-book format.

The Enceladus Mission: Is there really life on Saturn's moon Enceladus? *ILSE*, the International Life Search Expedition, makes its way to the icy world where an underground ocean is suspected to be home to primitive life forms.

The Titan Probe: An old robotic NASA probe mysteriously awakens on the methane moon of Titan. The *ILSE* crew tries to solve the riddle—and discovers a dangerous secret.

The Io Encounter: Finally bound for Earth, *ILSE* makes it as far as Jupiter when the crew receives a startling message. The volcanic moon Io may harbor a looming threat that could wipe out Earth as we know it.

Return to Enceladus: The crew gets an offer to go back to Enceladus. Their mission—to recover the body of Dr. Marchenko, left for dead on the original expedition. Not everyone is working toward the same goal.

hard-sf.com/links/780838

Proxima Rising

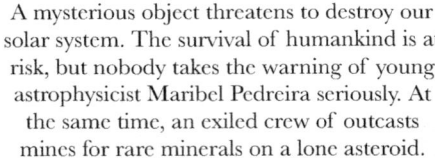

Late in the 21st century, Earth receives what looks like an urgent plea for help from planet Proxima Centauri b in the closest star system to the Sun. Astrophysicists suspect a massive solar flare is about to destroy this heretofore-unknown civilization. Earth's space programs are unequipped to help, but an unscrupulous Russian billionaire launches a secret and highly-specialized spaceship to Proxima b, over four light-years away. The unusual crew faces a Herculean task—should they survive the journey. No one knows what to expect from this alien planet.

hard-sf.com/links/610690

The Hole

A mysterious object threatens to destroy our solar system. The survival of humankind is at risk, but nobody takes the warning of young astrophysicist Maribel Pedreira seriously. At the same time, an exiled crew of outcasts mines for rare minerals on a lone asteroid.

When other scientists finally acknowledge Pedreira's alarming discovery, it becomes clear that these outcasts are the only ones who may be able to save our world, knowing that *The Hole* hurtles inexorably toward the sun.

hard-sf.com/links/527017

Mars Nation 1

NASA finally made it. The very first human has just set foot on the surface of our neighbor planet. This is the start of a long research expedition that sent four scientists into space.

But the four astronauts of the NASA crew are not the only ones with this destination. The privately financed 'Mars for Everyone' initiative has also targeted the Red Planet. Twenty men and women have been selected to live there and establish the first extraterrestrial settlement.

Challenges arise even before they reach Mars orbit. The MfE spaceship Santa Maria is damaged along the way. Only the four NASA astronauts can intervene and try to save their lives.

No one anticipates the impending catastrophe that threatens their very existence—not to speak of the daily hurdles that an extended stay on an alien planet sets before them. On Mars, a struggle begins for limited resources, human cooperation, and just plain survival.

hard-sf.com/links/762824

Impact: Titan

How to avoid killing Earth if you don't even know who sent the killer

250 years ago, humanity nearly destroyed itself in the Great War. Shortly before, a spaceship full of researchers and astronauts had found a new home on Saturn's moon, Titan, and survived by having their descendants genetically adapted to the hostile environment.

The Titanians, as they call themselves, are proud of their cooperative and peaceful society, while unbeknownst to them, humanity is slowly recovering back on Earth. When a 20-mile-wide chunk of rock escapes the asteroid belt and appears to be on a collision course with Earth, the Titanians fear it must look as if they launched the deadly bombardment. Can they prevent the impact and thus avoid an otherwise inevitable war with the Earthlings?

hard-sf.com/links/1433312

The New Tachyon Biography

> *"Do you not see they must move more quickly*
> *and go further, racing through many times*
> *the extent of space in the same length of time*
> *the sunlight takes to fill the sky?"*
>
> Lucretius

THIS IS WHAT THE ROMAN POET AND PHILOSOPHER LUCRETIUS wrote almost three thousand years ago in his didactic poem "De rerum natura" ("On the Nature of Things"). The work, which has largely been confirmed by modern science, primarily summarizes the ancient theory of the atom. It is not based on measurements in the microscopic range - which was impossible at the time - but on fundamental ideas such as "Where there is something, there can be nothing else" and in this way arrives at insights that seem astonishing today. However, these were later suppressed - because Lucretius also showed, for example, that gods are not needed to explain the world.

What about his idea of faster-than-light transmission? In his work, Lucretius refers to the concept of images, which he separates from light itself. How images are formed in the eye was not yet known at the time. He was convinced that images were transmitted almost instantly. He explained this vividly:

> *"This, too, seems a true and excellent example*

> *of how swift the motion is which carries*
> *images of things along: as soon as*
> *a bright water surface is first set out*
> *in the open air under starry skies,*
> *the world's calm and radiant constellations*
> *respond at once, appearing in the water.*
> *Do you not now see in how short a time*
> *the image falls from regions of the sky*
> *to places here on earth?"*
>
> Lucretius

Lucretius could not have known that the image of the stars had been traveling for billions of years at the moment the vessel was placed under the night sky and had, so to speak, only been waiting for that exact moment. I also find this thought phenomenally intriguing. At any given moment, billions of photons are just waiting to trigger an electrical stimulus in the eyes of an observer, creating an image in the mind that goes back millions, billions of years in time.

It should therefore be clear that Lucretius' speculations do not stand up to today's perspective. Nevertheless, it is worth reading his book to see what clear thinking was capable of two thousand years ago.

In science fiction, the possibility of faster-than-light travel has always been an important ingredient. It makes so many things easier, starting with the exploration of the universe. This is because the universe is so unimaginably vast. It has only existed for 13.8 billion years. If we assume that it has been expanding in all directions at the speed of light since the Big Bang, we arrive at a diameter of 27.6 billion light years.

But it's not that simple. Firstly, the universe is not a sphere, but almost flat. Secondly, in its early days it expanded faster than light. This does not contradict the theory of relativity, because there was no movement involved. Imagine an empty balloon. Draw two thick dots on it with a ballpoint pen. Now blow up the balloon. The dots stay in place, but still move away from each other. This is a good equivalent for the (long proven) constant expansion of the universe.

As the light spreads out, the space in which it is traveling

Tachyon: The Weapon

expands. The observable universe from which light can reach us must therefore be significantly larger than 13.8 billion light years. Scientists estimate a total diameter of around 93 billion light years. The distance from Earth to the core of the Milky Way alone is almost 30,000 light years. With a spaceship that is slower than light, we will never be able to explore space in its entirety.

People have never liked such externally imposed limits. Especially not science fiction writers, who have come up with all kinds of tricks or borrowed ideas from physics to allow their protagonists to fly faster than light. This ranges from shortcuts in space-time ("wormholes") all the way to warp drives (which are based on an artificial compression of space-time). Both "solutions" require negative energy, the existence of which has not been proven even to this day, in the 29th century. There are also references to "hyperspace", which ultimately corresponds to the wormhole concept, except that such a spaceship can create its own wormhole at any time and anywhere, through which it can leave our four-dimensional space-time.

However, our physicists still do not believe that ordinary matter can move faster than light. All known particles belong to two families: Firstly, we have tardyons (sometimes also called "bradyons" in scientific literature, and occasionally "ittyons"). They are always slower than light. The theory of special relativity proves this by showing that an infinite amount of energy would be required to bring a tardyon to the speed of light. This is because tardyons have a positive mass at rest.

But there are also particles to which this does not apply. Photons and gluons do not have a rest mass, nor do gravitons (which have not yet been observed). These are the exchange particles of three fundamental forces of the universe: gravity, weak and strong nuclear interaction, and electromagnetism. An interesting question in this context is why W and Z bosons, which mediate the weak interaction, are not also massless, but that is another topic. Due to their lack of mass at rest, photons and gluons can only move at the speed of light - no slower, but no faster either. Physics also calls them luxons, derived from "lux" meaning "light".

In addition to the speed they can reach, there is another exciting connection between the two families: how they deal with time. Tardyons always move forward in time. You know this because you are made up of tardyons: They age! Luxons, on the other hand, never age. You could also say that time stands still for them. Unless they die an unnatural death (for example, being absorbed by another particle), they live forever. Luxons do not decay, unlike tardyons, which all have a half-life, even if it is sometimes very long.

Couldn't there then also be a family of particles that basically move faster than light? For a very long time, this was a reasonable question. As late as 1904, the German physicist Arnold Sommerfeld wrote about electrons that moved both slower and faster than light. But then, in 1905, Einstein's essay "On the Electrodynamics of Moving Bodies" was published, which established the theory of special relativity, according to which the speed of light is the upper limit. After this, Sommerfeld was also convinced: "Superluminal speeds have no possibility of existing".

This scientific unanimity lasted until the 1960s. In 1962, Oleksa-Myron Bilaniuk, George Sudarshan and his student V. K. Deshpande thought a little further ahead. In a hypothesis they called "meta-relativity", they proposed the existence of particles that always move faster than light from the moment of their creation. The well-known physicist Gerald Feinberg eventually named these "meta-particles" tachyons in 1967 in an attempt to quantize them. But not everyone liked the idea. Isaac Asimov, one of the most famous science fiction authors of the time, published an article with the fitting headline "Impossible, that's all". On the other hand, Asimov's colleague, Arthur C. Clarke, defended the idea with an essay entitled "Possible, that's all". Asimov later admitted that he had been wrong.

This was followed by a phase of intensive theoretical discussion and a hectic search. At first, everything looked promising, as there was even a candidate for the tachyon: the neutrino, a neutral particle that only interacts via gravity and weak nuclear force. It was long assumed to have no mass. Experiments even seemed to confirm an imaginary mass for the neutrino - which is exactly what the tachyon has. However, this was due to a previously unknown interference effect of the detector crystal. Today, it seems more likely that the neutrino has a real mass, albeit a very small one. The particle could therefore contribute to solving another problem in cosmology - the search for dark matter, of which it could be a component.

Tachyon: The Weapon

However, this means that it could no longer be considered as a tachyon.

How do tachyons exist?

There is in fact more than one way to deduce the possible existence of a faster-than-light particle. Bilaniuk, Sudarshan and Deshpande derived it from the theory of special relativity, from which it arises as a possible mathematical solution.

This is relatively easy to understand. You probably remember Einstein's famous formula $E=mc^2$. Strictly speaking, this is a special case of a particle at rest in the reference system. In general, $E^2=(pc)^2+(mc^2)^2$ applies here. If you convert this according to the energy E, you get $E=mc^2/sqrt(1-v^2/c^2)$, where v is the speed of the particle. If this is greater than the speed of light c, then the entire term under the root becomes negative. The square root of a negative number is an imaginary number. If E is to be a real value and the denominator of the fraction is an imaginary number, what must the numerator contain? Also an imaginary number! The mass of the particle (more precisely: the rest mass) must therefore be imaginary. At the same time, the energy becomes a negative value, which many physicists do not particularly like. In this respect, the theory of relativity definitely does not prohibit faster-than-light speeds. It merely gives tardyons their upper speed limit and tachyons their lower limit, which they can never reach. And it requires an imaginary mass, whatever that may be.

Mathematical solutions are not necessarily what occurs in nature. On the other hand, physicists have often found particles that were initially predicted purely mathematically, such as the Z and W bosons and neutrinos. And so it was with the tachyon: in 2302, the Austrian physicist Alexander Thauer succeeded in proving its existence.

Thauer knew that there was evidence for it from another source: string theory. What are strings? Strings are simple objects from which all matter in the universe can be constructed. A string has an important advantage over the elementary particles (quarks and electrons) of the standard model: while the elementary particles are assumed to be point-like (i.e. they expand in 0 dimensions), a string is one-dimensional. It should be much easier to construct a clearly multidimensional space from components with one dimension each than from zero-dimensional points.

Simple observation shows that any geometric figure can be constructed from lines. On the other hand, you would need an infinite number of points to draw a line even one centimeter long (if you use a real pencil, you are cheating, because its points are not points at all, but small circles - as a glance through a magnifying glass shows).

The fact that no one has ever seen a string is due to the tiny size of these objects. Their typical length is around 1.6 * 10-35 meters in the Planck length range. No man-made instrument will ever be able to show objects of this size. However, this is not a problem as long as the theory perfectly predicts the observable reality.

However, a string alone is not enough to create matter - just as the mere existence of a guitar string is not enough to make musical sound. The vibrations of the strings are crucial. Each of these tiny objects can vibrate in several different ways. The stronger the vibration, the more energy it contains - and the larger the particle that manifests itself as a result. At least that's the short version of the explanation.

In fact, we know from playing the guitar that the length and tension of the string also play a role. A tightly wound string emits a different sound than if it is only loosely fastened. Strings also have a tension that decreases with the square of the length. This tension is comparatively huge - this proved to be one of the first problems theorists faced. Normally, it leads to energies around 1019 orders of magnitude higher than that of a proton. Strings with such high energies have not yet been discovered. Perhaps they only existed in the early days of the universe.

These energy ranges are also beyond what can be achieved with particle accelerators in the foreseeable future. Direct detection of individual strings is therefore unlikely. However, there are also oscillation modes with lower energy. Depending on the approach, this results in interesting particles: Gravitons, photons or even tachyons. Unfortunately, physicists can sometimes be nasty to other physicists. For a long time, they only considered a string theory (yes, there is not just one string theory, but a whole series) to be realistic (i.e. representing reality) if it did not produce tachyons. Or they made additions to their theory that removed tachyons from the picture. It was only after Thauer's groundbreaking work that they changed their minds.

Various quantum field theories (theories that explain our four fundamental forces in terms of quantum physics) also contain fields with complex mass, usually called tachyonic fields. Feinberg was the first to point this out in 1967. In the variant conceived by Feinberg, however, these possible states are nowadays regarded more as signs of an instability of the vacuum, which generally annihilates. This process, in which new particles with real mass are created, is known as tachyon condensation. The tachyons here are therefore merely symptoms of instability, and tachyon condensation corresponds to a second-order phase transition, such as in the Higgs mechanism, through which particles obtain their mass.

Properties of the tachyon

Researchers were unsure for a long time whether tachyons actually existed. Nevertheless, they knew from the outset at least roughly what they must be like. That is the least a theory must provide in order to be recognized as a theory: a roadmap for researchers who want to disprove or prove it. Incidentally, you cannot see a tachyon, even if it were somehow possible to visualize it. After all, it moves faster than light. Only after it has passed you could you perceive it, and as two images, especially if you were directly in its path. Both images would move away from you in opposite directions. One is subject to a strong red shift, the other to a blue shift.

However, when physicists talk about properties, they are not referring to a visual effect. We have already discovered the first important property: The rest mass of a tachyon is imaginary. The reason for this is described above. However, this does not affect its moving or actual mass or its energy. Depending on the tachyon's state of motion, it may well have a real mass and positive energy. This is simply because its energy is determined by its rest mass and its momentum (its speed). The contribution of the rest mass remains the same, but that of the momentum changes.

However, this happens in a very unusual way. If you want your car to go faster, you have to give it energy (accelerate). To slow down, you must take energy away (step on the brake). With tachyons, it is exactly the opposite. If you supply them with energy, they slow down. To accelerate them, you have to take energy away from them. This is a typical and unexpected property of these hypothetical particles. A tachyon with energy 0 would be infinitely fast. And you would need an infinite amount of energy to slow it down to the speed of light.

At the same time, tachyons move backwards in time. That's great for science fiction writers, but for physicists it's still hard to digest. After all, it could violate the principle of causality - the fact that the effect always follows the cause (see below for more on this). Even after Thauer's discovery, some researchers still believed that tachyons could not be real for this reason alone. Others assumed that tachyon waves, which act as information carriers and can be assigned to tachyons in quantum physics via wave-particle duality, only propagate at sub-light speed. In a sense, the recipient would receive an initial part of the information very quickly, but would only be able to piece together the whole picture once the wave had reached them completely, i.e. once even the slowest letter carrier had delivered their letter.

If tachyons were electrically charged, they would inevitably emit so-called Cherenkov radiation. Cherenkov radiation occurs when the speed at which a particle passes through a medium is higher than the speed of light in that medium (!). This is possible because light is slowed down more by some media than electrons, for example. It is only impossible to exceed the speed of light in a vacuum. Our tachyons would lose energy, become even faster, radiate even more - a domino effect would occur that would drive the tachyons to infinitely high speeds. Our world would probably be uninhabitable because of all this radiation. Fortunately, we do not observe any Cherenkov radiation from tachyons, so they cannot be electrically charged.

However, some researchers suspected early on that Cherenkov radiation can occur in tachyons under very specific conditions, namely when they pass through a medium in which the speed of light is higher than their own speed and which has a refractive index of less than 1. These are difficult but not impossible conditions to fulfill. The refractive index of a medium is normally above 1, but there are special metamaterials that meet this condition. Such material is what fills the tanks in the tachyon receivers on the moon and elsewhere. This is because an interaction with one of the basic forces known to us is necessary in order to be able to derive a signal from the tachyon current.

The weak interaction might also be considered. But this basic force is, as the name suggests, very weak, and it would take an enormous effort to build a tachyon receiver on that basis. Those who do not intend to do this (i.e. physicists) cannot rule out weakly interacting tachyons, at least from an experimental point of view. However, there is no evidence for this to date.

This also applies to gravity, although here we have the problem of imaginary mass. The extent to which two bodies influence each other gravitationally depends on the product of their two masses. What if one of the two masses is imaginary? The product and thus the attractive force then also become imaginary. But how does an imaginary force work in a real universe? Measuring it is not yet an option with today's technology. Another problem is the Cherenkov radiation caused by the gravitational effect. If the tachyon emits energy through the interaction, it speeds up, emits more radiation, speeds up again... The only way out of this dilemma would be for the gravitational exchange particles known as "gravitons" to be tachyons themselves. However, we currently know much less about gravitons - even their existence is unclear.

At least tachyons seem to stay completely out of one field: the strong interaction that holds nuclear particles together. If tachyons carried the necessary color charges, no basic component of matter would be safe from decay. In reality, however, neutrons, protons and so on are quite stable.

Tachyons and causality

As mentioned above, one might think that the transmission of information via tachyons violates causality. This seems to be suggested by thought experiments such as those developed by Albert Einstein and the physicist Richard Tolman. They are usually described as "Tolman's paradox" or the "antitelephone".

The story usually begins with two astronauts, Alice and Bob, who are far away from each other. Alice tells Bob in a tachyon message that she has an upset stomach from eating shrimp. The message reaches Bob. He replies with the warning "Don't eat any shrimp!", also via a tachyon message. Now you can calculate that - depending on Bob's and Alice's speed and the speed of the tachyon signal - Bob's warning reaches Alice before she has eaten the shrimp. But if she didn't eat the shrimp, she wouldn't have written her message to Bob, and Bob wouldn't have warned her, so she would have eaten the shrimp after all, and thus... a paradox.

This is of course unpleasant for those involved. Einstein and Tolman thus considered the impossibility of motion at faster-than-light speed to be proven. Of course, it is not. The twin paradox, which causes two people to age differently depending on their speed of movement, does not prove that relativistic time dilation and compression are impossible. Quantum physics also has a few paradoxes to offer. It appears that paradoxes are inherent to our reality.

The solution is in the story itself: A paradox only occurs when tachyon communication happens too fast. What is "too fast"? That depends on the relative speed of the communication partners and the speed of the tachyons. The former can be measured, the latter can be influenced: The less energy a tachyon has, the faster it becomes. So, all you need to do to accelerate it is to extract some energy from it using Cherenkov radiation. Of course, this also means that a tachyon transmitter cannot be set up just anywhere. All communication partners must know the location of the transmitter and receiver as precisely as possible. For this reason, it is always the last thing to be set up in a newly colonized star system, especially as such a transmitter also requires large amounts of energy.

The trick that Thauer's successors came up with makes Tolman's paradox manageable but does not eliminate it. For that, we need another clever idea. It has become known as the "reinterpretation principle". An observer cannot tell from the tachyon whether it is traveling into the past with negative energy or into the future with positive energy. If a tachyon of negative energy is absorbed somewhere, it looks exactly the same as if a tachyon of positive energy had been emitted. If the observer were now to try to detect a tachyon from the future (i.e. to have it absorbed by a measuring device, which would violate causality), this could also be reinterpreted as the act of generating this tachyon and

Tachyon: The Weapon

sending it in the positive time direction (which does not violate causality).

For some physicists, this is too much interpretation and too little proof. They claim that such paradoxes can only be avoided if tachyons cannot be detected at all from our world because they show no interactions whatsoever. In a sense, they would exist in their very own world, perpendicular to ours, which we theorize about but can never see. An argument against this (apart from the fact that you probably received this outline via tachyon communication) is that, according to our current state of knowledge, every mass (even an imaginary one) would have to interact via gravity. The two worlds would therefore not be separate, but connected via gravity. However, this would again make it possible to create paradoxes.

Where do tachyons come from?

So how do tachyons get into our world? Science can imagine various ways, and our engineers use a combination of methods. For example, they are created in pairs from nothing. In fact, particles are constantly forming and disappearing. The energy required for the formation of tachyons is not very high, at least when it comes to fast (and therefore low-energy) tachyons. More energy must be used to slow down the tachyons in order to be able to use them for paradox-free communication. The station on the moon works according to this principle. But there are also other suggestions. In particle accelerators, the bombardment of Z^0 bosons, for example, creates tachyons under the influence of a strong electromagnetic field.

Tachyons have also been searched for in cosmic radiation. They hit the Earth's atmosphere with high energy and at up to 99.99 percent of the speed of light, colliding several times with the molecules in the atmosphere. The particles resulting from these collisions continue to interact and generate even more particles. The phenomenon is known as an air shower (or "natural particle accelerator") and can be studied using various detectors. As early as 1973, Philip Crough and Roger Clay used a large number of particle detectors to identify a suspected faster-than-light particle in such an air shower - unfortunately, no one has been able to reproduce this result in the 800 years since.

The researchers have little hope of discovering tachyons today which could have been created shortly after the Big Bang. Theoretically, they could have played an important role back then. However, as their lifelines point into the past, they would have had to be very energetic (and therefore slow) to still exist today.

In 2018, Russian physicists Olga Chashchina and Zurab Silagadze put forward a different hypothesis. Do tachyons possibly also exist virtually? After all, there are behaviors in physics, especially in quantum physics, where effects occur at faster-than-light speed. This applies, for example, to entanglement, which Einstein rejected as "spooky action at a distance", but which has now been proven many times over. There are also tunnel effects in which light particles travel through a barrier in zero time, regardless of their density ("Hartman effect"). A moment ago, they were here, now they are there. They must have traveled the distance between the two locations at faster-than-light speed. It can also be calculated that every particle can become faster than light for a very short time. The length of this time depends inversely on the mass. For particles of very low mass (such as neutrinos), this time can be measurably long. Chashchina and Silagadze generalized this to mean that any particle can become a tachyon for a short time. However, the two physicists also arrived at a seemingly contradictory conclusion: tachyons exist, but do not propagate faster than light. "The tachyon is not a tachyon," they summarized.

Today we know that they were wrong. Nevertheless, your head may be spinning. Congratulations! Physics always manages to do that - that's what I like about it. Incidentally, if it were possible to generate tachyons much more conveniently, something like a tachyon engine would also be possible. Tachyons have an impulse, so they could propel a spaceship. However, this would not make the spaceship faster than light.

Alternatives to tachyons

The exciting thing is that tachyons are not the only type of particle that can move faster than light. On the one hand, there are superbradyons. These are particles with positive (!) mass and positive (!) energy that move in a vacuum at faster-than-light speeds. They "emerged" in the 21st century in the mind of physicist Luis Gonzáles-Mestres, who was looking for a new explanation for dark matter, dark energy and so on, i.e. an extension of the standard model of physics. He imagined the universe as a huge sea of faster-than-light superbradyons that only interact very weakly with ordinary matter, so that we are unaware of them. However, if they decay, they "create" the ordinary universe by emitting the particles we know until they reach a speed equal or close to that of light due to the continuous loss of energy. The superbradyons thus form a cosmological reservoir in which the relationship between inertial and gravitational mass (which are normally identical) would deviate from conventional physics. Superbradyons thusly also come into play as the cause of cosmological and astrophysical phenomena that are normally associated with dark matter and dark energy. However, no trace of them has yet been found.

And what about antitachyons, as used by Captain Janeway in the classic 2D series "Star Trek: Voyager"? Antiparticles can generally be obtained by exchanging the electrical and color charge of a particle for its opposite. A tachyon would therefore be its own antiparticle, because it has no color charge and (probably) no electric charge. Antitachyons are therefore quite ordinary tachyons.

Finally, I do not want to withhold a consideration from the physicists Chashchina and Silagadze mentioned above, mainly because of the comparison with which they introduce their existence. "There are beings who live south of the Himalayas (tardyons), who hover above the mountains (luxons) and who live north of them (tachyons). However, you can't rule out the possibility that one day you might come across an alien (even if you haven't met one yet) that comes from a planet where there is no Himalayan mountain range!" This type of possibly faster-than-light object differs conceptually from tachyons and therefore deserves its own name. The researchers call them "elvisebrions" ("elvisebri" means "fast as lightning" in Georgian). The elvisebrions would be very similar to the superbradyons of Gonzáles-Mestres. They would also be traveling in a realm of reality that is difficult for us to access. The two worlds could be connected by the Higgs field, which gives our particles their mass.

I hope I have been able to open at least a small window into the world of faster-than-light particles for you in this outline. As you have seen, tachyons are very special particles. Until the 23rd century, most scientists doubted that they really existed. For quantum mechanics at least, scientists like to refer to the "totalitarian principle". It says: "Everything not forbidden is compulsory." Tachyons are clearly not forbidden. But for physics, they have only existed since Thauer proved them beyond doubt. Science has not yet succeeded in doing this for all of its ideas.

Printed in Great Britain
by Amazon

62483645R00245